"A SPINE-TINGLING, CHILLING RIDE
INTO THE MIND OF A DEMENTED KILLER."
— Jill M. Smith, *Rave Reviews*

"RICO'S MISSING," SAID TERI.

When Selena didn't react to her words with so much as a raised eyebrow, Teri tried again. "He never came home. He just disappeared on Thursday and no one's heard from him since."

"How nice."

"Selena! What an awful thing to say."

Selena's perfect brow creased with that mild criticism, and her serene expression changed to one of bewilderment. "But it's the truth. Surely we can tell each other the truth."

Teri's stomach twisted at the thought of how Detective Kidder would interpret Selena's offhanded comment. "Selena, please — don't say something like that even in jest."

"Why? There's no one here but us. We both *know* you wanted to get rid of him, and now it looks like you got what you wished for." She giggled and gave Teri a playful poke.

Teri failed to understand what was so comical. Selena's silver eyes glowed with a joyous light, but Teri couldn't bring herself to share her pleasure. "Selena —"

"Oh, now, don't you worry." Selena patted Teri's shoulder and whispered breathily, "Your secret is safe with me. I'd never tell a soul."

POLITICAL ESPIONAGE AND HEART-STOPPING HORROR. . . .
NOVELS BY NOEL HYND

COME INTO MY PARLOR

MARILYN CAMPBELL

Pinnacle Books
Kensington Publishing Corp.

http://www.pinnaclebooks.com

One

"You'll get your money. The gallery just sold another one of the bitch's new paintings. Ya gotta give me more time," Rico Gambini pleaded into the telephone. "Just listen a minute. I've got a surefire plan. She won't hold out much longer. I'll make sure of it."

The "bitch" halted abruptly outside the bedroom door as she heard her husband's voice. Teri Carmichael Gambini had been preparing for a photo shoot in her studio over the garage when she spilled coffee on her blouse and decided to change. Closing her mind to the possibilities Rico's words suggested, the petite brunette stealthily retreated. She knew from past experience that confronting him would only waste time she couldn't afford today. Besides, their arguments always left her vibrating with anger and frustration, not exactly a state conducive to creativity.

Obviously, Rico was in trouble — gambling trouble — and he expected to convince her to bail him out — *again*. At least now she understood what was behind his recent efforts to charm her. If she hadn't overheard him just now, it probably would have worked, too.

She paused outside the garage of their White Plains home. Her favorite model, Selena, was already in the studio, getting into costume, and Teri wanted to compose herself before going up there.

She felt a soft pressure against her calf and glanced

down. "Well, hello there." Kneeling, she stroked the unfamiliar cat's gray and black fur and frowned when her fingers detected rib bones too close to the surface. "Poor baby. Have you been wandering very long?" The stray looked directly into her eyes, cocked its head, and let out a loud meow. "You're lucky summer came early this year. I suppose the others told you where you could find a free meal." The response was a shy purr that made her smile. "Well, you seem polite enough, but we have rules here. No digging in the garden, and stay away from the bird feeders in the backyard. If I find out you're bothering my birds, you won't be welcome back for breakfast. Got it?"

With a graceful arch of its back, the cat nuzzled Teri's palm once more, then took off around the side of the garage where the cat food was set out. Because of Rico's allergies, she couldn't have animals in the house, but there were plenty outside that had grown accustomed to her attention.

Substitute children. For the thousandth time she wondered if it would have made a difference if she and Rico had been able to have a baby. Her inability to conceive was only one of the thorns that had pricked his male ego, but it was a sizable one. Regardless of the fact that the doctors she went to gave her a clean bill of health, Rico blamed her. He refused to be tested since he had no doubts about his manhood. And he wouldn't consider adoption as an alternative.

With an audible sigh, she turned her thoughts to her young friend Selena, another lonely stray. By now she would be decked out in the low-cut blue satin gown Teri had selected. The cover being shot today was for a book set in Victorian England.

Five foot eleven, with a voluptuous body and waist-length platinum hair, Selena made an ideal subject for historical romance covers. With most models, Teri had to add lushness to the breasts to make them appear overflowing, or thickness and length to the hair.

None of that was necessary with Selena, but that wasn't the only reason Teri used her more often than any of the others.

Selena's eyes made her special. Almost colorless, they reflected a translucent silver when light hit them, giving her a haunted, mysterious look that Teri enhanced in her work. And Selena was sweet and extremely easy to work with.

For all those reasons, Teri chose to immortalize Selena in her *Women in History* series of oil paintings that the gallery was currently exhibiting. She knew some of the praise garnered was due to her exquisite model. During the long hours they worked together on the series, they developed a comfortable, personal relationship as well, even though Teri was fifteen years older. Or perhaps the relationship blossomed because of that age difference.

Teri was aware of the childlike dependency Selena occasionally demonstrated toward her, and she understood the cause. At twenty-one, Selena had already suffered the death of her father, her stepfather, and her mother. Teri's parents had also passed away, but she was much more mature than Selena. Under the circumstances, she had no objection to being Selena's surrogate mother figure.

As Teri expected, Selena was ready and waiting when she reentered the studio.

Selena smiled, then narrowed her eyes. "I thought you were changing. What happened?"

Teri grimaced at the dried beige stain on her white blouse, then fussed with the short ponytail at the base of her neck. "Oh, yes. I, uh, got distracted and forgot all about it."

"That's not like you. Rico's home today, isn't he? What did he do, pick another fight?"

Selena's breathy voice was gentle, but the way she straightened her shoulders and lifted her chin made her look as though she was prepared to duke it out with the man if asked. Teri shook her head and

7

changed the subject. "It wasn't important. I'm glad you're early today. I wanted to fill you in on something I'm trying. Actually, it started as a peace offering to Rico. He's been so nice lately . . ." Teri closed her eyes, then slowly opened them as she realized it had all been a lie. "Anyway, I have a photographer coming here to do the shoot today."

"A photographer? I don't understand. You do marvelous work. I thought you preferred to work with the models personally, rather than just painting from photographs someone else took."

Selena's Marilyn Monroe voice had altered to a girlish whine, a sure sign the change of plans did not sit well with her. Her whine was the only thing about Selena that was truly annoying.

"You're right. I do. But I promised Rico to cut back on my hours, and the most logical solution was to use a professional photographer, like most of the other cover artists do. This man is new, but he was highly recommended by the art director at Century Publishing. Since they're my biggest client, I agreed to give him a chance. I asked him to come here, though, so I could choose the poses and watch him work at the same time."

Selena made a little pout. "I don't like it. Men photographers make me uncomfortable. They all have this kinky idea that female models should think of their cameras as a sex organ. I'd rather continue working only with you. It's more personal."

Teri knew that. It was why she had asked Selena to come a half hour before the others. When Selena had first arrived in New York City a year ago, her exceptional looks had caused a flurry of excitement at the agencies. Although the unusual girl had moved to the big city to seek a career in modeling or acting, she was intimidated by the hustle and demands of mass media. Apparently, money had not been an issue, because Selena was renting an expensive apartment in Manhattan, as well as garage space for her new Cadillac. Yet once she modeled for Teri a few times, she stopped accepting assignments elsewhere. Teri had no doubt that a considerable amount of new cover work came her way strictly as a result of Selena's loyalty.

Teri stepped closer and took Selena's hand. "Look, I promise to keep your feelings in mind, but try to understand my side of it. I really could use the extra time for my other paintings. I'm starting a new series, you know."

Selena brightened immediately, but before she could inquire, a knock at the door interrupted her.

Hoping Adam, the male model, was arriving first, Teri opened the door. She got half her wish. Adam was one of the two tall men standing on the landing. Both were wearing black cowboy hats and gray snakeskin boots. The western apparel was Adam's look of the season, but the other man gave her the impression he had always worn clothes like this. Noting the expensive camera around his neck and the worn leather photographer's case slung over his shoulder, Teri ended her appraisal. "You must be Drew Marshall."

He touched the brim of his hat. "Ma'am."

"I'm Teri Carmichael." As she used her maiden name on her work, that would be the name he would recognize. "Come in." After making sure he and Adam had met, she introduced him to Selena. Teri caught the unsmiling glance Selena spared the photographer and prayed that she would not choose this session to start being uncooperative. "Adam, you're a lord of the realm today. The costume's hanging in the bathroom. To Drew she said, "I understand you've never done this type of work before, so I hope you won't object to a few suggestions."

He smiled, revealing straight white teeth. "Not at all, ma'am. In fact, I was countin' on it. I'll just get set up while he's changin'."

His deep-pitched drawl identified his home state as clearly as if the flag of Texas had been embroidered on his plaid shirt. Teri was debating whether or not to

9

tell him how she prepared for a shoot when he removed his sunglasses and hat and ran his fingers quickly through his wavy hair. Its salt-and-pepper color and the creases at the corners of his blue eyes gave evidence of a man who'd passed the age of forty or had a rough time of what years he did have behind him.

Adam, and several other male models Teri worked with, had such perfect features, they could be described as beautiful. They were always careful not to smile too broadly for fear of creating a wrinkle in their flawless complexions. Other men got the jobs because of their well-developed bodies. If their faces weren't handsome enough, Teri simply corrected whatever shortcomings they had.

She found herself appraising Drew as he walked around the room, checking the lighting from different angles. You wouldn't exactly call him handsome — his features were a bit too harsh — but he had an interesting face, one she'd like to paint . . . or get to know. As if he sensed her thoughts, he glanced over at her and grinned.

"I've got to tell you, Miz Carmichael, I was expectin' to meet an elderly woman here today."

Teri raised her eyebrows and ignored Selena's little snort. "Meaning me?"

His grin slanted a bit. "Your esteemed reputation gave me the impression I'd be workin' for one of the matriarchs of the business. The article in *Publishers Weekly* called you one of the most talented cover artists in the New York publishing community. From the number and quality of books they mentioned, I assumed you'd been at it for twenty or thirty years."

"She's also one of the best photographers in the business," Selena added proudly, "Which is why she's never bothered to use *outsiders* before."

Drew appeared not to have noticed the contempt in Selena's voice, and simply told Teri, "As I said before, I welcome any advice you might have." He glanced around the studio, noting the posters and oil paintings on the walls. "These are beautiful. Do you sell your work to anyone besides the publishers?"

"Occasionally."

Selena snorted again. "She's too modest. The Forsythe Gallery in Manhattan is currently exhibiting a series she did. It's the second showing they've had for her serious work. And, believe me, not only do her paintings sell, but the prices they fetch are very impressive."

Before Drew could compliment Teri again, Adam came out of the bathroom wearing black pants, a white shirt with a soft ruffle at his throat, and a gray frock coat.

"Okay, that's good," Teri commented as she checked the fit of the turnout. To Drew she explained, "The art fact sheets I get from the publishers range from very specific to very vague. I get as close as I possibly can with the costume, especially if it's a historical, like this one. I shoot them against a solid background, then fill the scene in on the canvas. Sometimes the art director tells me exactly what the surrounding area looks like and how they're to be posed, and other times I get only a general idea. Personally, I like to read the whole manuscript when I can get a copy in time. It gives me a better feel for the attitudes and facial expressions that are right for the story."

Drew nodded. "You mean like how Lord Davenport here wants to make Regina admit she wants him as much as he wants her?"

Teri laughed. "That was a pretty good guess."

"Not at all. I read Ann's copy of the manuscript last night."

Ann was the art director who had recommended him.

"You must be better friends than she let on."

It was Drew's turn to laugh. "We're cousins, and she told me you'd be impressed by my industry."

Teri was tempted to keep up the light banter. It felt so good to relax for a moment, but there was something about the way he was looking at her that made her uneasy. Instead of responding, she turned toward Selena and Adam. "For starters, let's try for a standard seduction pose. Adam, this girl has been driving you out of your mind for weeks. Every time you see her your masculinity responds, but she's found ways to keep you out of her lacy drawers. You know she's just as hot for you no matter what she claims, and you're trying to force the issue with a kiss. Selena, you don't want to give in, but your body is straining toward his even as you turn your face away. Adam, if you can't have her mouth, you'll take her throat. Drew, are you ready?"

Adam let out a high-pitched laugh. "From the way he's looking at you, I think he's more than ready." A wicked glare from Selena silenced him.

Drew cleared his throat. "Sorry. Your directing style just caught me off guard. Don't worry, I'll catch on."

After the first few poses, Drew made some suggestions, then gave a couple of directions of his own. Teri quickly decided that he had a good eye and backed off a little. Ann had been right: Drew did impress her. He might be new to this business, but his experience showed. His manner was casual yet efficient, and for the most part he had Selena and Adam moving like a veteran dance team. Every so often Teri thought she saw Selena giving him a dirty look, but she figured Selena would come around if she encouraged her to give the man a break.

As the shoot continued, Teri acknowledged that she and Drew worked well together. Their thoughts practically tripped over each other on the way to a decision.

After several attempts with one pose, Drew stated, "That's still not right."

"It looks fine to me," Teri countered.

"That's because you're seein' with your eyes. C'mere." Without removing the camera strap from his neck, he held it away from his chest for Teri to look through.

One moment she was concentrating on the way the camera would capture the image, and the next she was aware only of the man next to her. His hand rested lightly on her shoulder; as his head bent to hers, warm breath caressed her cheek. Swallowing hard, she labeled what that *something* was that she had noticed earlier: it had been so long since any man, including Rico, had looked at her that way. Curious. Interested. *Attracted.* And she had looked back without realizing that was what she was doing. Good Lord. Another man was the last thing she needed. Allowing mindless hormones to screw up her life once was more than enough.

Teri stepped away as smoothly as she could. "The expressions are wrong. Hold the position, but Selena, try a little more demure. Adam, more adoring."

Drew's camera clicked and whirred. "It looks good, but I don't think it'll work for this book."

She agreed, as she had with most of his ideas. If the pictures turned out as she expected, she could definitely use him in the future. Surely there would be no harm in doing one more session together. Then he could work in his own studio and have the final photos delivered to her for the painting. In the meantime, she would be certain to mention her marital status and take care not to stare at him too openly.

Drew wondered what had happened to the little lady. She had clearly been enjoying herself for a while there. Then it was as if she had curled into a protective ball. The fact that she mentioned her husband at three inappropriate times cued him into the fact that she wanted to be sure he knew she was off-limits. He hadn't been thinking of trespassing until she'd brought it to his mind . . . at least, not consciously. The easy camaraderie they had instantly established

13

felt right, and it was harmless as far as he was concerned.

At the end of the session, Teri maintained an aloof, professional manner as she told him she would like to work with him again. After both men left and Selena changed into her own clothes, Teri decided to have that talk with her right away. "Now, was that so bad?"

Selena shrugged. "No, I guess not, but probably because you were here."

"I really don't think he's the type that would suggest you have sex with his camera." Teri smiled, but it was obvious Selena wasn't convinced. "Look, I've never tried to hide the fact that you're my favorite, and I wouldn't want to upset you, as my model or my friend. How about if we have another session or two together and see how it goes from there?"

"All right. Did you like him?"

Teri felt her cheeks warm and turned away under the pretext of getting two cups from the cupboard. "I liked the way he worked. I'll have to see the photos to make up my mind about using him, though. How about a cup of tea?"

"Sure. He liked you. I could tell. And I don't mean professionally. I wasn't so sure about you."

Teri would have let it go if she hadn't caught the hint of a whine. Selena obviously needed reassurance of some kind. "Believe me, I've got my hands full with Rico."

That was all Selena needed to hear to shift her concern away from herself. "I knew something happened before. Why don't you tell me about it? Talking it out might help."

Sighing deeply, Teri let her shoulders sag a bit. Maybe Selena was right. As young as Selena acted some of the time, she could also be very level-headed, and she *was* discreet. A few of her and Rico's arguments had been within Selena's hearing, and no one else ever found out about them. Teri carried the two cups to the small dinette set and motioned for Selena to sit down with her. "You know Rico and I have had our problems in the past, but I can't take much more from him."

"I thought you said hiring a photographer was supposed to help."

"That's what I thought, too. But this problem has nothing to do with how much time I spend working. Ah, damn. As long as you're willing to listen, I may as well get it out of my system. About a year ago, I asked Rico for our joint savings account passbook, and he said he had misplaced it. He usually handled the transactions since the bank was on his route, but I had to go by there the next day, so I requested a new book. I was positive they'd made a mistake when they showed a balance almost ten thousand dollars less than I thought we had."

Teri's lashes lowered with remembered embarrassment. "I was furious with their incompetence. Finally, they ran a copy of the last couple of years' transactions. It was unbelievable. Money had been going in and out of that account as if it were an active business. Unfortunately, the balance column showed that whatever the business was, it was a losing one." She paused to take a sip of tea in an attempt to ward off the sudden chill she felt.

"When I questioned Rico, he confessed—a real heart-wrenching, Academy Award confession. As he put it, my success made him feel unmanly. Since I wouldn't quit, he wanted to bring more money into the house. He thought gambling was the answer. He never meant to let it get out of control, but he kept thinking he could make it all back on the next race, or the next number—whatever. He promised he was done with it as soon as he paid off the last losses."

"I've heard gambling can be as bad of an addiction as drugs and alcohol. There's even a Gamblers' Anonymous."

"Yes, I know, but the addict has to want to help himself. I believed him at the time, but a few days

15

later, I realized I didn't trust him. I went back to the bank. He had taken out another two thousand dollars the morning after we talked. I withdrew all but a hundred dollars. There was only a few thousand left, but I moved it to another bank and put it in my name alone."

"What did he do when he found out?"

Teri sighed. "He went berserk. Mind you, he never laid a hand on me, but he smashed every piece of our good china before he calmed down. Then he was sorry—but not so sorry that he stopped gambling. A month or so after that, he didn't deposit his check on payday. By the third week, I knew all his excuses, including the one about saving his money to buy me something special, were baloney."

"So you had it out again."

"You got it," Teri confirmed, making a disgusted face. "That time only a lamp was broken. He promised to get help, if I would just bail him out once more, to the tune of fifteen hundred dollars. I did, with the warning that it was the last time. I thought he was doing okay, until two weeks ago." She shook her head, still having trouble believing how easily he had fooled her. "I found out he had stolen a check from my business account, forged my signature, and almost wiped me out."

Selena's mouth dropped open. "This sounds more like a nightmare than a marriage. Can't you have him arrested for that?"

"I don't know. He's still my husband. After everything he's put me through, I don't love him any more, but I can't hate him, either. That night I asked for a divorce. He pulled out all the stops. The macho-man cried like a baby. He reminded me that our religion prohibited divorce, not that we've been especially devout Catholics all these years. He swore he loved me too much to let me go, and starting from that minute, he was going to prove it by being the best husband a wife ever had. But first, he needed a little financial

16

assistance." Recalling how shocked she had been at his incredible nerve, she rolled her eyes and gave a dry laugh.

"This time I refused. He told me he had gotten in over his head with some very nasty people. I saw real fear in his eyes, but I still said no. I was through bailing him out. In spite of my refusal, he lived up to his promise. For the last two weeks, he's been a paragon. We were like newlyweds again. Now I know just how low he's sunk." She took another sip of tea, and Selena waited patiently for her to explain.

"I overheard him on the phone when I went back to the house earlier. He still owes somebody money—maybe the same nasties he told me about. It's all been an act to get me to pay off his debts. The worst part is, I finally realized the reason he won't give me a divorce has nothing to do with our religion, or love. Where he used to resent my earning more money than him, he now wants to hang on to me for the same reason."

"Do you have a big life insurance policy?"

Teri looked at Selena in surprise. "What an awful thing to . . ." She stopped, recalling his words over the telephone: *she won't hold out much longer. I'll make sure of it.* She shook her head slowly, thinking of Rico's explosive temper and the handgun he insisted on keeping in the nightstand drawer. "No. He wouldn't. I don't believe he'd hurt me physically."

Selena shrugged. "Keep your guard up, just in case. If he gets desperate enough, he's liable to graduate from breaking things to breaking bones. Don't look so skeptical—I know what I'm talking about. I've read a lot of true crime stories. And remember, if it looks like he's about to change tactics and try some rough stuff, you can always hang out at my apartment in town."

Teri patted Selena's hand. "Thanks, hon, but I really don't think that'll be necessary. To be on the safe side, though, I'm not even going to confront him. Instead, I'm going to play along until I talk to an attorney. At least I should find out how hard it will be to get a divorce, knowing he'll contest it. Damn! I don't need this aggravation. How the hell am I supposed to work with this over my head?" She swiped at a tear threatening to escape her eye, then forced a smile when she saw how disturbed Selena was. "I'm sorry. It was really tacky of me to dump on you like this."

"Don't say that. What kind of friend would I be if you couldn't unload your problems on me?"

"I've only got one problem I'd like to unload. But he doesn't seem to be agreeable. You know what would be wonderful? If he met some hot, young chick that got him so worked up, he decided to leave me on his own."

"Is there any chance he's fooling around? You could hire a detective to follow him."

"Considering the way he flirts with the models when he gets the opportunity, I wouldn't be surprised if he's cheated on me along with everything else. But since he's been on this good behavior kick, I can account for every hour of his day. Of course, I suppose he could always fit in a quickie along his delivery route if he wanted to."

Selena got up and walked back and forth a few times. "Give me a minute. I've been told I have a very analytical mind. There must be some way to make this easier on you." She paced a little more, then abruptly returned to her seat. Her eyes sparkled with their unusual silver glints. "I've got it. I'll set Rico up. The way he slobbers over himself when he sees me, seducing him should be a cinch. Once I've got him hooked, you'll hire a detective to take some incriminating pictures and, *voilà,* grounds for a divorce."

Teri let out a squeal. "You're too much. I think sacrificing yourself to my husband might be a bit beyond the normal requirements of friendship." Picturing Rico and Selena together made her snicker. Not only were they extreme opposites in coloring, Selena was about four inches taller and thirty pounds heavier than Rico, but Teri had seen his reaction to the bigger woman, and slobbering pretty much covered it. When Teri vocalized her thoughts, Selena joined in. Giggling like schoolgirls, they were soon exchanging ideas about what Rico would do with so much woman after twelve years of sex with a pixie.

Selena amended her suggestion. "I was only thinking of leading him on, but you might have the key to a permanent solution. Sex with me would probably kill him, and then you wouldn't have to worry about how to get a divorce."

"But what a way to go!" Another tear squeezed out of Teri's eye, but this one was from laughing so hard. "If I thought for one minute that you could get Rico out of my life permanently by having sex with him, I'd not only give you my blessing, I'd double your next dozen paychecks!"

Feeling a hundred percent better for sharing a good laugh, Teri started telling Selena about her new series.

Selena smiled and nodded, but she wasn't absorbing Teri's news. Her mind was already occupied with the first step in her plan.

Two

Rico's breath caught in his chest when he saw who had been knocking at the back door. Just looking at her made his cock twitch.

"Can I come in?" Selena asked breathlessly.

"Oh, sure. Teri's up in her studio." He stepped aside, but as she entered, her body grazed his anyway.

"I know. I was up there all morning. She said you were off today."

Rico narrowed his eyes. "She sent you to see me?"

With a throaty laugh, Selena tossed her head, causing her pale hair to swirl around her. "Don't be silly. As possessive as she is about you? She thinks I went home, but I had this incredible craving all of a sudden. I thought you might be able to satisfy it."

Rico watched the tip of her pink tongue moisten her upper lip. For a year she had come and gone without giving him so much as a glance. Not that she had to look his way to turn him on. He had often broken out in a cold sweat simply imagining what it would be like to be in the male model's shoes, running his hands over all that soft flesh. Now, unexpectedly, she was close enough for him to smell her spicy perfume. He cleared his throat. "Craving?"

She appraised him from head to toe before meeting his eyes for a brief, seductive moment. Turning her back on him, she glided over to the refrigerator and opened the door. She bent over at the waist and peered inside. "I can help myself."

Without a doubt, she had the longest, sexiest legs Rico had ever seen. It was all he could do to keep from pressing himself against her ass as she rocked from side to side in her tight short shorts, but he held his ground. A few weeks ago he would have already had her flat on her back after such an obvious invitation. But he couldn't afford the risk now—not with Teri so close to giving in. And especially not with a girl who spent so much time with his dear wife. Besides, he wasn't sure he could trust a broad whose eyes glowed in the dark. After all, before this, she'd never shown any interest in him whatsoever.

"Aha! Found one." Selena showed him the apple she had unearthed. As she took the few steps back to where he stood, she slowly buffed the fruit's bright red skin on the section of tee shirt hugging her full breasts.

Rick was captivated by the sight of her nipples tightening into little points. As big as she was, he was surprised that she could go braless.

"Care for a bite?" she asked, holding out the apple.

With a level of self-control he hadn't known he possessed, he dragged his eyes away from her tits. He had to get rid of her before he exploded. "No. Thanks. I, uh, don't mean to be rude, but I was on my way out. I, uh, have an appointment."

Selena pouted prettily, but he wasn't buying. Maybe knowing Teri could walk in any moment was too great a threat for him. She took a big bite of the apple and sauntered toward the door. "Are you always off on Mondays?"

Her question threw him. "No. My days off change every couple of months. I got switched to Sunday-Monday last week. Why?"

"No reason. I was only thinking if you got bored sitting around the house while Teri's painting, we might catch a movie together . . . or something. I have a lot of . . . leisure time."

He knew he was going to regret it eventually, but he

had no choice. "I don't think so, Selena. It wouldn't be a very good idea."

She shrugged and stepped out the door. "Suit yourself."

Rico waited until her car was out of sight, then bounded up the stairs to Teri's studio.

Teri was mixing a shade of reddish-brown that refused to come out right when the door flew open. She twisted her head around but remained on the stool in front of her easel. "Rico? What's wrong?" A moment later he was behind her. Capturing her head in his hands, he tilted her backward and kissed her hard on the mouth. She made a whimpering sound and he freed her. "Rico!" His hands slipped under her smock as he nibbled her earlobe. "Will you stop? I'm up to my elbows in paint."

"You won't need your hands for what I have in mind." His fingers closed over her breasts, and he felt a stab of disappointment that they only filled his hands instead of spilling over. An image of Selena buffing the apple increased the ache in his crotch, and he ground himself against Teri's hip. Opting for what he did best these days, he lied out of necessity.

"I kept thinking about how good you were last night. Mister Wiggly doesn't want to wait till later to crawl back inside that hot little snatch of yours."

Teri's stomach clenched, but she refrained from shoving him away as she wanted to. A million years ago his dirty talk excited her. Now she could only think of how crude it was. Why couldn't he have grown up, too? "Please don't, Rico. Not now. I've got this color exactly right and I want to use it before it gets dry."

He kept nuzzling her neck while one hand slid down and squeezed between her thighs. "No problem. I'm too horny to make it last very long, anyway."

"I'd rather not stop at all. Besides, I think I may have an infection." She felt him tense, but he didn't withdraw his hands. "It might only be an irritation.

22

You know how much we've been at it these last two weeks. But I think I should see the doctor before I take a chance of infecting you."

He wasn't giving up that easy. Rubbing himself against her again, he murmured in her ear, "I like your mouth just as much. C'mon, mama. Your baby needs you."

Yesterday, she would have granted his request. Yesterday, she hadn't known what he really needed from her. Not only would he never get another penny from her, she wasn't going to let him use her any other way either . . . ever again. She took a deep breath and straightened her spine. "I am *not* in the mood."

She was busy, had an infection, and wasn't in the mood. About the only thing she skipped was a migraine. What the fuck was bothering the bitch now? Rico felt his temper rise, but he quickly checked it. A perfect husband would not rape his wife, no matter how much he wanted it. He backed away from her.

"Sorry I bothered you." His gaze moved to the twin bed on the other side of the room. "You used to like it when I was spontaneous. That was the reason we put that thing up here to begin with. Now I guess it's only another one of your props. And you wonder why I think you love your paintings more than your flesh-and-blood husband.

"We talked a lot about compromises in the last few weeks. I promised not to complain when there was no dinner ready, that I'd try to understand about, what'd you call it? Oh, yeah, your creative juices flowing into the evenings, while I sit alone with the television for company."

"I made a concession about that and you know it." She didn't want to have this conversation, but she also didn't want to let him know she was onto his deception. "I think the photographer that was here today will work out well."

"Hmmm. I'll believe it when I see it." He moved to her side and glared at the painting she was working

23

on. "And your name?"

She knew what he wanted to hear—that she would be putting her married name on her new paintings. This point was not negotiable, as far as she was concerned. "For the last time, Rico, I am not ashamed of your name. I started out using my maiden name on my art for my dad, and now that's the name that has developed a following. Why can't you let it go?"

He had heard her explanation before—how her father was the last of his branch of Carmichaels. It didn't matter to Rico. A good wife, one who respected him as a man, would use her married name at all times. But rehashing old arguments wasn't going to win her over. And at the moment he needed her money more than he needed her respect.

Reminding himself of his ulterior motives, he kissed her cheek. "Sorry, babe. I guess I've still got a ways to go to be the perfect husband. Tell you what, I'll pick up Chinese and you can eat whenever you take a break." He turned and walked away without waiting for her approval.

Teri turned back to her palette, but her mind refused to be distracted.

How could their marriage have gone so bad? If only she had not fallen so hard and fast in the beginning, or not been so anxious to give him all the attention he had lacked as a child. Twelve years ago, when they'd met, their future had glowed with promise.

At twenty-four, Teri had begun to believe she would be on the shelf forever. A short, hazel-eyed brunette with average features to match her average intelligence, she had dated her share of extraordinarily average, nice men. Her boring secretarial job fit the rest of her mundane life. She was primed and ready to fall for someone like Rico Gambini, with his dark Italian looks, sexy smile, and naughty suggestions.

Rico was the postman who delivered the mail to her office. The first time he saw her, he asked her to marry him. When she teased back that she preferred a courtship a little longer than two minutes, he agreed to wait two months, then ask again. And he had. They were so enamored, it never occurred to either of them that they might have differences that could not be worked out between the sheets.

In the years since, Teri could not think of one difference that had been worked out peacefully, let alone lovingly. Except when Rico wanted something very badly. Only then did he descend from macho mountain to placate her with a compromise.

A few years after they were married, he insisted she quit her job, stay home, and have babies, as a good wife should. As a concession, he agreed to her attending art school, thinking it would keep her busy until she got pregnant. He had even helped create a studio for her over the garage of their new home. It had never crossed his mind that she could use that training to earn a living.

His resentment of her career began the first time she received a check for a painting. He interpreted it as a sign that she didn't believe he could support her. That resentment escalated in proportion to her success, but she was willing to deal with his smoldering anger rather than give up her new career.

Despite everything, however, the making up that inevitably followed the arguments seemed to prove that their love was strong enough to weather any storm.

Until the last year or so, when Rico's gambling and lies had eaten away at Teri's love and trust in him. No amount of making up was going to bring that back again now.

Teri went to the desk to check her calendar. Since Rico's assault on her bank account, she had taken on more assignments than ever before. Three completed paintings were due in the next two weeks. If she worked from morning to night, nonstop, she could meet the deadlines. The first chance she would have to go see an attorney would be after that. In the meantime, perhaps she should start locking up her darkroom. There was no telling when he might realize how much he could get for some of her photographic equipment.

How on earth was she going to handle Rico for another two weeks?

Selena sat in her white Cadillac Seville at the end of Teri's block. When Rico didn't drive by after fifteen minutes, she knew his "appointment" had been a fabrication. The bulge in his pants attested to the quality of her seduction technique, so it had to have been her timing that was off. And the location.

Teri's comment about Rico getting a "quickie" along his delivery route triggered an idea. Selena drove to the nearest phone booth and made a few calls. Using the excuse that she wanted to write a letter commending her postman for his fine service, in a little friendly conversation Selena confirmed which branch Rico worked out of and what his regular hours were.

Considering the vast range of time in which her own mail arrived, she surmised a postman's lunch-break could be lengthened if he speeded up the delivery time.

Early the next morning, she set her plan in motion. Because she had no way of knowing where he might stop, Selena was in the post office parking lot when Rico got in his mail truck. Selena had acquired a collection of wigs to use when modeling. That day, she donned a curly black one and big sunglasses to disguise herself in case Rico should notice someone following him.

His route was in a residential neighborhood of single family homes, two-apartment complexes, and a strip mall. Selena had no problem tracking him along his morning route. Around eleven o'clock, he pulled into the drive-through lane of a McDonald's. As soon as Selena figured out he would be eating his lunch in

26

a parking space shaded by the building, she parked her car out of his view. Quickly she removed the wig, put on a big-brimmed floppy hat, and got out of the car.

One glance at her reflection in the window of the restaurant assured her that her denim shorts and red stretchy tube halter were scandalously brief—exactly as she intended. Ignoring the attention she stirred, she went inside, purchased a large diet soda, and exited on the side where Rico was parked.

As she neared his truck, she did a double take. "Rico? Is that you?"

With her hair all tucked up under a hat and those oversized shades, she wasn't automatically recognized by Rico, but her height, exaggerated by high-heeled sandals, and the body that was more out of her clothes than in, had caught his eye the second she'd walked out the restaurant door. The *I-just-had-sex-and-can't-quite-catch-my-breath* voice identified her with a swift kick to his groin. With great effort he forced himself to swallow the bite of hamburger in his mouth, then tried to sound casual.

"Hey, Selena—a bit away from your stomping grounds, aren't you?" He knew she lived in the city, and even if she had been working with Teri that morning, this area of White Plains would be out of her way.

"Kind of." She came alongside the open window where he sat. Purposefully, she shrugged her shoulders in such a way to cause the tube top to slip down a quarter inch. Rico's sharp intake of breath rewarded her effort. "My manicurist relocated to the shopping center down the street." She wiggled her scarlet fingernails under his nose. "See? Doesn't she do a marvy job? I swear, I'd follow her to the ends of the earth." Without waiting for a comment, she walked around to the other side of the truck and slid open the door.

Before Rico realized what she was up to, Selena shoved the mailbag off the seat and climbed in. He

27

knew he should object, but his brain got sidetracked as she pressed the cold soda cup to her throat and drops of condensation trickled into her cleavage.

"Oh, that's better. It's too hot to be outside today." She caught a large drop of water with two fingers and spread it slowly across her chest. Setting the cup on the dashboard, she leaned toward him and whispered, "Tell me, Rico, are you as hot as I am?"

Hot? An incinerator was blasting between his legs. He yanked his gaze up to her eyes, but when she removed her sunglasses, the promise of pleasure he saw there made his struggle that much harder. Why was she doing this to him? Why now? "Look, Selena . . ."

She stopped him by placing her hand on his upper thigh. "I've always heard women couldn't resist a man in uniform. You'd look good whatever you wore, but I think I prefer you in well-worn jeans, like yesterday. I could see exactly what was on your mind." Her fingers inched closer to his heat.

Rico grasped her wrist and placed her hand back on her own leg. "No! I . . . *we* . . . can't do this to Teri. I thought you and she were friends."

Selena gave him a bewildered look. Taking his hand, she brought it to her breast and pressed it there. "Friends sometimes share. Oh, Rico—I get so lonely. Men aren't as eager to get involved with me as you might think. They're afraid I'll be too much woman for them. But I wouldn't be for a man like you. I've wanted you since the first time I saw you. I don't want to pretend anymore."

His fingers flexed into her soft flesh. He wanted so much more than this brief touch. He wanted to strip the scrap of material away and bury his face in those two mounds. Her lips parted slightly and her lashes lowered as she closed the distance between them.

Another second and he would have tasted her . . . there, in a public parking lot, for anyone to witness his infidelity. He pushed her away. "Stay away from me, Selena. You're enough to tempt a saint, and God

28

knows I'm far from that. But I won't be unfaithful to Teri . . . no matter what. Our marriage means too much to me."

Liar! Selena mentally screamed. She would never have guessed he had so much willpower. Whoever he owed money to this time must really have his balls in a wringer. There could be no other explanation for his rejection. She still wanted to help Teri, but it looked like this idea had come to a dead end. Then again, perhaps his libido needed more time in order to overcome his good intentions.

"Okay, Rico. Have it your way." She got out of the truck and slammed the door. Before walking away, she leaned into the open window and blew him a kiss. "If you change your mind, my number's in Teri's address book."

Three days after their introductory session, Drew brought the developed pictures to Teri's studio. Again he was attired in a style customary for his home state.

"Very nice," she murmured as she spread the prints out on the table. "Now, which three would you offer to Ann for the book cover?"

Without hesitation, he set two prints aside, then pointed at two others. "I'm torn between these two."

Teri smiled and chose the third. "You're a natural, Drew. I hope you'll have time to do more work for me."

He ran his fingers through his silver-streaked hair and grinned sheepishly. "I don't think time'll be a problem. Look, I'd feel a whole lot better here if I laid all my cards on the table. I'm sure Ann told you I'm new in town. I arrived from Fort Worth only the day before you offered me this assignment. I don't even have a place to work yet. But there's more to it than that . . . these pictures represent my first paying job as a photographer."

"You're kidding! You showed all the expertise of a pro."

"Let's say I was a professional amateur. I . . . won a few awards . . . in my younger days."

"Well, I'm glad Ann sent you my way first. I predict you'll have more business than you can handle one of these days. What did you do in Fort Worth?" When he grimaced and glanced away, she apologized. "I didn't mean to pry."

"It's not that. I just wasn't sure what you meant by 'do.' "

She recognized avoidance when she heard it, but she pushed anyway. "If you weren't a photographer, what did you do for a living, or are you one of those lucky Texans who discovered oil in his backyard?"

He laughed out loud at that. "Don't I wish. At least then I'd be livin' in some fancy hotel suite instead of campin' in Ann's son's room."

"Oh, dear. No luck finding an apartment, huh?"

"Nothin' on my budget in the city. But I saw a couple places in between here and there that I figure to check out on my way back today. By the way, can you recommend a processin' lab? The one that did these warned me they rarely do work this fast."

Teri wondered what kind of profession he had had that he'd rather not discuss. She decided to respect his right to privacy and jerked her thumb toward a closed door with a red lightbulb above it. "That's the best one I know. I do my own developing. You're welcome to use my facilities anytime. Especially if I'm your number one client." She opened the door to the darkroom. "See? Just like downtown."

Drew stepped inside and scanned the equipment. "This is great. I can't wait to set up my own. I'm not crazy enough to refuse your offer, but I will insist on payin' rent of some kind."

As he stepped back out of the cramped room, Teri said, "You can pay for your own supplies. In a way, this works out very well." She briefly explained Selena's reluctance to model for anyone but her, and her own desire to make the transition as easy as possible for her favorite model. "So, I gather you won't mind coming here to do another session together tomorrow."

"It would be a pleasure, ma'am."

Teri chuckled. "You know, I *do* like the way you say that, but I think it would be quite proper for you to call me Teri . . . considering the fact that we'll technically be sharing quarters for a while."

Drew's fingers combed his hair again. When Teri noticed the sheepish look that accompanied the gesture, she determined it was more of a nervous habit than primping on his part. "Yes?" she prompted.

"Do you do that a lot?"

"What?"

"Anticipate someone else's thoughts?"

"Hardly!" She laughed and rolled her eyes. "Reading minds would have kept me out of a lot of trouble." A frown threatened to take over her smile, but she instantly pushed thoughts of Rico out of her head. "Unfortunately, I take everyone at face value, and your face looked like you had something else you wanted to say, that's all."

"Yeah, well, it's about the other day. I had the feelin' I did or said somethin' to offend you — that you thought I was comin' on to you." He thought her blush was one of the prettiest sights he'd seen in ages. "I wasn't. At least not intentionally. I'm not . . . I mean, I wouldn't . . ." Drew sighed. "I was married to the same woman for a long time. It's been quite a while since I made a pass at a woman, I guess I may have . . ."

"It's all right. I'm a little sensitive myself at the moment. I realized afterward that I overreacted." She held out her hand and he shook it firmly. "Friends?"

"Friends."

For some time after Drew left, Teri had trouble keeping her mind on her canvas. Not only was he an

31

incredibly good-looking man with an accent that dripped liquid heat into her pores, he was a gentleman in the true sense of the word.

That was something Rico wouldn't comprehend without a guidebook. At least her husband was still trying to impress her with his good behavior. And he had bought the lie she'd told him about seeing her gynecologist while he was at work. An imaginary infection had granted her ten days of abstinence. All she had to do now was ignore his hangdog expression when she refused to stop working and join him when he went to bed each night.

Her main hope now was that whatever the rest of his "surefire plan" was, it didn't escalate too soon. She needed a little more time to prepare for a new life . . . without him.

Drew returned the next day with a surprise. Ann and Lettice, the editor for the book they were working on, had decided to sit in on the shoot. It had been a while since anyone from Century had done that, and Teri was extremely pleased that they would take the time. They often complained about her living so far outside the city, but that never stopped them from using her work.

This book was a western with two strong-willed characters who fought with each other through most of the story. Selena was in a long skirt and camisole. Pete, the male model, was chosen for his well-defined muscles; he was shirtless and his skintight jeans were unsnapped and slung low on his narrow hips.

"They're perfect!" Lettice exclaimed immediately.

Ann beamed. "I told you, you could leave it to Teri. She never fails me."

Teri accepted the praise with a smiling nod. "Okay, kids, let's get to work."

After the first few minutes, their audience was forgotten and Teri and Drew were orchestrating the models' performance much as they had the first time.

Teri heard the sound of the door opening and turned in time to see an extremely menacing character enter her studio. The man was about six feet tall, but his broad shoulders and bulky arm muscles made him appear bigger. Coarse black hair hung straight to his shoulders. A bushy Fu Manchu moustache and reflective wraparound sunglasses hid most of his face. The large gold hoop hanging from his right earlobe caught the light as he surveyed the inhabitants of the room.

"Mrs. Gambini?" His voice was as rough as his appearance.

Teri took a step forward. "I'm Mrs. Gambini. I didn't hear you knock."

"I didn't. I was lookin' for your husband, but you'll do."

It was difficult to tell with his mirrored glasses, but it looked as though all the man's attention was focused on Selena. "Excuse me," Teri admonished sternly. "We're in the middle of a shoot here. If you would like to leave your card, I'll have Rico call you when he gets home."

The man's lip curled up into a sneer. "My card? That's cute." He turned his head toward an unfinished canvas. "I heard you was an artist. Not bad."

Teri wanted to order him out, but like a coiled snake, he emanated a capacity for deadly violence. "Who are you? What do you want?" she asked quietly.

"I guess you could say I'm in the insurance business. Yeah, right. I'm checkin' out your property for insurance purposes. Like, I see you got a lotta paint here. Now paint is a very flammable substance, ya know. This whole place could go up" — he snapped his fingers at her face — "like that. Ya oughta consider lockin' your door, too. Never can tell who might wander in when you're . . . all by your lonesome."

Teri gasped. There was no doubt that he was threatening her. The reason was not that hard to fathom. She needed to hear it said aloud, but no sound would form in her throat to ask for an explanation.

The man strolled to the open door, then turned back to her one last time. "Your hubby owes a debt to a certain Irishman. Tell him he's got four more days, till five o'clock Tuesday. If I were you, lady, I'd be thinkin' how to help him with his problem . . . for your own sake."

He was gone several seconds before anyone moved, then everyone spoke at once.

"Please!" Teri cried to stop their conjectures. She was thoroughly humiliated by the fact that the incident occurred in front of people she worked with. "I have no idea what he was talking about, and until my husband gets home, there isn't much sense in speculating. Now let's get back to work."

Selena kept one eye on Teri as the morning progressed. She could see that fear still had a grip on her, but Teri was doing her best to conceal it. This woman was the best friend she had. She loved Teri as much as she'd loved her own mother. And Teri was hurting because of a man.

Just as her mother had been hurting.

Selena despised Rico for putting Teri into such a precarious and embarrassing position. She had to find a way to get Rico out of Teri's life. Thoughts of vengeance gave Selena the impetus she needed to come up with phase two of her plan.

Three

"I don't want to hear any more of your apologies, Rico! That animal was in my *studio!* He as much as threatened that he'd burn the place down if you didn't pay up." So livid she couldn't choke out another word, she slapped his face with all her pent-up fury. A split second later the back of Rico's hand lashed her cheek.

The moment he'd done it, he knew all hope was gone. He reached for her, but she jerked away. "God, Teri—I didn't mean to do that. This whole thing's got me so nuts, I don't know what I'm doing anymore." He collapsed on the sofa and buried his face in his hands.

Teri glared at him, her chest heaving with anger. "And I don't care anymore. It's over, Rico. We're through. I want you out of my life."

A sob escaped his throat—one he didn't have to fake for her benefit. When he looked up at her, real tears filled his eyes. "They're going to kill me, Teri. I didn't know who I was involved with until it was too late. These guys don't believe in payment plans. And they don't just nail your knees to the floor when you don't come through. If you don't pay these guys, you disappear . . . in pieces. Ya gotta help me, babe, one more time, and then I'll get out of your life . . . if that's really what you want."

She saw the naked desperation in his eyes, smelled his fear, and felt absolutely nothing. Even the anger had left her. Where there was once so much love, now there was only numbness. Her voice sounded as hollow as she felt. "How much? How much will it cost me to be rid of you permanently?"

Rico pressed the heels of his palms to his eyes. He could hardly believe his ears. The life raft she was holding out had a hole in it, but it was the only one in sight. Keeping his eyes downcast, he mumbled, "Seven grand . . . *in cash.*"

Teri gritted her teeth. Seven thousand dollars was twice what she'd received from the gallery that day. She could refuse, and risk having her studio burned to the ground. She could bail Rico out, and trust him not to contest the divorce when the time came. Forced to choose the lesser of two evils, she said, "All right, Rico. I'll have the money for you by Tuesday morning." The only punishment she could mete out was to make him sweat it out until the last minute. "I suggest you start looking around for a place to live, because I want you out of this house one minute after you have the money in your hand. In the meantime, I'll be sleeping in my studio."

Selena laughed at the image in her bedroom mirror. It had taken the rest of the day after she left Teri's, but she had done it. No two pieces of the costume had been purchased in the same place. The ugly black wig, thick moustache, wraparound glasses, and gold earring looked like duplicates of the originals. Only the hoodlum's clothes had to be revised to allow for additional padding. An old black vinyl jacket and gloves hid her feminine arms and hands, and dark beige makeup altered her ivory complexion. If the guy who had threatened Teri were standing beside her now, they'd look like twins.

It pleased her sense of irony that the thug should have a role in her little play, albeit in absentia.

She had come to the conclusion that her previous

attempts to seduce Rico had failed partly because he'd had time to consider the consequences of his actions. Even if he had succumbed to her flirtation and agreed to a rendezvous, he could change his mind before the appointed time. The solution was simple. Rico must not be given time to think, let alone resist.

She could effectively implement her plan without having sex with Rico. She hadn't actually promised Teri that she would go that far, but she couldn't forget what a kick Teri had gotten out of the imagined scenario. One day she might tell Teri what she had done for her, then they would share a laugh even greater than they had that day. No sacrifice was too enormous if it insured Teri's happiness.

Just as she had ensured her mother's.

Saturday morning, in her man's disguise, she drove out to White Plains again. Phase two required an apartment in one of the two complexes along Rico's delivery route. Her first choice was the larger one, but she was turned away because there were no vacancies. She suspected her rough appearance was the real reason. The other building had only about thirty units, but it was not as well maintained, and the parking lot was only half full. Leaving her car at the shopping plaza a few blocks away, she walked the short distance and claimed to have taken a bus.

The manager was too happy about getting three months' rent in cash, plus an advance deposit for use of the building's utilities, to demand identification or references, especially when his new tenant informed him he would need the furnished apartment for only one month, since he was leaving town.

The next part of Selena's plan required infinite patience, but freeing Teri was worth any effort required. When Teri had told her she would be completely tied up painting for the next week and would not need her to model, Selena decided to set her scheme in motion. She had nothing better to do than sit and wait for Rico to walk into her trap.

On Monday she scrawled four words on a sheet of paper, folded it, and sealed it in a letter-sized envelope. Once again dressed as the thug, she went to the post office and mailed the envelope to the apartment she'd rented, with return receipt requested.

Then she waited.

Tuesday morning Teri had the money ready for Rico. As he made his rounds, he couldn't help but consider how far he could run on seven thousand dollars. In the end, however, he paid his debt and headed home. This last scare had finally shaken some sense into him. He was through gambling—with his life or his love.

In spite of how far apart they'd grown, he couldn't leave Teri to deal with the mess he'd made. He was still a man, and she was still his woman. If only she could understand how her success emasculated him, and how jealous he was of all the men she worked with. Those were the reasons he'd fucked up—the gambling, the lies, the women. But it was all over. He loved Teri and almost lost her.

The only thing left to do now was to get her to forgive him. At the moment it looked like an impossible feat, but somehow he would earn Teri's trust again. The love they had once shared was too special to flush away in a divorce court. He had already bought himself some time by convincing her he hadn't yet been able to find a place to move.

Selena knew this had to be the day. The letter had not been delivered Tuesday or Wednesday, but she hadn't really been expecting such speedy service. The certainty that the time was nearing had adrenaline thrumming through her system. When the doorbell finally rang, she almost forgot to look through the peephole to make sure it was Rico before opening the

38

door. As soon as she saw that it was him, she deepened her voice and called, "Just a minute."

Closing her eyes, she inhaled slowly. It had been a long time since she had stepped into her chosen role. A fresh surge of exhilaration filled her as she reveled in the forgotten sense of power. This day's challenge would see her vanquish another enemy.

She turned the lock.

Rico's mouth gaped as the door opened in front of him. For a moment he thought he was hallucinating. Standing there, with nothing but her long hair to cover her luscious curves, was Selena. The impact of seeing her unexpectedly . . . and undressed . . . left him speechless.

"Hello, Rico. I've got something for you." She grasped his arm and pulled him inside.

He watched her close and relock the door before he thought to protest. "Selena, I . . ."

Before he could orient himself completely, she pressed his body back against the door and claimed his mouth in a searing, tongue-probing kiss. The mailbag hit the floor with a thud as his fingers released the certified letter. When his own body joined her assault, any objection he might have had was overruled.

Now that he had finally given in, he couldn't touch enough, couldn't taste enough, as quickly as he needed. Not wanting to remove his hands from the flesh she so willingly offered, he allowed her to remove his clothing. When she knelt before him to pay him the ultimate homage, he could barely tolerate the mind-boggling pleasure. She used her tongue and teeth to drive him to the brink of insanity, only to leave him hanging there as she rose to her feet.

She led him into the bedroom and slowly crawled onto the bed. Holding her breasts up to him, she asked, "Do you want me now, Rico?"

He emitted a low growl as he pressed her backward and took one big nipple into his mouth. He was already about to burst, but he wanted to hold on to the feeling a while longer. Controlling the urge to bury himself deep inside her and be done with it, he made himself savor each of her feminine secrets. She moaned and squirmed beneath him, heightening his desire with each of her kittenish sounds.

Suddenly, as if he were weightless, she flipped him onto his back and mounted him. He cried out with surprise and intense pleasure as she enveloped him completely, but prevented him from thrusting.

"No," she whispered. "I'll do it. You just enjoy yourself." And with those words she leaned forward, pressing her breasts to his face and creating a silken curtain of white hair around them.

With agonizing deliberation, she tightened her vaginal muscles, eased herself to his very tip, then made him wait for the moment when she would descend and begin again. He had never had a woman tease him into such a state. He hadn't even come and he was thinking of how soon he could manage a repeat.

His climax began slowly and built rapidly into an explosive finish that almost stopped his heart. In some far corner of his mind he was aware that her hand had slipped beneath the pillow and back out, but he could barely breathe, let alone open his eyes to see what she was doing. He felt her raising her upper body, and smiled when her muscles gripped him again and he was able to give her a valiant salute in return.

Selena sneered at the macho pig as she raised the knife in her hand. His egotistical grin contorted as she punctured his jugular and slashed his throat.

Four

Selena's thighs clenched around the body until the involuntary twitching ceased. The initial spurt of blood settled into a low-pulsed flow as Rico's life oozed out onto the mattress. Indifferent to the blood splattered over her body or the semen dripping down her thigh, Selena got off the bed and reached for the three items she had hidden beneath—a wooden cutting board, a meat cleaver, and three large self-locking plastic bags.

She centered Rico's right hand on the board, then whacked it off with the cleaver. Raising it by a finger, she let the blood drain from the appendage, then dropped it into the bag.

In one of the many true crime novels she had read, a branch of New York's Irish mob kept the hands of someone they killed to use his fingerprints on some future job. Since the thug had mentioned "a certain Irishman," Selena decided this act would firmly tie Rico's murder in with that mob. Also, the idea of using the fingerprints had intrigued Selena enough to risk keeping such clear-cut evidence of her accomplishment. She stared critically at the body on the bed and decided she had done a professional-looking job. She severed Rico's left hand, put it in another bag, then secured her tools in the third.

It was vital that she not leave any clue behind that might insinuate that this was anything but a mob hit.

41

She had brought everything she would need ahead of time. She began the tedious chore of cleaning up the blood. Then she searched for any long hairs on or around the bed and took them into the shower with her. When she was through scrubbing herself, she pinned her hair tightly to her scalp, then flushed all the loose hairs down the drain. Next she covered every inch of the apartment with a hand-held vacuum. After that, she used a cloth soaked in ammonia to wipe every surface she might have touched during her brief stay.

She had a few final details to arrange. It could be days before anyone would discover the body, and she wanted to be sure it was still somewhat identifiable without the fingerprints. To slow the decomposing process, she turned the air conditioning down as cold as it would go, closed off all the vents except the one in the bedroom, and shut that door. Her fascination with the criminal mind pushed her to perform one more eccentricity, just to confuse the police. When she left the apartment carrying all her belongings in a bag similar to Rico's mailbag, she was wearing her man's disguise with two variations.

Although it was a snug fit, she had put on Rico's uniform shirt. The black wig was tied in back and tucked inside the shirt collar. If someone witnessed her departure from the apartment complex, it would be the postal uniform that would be remembered. If that someone was very observant and knew what the regular postman looked like, that witness would be supplying the information Selena wanted given. The description of the man who had left the premises in Rico's mail truck would fit that of the thug that had threatened Teri and rented the apartment.

It took only a bit of common sense to deliver the mail for the next several blocks. The riskiest part came when Selena reached the shopping plaza where her car was parked. She had to carefully choose the moment to abandon the truck and leave without being seen. Nature sided with her that day—a sudden cloudburst had shoppers dashing into stores or cars, more intent on keeping dry than observing a mailman. It also kept the store managers from wondering why the mail truck was outside though no mail was being delivered.

Later that night she would dump her tools, disguise, and Rico's belongings, except for his keys, in the murky East River, but for the moment, Selena had to make the transformation back to her usual appearance by the time she entered the parking garage where she kept her car.

Only when Selena had locked and chained her apartment door did she permit herself to relax. She stored Rico's hands in the back of her freezer, put his keys in her special souvenir box, then methodically reviewed her activities, assuring herself she had overlooked nothing. Besides disposing of the remaining evidence, there remained one small detail. With a satisfied smile, she opened the envelope Rico had delivered to her and smoothed the creases from the paper within.

She had to find the right place for it. Taking the paper and a thumbtack into her bedroom, she smiled as she always did upon entering this place of purity. The French provincial furniture was just a shade off the snow-white of the ceiling, walls, and carpet. With a critical eye to perfection, she studied the only adorned wall—the one opposite her elegant canopied bed. Teri's new painting, which Selena had purchased anonymously from the gallery, held the center position. Surrounding it were posters of the covers she had modeled for and a collection of newspaper and magazine articles about Teri Carmichael. It required a bit of rearranging, but eventually she managed to make a space for her new addition within a square formed by the articles.

For a final inspection she crawled onto her bed with its white eyelet spread and canopy and picked up

43

the pretty porcelain-faced doll lying on her frilly white pillow. As she hugged her oldest and very best friend, her knees automatically folded up to her chest and her thumb slipped into her mouth. Softly sucking, and rocking back and forth, she read and reread the four words that made up her vow:

I AM THE PROTECTOR

And she remembered the day she had first learned what those words meant to her . . .

"I'll protect you, Juliette. Don't cry," Selena whispered to her favorite doll as she slid the closet door almost closed. Selena thought herself brave for a five-year-old, but not so brave that she could stay alone in total darkness. Without that sliver of light, she might imagine that the soft ribbon hanging from the dress above her head was a spider's web brushing her cheek instead.

"Now, Juliette, you know we must be very quiet, just like Mommy told us the last time. She'll make sure he doesn't find us again." Curling herself into a ball in the corner, Selena wiped her runny nose on her sweatshirt sleeve and reminded Juliette not to sniff aloud. Her parents' voices carried clearly from the living room downstairs. The angry words that her father had shouted only moments after arriving home had been warning enough.

She only wished she'd had time to go to the bathroom before hiding. The memory of how he'd hurt her the last time she'd had an accident made the tears fall harder. To keep from thinking of how much she had to go, she made herself listen to the argument going on outside her room.

"It's none of your goddamned business where I was tonight. I don't have to—"

Selena missed the rest of what he said because of

the loud crash. She supposed he'd tripped and knocked something over and broken it. That sometimes happened when he came home late like this. And she also knew that besides being clumsy, he would smell bad and squint and blink a lot, like he couldn't see very well.

Her mother's voice was softer, and she couldn't make out the words at first, but then they suddenly became clear. Her parents had come into her bedroom.

"I *told* you, she's not here," Selena's mother said in a strange, scary voice. "She's . . . visiting my sister tonight."

"Your sister! What'd I tell you about her?"

"Lenny, please—"

"She's probably teaching my kid how to shoot up right now. If you were any kind of decent mother you wouldn't let that crazy cunt near her. I can't work my ass off all day and teach you how to do your job, too."

"I—"

A hard smack cut her off, and when Selena heard her mother's cry, she had to peak out through the narrow opening in the closet. Her mother had fallen on the bed. She was pressing one hand against her cheek and looked terribly afraid. Daddy's back was to Selena, but she could tell he was taking off his belt. She knew how bad that belt could hurt and wanted to stop him from hurting her mother that way.

She was about to push the closet door open when her mother looked right at her hiding place.

"*No!*" her mother screamed, just as the wicked belt whipped through the air. But Selena understood the order was for her and she obeyed. She knew it was her mother's only way of protecting her. In spite of the fear and hatred making her small body shake, she stayed quietly in her place long after her father left the room and her mother lay still on her bed.

Someday, she promised Juliette, *he'll be sorry. I*

45

won't always be so little. This time her mother had protected her, but Selena vowed there would come a time when she would take care of her mother.

How will you do it? Juliette asked in the musical voice that only Selena could hear.

"I don't know. He's so very big."

I'll help you. And when you do all the things I say, you will become the Protector.

Selena liked the sound of that so much, she gave Juliette a happy hug. When she thought it was finally safe to come out of hiding, she became aware of a problem that made her tears start all over.

She had wet herself again.

Five

Teri came awake with a start, as if she had forgotten to set her alarm for an important appointment. She yawned and rubbed her eyes before focusing on the clock on the studio wall. It was only six-thirty, and she had no appointment. Surprisingly, she had slept more than a couple of hours. The narrow bed she had been trying to rest on for the past seven nights groaned as she pushed herself into a sitting position. "My sentiments exactly," she grumbled as she massaged her lower back. Rico assumed it was his charm breaking down her resistance, when in fact it was thoughts of their king-sized, extra-firm mattress enticing her back into the main house.

She wondered when he had gotten home last night, or rather, this morning. It was the first time in weeks that he hadn't come straight home after work. Perhaps he had found a suitable apartment and—No, she didn't believe for a minute that he was really looking. At one A.M., she had cleaned her brushes and gone to bed without having heard his car. A quick glance outside at the empty driveway let her know he had either come and gone while she'd slept, or he had never come home at all.

Now *that* was unusual. From time to time he'd come home late with one asinine excuse or another. Occasionally a hint of perfume clung to him. And occasionally someone else drove him home because he was in no shape to drive. But he *always* came home.

Teri made herself examine how she felt about his being out all night. Jealous? The complete absence of that feeling confirmed she was doing the right thing in seeking a divorce. However, he had been her husband for twelve years, and she couldn't help but be concerned about his welfare. Especially after the lethal warning she had personally received.

Chilly fingers of suspicion scraped her spine, bringing to mind an unwelcome possibility.

Surely he had paid them back. He'd sworn he'd given them the money on Tuesday, right after he'd cashed her check. As frightened as he was, she couldn't believe he would try to evade them. But what if, like the addicted gambler she now knew him to be, he had thought he could double or triple the money she had given him, and used it to make a bet of some kind? Why hadn't she thought of that before and insisted on going with him for the payoff?

She shook herself. One meeting with an obnoxious hoodlum was enough for a lifetime.

Her fretting was probably a waste of time. As usual when she was working, the phone in her study was not plugged in. Rico must have called and left a message on the answering machine—she had forgotten to check it last night. As she pulled on her robe and headed out of the studio, she hoped that was the case, but the uneasy sensation she had awakened with would not go away.

Teri relaxed slightly when she saw the flashing red light on the machine. Playing back the messages, she scribbled names on the pad next to the phone: Gary, a co-worker of Rico's, wanted him to call as soon as he got in; someone named Horse had some interesting advice to share; Drew and Selena each said they'd see Teri the next day if she didn't call back; and there were two calls—at six and eleven o'clock—from Mr. Kelly, Rico's supervisor at the post office. He sounded furious. Teri made a note of both numbers he left.

Walking through their bedroom to the shower confirmed what Teri had guessed: Rico had not been home last night.

Showered and dressed, she had just fixed a cup of coffee when the phone rang. She grabbed it before the second ring.

"Rico?"

"No! This is Kelly. Where the hell *is* that bastard?"

"Mr. Kelly?" Teri forced herself not to respond as crudely. "This is Rico's wife. He's not here, and I don't *know* where he is right now."

"Did he ever get home last night?"

"I don't see—"

"Look, Mrs. Gambini, I'm sorry if I'm upsetting you, but Rico's in deep shit if he doesn't get in here *pronto*."

Teri took a deep breath. "And *I'm* sorry, Mr. Kelly, but I haven't seen or heard from Rico since yesterday morning. You will undoubtedly talk with him before I will, so you can stop leaving obscene messages on my machine."

"Oh. I see." His tone indicated that he did indeed.

She wished she understood as well. Mr. Kelly's call had aggravated her already nervous state, but it made her realize she wanted to be left alone today. Before returning to her studio, she called Selena to save her the trip out to White Plains. Teri could hear the disappointment in Selena's voice, but there was something else she couldn't identify.

"Are you *sure* you don't want me to come up? Just to keep you company? It's no trouble," Selena managed to insist with barely a suggestion of a whine.

"No, really—I've got to finish this painting for Century today, so I don't have time to do the shoot we discussed. Monday will be soon enough."

"But, um, how's everything going with Rico?"

Teri paused. Selena asked that question in every conversation lately, and Teri had begun to regret having confided so much to her. She found it more comfortable to give the same noncommittal answer each time. "Fine. Everything's fine. I do have to get to work now, hon. I'll see you Monday." Teri knew if she could see Selena now, she'd be pouting, but she didn't have the patience to soothe her young friend today. She'd make it up to her later.

She depressed the hang-up button and was about to call Drew when she realized he hadn't left a number. She thought of calling his cousin Ann at her office, then decided against it. There was really no valid reason he couldn't use the darkroom today while she was painting, as he had done two other times this week already.

After putting out some cat food and refilling the bird feeders, she went back inside her studio and tried to use her painting to block out all thoughts of Rico. He was a full-grown man and she was no longer his caretaker. When he finally came home, she swore she wouldn't even ask where he had been.

Teri had almost convinced herself to stop worrying about him when she heard the sound of a car's engine in the driveway. She looked out the window expecting to see Drew, yet hoping it was

50

Rico. Instead, there was a blue-uniformed officer getting out of a white and blue police car. Her stomach clenched with the certainty that something had happened to Rico. She had been fighting it all morning, but that hadn't kept the truth away.

Then again, what if Rico hadn't paid his debt and this was another messenger from that "certain Irishman"? Her perverse memory called up stories of criminals pretending to be cops. Might a killer also steal a police car to flesh out his disguise? For one cowardly moment she considered staying within her locked studio, but her common sense told her that would only postpone the inevitable. With trembling fingers she unlocked the door and stepped out onto the landing as the officer approached the front door of the house.

"Officer?" she called down, and waited for him to locate the source of the summons. When he returned to the driveway and looked up at her through his dark aviator glasses, she noticed how his right hand rested on the top of his holster. Again, she had to force herself to speak. "May I help you?"

"I'm looking for Mrs. Rico Gambini."

Swallowing her cowardice, she descended the stairs to join him in the driveway. At least that way she was out in the open, on level ground, in case he turned out to be a fraud. "I'm Mrs. Gambini. Has there . . . been an accident?" She held her breath, waiting for his answer.

"Not that I'm aware of," he replied in a way that made Teri think he had dropped the word "yet." "Is your husband at home?"

"No." She made a mental note of the number on his silver badge, then decided to answer his next question before he asked. "I haven't seen or heard from him since yesterday morning."

51

"Is that normal?"

She shook her head. "No. He's never stayed out all night before, but—" She shrugged, leaving the insinuation hanging, and looked away from the reflection of herself in the man's glasses.

"But?"

Suddenly she was tired of having questions thrown at her. She returned her irritated gaze to the officer. "My husband and I have had some problems lately. Now, why don't you tell me what this is all about?"

He hesitated a moment, as if trying to decide if she was worthy of any information. Using a minimum of movement, he slowly extracted a notepad from his back pants pocket and a pen from his shirt. The sight of him preparing to write down anything she might say unsettled Teri that much more before he finally explained.

"Last night we received a report of a postal truck abandoned in the Village Shopping Plaza. This morning, their postal supervisor confirmed that it was one of theirs."

"Mr. Kelly?"

He glanced at his pad and nodded. "Mr. Kelly said the truck had been assigned to postal employee Rico Gambini, and that said employee had not returned at the end of his shift yesterday."

Teri's mouth dropped open. "Why didn't Kelly call the police yesterday?"

"Apparently he thought he was covering for a friend who just got waylaid. Kelly also advised that he had already spoken to you about your husband's whereabouts and received the same answer as you gave me."

The knot in Teri's stomach tightened. "What should I do?"

"Tell me, Mrs. Gambini, were the problems between you and your husband sufficient to cause him to take off?"

She frowned, thinking again of the seven-thousand-dollar check she had handed Rico a few days ago. Maybe it was enough to tempt him to gamble, but it was certainly not enough to run away on. "I don't think so. I couldn't even convince him to move out of the house."

"Any other problems that might have caused him to abandon his truck and disappear on his own?"

On his own? As opposed to, with someone else's help? Teri considered telling the officer about the gambling and the animal that had threatened her, but the consequences of pointing a finger at someone so dangerous without any proof were too great. She still held on to the possibility that Rico might show up later today with a screaming hangover and empty pockets. She elected the coward's answer. "I'm really not sure."

The way the officer's mouth curved downward suggested he didn't believe her one bit. "Well, that's about it, then. Thank you for your help." He put away his pad and pen and walked back to his car.

"Just a moment," Teri called as he opened the car door. "What are you going to do now?"

"Basically, the post office has their truck back. Unless they file a formal complaint against your husband, that's the end of it. My coming here this morning was a routine follow-up on the abandoned government property."

"But what if . . . what if Rico doesn't show up today?"

"After twenty-four hours, you can file a missing person's report. Then someone might be able to track down when he was last seen."

Teri was about to ask another question when Drew's car pulled into the driveway next to the police car. She watched the officer back away and tried to give Drew a pleasant greeting. It fell short, and he noticed immediately.

"Good mornin'," Drew said, eyeing the retreating vehicle. "Trouble?"

She would have lied without hesitation except for the fact that he had been part of the audience that had witnessed her previous humiliation. But that didn't mean she had to tell him any details. "I don't know yet."

A big gray tomcat that had been crouching beneath the stairs throughout her discussion with the police officer now sauntered out to inspect the new arrival. When the animal rubbed itself against Drew's snakeskin boot and meowed, he leaned over to pet the creature's furry head. The little kindness earned a mental nod of approval from Teri. Her gaze moved to the photographer's case slung over his shoulder and the shopping bag in his hand, and she changed the subject. "Do you have a lot to do today?"

His grin gave her spirits a little lift. Yes, thank heavens. Having Ann on my side is getting my new career off the ground in a hurry." Holding up the bag, he added, "I picked up a few props for two still-life covers I've been assigned. I sure wouldn't object to any advice you might be willin' to part with." This time his smile was accompanied by a wink. So far, Teri hadn't been able to keep herself from offering her advice whenever he worked in her studio. Each time she did, she apologized for interfering and he assured her he appreciated her help. When he didn't push her any further about the police visit, she was the appreciative one.

On the climb back up to her studio, Teri replayed her conversation with the police officer. Maybe she should have told him about Rico's gambling. If there was a question of foul play, she wouldn't have to wait the full twenty-four hours to report her husband missing. But that only brought her back to the potentially dangerous role of accuser: was she willing to go through mug shots looking for the man who had threatened her? She realized her fearful reaction to the idea was probably what that animal had counted on when he'd confidently issued his veiled warnings in front of witnesses.

Damn! How could Rico have involved her in something so awful? It now seemed entirely possible to her that Rico had blown the money and was hiding out somewhere. In fact, he would probably be calling any minute, begging for her help. The mere thought of his daring to ask her for more money riled her so much, most of her fears fled from her mind, but as soon as she entered her studio, she plugged in the phone, just in case.

Drew gave a soft whistle of appreciation when he saw the nearly completed painting on Teri's easel. "You are one talented lady, ma'am."

Teri smiled her thanks for the compliment as she donned her painter's smock. That Texas drawl of his was enough to dispel the last of her fears. She was suddenly very glad she hadn't had his phone number to stop him from coming today. "You didn't leave your number on my machine. Are you still staying at Ann's?"

He was busy spreading out the contents of his shopping bag on a table as he answered. "Nope. As of yesterday afternoon, I moved into a place in Tarrytown. It's just a furnished efficiency, but it's all I need at the moment. Unfortunately, I won't have a phone in until later next week. So Ann is still acting as my message center."

"You're lucky to have her."

"Don't I know it. She says she has a weakness for lonely cowboys."

Teri chuckled. "Her and a few million other women." When he turned his head back to her and raised one dark eyebrow, she quickly added, "It's one of the so-called feminine fantasies, which is why historical western romances are so popular."

Turning the rest of his body toward her with his hands fisted on his hips, he gave her his full attention. "You mean women find something romantic about cleaning stables and listening to cattle moan all night?"

She laughed at his disbelieving expression. "More like they imagine riding double on a horse across the wide-open prairie, under a starry sky, with a barely civilized but immensely capable man." Her mind flashed an image of Drew as that cowboy with her cradled in front of him, between his spread thighs. She laughed again, this time at her overactive imagination, and started preparing her paints. "You'll get the full picture if you keep reading all the manuscripts for the covers we do."

But Drew wasn't ready to abandon such a fascinating subject. He brought a stool up next to hers and perched on it with one boot heel hooked on the upper rung. "Tell me more about these feminine fantasies."

She thought he was teasing her, but his blue eyes were bright with sincere interest. "You really want to know?"

"Sounds like the kind of inside information that could come in mighty helpful." Then, with a wink, he tacked on, "In my new line of work, that is."

Teri groaned as she realized he *was* teasing a

little, but she didn't feel threatened by him. It had been so long since she'd relaxed around a man that she couldn't remember how to counter innocent innuendo. She opted for a serious answer to his reasonable request. "The most successful plots of the romance novel hone in on some feminine fantasy, and the untamed cowboy is one of them. There's also the captor/captive angle, where the heroine is more or less forced to do what she wanted to do anyway, but couldn't for one reason or another."

"That one sounds twisted."

Teri pursed her mouth thoughtfully. "It does have to be handled just right, but I'm sure you'll understand better after you've read one."

Drew leaned forward, crossing his arms over his bent denim-covered knee. And what about you, Teri? What's *your* fantasy?"

His deep voice had softened; it made Teri think of black velvet brushing against her skin. Her common sense told her not to answer, to get to work, to send him back to his side of the room. Her rebellious emotions demanded she answer and extend the luxury of his freely offered attention a little longer. "I . . . I don't know," she hedged with a shrug.

His finger, stroking her cheek, felt cool against her warm flesh. "I do believe you're blushin', ma'am. C'mon, tell ol' Drew which kind of fantasy rings your chimes."

She laughed at his "down-home" slang. "Why don't you get to work, cowboy?"

"Cain't. Once my curiosity's aroused, it's like an itch that needs scratchin'. But I'll make you a fair trade. You tell me yours and I'll tell you mine."

The twinkle in his eyes was contagious, and Teri found the nerve to tease him back. "All right. My fantasy is to be on an island where there are no men at all. That way, I might get some work done!"

Drew's hand covered his heart. "You wound me deeply. But I can take a hint." He rose from the stool, then lowered his head so that his departing words tickled her ear. " 'Course, now you'll be wonderin' all day just what *my* fantasy is."

As he sauntered back to his paraphernalia, she rolled her eyes and shook her head, but let him have the last word. A few minutes later, when the tint she was blending looked about right, she realized she was still smiling. What kind of existence did she have, that smiling had become a noteworthy event? Why, the last time she'd had a good laugh was—Her brush froze in midstroke. It wasn't that long ago. Only about two weeks. When she and Selena were joking about . . . *about how to get Rico out of her life permanently.*

She daubed her brush carefully on the canvas, creating a slightly raised area within a purplish cloud. Her moment of levity was over. Rico was back, at least in her head. With Rico, she had never been able to tease and walk away. He was the kind of man who only touched or cuddled as a prelude to sex. Now that she thought about it, the only time he even talked nicely to her was as a form of foreplay. Drew talked to her; today he even teased her and encouraged her to play, without making her feel obligated to perform a personal service for him in return.

Like a fire bell, the reason clanged in her brain. His little act had fooled her completely, at least at that moment. Each time she had seen him before, he was kind and extremely polite, but there was nothing playful about him. If anything, she had noticed a sadness that overcame his expression

58

when he was certain no one was watching. The teasing male routine, with those not-so-subtle yet utterly safe innuendos, was all for her benefit. Rather than badger her to explain about the police officer or pretend he wasn't interested, he distracted her from her worries.

She could not think of a single time when Rico had behaved so intuitively. In their relationship it had always been her responsibility to keep her antennae tuned to his needs if she wanted peace.

Peace . . . was such a state ever going to be hers again? She had thought getting a divorce was going to bring enough additional anxiety into her life. What was she going to do if Rico really had disappeared? When she had made that offhand comment to Selena, she hadn't imagined it actually happening or the problems his "getting out of her life" could create.

With a sigh, she set down her brush, wiped her hands, and walked over to the table where Drew was arranging some items on a swatch of ivory satin. When he turned to her, she held out her hand.

He accepted it, but raised a questioning brow.

"Thank you," Teri said with a poor attempt at a smile. When he grinned back, she knew she had guessed right.

"Shucks. 'Tweren't nothin', ma'am."

Her smile grew. "Stop that. You had me going there for a minute. You really *are* going to be my friend."

He enclosed her small hand between both of his and squeezed gently. "I'll keep up the witty cowboy repartee if you'll keep smilin' for me—unless you'd rather talk about what's causin' those unsightly worry lines across your forehead."

She wanted to laugh it off, but he was looking

at her with such tenderness that she choked up instead. She turned, but his hands held her in place.

"Easy," he murmured, tugging her back.

Her lower lip quivered, then her eyes filled with moisture. *Oh, God, no . . . not now.* But the Almighty must have decided against saving her pride. Teri burst into tears.

Drew released her hands so that he could wrap his arms around her. He held her close as she sobbed against his chest. When her crying lessened to an occasional ragged breath, he stroked her back and hair, and rocked her slowly from side to side as if she were a small child.

Teri had never felt such comfort at the hands of a man, and it took all her willpower to give it up so quickly. But the sharp reminder that she barely knew Drew gave her the strength to pull away.

"I am *so* sorry," she said, swiping at her cheeks with her fingers. "I guess it's been building up for so long now, and after this morning—" He released her and went over to her worktable for a tissue. After she'd dried her face and blown her nose, her eyes widened at the huge wet spot on his shirt. Lifting the hem of her smock, she rubbed it frantically against his chest.

"Whoa," he said with a laugh and stilled her hand. "I'm okay. It's drip dry. But now you have to pay the penalty."

She frowned as he led her back to her stool and again sat next to her, but he was right. She wondered if it was written somewhere that if you let someone see you cry, you had to explain yourself. He didn't insist. Somehow, she knew he never would. And for that reason she told him why the police officer had come to see her.

He listened to what she said and guessed at

what she kept to herself. "Did you tell him about the hood who threatened you?" When her eyes flew open in surprise, he knew that answer, too. "Teri, I was here. Remember? Pretending it didn't happen doesn't make it so. That guy promised violence because of something your husband owed someone. Do you know what it was all about?"

Taking a deep breath, she decided she needed advice, and Drew seemed willing and able to offer it. She told him about her husband's gambling and the check she gave him for what was supposed to have been the last payoff.

"Are you certain he made it?" Drew asked, voicing her own doubts. When she shook her head no, he grabbed her hand and pulled her upright. "C'mon. Let's go."

Confusion caused her to dig in her heels. "Where?"

"The police, of course."

"But the officer said twenty-four hours."

"Teri, even from what little you just told me, it seems pretty obvious. Either your husband didn't pay off his debt and the bad guys caught up with him, or he's taken off on his own, in a big hurry, which also sounds like he didn't pay up, but means that *you* could be in danger."

She freed her hand to unbutton and remove her smock. "But couldn't there be some other explanation?"

"Sure. It doesn't sound like your marriage was going smoothly. Maybe he ran off with someone else, in the middle of a work day, without his car or any luggage."

"No. That sounds crazy. Besides, he promised me an uncontested divorce in exchange for the check. He was the one that didn't want to end our marriage."

61

"You had already asked for a divorce?" he asked with surprise.

"Yes, but—"

"No more buts." His look was one of total exasperation as he tugged on her hand and she pulled back again.

"Wait! What if these 'nasties,' as Rico called them, come after me because I've accused them of something?"

Drew gripped her shoulders and gave her a small shake. "You have no choice. They may be coming after you anyway. Now let's go."

Detective William F. Kidder tilted his head to the left so that his good right ear had a better chance of picking up everything being said by the woman across the desk. It didn't really bother him that his once flat stomach now protruded over his belt or that what little hair he had was snow white. His hearing was the defect the department was using to force him out of the job that was more important to him than life itself. True, he had never worked in the big city, but even in White Plains he had solved more than his share of homicides in the past thirty years.

In his mind, there was nothing that compared to the thrill of the hunt and, even though there was no body to confirm Rico Gambini's demise, Kidder's bloodhound nose detected the scent of a fresh kill.

When Mrs. Gambini and Mr. Marshall first came into the station, the desk sergeant took their report. However, when he had assimilated the words "threat," "Irishman," and "missing gambler," he wisely asked Detective Kidder to sit in. The first thing Kidder had done was to ask Mrs. Gambini to tell him everything she had told the sergeant. That broad's nerves were on the outside of her skin, and it wasn't only because she disliked having to repeat herself.

Kidder listened to Mrs. Gambini's facts and hypotheses, some of which her cowboy companion confirmed. Then he asked a few more questions of his own and told them he'd be in touch as soon as he learned anything. He suggested Mrs. Gambini might look through the rogue's gallery for her threatening visitor, but he didn't insist she do it today. There would be time for that later.

Kidder watched Mr. Marshall assist Mrs. Gambini out of her chair with the gentlest care, then rest his hand on the small of her back as he escorted her out of the office. When the couple left the area, Kidder turned to the desk sergeant, who had been scribbling notes ever since he'd joined them.

"You want to be a detective, don't you, Parkins?" The young man nodded. "Did you make note of what you just saw?" Parkins's freckled face and narrowed auburn brows betrayed his uncertainty. "I mean, the way they looked at each other? The way he touched her?" He massaged his loose jowls as he let his conclusion sink in.

"I may be old-fashioned, but I consider it bad form for a woman to bring her lover to the police station to report her husband's disappearance."

Six

Neither Teri nor Drew made an effort to cut the tense silence during the ten-minute drive to Teri's house. There, Drew insisted on going inside with her for a tour, but Teri saw through his flimsy excuse.

"Drew, honestly, I appreciate your support this morning, but this isn't necessary. I'm sure no one is lurking in my bathroom shower, waiting to spring out at me. However, I do think I at least owe you lunch, so have a seat and I'll make some sandwiches for us."

In spite of her confidence, he made her stay behind him as he took a look in every room and closet before agreeing to return to the kitchen.

"You're a regular knight in shining armor, aren't you?" Teri quipped, waving him toward a chair.

He flinched as if she had struck him. "Hmmph. I would have felt a lot better doin' that if you hadn't mentioned the shower. I'm afraid the movie *Psycho* put a permanent dent in any armor I may have."

"*Ooh!* And you braved the shower monster to protect little old me?" She batted her eyelashes at him, then opened the refrigerator door. "So, Sir Drew, do you prefer ham or turkey?"

Rather than sit down or answer, he walked over to her and pushed the door closed again. "You don't have to do this, Teri."

She cocked her head at him. "You're not hungry?"

"I'm not talking about lunch. I mean the smiles and little jokes. It's okay to be scared."

"It is?" she asked, letting her smile slip away. His eyes held a promise of secrecy concerning her weakness.

"Yes, it is. I'm an expert on the subject. Even knights in shining armor can be afraid of nonexistent things. But in your case, the danger is very real. So don't hesitate to ask for a little protection."

With that, he opened his arms and she stepped into them without thinking. As he gave her the safe comfort of his embrace, she sighed. "I could get used to this, you know," she whispered. In response, he tightened his hold for a brief moment and rested his chin on the top of her head.

Beneath her cheek she felt the steady beating of his heart and wondered why it seemed so right when everything else about this was wrong. Her husband was missing, possibly even dead. Some maniac could arrive any minute to burn her house down or worse. And a virtual stranger was holding her in his arms for the second time that day. Like she belonged there.

Only when she detected an increase in his heartbeat did she realize that his reaction to their embrace might be very different from her own. At her slightest movement, however, he stepped back.

"Are you goin' to be okay?" he asked, lifting her chin with his finger and searching her face.

"Mm-hmm. Thank you again. I'm certainly fortunate to have crossed your path just when I needed a few good hugs."

He gave her a slow smile. "There's plenty more where that came from."

She smiled back, but his words only compounded her concern that he might eventually be expecting to share more than a friendly hug. He was acting out of consideration now, but he was still a man. Not only was it extremely inappropriate to think about such a thing at the moment, she never intended to have another relationship built on lust.

"Oh, jeez!" Teri blurted out. "I forgot to check the machine." A moment later she played back the one message left while they were gone: "Teri. This is Selena. Please call me as soon as you listen to this message. You know, you really ought to plug in your studio phone when you're alone. What if something important happened and someone was trying to reach you? Call me. 'Bye."

Teri reset the tape and went to the kitchen, where Drew was investigating the inside of her refrigerator.

"It was only Selena," she said, nudging him out of the way.

"Yeah, I recognized the heavy breathing."

She pulled out the sandwich fixings and again asked his preference.

"Turkey's fine. And I'll take some of that lettuce and tomato, on whole wheat bread. Have you got any Thousand Island dressing?" Again he dipped his head inside the fridge.

"Yes. Now please sit down and let me do something for *you*. Or are you one of those people who consider the contents of refrigerators vastly intriguing?"

He laughed aloud. "Guilty as charged." He sat quietly, appearing completely relaxed, while she turned a quick bite into a work of luncheon art with the aid of olives, pickles, and chips.

"Selena sounded pretty anxious to hear from you," Drew said between mouthfuls.

"She's always like that. Oh, that didn't sound very nice. I don't mean it in a bad way. Truly. She's just, well, in many ways she's like a lost little girl. She has more or less attached herself to me."

"I noticed. She's a one-woman Teri Carmichael fan club, from what I've seen so far."

Teri nodded. "I know. I'm not sure what I ever did to deserve such blind devotion, but my ego appreciates it. There are times though, when . . . oh, never mind."

"What?"

"Nothing. It's petty."

"Good. Say somethin' petty and mean. If only to assure me you're not a total saint and Selena has a flaw beneath that glamorous exterior."

Teri was oddly pleased that his reference to Selena didn't sound as if he was captivated by her sensational appearance, as most men were. "It's just that there are times when she seems to want more from me than I'm willing or able to give."

Drew raised one eyebrow, but held his tongue.

"No, no. Not like that. I think I could tell if she, um, wanted something physical from me. No, it's more like she wants the lion's share of my time and attention. If I'm not mistaken, I think I'm her only friend, and she wants me to be the same with her. I'm not even sure she works for anyone else. Most of the time I don't mind, but occasionally—"

"You feel smothered?"

Teri nodded thoughtfully. "Yes, I think that describes it."

"Like Brenda."

"Oh?" Teri didn't want to pry, but he had never revealed any personal information beyond where he was from. She wanted to hear more. When he didn't expound, she could not resist prying a little. "Would you care to explain that?"

He hesitated for a moment, then gave a dry laugh. "Brenda's my ex-wife, and, as a matter of fact, I came up with explanations for her behavior for about fifteen years. I gave it up the last three years before the divorce and let her try to explain mine instead."

Teri quickly added up eighteen years of marriage, but that still didn't tell her how long ago they'd divorced, or why, or how old he was; nor could she follow the cryptic remarks he did make. She opted for what she thought was the least offensive inquiry. "Do you have children?" She saw the sadness she had noticed before and half expected him to say no, that like her, he'd never experienced that joy, but that wasn't the case.

"Yes. Two. Drew, Jr.; he's fifteen. And Jennifer; she'll be thirteen soon. They live with their mother in Fort Worth." He looked at his plate, at the clock on the wall, out the window—everywhere but at Teri.

"They're great kids, but we had them for the wrong reasons. Brenda was several years younger than me when we got married, so I figured she still needed some time to grow up. But she wasn't interested in growin' up. Instead, she grew more dependent every year. She didn't want to do anything on her own, not even a hobby. If she could have gone to work with me every day, that would have tickled her pink. I pushed her into havin' kids, thinkin' it would give her someone to dote on other than me. Dumb idea, huh?"

"Well, I suppose it made sense to you at the time. You're not the first person who thought children could heal an ailing marriage. I know."

"But you never tried that."

She smirked. "Oh, we tried. It just didn't produce results. I guess it turned out for the best after all."

Drew moved the conversation to more neutral ground, but Teri was pleased to have extracted at least a few personal tidbits from him. After lunch, at Drew's strong recommendation, they went back up to the studio to work. Teri returned Selena's call before she got involved in her painting again.

"Hi, Selena. It's Teri."

"Did you hook up your extension phone?"

Teri laughed. "Yes, but I'll never get this assignment done today if I don't keep at it. Did you need something?" Teri listened to Selena take a breath before speaking.

"Actually, I can't explain it. I had this strong urge to talk to you and make sure you were okay. You know?"

Teri almost told her she was not okay, but that Drew was with her, except her intuition told her neither bit of information would please Selena.

"Yes, I know. I really must get back to work now."

"Well-l-l. All right. Promise you'll call if you need me . . . for anything."

"I promise. I'll see you Monday." As she hung up the phone, she thought she'd worry about what to tell Selena Monday, when that day arrived.

By late afternoon, Teri and Drew both finished their work without further interruptions, and he offered to take her to pick up Rico's car from the post office parking lot. As they left the house, Drew suggested they have dinner first at a nearby restaurant. She justified her quick acceptance by telling herself they were merely two friends sharing time. If it were a date, it would have been planned ahead of time, and it wouldn't have been at a well-lit family-style restaurant like this.

Throughout their meal, they each made an effort to keep the conversation light and the topics general and far away from ex-wives, children, and missing husbands. Teri could not help but notice that, although she talked a lot about her work, Drew carefully avoided any mention of his former career. The more time she spent with him, the more curious she became about his life, but he didn't seem the least bit inclined to fill her in. On every impersonal subject, however, he was knowledgeable, expressive, and often humorous.

And she wished she'd met him a lifetime ago.

Teri's conscience demanded she pick up the tab and, after a brief debate, Drew agreed to split it with her.

From the restaurant, they went to the post office, where Teri pointed out Rico's car.

"I want to thank you again, Drew . . . for everything. You were right about working this afternoon and having dinner out of the house. It was a lot better than sitting around waiting for the phone to ring."

"Good. A lot of people wouldn't be so rational in your situation. Now, you take his car back home. I'll follow."

"You don't have to do that. I'll be fine."

"I'm sure you will, but it'll make me feel a whole lot better knowin' you got home safe. In fact, if you'd like me to stay—"

"Stay?" Teri's eyes widened.

"Since I'm such a gentleman, I'm goin' to pretend I didn't notice how you misconstrued my perfectly gallant meanin' and go on. If you'd like me to stay in the studio tonight—while you're in the house—I'd be glad to."

"Oh my, no, that wouldn't be a good idea. I mean, what if someone—"

" 'Nuff said. But since you can't call me, I'll give you a call or two over the weekend, if that's okay. For my own peace of mind."

"All right. Will you be working Monday?"

He slapped his forehead. "Ah, dang! I almost forgot to ask—would you mind if I had two models come up in the afternoon for a shoot? We could go elsewhere, if it's a problem."

"Not at all. No matter what happens, you can use the studio." She didn't need to itemize the possible things that might happen by Monday.

As promised, he followed her home, then checked out the interior of the house and studio before leaving her alone.

"Fool!" Drew said aloud to the empty apartment. He was ten kinds of fool. The one thing the psychiatrist warned him not to do—right after no more booze and no more drugs—was no more codependent relationships.

"Be aware," the clinic doctor had stated, "besides being an addict, you have a caretaker personality. You're very vulnerable to people who need your help."

In other words, he was a sucker for a hard-luck story or a damsel in distress. He had married Brenda believing she needed rescuing. But the only rescuing she had needed was from her own insecurities and helplessness. When he finally quit trying to help, she thrived. *He* ended up nearly killing himself, and four hundred other innocents along with him. Hardly justifiable.

"Vulnerable" seemed to summarize a lot of things he was feeling. Perhaps he would have been

71

vulnerable to any damsel at this point, distressed or otherwise. Six months had passed since the divorce, a large portion of it spent in the rehab clinic. Before that . . . he couldn't be sure when the last time was that he and Brenda had made love. No, that wasn't right. He wasn't sure when the last time was that they had sex. They hadn't made *love* in a decade. Until spending time with Teri, he had thought his sexual needs had retired from the active world.

Vulnerable or not, he couldn't simply turn away from Teri, could he? Or remain indifferent to her problems, knowing she might be in serious danger?

In defense of his vulnerability, he told himself Teri wasn't anything like Brenda. Teri was bright and creative, and seemed to be entirely self-sufficient. If anything, it sounded like she was the caretaker in her relationship. Drew thought it was a shame he'd had to meet her when her defenses were so depleted she was grateful for any morsel of security dangled before her. If they'd waited a few months, until after she'd recovered from losing her husband, they might have been able to make a go of it together.

Thoughts of her husband made him angry all over again. What an asshole her husband must have been! How could he have used her that way? Hadn't he known what a prize he had, right in his own bed? Drew realized he already thought of Rico Gambini in the past tense, but then, so had the police.

No matter whose fault it was, however, Teri was now another damsel in distress, and even though her distress was much more genuine than his wife's had ever been, he couldn't be sure if that wasn't the primary feature that had attracted him. For

Teri, he was little more than the security blanket of a child lying awake in her darkened bedroom. Though the situation was scary, she'd probably get through it fine without his assistance.

Nevertheless, he couldn't turn away. He did decide it would be in their best interest however, if he found a less intimate way of comforting her in the future.

Teri went into the kitchen and poured another cup of coffee out of habit. It certainly wasn't out of need; her nerves were stretched so taut her ears were ringing.

She had lain down in her own bed last night, but as tired as she was, she could only doze for short periods at a time. Then some nightmarish image would jolt her awake again. The animal and his dark wraparound glasses played a key role, as did Rico. But at one point, she remembered dreaming of Detective Kidder. The intense concentration he had directed at her in the police station became a suspicious glare in her brief dream. Had he really looked at her like that, or were her fears blowing everything out of proportion?

Perhaps she should have asked Drew to stay after all. Having someone nearby might have given her enough security to allow her some rest. But the final dream before she got up had proved that that could have been a serious mistake. When she had refused his offer, she had been considering how it would look to the neighbors, or worse, how Rico would react if he did happen to wander home. But those possibilities took a backseat to her greater concern.

She couldn't trust herself. If he had been in the studio last night, she would have gone to him—

maybe for reassuring conversation, perhaps for another comforting hug—but alone, in the middle of the night, she might have asked for more.

The chime of the doorbell caused her heart to trip. She set down the coffee mug and took a deep breath. Whoever it was, she needed to calm down.

The identity of the visitor made that feat impossible. Through the peephole Teri recognized Detective Kidder, and anxiety gripped her throat. There was only one reason she could think of to explain why he would be at her house at eight o'clock on a Saturday morning: he had news of Rico.

On the other hand, the fact that he was dressed in a casual short-sleeved shirt instead of a jacket and tie, as he had been yesterday, suggested he was off duty. The dream image of him ran through her mind, increasing her fear of what he had to tell her. With great effort, she forced herself to unlock the door and partially open it.

Detective Kidder's gaze scanned her and the room beyond before he greeted her. "Good morning, Mrs. Gambini. Glad I didn't wake you. We met yesterday." When she didn't acknowledge him, he elaborated. "At the police station. I listened to your report."

Teri wondered if police had always had the ability to strike terror in her heart, or if it was only a result of the circumstances, but it took every ounce of courage she could muster to make her vocal chords function. "Yes. I remember." Her voice cracked on the last syllable and she cleared her throat. "Detective Kidder, wasn't it?"

"Right," he said, not smiling. "Could I come in for a few minutes?"

She finally regained some control over her thoughts and opened the door wider. "Of course.

Please." Stepping back, she waved him into the living room. "Have you found Rico?" she asked as soon as she closed the door behind him.

He didn't answer. Instead, he walked further into the room, moving his head as a camera would pan a scene. She was close to screaming at him for an answer when he turned around. Her expression must have been readable, because he immediately looked contrite.

"Sorry, I didn't realize you were speaking." He took something out of his shirt pocket and affixed it to his ear. "I forgot about this."

She stared at the hearing aide and wondered why she hadn't noticed it yesterday. He answered her, as if he had clearly heard her thoughts.

"Vanity. I hate needing this thing—especially around the youngsters at the station. They think the old man ought to be put out to pasture as it is." He made an adjustment to the aide, then gave her a brief, close-mouthed smile.

It didn't go far to relax her. "Detective—" When he turned his head slightly, she raised her voice a bit. "Do you have news about my husband?"

"I guess that would depend on your definition of news. Is that coffee I smell? I hate to ask, but I left my house so early this morning."

Why was he being so evasive? Although she felt like shaking him until his teeth rattled, she decided she'd better let him tell her what he had to say in his own way. "It's a fresh pot. How do you take it?"

"Light and sweet. Please," he added as an afterthought, followed by another tight-lipped smile.

A minute later, Teri was back with a mug of steaming coffee, but Kidder was nowhere in sight. Assuming he needed to use the bathroom, she set down the cup and paced impatiently. When another minute passed without the expected sound of running water, she headed down the hallway.

At the same time as she noticed the vacant guest bathroom, Kidder stepped out of her bedroom at the end of the hall. "Were you looking for something, Detective?" He didn't look nearly as guilty as Teri thought someone should look when caught snooping.

"Nice house. My late wife liked Oriental, but I always thought it was too fancy. Wish she'd seen this—kind of Southwest desert and American Indian. Did your husband help pick it all out?"

She'd completely lost her patience by the time they returned to the living room. "No. He didn't care one way or another. *Please,* Detective, tell me what's going on!"

"Isn't that your husband's car in the driveway?"

"Yes," she hissed. "I picked it up last night."

"Have a seat, Mrs. Gambini," he firmly suggested, as if they were in his office instead of her home. She complied only so that he'd get to the point.

"We haven't located your husband, but we have a few ideas. Yesterday afternoon I spoke to the merchants at the Village Shopping Plaza. Two of them remembered seeing the postal truck pull into the parking lot. It seems your husband was running later than usual and they had had their eyes peeled for him. Unfortunately, as he was parking, it began to rain, and neither of those witnesses saw Mr. Gambini get out of his truck. One of them was the woman who reported the abandoned vehicle later Thursday afternoon."

"Do you mean to tell me he simply disappeared from a busy shopping center—one where a lot of people know him by name, by the way—and not a soul saw what happened to him?"

Kidder raised his arms in a helpless gesture. "It goes like that sometimes. People racing around with their minds on their own business, a sudden downpour, and who knows? I have a few more people to question at that plaza. I also got a map of your husband's usual route and his approximate timetable, from his supervisor. Since no one has reported seeing him after he was at the shopping plaza, I figure the next best thing is to try to reconstruct his day, working backward. You said yesterday that you didn't see or hear from him after he left for work in the morning. Is that correct?"

"That's right."

"Is that usual?" Her frown encouraged him to explain. "Did he ever call or come home during the day? Like, for lunch?"

"Rarely. He always said he'd rather stick to his routine of working straight through and finishing early."

"He was a punctual man, then?"

Teri didn't care for his use of the past tense. It seemed . . . indelicate. "When he wanted to be," she answered, thinking of the days he didn't come directly home after work.

"Hmmm, yes. That would agree with what the witnesses said about his work habits. So, tell me, Mrs. Gambini, why do you suppose he was running so late Thursday? They said it was almost two hours."

Her brows raised in surprise. "Two hours?" Rico could have done any number of things in two hours. "I told you, he gambled. He owed all that money to someone. Maybe he didn't pay them back Tuesday when I gave him the check. Maybe he met with them Thursday morning instead. That might have delayed him."

"Or caused his disappearance, he said, completing what she was thinking. "Would you mind answering some personal questions for me, Mrs. Gambini? It would help me get a better picture of the man I'm trying to locate."

"I understand. What would you like to know?"

"First, why don't you just tell me whatever comes to mind about him? You never know what little detail is going to help me later on."

For the next half hour, Teri filled him in on the facts about Rico's life, few of which seemed to have any bearing on his disappearance. But when Kidder started probing into their marital relationship, she grew defensive. He made her feel like she was under an interrogation lamp, like an incorrect answer could automatically convict her of some horrible crime.

"Did you and your husband fight? About his gambling, or anything else?"

"Doesn't every couple have their share of arguments?"

"But you stayed married in spite of his gambling."

She rapidly weighed the consequences of her next words and decided to tell him a partial truth. "We were getting divorced."

It was the first thing she had said that caused his deadpan expression to alter with interest. "I see. Do you work outside the home, Mrs. Gambini?"

"I'm an artist. My studio is above the garage, so I guess the answer to your question is yes."

"An artist! How I envy creative people. I have absolutely no talent myself, but I sure can appreciate it. Would you let me take a look at some of your work? It would be great to go back to the station and tell the boys I met a real artist today."

Teri would have preferred that he just go back to the station right now, but at least a tour of her studio would get him out of her house, and maybe on his way.

After she escorted him into her workroom, however, he seemed only slightly interested in the paintings themselves.

Pointing to the closed darkroom door, he asked, "What's in here?" and then opened it to look inside before she could answer.

When he finally left, a few minutes later, she took another look at her studio, trying to imagine it from his viewpoint. What had he been looking for? She went back downstairs and walked through the house asking the same question.

In her bedroom she grimaced at the unmade bed, the open closet door, and the clothes and shoes she had dropped on the floor last night. Then she remembered his question about Rico's car. Could he have suspected that Rico was not really missing, but hiding right here in his own house? What reason would she have for trying to mislead the police that way?

She played with the idea of a fraudulent insurance claim. That would make sense if they were planning to use the money to pay off a big gambling debt of Rico's or to run away to South America. But didn't the insurance company require a dead body before they paid any benefits?

The other possibility that came to mind was that she and Rico could be using the police to convince the bad guys of his disappearance so they would get off his back. The problem there was, that might not stop them from taking revenge on her or her belongings. So that didn't make much sense either.

A third and more frightening alternative was

that Kidder suspected she was personally responsible for Rico's disappearance, and was looking for evidence of some kind. He had asked a lot of questions about their marriage. But telling him about the forthcoming divorce should have convinced him that violence was unnecessary—they'd soon be legally separated anyway. As long as Kidder believed Rico wanted the divorce, there didn't seem to be any logical rationale behind her doing Rico any harm.

So, what was Kidder looking for?

Kidder turned on the hand-held tape recorder as he drove away from the Gambini house. He had discovered long ago that people talked more freely if they didn't think he was taking notes. Thus he had begun verbally recording his impressions immediately after an interview ended. Fortunately, his memory hadn't gone the way of his hearing.

He shook off his initial disappointment about the way this interview had gone and instead considered the challenge that lay ahead. It would have been all too easy if the morning had turned out the way he'd expected.

His early morning, impromptu visit had served only to unnerve Teri Gambini a little more. He hadn't found Drew Marshall breakfasting in the kitchen or lounging in her bed. There was no pair of wineglasses in the sink signifying a private celebration, nothing anywhere that supported his instinct in this case. He could be wrong, but he seldom was. Time would tell, of course.

His nose said she hadn't been completely honest with him. On the other hand, she had told him things that a woman guilty of knocking off her husband normally wouldn't reveal. That might

80

make sense if it hadn't been her hand that had done the dirty deed, but her lover's.

Even though this wasn't technically a homicide case yet, he had a long list of ideas and questions to be investigated. He would begin by tracking down Rico Gambini's missing two hours. After that, he would start searching for motives and opportunities among every possible suspect. He would work around the clock. Sooner or later the *corpus delicti* would turn up.

And Detective William F. Kidder would be ready for it.

But it had to be soon. He desperately needed to crack one more big case fast. That would sure show those administrative rocket scientists that the old man still had what it took to be a detective. A desk job in the property room! He hadn't received the official transfer notice yet, but that was where rumor said he was being shipped. They might as well exile him to Siberia. He would be cooped up in that stuffy room all day long, then go home to his silent house, all cluttered with the gewgaws his wife had loved and he hadn't had the stomach to throw out. The mere thought of that kind of existence had him considering how the wrong end of his gun would taste.

Once that fatal notice reached his hands, he would have two weeks to report to his new assignment, two weeks to solve a crime that might normally take months or even years. But that was exactly the kind of grandstand play he needed to convince Administration to postpone his transfer.

If he were to take everything Teri Gambini said at face value, the obvious perpetrators were the Irish mob and the motive was revenge for an unpaid gambling debt. He would check it out as well as anyone could, but his nose told him that was a little too pat. It was very convenient for a murderer, or murderess, to blame a homicide on some unknown person in a known criminal element. A body might never be found, or even searched for, and if it was, there would be few clues, if any. It would have been a professional hit, void of the errors caused when human emotions were involved. But just the suggestion that it was a mob elimination was enough to keep some detectives from even looking for the body. A really lazy detective, one who didn't have his job on the line, might put the file aside and chalk it up as unsolvable.

But not Detective William F. Kidder. He didn't take things at face value. And he rarely accepted the obvious, especially when his job was on the line.

Fortunately for him, two less obvious suspects had fallen right in his lap. They had made one major error beside letting him see how they cared for each other. Having five witnesses to the alleged thug's threat was overkill. Kidder figured the man could have been hired to dress up and reel off the standard threatening words, but Kidder didn't buy the idea that one of the mob's errand boys was quite that stupid. A single witness, made to overhear the incident accidentally, would have been far more credible. The two suspects he had in mind, however, would have been acting on emotion, not intellect.

And between the two of them, Teri Gambini was clearly the weaker. It wouldn't take much to break that nervous little broad. Why, he bet he could have her babbling a confession in less time than it took to clean his weapon.

Seven

As the sun rose Monday morning, Teri was no closer to getting any answers. She had no idea where her husband was, and she still couldn't imagine what Detective Kidder had been looking for. Nor had Kidder been in touch with her again over the long weekend. She hoped the lack of new information was only because the detective didn't work on Sunday and not because he hadn't been able to find any leads. With each passing day she grew more certain that Rico had met with some terrible fate, but the lack of any proof to back it up had left her in a nervewracking limbo. Selena's very early arrival at the studio didn't help any.

"Teri! You look absolutely awful," Selena exclaimed without her usual tact. "Do you have the flu?"

For a brief moment Teri was tempted to say yes and let it go at that. She wasn't sure she was up to repeating everything again and then convincing Selena not to worry about her. But eventually Selena would find out the truth and be hurt that Teri hadn't considered her enough of a friend to confide something so important. "No, it's not the flu. I've had a rough couple of days."

"Oh?"

Teri sat down at the small table and Selena followed her lead. "Rico's missing." When Selena didn't react to that with so much as a raised eyebrow, Teri reworded her statement. "He never came home. He just disappeared on Thursday, and no one's heard from him since."

"How nice."

"Selena! What an awful thing to say!"

Selena's perfect brow creased with that mild criticism, and her calm expression altered to one of bewilderment. "But it's the truth. Surely between the two of us we can speak the truth."

Teri's stomach twisted at the thought of how Detective Kidder would interpret Selena's offhand comment. "Selena, please. Don't say something like that, even in jest."

"Why? No one's here but us. We both know you wanted to get rid of him, and now it looks like you got what you wished for." Her face broke into a rare ear-to-ear smile. "And you don't even have to double my paychecks." She giggled and gave Teri a playful poke.

Teri failed to understand what was so comical, but Selena was quick to fill her in.

"Don't you remember what you said? It was exactly two weeks ago. We were sitting right here, having coffee. You had just found out Rico had been lying to you again, and you said, 'If I thought for one minute that you could get Rico out of my life permanently by having sex with him, I'd not only give you my blessing, I'd double your next dozen paychecks!' Then we laughed so hard you had tears in your eyes. It was one of the best times I've ever had!"

Selena's silver eyes glowed with a joyous light, but Teri couldn't bring herself to share her pleasure in recalling the conversation. She remembered it all right, but with an enormous amount of guilt that she'd ever had such a wicked thought. But Selena not only remembered it, she'd memorized the exact words. And for Selena to call it one of her best times seemed to make the bad joke that much worse. "Selena—"

"Oh, now, don't you worry." Selena patted Teri's shoulder and whispered breathily, "Your secret wish is safe with me. I'd never tell a soul."

"Well, it's just that there's this detective—"

"What?" Selena's eyes abruptly filled with anger. "I had to report Rico's disappearance to the police."

"But I wanted . . . I mean, why didn't you call me? I would have handled that for you, or at least gone along with you. Really, Teri, you shouldn't have tried to take care of this on your own. It was quite selfish of you, you know. After all, that's what best friends are for."

Teri couldn't understand what had caused Selena's anger, but as her irritated expression was replaced by a hangdog look of devotion, she realized the young woman felt left out. She again decided not to mention that Drew had been with her. In a far corner of her mind, she noted that Selena had added the word "best" to their friendship.

Teri tried for a diplomatic excuse. "I didn't want to drag you out here on your day off. The only reason I even mentioned it is because this detective came by and, well, he made me a little nervous. I don't think he'd think our conversation was all that humorous." Now Selena looked crushed. Teri sighed; she simply couldn't win today.

"I would never, *ever* do or say anything to hurt you, Teri. You must trust me about that."

Teri mentally squirmed under the piercing gaze Selena fixed on her. She suddenly needed some breathing room and got up from the table. "What do you say we get to work? I need to get my mind busy."

Selena brightened immediately. "Great! What are we doing today?"

"I just wanted to do some sketches for an idea I had. It would help if you had short curly hair. I think there's a red wig like that in the prop cabinet."

As usual, once Teri started working, she lost track of time, and Selena never complained, no matter how long she had been holding the same pose. It was late morning when a knock on the door interrupted them. When Teri saw that it was Detective Kidder, her first hope was that he had news about Rico. Her second was that Selena would be true to her promise.

This time, as soon as Teri let him in, he was ready to get down to business. This time, Teri did the stalling. She didn't want to take any chances with Selena. God knew what she would say with the intention of defending her.

"Detective Kidder, this is my model, Selena. We were right in the middle of working, but if it's something urgent . . ."

"No, nothing yet. I'll only keep you a few minutes. I was wondering—"

Teri cut him off by turning to Selena and saying, "Selena, why don't you relax for a few minutes. I'll go outside to talk to the detective."

Selena glided past the two of them with a flip of her wrist. "Stay here. If you don't mind, I'll go out for a walk instead. I'm rather stiff from this morning."

Teri flushed, both from the awareness that Selena knew she didn't want to talk in front of her and the reminder that she had thoughtlessly caused Selena some physical discomfort.

Selena closed the door behind her and descended the wooden stairs with a heavy foot. A moment later she tiptoed back up and pressed her back against the wall next to the door, grateful for the warm spring day that had made Teri open the window. She could hear the conversation as clearly as if she was inside with them.

"Light and sweet, right?"

So Teri was fixing the detective a cup of coffee. Good—she hadn't missed anything important. She supposed it was natural for Teri to want to talk to the officer in private, but it hurt all the same. She wanted to share every moment of this victory with her dear friend, which included dealings with the police. Teri simply wasn't mentally equipped to side-step the kinds of questions they might ask. *She* was.

Teri was acting most peculiarly. Selena had thought she'd be happy about her freedom, but she seemed very upset instead. She hadn't even laughed over their private joke. That was the moment Selena decided not to tell her about what she'd done for her. She realized then that Teri didn't want to know the details any more than her own mother had.

As part of her mind recorded the conversation going on inside the studio, her gaze drifted down the wooden steps, and she recalled another flight of stairs and another time she had stood listening . . .

Eight-year-old Selena stood outside her father's room for several seconds and listened to his loud snores. As her mother would say, the drunken son-of-a-bitch was passed out again. She only hoped she could wake him up at the right time. Juliette's plan counted on that.

But he couldn't wake up too soon, either. So she stayed as quiet as a little mouse while she went back to her room and pulled her special box out of the closet. She hadn't known when she would need the things in the box, but Juliette had told her to be ready at any time. Even when she took something out to play with it, she was always very careful to put it back in the box. And the time had finally come for her to use it all as Juliette had planned.

Mommy didn't work in the evenings very often, and when she did, Selena usually stayed at a friend's house or with her aunt. She was lucky tonight, though. No one had been able to take her. It hadn't been too hard for Selena to make her mother believe she'd be okay if she stayed home. She promised to hide if Daddy started getting drunk-mean.

Just as Juliette had told her to, she carried the box to the stairs and went to work. Very carefully she took out each thing and placed it on a step. First one roller skate, then another on the next step, six marbles on the next, then three golf balls after that, and so on, until she was on the floor and her box was empty.

The stairway was too dark for her to see how it looked when she was finished, but she knew she mustn't turn on any lights. Everything had to be just right for the plan to work. Clinging to the polished railing, she carefully made her way back up the edge of the stairs to her father's bedroom.

Then she screamed at the top of her lungs.

"Daddy! Daddy! Help!"

As soon as she heard him groaning and the bedsprings squeaking she climbed onto the railing and slid to the bottom.

"Daddy! Help me! There's a fire in the kitchen!"

She moved to the side of the stairs and waited for his feet to appear at the top.

And watched him fly through the air like some great, clumsy bird.

As Selena saw his body crash down only to bounce and tumble the last few steps to the floor, she thought she'd have to remember to tell Juliette that the first roller skate was the only thing they had needed after all.

She waited to make sure he wasn't going to get up before walking over to him. She needn't have worried. As soon as she saw his half-open eyes staring at the ceiling, she knew it had worked.

Just like in the movie she and Juliette had seen.

Smiling, she remembered the next part of the plan. She had to make sure every single thing was returned to the box before putting it away in her closet again. The only problem she had was when she had to search under his body to find one last marble. He was much heavier than she'd thought he'd be.

She was sound asleep when her mother came home, but she woke up when she heard crying. She couldn't understand why being rid of their enemy would cause her mother to cry, but it made her decide to hold off telling her mother the secret for a little while.

At the first hint that Detective Kidder was finished poking and prodding at Teri, Selena abandoned her memories and crept back down the stairs. She didn't like this police officer any more than the others she had dealt with in the past. When he came outside and saw her, he asked if she could describe the thug who'd threatened Teri in front of so many witnesses. Putting on her "dumb blonde" routine—even though she was still wearing the red wig, she gave him a vague list of characteristics, as if she could barely recall the incident, even going so far as to stupidly ask if it was important. She made quite sure, however, that what she did say matched perfectly with the disguise she had created.

After he had gone and she and Teri had resumed their earlier positions, Selena encouraged her to relate the conversation as if she hadn't heard every word.

Teri continued to sketch as she talked. "He seems to think the missing two hours are very important. So far he's narrowed it down but hasn't yet figured precisely where or when the time was lost. He wanted to know if Rico might have been having an affair with someone along his route. That could explain the time."

"What did you tell him?"

"The truth. I don't know *how* he would have managed it when I could account for every hour of his day these last few weeks."

"Except for last Thursday," Selena said with a laugh.

Teri winced at Selena's continued attempt to make light of the situation. She had never known Selena to enjoy black humor, and Teri didn't appreciate it, even when she wasn't personally involved. Rather than scold her and appear oversensitive, she told Selena the one other important thing she and the detective had discussed. "He wants to confirm my description of the animal who threatened me that one day when you and everyone else were here."

"Yes, I know. He stopped me outside. I gave him my home address and phone number in case he has any more questions."

Teri hoped that was all she'd given him. "Good. I didn't want to give it to him. I know he thought I was being difficult, but I really hate getting everyone else involved in this. Especially Ann and Lettice. They're business associates, for God's sake. I finally gave him their office number. I offered to go to the station and look at mug shots to see if I could find the guy, but he said that could wait until we were certain, uh, you know."

Selena nodded her understanding. She also would

have preferred not to bother those people. It was embarrassing to Teri. She had to give the detective credit on one point, though. She hadn't thought anyone would notice if their mailman was late. Her own was notoriously erratic. But Rico's dependability on the job was turning out to be an unexpected blessing. Instead of having to wait until someone reported a bad smell coming from the apartment where Rico was rotting, it looked like Detective Kidder was going to track him down in no time.

Teri seemed very disturbed about not knowing for sure what had happened to her husband. Since Selena had decided it was best not to tell her just yet about the favor she'd done her, only discovery of Rico's body was going to calm that sweet woman and get her life back to normal.

Once the corpse was found, that should also take care of Detective Kidder and his annoying questions. One look at the stumps at the ends of Rico's arms and any cop around the New York City area would automatically know the Irish mob was responsible. And that the crime was unsolvable.

Before Selena left an hour later, she stuffed the red wig into her purse. She wasn't sure how bright the detective was, but just in case, she would be sure to wear it if she had to meet with him again. It wouldn't do to have him know how easily she could change her appearance.

Drew and his two models showed up shortly after Selena had departed, and Teri relinquished the studio to them. She had the strongest urge to clean her house and rationalized that the physical exertion would probably do her some good.

Her urge paid off. When Drew knocked at the kitchen door to tell her they were finished, her spirits had risen enough to greet him with a genuine smile. "Do you have time to come in?"

"Sure. My microwave dinner will wait for me."

"A microwave dinner? I think I can offer better than that."

"I accept," he said with a grin that revealed he'd been angling for the invitation.

Teri raised both eyebrows and laughed. "In that case I suppose you don't care that it's escargots and sauteed frogs' legs, with a side of slimy fried okra."

He walked in and set his hat on a chair. "I think I'll just stick with the okra, thank you."

"Yecch! I should have known a cowboy would have no sense of taste. I can tell you, that's the one food you'll never find in my kitchen!"

"So, how's it goin'? When I first saw you today, you looked like you'd lost your best friend. Ah, jeez, I'm sorry. I didn't mean it like that."

"Hey, no problem. I've already realized what a perfect gentleman you are." His concern for her feelings made Selena's lighthearted remarks sound cruel by comparison. Drew had called her several times over the weekend, as promised. Each call had been brief—he had only wanted to make sure she was okay—but hearing his soft drawl had somehow comforted her in an otherwise panicky situation.

"Have I thanked you yet for keeping tabs on me this weekend?"

"A dozen times. And a dozen times I've told you it was my pleasure, ma'am."

"It's good you added the ma'am, or I might have doubted your sincerity."

"That reminds me, my new neighbor says hello."

"It was nice of her to let you use her phone." She probably welcomed the opportunity to have you in her apartment, Teri thought with pure female insight. "Maybe she's another cowboy lover."

He laughed. "Yeah, come to think of it, she was

eyein' my, uh, *boots* with a heap of interest." When Teri smirked at him, he added, " 'Course, it was hard to tell exactly what she was lookin' at through those thick bifocals." He winked and Teri threw a potholder at him.

"How's steak and fries sound?" Teri asked, opening the refrigerator.

"Much better. By the way, the phone company promised I'd have my phone line turned on tomorrow, so you should be able to call that number I gave you soon."

"Great. Detective Kidder came by—"

"Again?"

She nodded. She had told him about the first visit without making a big deal about it, but Drew had read between the lines.

"What did he want this time?"

She quickly related their terse discussion. "He asked for a number where he could reach you to ask you a few more questions about that animal who threatened me. I don't think he believed me when I told him you didn't have a phone yet."

"I'll call him. What's his number?"

She handed him the detective's card. "I doubt if he's in now. It's after six. I'm sure it can wait until morning."

Drew hesitated, then went ahead and copied the number on the card for tomorrow. They both managed to push the detective out of their conversation until, in the middle of clearing the table after dinner, that man once again appeared at Teri's door.

The sight of him spoiled the relaxed mood Teri had worked so hard to achieve.

"Detective Kidder? I didn't expect to see you again today. Do you have some news?"

"No. Sorry. But the police officer cruising this neighborhood saw a strange car in your driveway for this time of night and reported it. I wanted to follow it up personally and make sure you were all right."

"I don't understand," Teri said as she ushered him inside.

"We placed a watch order on your house after you gave your report. Under the circumstances, any suspicious activity will be immediately called in and brought to my attention . . . in case it looks like a backup is needed."

"Oh, I see. Well, thank you, then. I appreciate your prompt attention and concern, but as you can see, I'm fine. The car belongs to Mr. Marshall." She turned to nod at her guest and was surprised to see him hovering close to her shoulder.

"Yes. I remember Mr. Marshall. We met at the station. Have you gotten your phone installed yet, sir?"

Drew took a breath that seemed to make him grow an inch in height. "No. And I don't —"

"Detective," Teri interrupted, not wanting Drew to cause a problem by calling the officer to task for his bad manners. "Didn't you want to ask Drew some questions? About the man that threatened me?"

"Yes, I did. Would this be a bad time?" Kidder looked from one to the other.

Teri answered. "Not at all. I'll go finish the dishes."

Kidder held up his index finger. "If you don't mind, I'd like to speak with the both of you." He encouraged them to sit on the couch while he stationed himself in a seat across from them.

For the first time, Teri saw Kidder preparing to take notes.

"First off, Mr. Marshall, you're aware that you are a key witness in what may very well become a homicide case. We have your address on the report, but I need a phone number where I can reach you."

94

Drew gave him the number that would be working the next day. Kidder wrote it down, then set his notepad and pen on the coffee table between them. "Regarding the thug, have you remembered anything else about what he looked like or said?"

Drew paused and glanced at Teri, who gave him a little shrug. "No. Guess I told you 'bout all I could last week."

"Uh-huh. Now, I'd like both your ideas on this. Why do you suppose he made such clear threats in front of all those people?"

Teri thought the detective's body looked at ease, but his eyes were intently watching Drew and her. She had the impression he was looking for a specific reaction. Again, she replied first. "I was so upset when it happened, all I could think about was how embarrassing it was. But later, I wondered the same thing. Then I realized I was too frightened by what he could do to me to complain to the police. I wouldn't have ever mentioned it if Rico hadn't disappeared. I guess he was used to that reaction from people like me and that was why he wasn't worried about witnesses. I mean, he wasn't the kind of person you wanted to make an enemy of."

Drew agreed with Teri's assumptions and added, "He was in and out so fast, I didn't even have a chance to gather my wits, let alone challenge him. I got the idea he hadn't been expectin' an audience, but once he was in the door it was too late to back out gracefully. I doubt if he wanted to take a chance on coming back again later."

Teri's eyes widened at the realization that Drew had even contemplated something as dangerous as challenging the animal. When her gaze touched on Kidder, she noticed that tight little smile she was beginning to despise.

Kidder picked up his pad and pen again. "As I said before, Mr. Marshall, you are a key witness,

95

and as such, you need to provide me a little more information. Background, that kind of thing." He made a sound that was almost a chuckle. "Have to make sure you're reliable and all that."

Teri's ears perked up. She wasn't sure why Kidder needed it, but *she* was interested in any information Drew might relate. Drew's eyes narrowed at Kidder and he sat forward, his body noticeably rigid, but he didn't refuse outright. Kidder appeared not to notice Drew's hostility as he asked his first question.

"Your accent's not exactly New York, Mr. Marshall. Where are you from?"

"Fort Worth."

"Former address?" Drew gave it, and Kidder wrote it down.

"When did you move here?"

"Almost three weeks ago."

Kidder looked surprised. "So recently? Doesn't say much for our fair city when a newcomer moves in and gets involved in a possible homicide almost immediately, does it?"

Teri was stunned at the way Kidder hinted that there might be some connection between Drew's arrival and Rico's disappearance. But Drew fielded the comment with sarcasm.

"Actually, I had a few friends in Texas who thought *I* would be a victim if I moved here. New York City doesn't exactly have a sterlin' reputation in other parts of the country."

Teri could tell that Kidder didn't find Drew funny, but he let it drop.

"Are you married? Have any children?"

"Divorced. Two children. They're in Fort Worth with my ex-wife."

"At the address you gave me?" Drew gave him a stiff nod and Kidder made another note. "And how long have you known Mrs. Gambini?"

96

"About two weeks."

Kidder's expression bordered on shock. "Really? I would have thought you'd known each other for quite a while, what with your escorting her to the station last week and all. So, how did you two happen to meet a week before Mrs. Gambini's husband disappeared?"

Teri didn't care for the insinuation and spoke up. "I hired Mr. Marshall, through a mutual acquaintance, to do some work for me, and I'm very grateful that I did. Not only is he an excellent photographer, he's been a big help with this"—she struggled for the right word—"situation."

Kidder gave another one of his non-smiles. "I can tell. Everybody needs a shoulder to lean on at times. Tell me, Mr. Marshall, did you have your own photography business back in Texas as well?"

Teri could feel the tension radiating from Drew's body as his fingers curled into fists and relaxed again. Part of her wanted to call a halt to any questioning that would upset him, but another part of her waited expectantly for his answer.

"No," Drew said quietly. "I wasn't workin' as a photographer then." Kidder angled his head, also waiting for more. "I worked . . . for the United States Government."

"Oh?" Kidder was clearly intrigued. "You say that rather cryptically, Mr. Marshall. Were you involved in some top-secret work?"

Teri saw a faint flush cross Drew's cheekbones and thought he was clenching his teeth. She wanted to take his hand, tell him it was okay, he didn't have to tell the nosy detective anything. But it was not her place to do that, so she waited again and watched him take a deep, slow breath.

"No, Detective," Drew said in a hollow voice. "Nothin' secret 'bout it. I just don't believe in

97

lookin' backward. And that was one job I'd rather forget about."

Teri felt relieved when Kidder didn't push Drew on the subject, but her relief was followed by a pang of disappointment — she still didn't know what Drew had done for a living.

Kidder asked Drew a few more general questions, then apologized for interrupting their evening. As he was about to leave, he turned back to them. "Mrs. Gambini, I almost forgot. I think I've pinpointed the lost time I told you about. In his deliveries up to and including the manager of an apartment complex, Rico was apparently on track. After that he was running late.

"The manager was fairly certain that was the day he and Mr. Gambini exchanged a few words about the Mets' chances this year, but he had to do some repair work in one of the units after that and didn't notice when your husband left. There aren't that many tenants in the complex. Only a handful of people were in this afternoon when I was there, though, and none of them had seen the mailman at all. The manager said most of the tenants work during the day, so I'm going over there again early in the morning and try to catch some of those I missed today. Who knows? Maybe one of them saw something I can use."

Tension pulsed in the room for several seconds after Kidder left.

Without thinking about it Teri scooted close to Drew, got up on her knees, and put her arms around his shoulders.

Instead of accepting her hug, he stiffened and pulled back to stare at her. "What's that for?"

Teri dropped her hands and sat back on her feet with her head down. "I thought you needed a hug. I didn't know that only worked one way."

He closed his eyes and sighed as he ran his hands

through his hair. After another slow breath, he looked at her again. "That obvious, huh?"

She shrugged, not wanting to add to his discomfort.

"Okay, I'm ready. I'll take that hug now, ma'am . . . if it's still bein' offered."

Teri smiled and leaned forward to envelop his upper body once more.

"Feels good," he murmured near her ear.

"I owe you."

For a long moment, neither said a word. When his hands pressed against her lower back, she automatically shifted so that they were chest to chest, and the consoling hug became a tender embrace.

"Teri, we have to talk," he said softly, but the hands stroking her spine whispered other suggestions, and she snuggled more comfortably into the contours of his body.

She didn't want to talk . . . or think. She'd done enough of that in the last few days. This was much better, just feeling—giving and taking without questions or recriminations. Apparently Drew didn't feel the same way.

Gently disengaging her arms, but still holding her hands, he waited to speak until she slowly raised her eyes to his. "I'm sorry I handled Kidder so badly."

"Sorry? He's rather rude. You didn't say anything to be sorry about."

"I'm afraid it's what I didn't say. I should have just told him what he wanted to know, but—" He looked away from her. "Lord knows I've tried, but I can't stop bein' defensive about it. I'm sure my reluctance to talk was taken the wrong way, and now he'll start diggin' on his own."

"I don't understand. What difference would it make what you did back in Texas?"

"I'm not sure, but I can recognize a man on a

99

huntin' trip when I see one. I just can't tell what he's huntin' *for.*"

"Funny you should say that. I got the same feeling myself." She told him about Kidder's inspection of her house.

Drew offered a possibility; she hadn't thought of it before, but wanted to believe as soon as she heard it. "Maybe it's his investigative style to gather every fact he can, regardless of whether it's relevant. I can't fault him for that. But I'm afraid he's goin' to come up with somethin' that could reflect on you."

Teri was dumbfounded. "That's ridiculous! Whatever you did in Texas has nothing to do with me."

Drew looked into her eyes and made a judgment call. "It does if your so-called key witness is a convicted felon."

She gasped and covered her mouth with her fingertips too late to smother it.

"And a drug addict. And let's not forget, I almost killed four hundred people!"

He turned his head from her and tried to pull his hands away, but she held tight.

"Drew. Drew, look at me." He did as she ordered, but his look was defiant. He was clearly prepared for a nasty tongue-lashing. "You can't say things like that and not explain. It's against the rules."

"Hmmph. Whose rules?"

"Mine. I make them up as I go along. Now talk." She sensed him wavering between getting up and walking out, and unburdening his soul. She encouraged the latter. "The man I've gotten to know these last two weeks couldn't possibly have done those things. Unless, of course, he was possessed by the devil. Is that what happened to you, Drew? If you tell me it is, I'll believe you, you know. I've already drawn my own solid conclusions about you, and I'd believe anything you say."

He shook his head. "You're too much. How could your husband have been such a fool to treat you the way he did?"

"You're detouring."

"You're right. I haven't told all of it to anyone—except the psychiatrist. Oh, did I forget to mention I was also committed?"

"Drew, you are quickly starting to lose some of that credibility I referred to."

"It's all true, darlin', and I'll tell you 'bout it if you really want me to. The way I've been thinkin' 'bout you, it's probably better if you find out right away. But first, I want to let you off the hook. I don't need your disgust or your pity. After you hear all the gruesome details, you are free to avoid me at all costs, and that includes canceling our agreement about the studio."

"All right. No disgust, no pity, no moralizing of any kind. Spill."

Again he tried to free his hands, but she refused to break contact.

"Okay. Remember, you asked for this." It took him another few seconds before he began. "I was an air traffic controller. You've probably heard about the kind of stress that goes with that career. I might have handled it fine if my marriage hadn't been such a strain on my patience. I told you how my wife was. She never made a single decision on her own. I even had to go grocery shoppin' with her, or do it myself, because she didn't know which bathroom cleanser I preferred." Remembered frustration showed clearly on his face.

"After the kids were born, it only got crazier. She'd leave messages at the tower a couple of times a day, insistin' it was an emergency. Usually it was for somethin' as stupid as whether I wanted steak or pork chops for dinner. All that time I kept tellin' myself, if I just help her get through this stage or

101

that, she'll be standin' on her own two feet in no time."

Teri squeezed his hands. "You aren't the first person who thought like that. I know. I've been bailing Rico out for years, and every damn time he promised it was the last. I never really believed him, but I wanted to so much, I always forgave him again."

He tried to smile, but it wasn't convincing. "Sounds like we're quite a pair. Anyway, at first I eased the stress with a drink after work, and then a few more. Before long, I started bringin' hundred-proof cocktails to work in my thermos. The problem was, the alcohol made me too drowsy to stay as alert as the job required."

Teri squeezed his hands a little harder this time. "But it didn't stop there, right?"

He met her concerned expression with one of self-disgust. "Right. When a co-worker introduced me to cocaine, I fell in love with the drug. It was perfect. I was relaxed, alert; I could handle the job, my helpless wife, two growin' kids. All I needed was a little snort now and then. The only problem was the expense."

He made a move to rise and she let him slip his hands from hers. He walked over to the picture window and stared out, but she knew that he was seeing his own nightmares.

"Pretty soon I had to find a few customers of my own to support the habit. I didn't know it at the time, but I'd turned into Dr. Jekyll and Mr. Hyde. Brenda and the kids were terrified of me. I still don't remember doin' half the things she said I did durin' that time. I doubt if the kids'll ever forgive me."

"Haven't you talked to them?"

Drew shook his head, but he kept his back to her. "Not since the arrest . . . almost seven months ago. I haven't had the nerve."

Teri determined to discuss his negligence further at a later date. "Why were you arrested?"

He turned then, and she watched him physically prepare to withstand the disgust he expected her to respond with. "The arrest was for possession. But what happened before the arrest was the greater crime." He paused and gathered the confidence to tell her the rest. "I'd been usin' for about a year. Never too much at one time, mind you. I always believed I had it under control. Of course, that's what all addicts tell themselves on the way downhill."

She got up and walked over to him. With the briefest touch on his cheek, she let him know he could tell her the rest, but only if he wanted to.

As if he was afraid of what his hands might do, he shoved them into his front pockets and again looked out beyond the window. "I froze one day. On the job. I was lookin' at my screen, talkin' to two separate pilots on my headset, and I panicked. I saw blips that weren't there and couldn't find the planes I knew *were*." He paused, and she tried to wrap her arms around his waist from behind, but he moved away from her and crossed back to the couch as he continued.

"There's no room for panic or hesitation in that job. If it hadn't been for the guy next to me knockin' me out of my chair and takin' over, I'd have killed everyone on those two planes. You see, I was bringin' both pilots in on the same runway, at the same time, from two different directions. They wouldn't have been able to avoid the collision I was settin' up without realizin' it."

"Oh God, Drew, how awful. I can understand why you don't like to talk about it. But you mustn't let it keep eating away at you. No one was actually hurt, were they?"

He slumped down onto the couch as if the weight

of his confession was more than he could bear. She sat beside him.

"If you mean did the planes get down safely, then yeah, no one was actually hurt. Unfortunately, this little tale gets worse. I was so out of the real world, I got up from the floor and tried to beat the hell out of the guy who had saved all those people. They had to call Security to restrain me and get me out of the tower. Cocky bastard that I was, I had my stash right in my pants pocket. I was lucky they only got me for possession. Even though I had enough on me to make it a felony, they hadn't caught me sellin' the stuff, which had been a definite possibility that day."

When he paused, she reached for his hand once more, and he gave in to her. "The judge accepted my attorney's defense that I was in a high-pressure job. He had me committed to six months in a state institution—more kindly referred to as a rehabilitation clinic—under psychiatric care. I came straight to New York when I got out."

Teri didn't know what to say. She had promised she wouldn't pity him, but she felt sad nonetheless. And she could tell by the way he looked and talked that he hadn't yet forgiven himself for falling apart. She released his hand and attempted to hug him again.

A second later his arms were tightly wrapped around her as well. "No disgust?" he asked uncertainly.

She leaned back to let him see she was sincere. "No disgust, but I can't say the same about the pity. Not for you. You're a grown-up man. Eventually, you'll adjust. But I feel sorry for those two kids who've been deprived of a wonderful father."

"I can't make it up to them."

"Yes, you can. When it's time, you will. And you're not getting out of our agreement. I'm counting on those rent payments you promised." She paused and softened her voice. "And I'm also counting on having you around to give me a hug when I need it."

He didn't say a word, but only leaned toward her and briefly touched his lips to hers. "You're incredible," he said, his gaze fixed on her mouth. When he drew close again, Teri met him halfway. This kiss was shared, a preliminary exploring by both of them, a mutual, unexpected discovery of underlying heat too long held back.

The appreciative kiss suddenly became open-mouthed and hungry. Teri held nothing back from him, nor did he from her, yet it wasn't enough.

And it was much too much.

She broke away, panting more from the effort the decision required than her unsatisfied desire. "I'm so sorry, Drew. I didn't mean for that—"

"No, *I'm* sorry. I should have known better."

"It's not that I don't—"

"I know." He held her tightly one more time, then eased her away. "But the timin' stinks."

Teri smiled crookedly, grateful for his understanding, in spite of his own emotional turmoil. "Can I have a raincheck?"

He stood up and took her hand to draw her up as well. "Darlin', you can have a whole passel of rainchecks. I'd just feel a lot better if you'd wait to cash 'em in until you're sure about why you want 'em."

Detective Kidder was prepared for a long night ahead. It had been years since he'd done a stakeout in his car. Instead of taking a city vehicle tonight, he used his own nondescript gray compact. He parked on the street across from the Gambini house, where he blended in with a line of other cars like his.

He was eager to get into the station tomorrow. He had intended to check Marshall out, but he had had nothing to go on before. He now had Marshall's Texas license plate number and knew he had been a civil servant in Fort Worth. He hadn't needed to insist on any more answers from the man. Tomorrow the computer would cough up every detail of Marshall's life. One of the costs of a cushy government job with big fringe benefits was that you gave up your right to privacy. He wondered if he'd so easily disprove their claim of having met only two weeks ago.

In the meantime, any number of things could happen before tomorrow. One, Marshall could stay all night, which would confirm the theory that they were lovers. Two, one of them could take off because of something he'd said, in which case he intended to tail him—or her. If luck was with him, that person would head straight to the apartment complex—he had purposely avoided naming it—or some other nearby location, to make certain no incriminating clues had been overlooked. And three, and most preferable to Kidder personally, was a combination of the first two.

He was only slightly disappointed when the front door of the house opened and Marshall stepped out barely an hour after Kidder had left them alone. He raised his binoculars to observe the farewell.

Mrs. Gambini remained framed in the doorway with the light behind her. She touched Marshall's cheek, reassuring him of something. The cowboy turned to leave, then spun back around and pulled her into his arms. The kiss was brief, but loaded with dynamite.

And Detective William F. Kidder now held the detonator that would blow it sky-high.

106

* * *

The ringing telephone woke Teri from the first sound sleep she'd had in weeks. She almost ignored it.

"Hello?"

"Mrs. Gambini? This is Detective Kidder. I think we found your husband."

Eight

"That number is not in service at this time."

"Damn!" Teri replaced the telephone receiver with a shaky hand. She knew, even before she dialed Drew's new number, that it'd be a miracle if the call went through. It wasn't very brave, but she didn't want to do this alone, and he was the only person she wanted with her.

Between Rico's demands and her work, she hadn't formed any relationships she could call close — except perhaps with Selena, but even that odd friendship had developed because of her work. She had no relatives that she wanted to involve. Her grandmother was still alive, but in a nursing home in Camden, New Jersey, barely able to feed herself, let alone give Teri any support. Rico's family had never approved of her to begin with, and when, after a few years, no grandchildren were born, they stopped talking to her completely. She would screw up her courage to deal with them after she'd made the funeral arrangements.

Asking for a neighbor's assistance was also out of the question. She got along with all of them, but everyone, herself included, always seemed too busy to form any strong friendships.

She had met Drew only weeks ago, and yet she felt more of a bond with him than she did with any of the others — including Rico.

The passion that had sparked between her and Drew last night had been smoldering since the moment they'd met. She had sensed it and had been determined to ignore it. Foolish woman.

If the first kiss had been a test, and the second discovery, the third had been a promise of things to come. She had gone to bed with his taste on her lips and the need for more of him humming through her body.

Stop thinking about it, she commanded herself. Her husband's body was in the morgue, awaiting her identification. A good wife would be overcome with grief upon learning of her husband's murder.

But grief was not what she felt — only relief that her being in a state of limbo had come to an end. And regret that Rico had destroyed what feelings she had once had for him. And anger that he had been so irresponsible as to get himself killed and leave her to deal with the morbid details. But not grief.

For another moment she considered what she had to do that day. When thoughts of Detective Kidder and his endless questions entered her mind, she picked up the phone and dialed Selena's number. Having a friend, even one who occasionally made her uneasy, was better than going it alone. She only hoped Selena would leave her newly developed sense of humor at home.

The overweight woman behind the scarred, wooden desk glanced at her calendar and back at Teri. "Detective Kidder said he would be here at two and you were to wait for him. It's only a quarter to. You can have a seat over there." She pointed to a row of bright orange molded plastic chairs against the wall, then resumed her typing.

Teri figured working in a morgue probably didn't nourish friendliness. She and Selena sat down. The chairs were the only spot of color in the beige reception area, but at least it wasn't the sterile white with metal fixtures she had expected.

Selena patted Teri's hand and Teri smiled her thanks. She shouldn't have worried about Selena's behavior. Except for her nonsensical explanation about why she was wearing the red wig, Selena was back to being her usual caring self, wanting to do whatever she could to make this easier on Teri. She had offered to view the body for her, but Teri knew that was something she had to do herself to put her uncertainty to rest.

With each minute that ticked by, Teri's nervousness increased. Kidder had warned her that the body had begun to decompose and, if she preferred not to look at it, they might eventually be able to confirm the victim's identity by his dental records, medical history, and her description of Rico's physical traits. She recalled him saying something about not having fingerprints to work with and supposed that was because of the decomposition he had referred to. He had insisted he would fill her in on everything else at the morgue.

Before bringing Mrs. Gambini back to the autopsy room, Detective Kidder checked to make sure the body was in place. He was pleased that she had insisted on personally identifying her husband, since it was what he wanted, too. This way he would be able to put a little more pressure on her and, at the same time, he'd be able to observe her reaction to the butchering the man had suffered.

One look at the body had told him she probably didn't do the damage herself; it had taken someone much bigger and stronger, both physically and emotionally. But that didn't mean she wasn't aware of who that someone was. Faced with the grotesque evidence, she might be so horrified by what her lover was capable of that she'd point her finger at the perpetrator and throw herself on Kidder's mercy. He smiled at the thought.

He had arrived at the apartment complex at seven A.M. in hopes of catching the tenants while they were getting ready for work. With a little coercion, he had convinced the slovenly manager to take him from door to door to vouch for him, thus speeding up the interviews.

As it turned out, one of the tenants had had a doctor's appointment that day and recalled pulling into the parking lot just as the mail truck was driving out. Because that was about two hours after the manager had reported talking to Gambini, Kidder was fairly certain that the postman had spent his lost hours somewhere in the complex.

Unless someone he'd questioned was lying—and his nose told him no one had—his search was narrowed down to the vacant apartments and two others where the residents hadn't been home. The threat of building inspectors swooping down on him pushed the reluctant manager into opening those units with his passkey.

Kidder had known what they would find the second the manager opened the right door. Nothing on earth smells quite so horrendous as decaying human flesh. The air conditioner's thermostat had been turned down as far as it would go, keeping the temperature in the near-frigid range. That, combined with the massive loss of blood, had prevented the corpse from decomposing as rapidly as it normally would have.

The cold also kept the maggots from appearing, much to Kidder's relief. The only aspect of working homicides that his stomach had never become accustomed to was those repulsive, squirming worms that fed on death. For that small bit of unintended thoughtfulness, he thanked Gambini's killer.

Since he had traced the lost time by process of deductive reasoning, it didn't matter that the cold might

111

have hampered the medical examiner's ability to pinpoint the exact moment of death. In that, Kidder believed he had won a point over the murderer.

He also believed someone else had left the complex in Gambini's mail truck, even though no one had recalled seeing someone other than their regular postman on that day.

Discovery of the body had thrown a few kinks into his well-developed hypothesis about this case, however. For instance, the hands had been neatly chopped off, indicating a separate weapon had been brought in specifically for that purpose. Perhaps the murderer had been trying to delay identification by eliminating the possibility of obtaining fingerprints. Likewise, he must have expected the cold temperature to hold down the smell enough to delay investigation for some time, as well as throwing off the time of death. All these delaying tactics might serve a purpose if the culprit was really part of the mob and using the time to make an untraceable escape.

He had heard of cases where the Irish mob had cut off a dead man's hand to use the fingerprints on a future crime. But when they started hacking up a body, there was seldom anything left to be identified. So he was back to the question of why the hands were missing.

There was that overkill factor again.

Another kink came from the apartment manager. The man who had rented the apartment where the body was found had matched everyone's description of the thug who had threatened Mrs. Gambini.

It would wreak havoc with his life if this actually turned out to be a mob hit, but it looked like he was going to have to get Mrs. Gambini to look at the mug shots after all. He worried over that for a moment, then relaxed when he came up with a plausible answer for the matching descriptions.

If the lovers had paid someone to play the thug for their co-workers, that man could also have been paid to rent the apartment, and make a few appearances at the complex to firmly establish the cover, not knowing, or not caring, what the apartment would be used for. In that case, Kidder was certain Mrs. Gambini would not want that man to be found. When asked, she would undoubtedly look at the photos without any intention of pointing out the pretender. And, in a way, Kidder would have won another point.

Thinking along those lines, he realized there could be a plausible answer for the hands also. Mrs. Gambini had been insisting all along that he look toward the Irish mob for answers to her husband's disappearance. What better way to pin it on the group than to leave a calling card like the missing hands? Anyone with money for a newspaper or a paperback book could have read an article or the recently published novel detailing the mob's messy business practices.

Overkill. That was one of the problems when human emotion came into play.

"Good afternoon, Mrs. Gambini."

Kidder's voice startled Teri out of her contemplations.

He nodded to Selena. "How nice of you to keep your boss company. This is such a difficult thing for the loved ones to go through." He pulled a chair away from the wall and sat down across from Teri. "I didn't want to give you the details over the phone, but before we go inside, I want to let you know what to expect."

Teri nodded and felt her stomach clench with dread.

"Have you ever seen a dead body?"

Teri nodded again, picturing how her father had looked after his fatal heart attack. "In a funeral home."

"Well, this is nothing like that, I assure you. Even though this corpse isn't nearly as bad as some I've dealt with, it's still rather gruesome."

"It doesn't matter. I need to see it to know for sure. You said on the phone you'd fill me in on how and where you found him."

Kidder gave her a brief summary of what had led to the discovery. Then his flat expression changed to what Teri thought might have passed for sympathy, but she didn't buy it.

"Believe me, Mrs. Gambini, if I could spare you the details of how I found him I would, but you should be aware of exactly what happened to him."

She could not find the courage to do more than silently wait for him to go on. The truth was that she really didn't want to hear anymore.

"When I found him he was naked, stretched out on his back on a bed. He had lost a great deal of blood—the entire sheet beneath him was blackened with it, but I doubt if he suffered overmuch. His throat had been sliced from one side to the other."

Teri's hand flew over her mouth, muffling the whimper she made. Immediately Selena's arm was around her.

Kidder cleared his throat. "I'm afraid that's not all of it. Both his hands were cut off."

"Oh, my God," she cried. "I thought they only did that to thieves in the Middle East! Rico told me those people would make him disappear in pieces if he didn't pay up, but I didn't believe him."

Kidder looked at her curiously. "Is that why you think it was done? Because the mob considered him a thief for not paying what he owed? Hmmm. That could make sense if they wanted to make an example of him, but why do you suppose they would take the hands with them?"

"You mean . . ." Teri gulped down the bile rising in her throat. "You mean his hands weren't with the body? Why would anyone take them?"

114

Selena tightened her hold a little, as if she was afraid Teri would collapse without her support. In an uncertain, childish voice, Selena answered the question both of them had asked. "Somebody told me about a scary story they'd read not too long ago about the Irish mob cutting off a man's hands. I don't remember why, though."

Teri was bewildered, not only because of what Selena said, but also because of how she said it. She was doing what she usually called her "dumb blonde" routine in spite of the red wig, and if there was one thing she knew about Selena, she had an incredibly good memory. If someone told her about a story, it was more likely she remembered every word that person had said.

Kidder seemed to be considering Selena's suggestion, but he made no comment on it.

"Well," he said as he stood up and adjusted the waist of his slacks beneath his paunch, "if you're sure you're up to this, I'll take you back to the autopsy room."

Teri and Selena rose and followed him down a long corridor. Selena took two fine white handkerchiefs out of her purse and handed one to Teri. "Here. Use this to cover your nose and mouth."

Teri had noticed the faint aroma of formaldehyde in the reception area and wrinkled her nose as it grew stronger in the hallway. But she hadn't been prepared for the chemical blast that hit her as they entered the autopsy room. She covered her lower face as Selena suggested and blinked away the moisture that protectively filled her eyes.

Kidder bobbed his head in understanding. "Believe it or not, this is a lot better than the apartment where I found him."

She shivered against the freezing cold as he led her across the concrete floor to the only metal examining table with anything on it. A large green sheet hid the body from Teri's immediate view. Her breathing

115

slowed, then halted completely when he drew back the cloth.

Teri's eyes slammed shut against the unholy sight he revealed. Her senses screamed at her to run away. Her mind demanded she not be a coward about this.

"Mrs. Gambini? Are you going to be all right?"

She took a small breath through the hanky and the stench rising from the body overpowered the formaldehyde. But if she didn't breathe, she was going to faint. And if she fainted, she was just going to have to do this all over again. She drew a deeper breath into her mouth, then forced her eyes open.

The curly black hair was Rico's. The rest of the head on the table was a monstrous distortion of her husband's—swollen out of its usual shape with skin that looked as though a mad artist had painted it—a sickly yellow down the center, with some plum blotches on the sides of the face. The rims of the ears and the skin along the sides of the neck were dark purple.

And beneath the chin, a hideous black slash gaped at her like a misplaced, mutilated mouth.

"It's him," she heard herself say. "It's Rico. Can I go now?"

Until she turned to leave, she hadn't realized Selena had been holding her up the whole time. Her legs were so weak, they almost gave out with her first step, but soon, with Selena's help, she made it back to the reception area to sit in one of the orange chairs again.

She knew she must have looked pretty bad when the unfriendly receptionist rushed off to fetch her a cup of water. It was minutes after her body stopped vibrating before she could speak.

"What now, Detective?"

"Your husband's body is in the hands of the medical examiner. It'll be gone over with a fine-toothed comb—and I mean that. At the same time, Forensics has already sent someone to the apartment to scour

116

for clues. I'll let you know the results of both reports as I get them. In the meantime, as soon as you're up to it, I'd like you to come into the station and look at some pictures. It's time to look for your thug."

"Since when do we take people into the autopsy room to view a mutilated corpse of a family member? Damn it, Kidder, you *know* that's not the procedure in a case like this! It was completely unnecessary to put the wife through that."

Kidder bowed his head while his captain vented his spleen. It was best to let the man get it all out of his system before defending himself. As precarious as his current position was, he didn't need to cause any more waves by being argumentative.

For a terrifying moment when he had first returned to the station from the morgue and was told Captain Hart wanted him in his office pronto, he had thought his transfer had come through. A little verbal reprimand was nothing compared to that.

He had no problem with a set-down from this man. Although Hart looked years younger than Kidder—he still had all his hair, and frequent exercise kept his large body in shape—they were almost the same age. It was only when the young pups started flexing their muscles that he regretted never having had the ambition to move up the police ladder as Hart had.

"Kidder!" Hart exclaimed.

His head popped up.

"Put that damned thing in your ear so you can hear me. I don't have time to waste talking to myself!"

"Yes, sir." He quickly affixed the aid to his ear and leaned forward, assuming a position of complete attention.

"Did you hear any of that?"

"Yes, sir. And I can explain. I warned Mrs. Gam-

117

bini how it would be. I tried my damnedest to talk her out of going down there, that it wasn't necessary, but she was very insistent. Threatened to sue the city if I didn't cooperate. Under the circumstances—"

"All right, all right. It's over with now. How did it go?"

"She confirmed that it was Rico Gambini. All things considered, she held up unbelievably well."

"Meaning she didn't faint or get sick?"

"Or have hysterics. Not even a tear."

"You know, that's not so unusual. She's had days to deal with his possible death. I've gone over the report she filed. Have you had any luck tracking down the thug?"

"Mrs. Gambini will be in tomorrow to look at some pictures. But I don't expect her to find him."

"Hold it right there. Are you telling me she hasn't looked through the mug shots yet?"

"No. It really wasn't necessary before."

Captain Hart slapped his big hand on his desk. "Christ! You had six witnesses to a threat that clearly tied in the mob and you didn't follow it up? What were you waiting for? The guy to walk in the front door and confess? He's probably so far underground now, we'll never find him."

Kidder felt the heat rise in his face. Hart had no right to question his tactics with the excellent arrest record he had. "There was no victim before today. If there really was a thug, I didn't want to scare him into hiding by asking a lot of questions, when I had nothing yet to hold him on."

"You said *if.* Why?"

Kidder proudly related his theories about Mrs. Gambini and her lover.

Hart's frown grew as he listened. "Forget it. You have no evidence to support that line of thinking. We can't arrest people because of the way they look at each other."

"But I saw them kiss! They're definitely lovers. I

haven't had time to disprove their claim that they met just two weeks ago. But I will—I just need a little time. And Teri Gambini's soft. A little more pressure after what she saw today and she's going to crack wide open."

Hart shook his head. "You haven't *got* more time. And the *department* doesn't have time for its detectives to be chasing smoke when there's a mountain of evidence pointing to this being a mob hit. I usually go along with your instincts, but in this case, I'm afraid you're letting personal problems influence your judgment."

Kidder wanted to know precisely what he needed to deny. "What's that supposed to mean?"

Hart sighed and sat forward. "Look, Bill, it's just the two of us in here. We've known each other more years than two of our rookies' ages added together. Ever since Lydia left you—"

"Lydia's dead," Kidder interrupted in a flat tone.

"No, Bill. She *left* you. I'm not your shrink or your bartender, and I have no intention of playing either part now. I've heard you refer to her as your 'late wife' and I didn't correct you. I didn't think you needed anyone butting into your private life and making things more difficult for you. Maybe I should have, because it looks like your private life is now affecting your professional one."

Kidder bolted out of his chair. "I don't have to listen to this. I thought we were pals."

"Sit back down, Detective Kidder. Right now I'm not your pal, I'm your captain, and that's an order." He waited for Kidder to obey, then went on. "You've handled four male homicides since your wife left you for another man. And in every case you were convinced the dead man's wife and a lover were the perpetrators. In one case you were half right. The wife did kill him, but it was self-defense and there was no lover, only a violently abusive husband. The other three cases had nothing to do with wives and lovers.

"You've lost your objectivity where wives are concerned. Because you eventually got to the correct solution in spite of your bias, I let it go in the past. But not this time. I want you to leave that woman alone and spend the next two weeks looking for more evidence to tie this one to the mob. It would be quite a feather in our cap if we could bring in one of their soldiers. There's no telling who else that could net."

Kidder heard nothing past the words "two weeks," but he wasn't about to ask what that meant. Nor was he about to toss out his theories on the Gambini case. The captain was all wrong. Detective William F. Kidder was as unbiased today as he ever was before his bitch of a wife started fucking her dry cleaner.

Teri Gambini and Drew Marshall had committed a premeditated murder—he was certain of it and more determined than ever to prove it. Now he not only had to justify that he wasn't too far over the hill to be a good detective, he had to show his captain that his instincts were still on target. When he realized Hart had stopped talking about the mob and was looking through a stack of papers, he held his breath. He knew what the man was taking out of the pile even before he saw it.

"I know you're not happy about this, Bill, but there's nothing I can do." Hart's expression was contrite as he passed the official administrative form across the desk. "This is your transfer notice. You report to the Property Room in two weeks."

Even with his bad hearing, Detective William F. Kidder could hear the clock of time running down.

Nine

Selena opened a cabinet in Teri's kitchen. "I could heat up a can of soup for you. You should put something in your stomach."

Teri shook her head. "No. *Really.* I don't think I could keep it down. Didn't that upset you at all?" Teri asked as they both went out to the living room.

"Not much. I've got a strong stomach, but also, I kept thinking about what a louse he was to you."

"Well, I know that, but I never . . . I mean, I wanted him out of my life, but I wouldn't wish that kind of death on anyone."

Selena raised one brow, then shrugged. "Next time you make a wish, I guess you'd better be more specific."

Teri tried to adopt a little of Selena's blasé attitude to calm herself down. "Like the old saying: Be careful what you wish for—"

"You might just get it," Selena finished with a laugh. "Since I can't fix you anything to eat, do you want to go anywhere? Watch television? Play cards?"

Teri forced a smile. "No, thank you, hon. Another time, I promise. You've been an enormous help today, but I think I'd like to be alone for a while. Besides, I have a screaming headache. I can't tell which was worse, the tension or the formaldehyde. I'd kind of like to take a few aspirins and lie down."

Selena patted Teri's shoulder. "I understand.

Would you like me to run a nice steamy bubble bath for you before I go?"

"Oh, no. Thanks for the idea, though. I might try it if the aspirin doesn't do the trick."

"Okay. If you need anything at all, I want you to call me. Anytime. Promise?"

"Promise."

"I promise you, baby, nobody will ever hurt you again."

Selena hugged her mommy's neck. "And I promise nobody will ever hurt you again, either." With her finger she wiped a tear from her mother's cheek. "Why are you still crying? The funeral's over. We don't have to pretend we're sad anymore, do we?"

"No, baby. We don't have to pretend about anything anymore. And we don't have to be afraid anymore, either. I just need a little time to adjust. It'll be you and me from now on. You'll see. We'll go places together and have such fun!"

Little Selena liked the sound of that a lot, but she'd seen too many promises broken in her life to count on her mother's words. She decided she'd wait and see if this promise could be kept any better than the others.

Teri heard the doorbell and groaned. When the aspirin hadn't worked, she had poured herself a large goblet of wine and filled the tub up with hot water and a handful of strawberry-scented bath crystals. She had hoped the fruity aroma would get rid of the disgusting one that lingered in her nostrils. With the radio tuned to elevator music, she had been determined to unwind.

Now her glass was empty. The water had cooled, the bubbles disintegrated. The doorbell chimed again. Feeling fairly mellow, she could have ignored it, except for one possible consequence: if it was Detective Kidder and she didn't answer, he might think she had gone out. Without understanding why, she was certain he wouldn't approve of that. Imagining how her lack of response might make him suspicious, she climbed out of the tub, opened the bathroom door, and shouted, "Wait a minute!"

Pushing herself to move faster than her relaxed muscles wanted to, she wrapped her damp body in her full-length pink terrycloth robe, stuck her feet into the matching slippers, and shuffled to the front door to peek out. Expecting to see Detective Kidder through the peephole, she was relieved to see Drew instead.

He was not as pleased to see her, however. As soon as she opened the door he berated her. "Why didn't you answer the phone? Or at least call me back?"

She blinked at him, trying to clear the wine-induced fog and the Drew-induced bewilderment. "When did you call?"

"All afternoon. I left messages."

The fog cleared. "Oh, God. I'm sorry. I forgot to check the machine when I got in. Then I was in the tub, and—" She spun away to take care of her oversight, leaving him standing outside the open door.

"Teri!"

She froze in her tracks and swiveled toward him again.

"I drove like a crazy man to get here. May I at least come in?"

Closing her eyes, she pressed her fingers to her temples, partly because her head was spinning and partly because she realized how silly she must seem to him. The wet strands of hair flopping over her hands reminded her she didn't look her best.

He didn't wait for an invitation. In three strides he crossed the threshold, closed the door, and wrapped his arms around her. The next instant he was sorry he hadn't waited longer. She was warm and soft and smelled like strawberries. And when she instinctively burrowed more comfortably into his embrace, the knotted tie of her belt scraped his lower regions, making him think things he'd sworn he wouldn't. But holding her felt too good; he couldn't push her away. "Where were you today? Workin'?" He felt her shake her head against his chest. "Where?"

"You didn't really drive here like a crazy man, did you?" she murmured into his shirt.

"Yes, I did. I was worried sick about you. As soon as my phone was workin', I started callin' you. When you didn't pick up the last time, I reckoned I'd drive by . . . just to make sure you were okay."

She sighed aloud. "They found Rico today."

Without thinking, his arms tightened their hold. He was suddenly afraid this might be the last chance he'd have with her.

She lifted her head to look at him as she explained. "I tried to call this morning. I wanted you to go with me, not Selena."

"Go where?"

"To the morgue."

The bunched muscles in his arms relaxed. "He's dead, then." She nodded. "And you had to identify the body?" Her head slowly raised and lowered once and she swallowed hard. "Bad, huh?"

"Oh, Drew. You can't imagine what he looked like. Detective Kidder told me I didn't have to do it, but I couldn't stand waiting any longer to find out for sure. Now I wish I hadn't. I think the image and smell will haunt me the rest of my life."

He drew her over to the couch and sat down beside her. "Do you want to talk about it?"

She hadn't thought she'd ever want to talk about it, yet once she started, she told him everything: about Kidder's discovery, how the body looked, and how Selena helped her through it all, in spite of her peculiar moments.

Drew didn't touch her throughout the telling.

124

Somehow it seemed improper for him to offer physical comfort while she spoke of her murdered husband; but it was impossible not to hold out his open hands for her after she finished. She placed her hands in his without moving any closer, and he gave them a quick squeeze. "Have you eaten today?" he asked in a concerned tone as he stood up.

"No. And I don't want to. I can't."

"Then how about a drink?"

She cocked her head at him.

"Not for me. For you." His eyes narrowed a little. "Don't worry. I don't foam at the mouth when I see someone else drinkin' what I can't have."

With a cluck of her tongue, she returned his frown. "I didn't—"

His finger pressed against her lips before she could say another word. "No, that's right. You didn't. I'm too sensitive and you're easy pickin's tonight. Some wine, maybe?"

"That's fine." She started to rise and he waved her back down.

"Let me."

"The wine's in the fridge, and I had a glass in the bathroom."

He winked at her and headed down the hall. The smell of strawberries led him to the empty goblet. Seeing the tub full of cloudy water made him fully aware of the fact that she had been in it when he arrived. The bulky robe and slippers she wore left nothing exposed except her head and hands. He hadn't let himself consider what was underneath until that moment. And there wasn't a blamed thing he could do about it that night.

He lifted the drain stop, then carried the glass to the kitchen. Like her guardian angel, he sat beside her while she sipped her wine; he listened sympathetically whenever she needed to repeat something she'd already told him. When her glass was almost empty and her eyes began to droop, he tucked her robe securely around her legs and picked her up.

"What're we doin' now?" she slurred, trying to focus on his face.

"I'm just goin' to tuck you in, ma'am. And you're goin' to take a long nap."

"I can walk." Rather than struggle to be let down, however, she snuggled closer.

"I know you can," he whispered as he laid her down on her unmade bed, took off her slippers, and pulled the sheet over her. He thought she'd probably be more comfortable without the robe, but he wasn't strong enough to remove it for her. Fighting the temptation to lie down beside her, he kissed her forehead and tiptoed to the door.

"Drew?"

He moved back to the side of the bed and looked down at her worried face. "What is it, darlin'?"

"Please stay."

Oh, darlin', he thought, *how I wish you knew what you were sayin'!*

She opened her eyes a fraction to look at him. "I don' care what the neighbors think tonight. I'm scared an' I don' wanna wake up all alone again. *Please.*"

His heart came up into his throat and he gulped it down again. With a stroke on her velvety cheek, he tried to sound reassuring. "All right. I'll sleep up in the studio."

"No! Not the studio. Too far!"

"Okay, okay," he said quickly to chase away her fears. "I'll be out on the couch if you need me."

"Guest room."

"Fine. Now go to sleep," he ordered gently, and started to leave again.

"Drew?"

He took a deep breath. Maybe he should have poured her another glass of wine. "Yes?"

"May I have 'nother g'night kiss?"

He rolled his eyes heavenward, but gave her an-

126

other peck on her forehead anyway. Her drunken glare told him that it had not pleased her, and he lowered his mouth to hers, giving her the kind of kiss she had wanted in the first place. Right or wrong, when he left the room, his damsel was sound asleep, with a perfectly contented smile on her pretty face.

In his car Kidder smiled gleefully as the numbers on the digital clock changed to two A.M. and the last light in the Gambini house was turned off. Drew Marshall's car was still parked in the driveway. Talk about not waiting to bury the body! These two must think they'd gotten away with murder, to flaunt their affair so soon! He laughed aloud at his own play on words.

Too bad he couldn't tell Hart about this. But he'd promised the captain he'd back off Teri Gambini and concentrate on the mob angle for his last two weeks as a detective. He would present only a completed investigation with all the evidence he'd accrued against the couple. Then he would prove without a doubt that his transfer was a mistake and that Hart's opinion about his being biased was completely crazy.

Kidder played with the idea of hanging around until dawn to pay a surprise visit to the confident pair, but he decided it was too soon to tip his hand. He had no doubt there'd be plenty of other opportunities to catch them in the act.

Teri opened one eye and squinted at the illuminated clock on her nightstand. It was only four o'clock, but she felt well rested . . . except for the headache. The dull pounding reminded her of why she should be so well rested. She had gone to bed at an hour when other people were just sitting down to dinner. No, that wasn't entirely right. She had been *put* to bed. By Drew.

Embarrassment rushed through her as she recalled how foolish she'd been. She wasn't sure which was worse—having been too drunk to walk, or begging him to kiss her goodnight. She hadn't drunk enough wine to forget either his gently tucking her in or his passionate kiss.

The house was quiet. Had Drew stayed as she'd requested? Of course he had. A gentleman never breaks a promise to a lady. And Drew was a perfect gentleman, from head to toe. The fact that she was still in her robe could attest to that. Thoughts of what he might have done were he not such a gentleman drove her from her cozy nest. Bathroom, clothes, aspirin, and coffee were in order.

One glance into the vacant guest bedroom had her tiptoeing into the living room, where she found Drew sprawled on—and off—the couch. Guilt that she had caused him a difficult night added to her embarrassment. As quietly as possible, she went to the kitchen and started the coffee. It had barely begun to drip when Drew joined her.

"Mornin'," he said in a hoarse voice, raking his mussed hair off his forehead. "Smells good."

In that moment Teri decided he looked just as good rumpled as when he was perfectly neat and pressed. It made her wonder if he ironed all those embroidered cotton shirts he wore. "Good morning. Would an apology be acceptable, or should I throw myself off a cliff as penance?"

The bleariness had not quite left his eyes, but he managed to wink at her anyway. "A cup or two of that coffee is all I ask, ma'am."

"I apologize anyway. I don't usually . . . behave so badly." She turned away from him to get two mugs from the cupboard. Drew's hand on her shoulder brought her around again.

"Teri, you don't *usually* have to go through what you have in the last week. Apologies are for strangers, not friends. At any rate, it was my pleasure to be of service." When he saw her flush, he brushed her lips with his thumb. "All of it."

She restrained herself from throwing her arms around him to show him just how much of a pleasure it had been for her. Instead, she ignored the fluttering in her stomach and fixed their coffee. As she carried the hot mugs to the table, she said, "I'm glad you find being in my service so pleasurable, because I have another favor to ask."

"Sure. Whatever," he said, in a way that told her she didn't have to explain if she didn't want to.

"I have to go to the police station to look at the mug shots. And then there's, um, the arrangements for Rico. I'd like to get it all over with today—after the sun comes up, of course."

In answer to her unspoken request for company, he toasted her with his cup. "Before we get started, though, I'd best make a trip to my apartment. I don't think this shirt has another twelve hours, wear in it."

"This should keep you busy for a few hours," the young police officer said with a laugh as he set the fourth voluminous binder on the table in front of Teri and Drew. "Just let me know if you see anyone who looks familiar. When you're done with these, I have plenty more." They each chose a book and began their search.

Teri thought the task wouldn't have been half as bad if the suspects weren't such a motley crew. In her secure middle-class life, she had never had to come in contact with the dregs of humanity. After studying hundreds upon hundreds of faces, she knew how fortunate she was to have been sheltered from animals like these.

Four hours later, Drew struck paydirt. "Teri, look at this one."

She leaned toward his book and gasped. "I think

that's him. Of course, he had those wraparound sunglasses on, so it's hard to tell about the eyes, but it's the same mangy black hair and moustache. And the nose. I remember noticing how it looked like it had been broken a few times. And that even looks like the same earring he wore the day we saw him."

A few minutes later, Drew had told the officer of their success, and that man passed the news on to a superior.

A big, gray-haired man came into the room and shook hands with Teri and Drew. "Hello. I'm Captain Hart. Detective Kidder told me you'd be coming in. I realize this is a terrible imposition at a time like this, but we can't afford to drag our feet, now that we know we're dealing with an obvious mob hit. The trail goes cold awfully fast."

"It's no imposition, Captain, truly. I only wish I had reported the threat at the time. It may have—"

"Tut-tut," the captain interrupted. "Mustn't blame yourself. Had you done something sooner, you may have ended up being a target as well. As it is, I want you to report any suspicious activity around you. I'm not trying to alarm you, but until we check out your man, you should stay on your toes."

Teri sagged in her chair. Why hadn't she thought about the fact that she might still be in danger? That this creep could now come after her for pointing him out? That was exactly what she'd been afraid of to begin with, but after they'd found Rico's body, she'd somehow lost sight of the danger to herself. Why hadn't Detective Kidder mentioned that?

The captain told her the medical examiner would let her claim the body by Friday and promised that Detective Kidder or another officer would keep in touch. They thanked him, then left to attend to the second item on Teri's agenda.

It did not take too long to make arrangements for a private graveside service and burial on Saturday. Drew stayed by her side during those sensitive decisions and remained with her while she went through her list of calls to relatives, Rico's employer, and some acquaintances she thought would want to be notified. A few more phone calls let her clients know she was taking some time off. She was glad she had pushed herself so hard to finish all her assignments last week. There didn't seem to be one ounce of creative juice or anything else left in her body. She felt totally empty.

In the midst of her calls, Selena rang in. Teri thanked her again for her help the day before, but guessing that Selena would feel left out again, she omitted the news that she and Drew had identified the thug to the police.

"I've made the burial arrangements for Saturday. Under the circumstances, I want to keep it private, but I'd like you to come, Selena." Teri hadn't meant to make it sound like she was inviting her to a party, but Selena's response made her uncomfortably aware that a party was how Selena interpreted it.

"I wouldn't miss it for the world. Do you need anything today? Company? Groceries?"

Teri shook off her concern. Selena was just trying to be the best friend she knew how. "No, hon, but thanks for asking. I promise I'll call you if I do."

"Well, okay, then," Selena whined, obviously displeased about not being given anything helpful to do.

"On second thought, I do need a favor." Teri sensed Selena brightening immediately. "I don't own a plain black dress, and the last thing I feel like doing is shopping. Do you think you could pick me out something suitable in a size 7?"

"Of course. I'll go look right now and bring by whatever I find later tonight."

Teri glanced at Drew and knew that dinner for three was not what she wanted that night. "Tomorrow or even Friday would be soon enough. I have to drive over to Jersey and have dinner with my grandmother tonight. I don't know when I'll be back."

After a few more assurances, Selena sounded quite satisfied as they said goodbye.

"Well," Drew said, rising from his place on the couch, "if you're goin' visitin', I guess I'd better mosey on home."

"I'm not." She walked over and sat down on the couch.

"What?" he asked, sitting back down beside her.

"I'm not going anywhere. I lied to Selena."

Drew's eyebrows rose as he laughingly scolded her. "Why, shame on you, Miz Carmichael. An' here I thought you were such a *good* girl."

Teri lowered her lashes. "I always have been, but lately . . ."

He touched her chin to get her to look at him. "Remember, I understand about feelin' smothered."

She shook her head. "It's not that. Although my breathing is definitely being affected." She took a deep breath, as if to prove her claim. "I didn't lie to Selena just to keep her from crowding me. I did it because I wanted to be alone . . . with you." His narrowed brows made her explain. "I know. It's awful and wicked. My husband of twelve years was just brutally murdered. I spent the whole day looking for his killer and making arrangements to bury him. I should be distraught, overcome by grief, anything but what I'm feeling."

His fingers combed through the hair at the side of her head. "And what is it you're feelin' that's so awful and wicked?"

Could she tell him more than she already had? Would he be shocked to learn that she felt as relieved to have Rico out of her life as she was saddened by his death? She looked into his eyes and saw the same fire that was burning within her soul, and she dared to tell him what she was really feeling. "Need."

He withdrew his hand and leaned his head against the back of the sofa. "I was afraid you were goin' to say that."

Teri felt a rush of embarrassed panic over being so bold. "You don't . . . want me?"

"Oh, darlin'," he said with a dry laugh, then sat up and took her hands in his. "If I didn't think I'd explode, I'd have you run these talented little hands of yours all over my body to let you find out for yourself just how much I want you. And I'm not only talkin' 'bout the obvious. You can probably see that with your eyes. I'm talkin' 'bout the fact that I'm purely vibratin' with the need of you. Problem is, I don't think your need and mine are in synch."

"You're confusing me."

He lifted one of her hands and kissed the fingertips, then her palm. "I want more from you than today. I want more than to be someone you turned to for a quick fix, then felt too guilty about it to go on from there. I can't afford to make the same mistake twice. And you can't afford the guilt right now."

She let his words sink in, she completely understood his concern. How could he be sure of her when she wasn't sure of herself? Barely two weeks ago she had thought she'd never let another man into her life. "You're right. I know in my head you're right. But understanding doesn't make the ache go away. Please, Drew." She raised her hands to his cheeks. "Just a little more than nothing."

He closed the distance between them, but stopped an inch short to say, "I never should have let you know how little willpower I have."

His lips slanted over hers in a mating that spoke of much more than two mouths touching. This time there were no exploring caresses or tentative tastes. They each knew what pleasure the other held and anxiously reached for it. As if their bodies had practiced together for a lifetime, they moved in harmony, without the need for conscious thought, until they were stretched out on the sofa, fitted one to another, as they were meant to be . . . until each felt the other's driving need as powerfully

133

as each felt his own.

Her hands discovered the resilient strength of his muscled shoulders and back, the ungiving hardness between them, and the vibrating need he had spoken of.

His hands discovered the softness that concealed her strengths, the sensitive places that made her purr, and the damp heat she had so honestly confessed to.

And they both knew they had to stop.

As if they had both heard the same warning sound, their hands stilled and moved to less responsive areas. A moment later the endless eating kiss gentled to one final caress.

Drew grinned at her. "Just a little, huh, darlin'? A little more and I'da been visitin' St. Peter at the gate."

She hid her face in his shoulder. "I'm sorry. I didn't mean to get so carried away."

"*We,*" he corrected, making her meet his gaze. "*We* got carried away. But just think what we have to look forward to next month."

She blinked at him. "Next *month?*"

"Well, maybe three weeks."

"You're crazy, you know that?" She gave him a peck on the cheek. "But it's a good crazy."

"It's goin' to be a bad crazy if we don't put some air space between us soon. What do you have to do around here that falls into the *un*stimulatin' category?"

They managed to occupy themselves with a board game, a video, and dinner, but the fire between them smoldered and sparked through it all in spite of their pretending it was safely banked.

As they kissed goodnight and fought to keep their desire confined to their lips, Drew voiced the words Teri was thinking.

"Two weeks."

Ten

Drew had work to do the next day, but Teri still had company. Selena had found three dresses and brought them by for Teri to choose, along with an array of accessories.

"You didn't need to bring so much. Whatever you picked would do fine," Teri told her, unable to work up the enthusiasm to match Selena's mood.

"Is that the thanks I get for spending half a day searching for the perfect outfit for today's grieving widow?" she giggled, completely ignoring Teri's disapproving frown, and breezed on by, her arms filled with bags. She glanced back once to make sure Teri was following her to the bedroom. "Well, let's go. The fun doesn't start till you try everything on."

"Do I need to remind you that this is a *funeral* we're going to, and not a social event?" The harshness in Teri's voice made it clear she wasn't amused.

"No," Selena snapped back as she tossed the bags on the bed. "But maybe I need to remind you who you're talking to. I've done my very best to help you through this, but I refuse to pretend we feel something we don't when we're alone."

Teri gritted her teeth against another biting comment and reminded herself one more time that Selena was very young and just trying to help lift her spirits.

"By the way," Selena added, a little more kindly,

135

"you look a hundred times better today. You must have had a good rest last night after all."

Teri felt her face flush and quickly picked up one of the dresses to examine. For a moment she wished she could share the secret of why she had rested so well, but thoughts of their last confidential conversation warned her against it. Feeling bad for not showing Selena sufficient appreciation, when it was really her own conscience bothering her, prompted her to say, "I have you to thank for that, hon. After you left, I poured myself a quart of wine and took a long soak in a sweet-smelling bubble bath. It worked wonders." For this half-truth Selena awarded her with a smile that lit up the room.

"You see? You should listen to me more often. And this is my next bit of advice: try everything on and forget about the real reason you're doing it. Have some fun!"

Teri made an effort to do as she was told, if only to keep Selena content. Personally, she thought she owed Rico's memory a little respect after her behavior last night. The problem was, she didn't feel guilty enough to pay her late husband that tribute. It was fretting over that lack of guilt that had sharpened her tongue today, and she determined not to take it out on her young friend again.

Selena eventually made all the choices for Teri. "Now try on the hat."

Teri lifted the smart little hat with its fine black net veil and set it on her head.

"No, no, no," Selena said, taking it from her. "Your hair's all wrong for this hat. Sit down. I'll need your brush and lots of hairpins."

"Really, you don't have to do my hair. I'll figure it out."

Selena laughed. "Right. That's why you wear a ponytail half the time and leave it hanging straight the other half. Don't worry, I know what I'm doing.

I used to do my mother's hair for her all the time."

Teri gave in and got her what she needed before sitting down at her vanity. She wasn't used to all this pampering. First Drew, and now Selena. Visits to beauty salons were few and far between since all she ever needed was an occasional trim, and she usually did that herself. But as Selena applied the hairbrush with slow, smooth strokes that massaged her scalp, Teri decided this was something she could easily become accustomed to.

She watched with fascination as Selena brushed and pinned every hair into a severe twist at the back of her head. "Did your mother have long hair?" she asked.

Selena answered through teeth clenched around several hairpins. "About the same as yours. It was almost the same shade of brown, too. Someday I'll have to bring the picture of her when she was about your age. I remember thinking how you reminded me of her the first time we met. Though you might guess that she was much taller and heavier than you are. Both my parents were big people, but I got my coloring, or I should say lack of coloring, from my father."

Teri caught the wistful tone, and her caring heart again felt sympathy for the girl who had lost her parents at such an early age. When Teri's mother died after many years of suffering with cancer, Teri and her father easily consoled each other. But remembering the tremendous loss she'd felt when her father had died the year before, she asked, "Do you still miss them?"

Selena inserted one last pin and met Teri's gaze in the mirror. The haunted look Teri had often tried to capture on canvas seemed more pronounced than ever before.

"Miss them? Not him. He was a drunken bastard. It was a relief to both my mother and me when he

137

died. You see, that's why I understand how you're feeling about Rico. But her? I didn't think I'd ever get over losing her." Selena's hands absently began massaging Teri's shoulders and neck. "She had a heart attack, you know. So young! She was only a year older than you are now. But I don't miss her as much as I did at first. After all, I have you to care for now, don't I?"

Teri was not nearly as disturbed by the strange statement as she was by the image she saw reflected in her mirror. Selena's eyes gleamed like polished silver, and while her thumbs were massaging the base of Teri's neck, Selena's fingers had laced themselves around her throat. Before actual fear set in, however, Selena moved away to fetch the hat.

A moment later Teri told herself that her mind had been playing tricks on her. Selena was smiling and cheerful as she adjusted the headpiece and veil. And a few seconds after that, a new reflection shelved thoughts of the other.

She had told Drew that she was wicked. The woman staring back at her in the mirror truly looked the part of the merry widow. All she needed was diamond studs in her ears and blood-red lipstick, and she could pose for one of the glitzy covers she'd photographed on occasion.

"Good God! I don't know, Selena. I don't look very grief-stricken, do I?"

"No. But then, you really aren't, are you?"

Teri grimaced. "I won't lie and say I'll miss him. But at the same time, I wouldn't want other people to know that. I can't explain it, exactly, but I still have the feeling Detective Kidder didn't trust me. Now that they found Rico the way they did, I assume he'll leave me alone, but he made me so uncomfortable. I wouldn't put it past him to show up at the burial services to see if I cry."

Selena's eyes narrowed. "You could be right

about him. I didn't like him, either. We should be prepared. Can you force tears? For appearance' sake?"

"I don't know. I cry at the dumbest times and can't when I should."

Selena laughed and squeezed Teri's shoulders in response, then began undoing her handiwork. "That's okay. All you need is a pinch of tobacco and an unironed hanky that looks like you've been using it all morning. Tobacco can make your eyes tear if you need some help bringing on the water-works."

Teri didn't promise to go to all that trouble just to make the proper impression, but she did wonder how Selena managed to know so much about the strangest things.

Kidder could not remember ever being so over-joyed at *not* obtaining information. He had spent most of the three days since they'd found Gambini's body pumping the old fraternal network of police acquaintances. He'd put out the word that he wanted to confirm a mob hit and find out where an ex-con named Vince Nunzio, who was supposedly working for an Irishman, hung out.

The system had nothing to do with courts of law and administrative procedures, and everything to do with solving crimes the old-fashioned way—with one's nose. Of course, to put one of the scumbags away, a detective still had to present the proper evidence, but it saved a lot of time when you knew who the guilty party was to start with. Then you simply had to come up with the proof to back up the truth. It usually worked.

This time it worked in reverse. Word on the street was that Rico Gambini had paid his debt to the Irishman as he was supposed to. He was too good a customer for them to off him for being a little late. They might have hurt him, but with the man dead, they'd lost a good source of income that had promised to get even better. On the other hand, they were glad to take anonymous credit for the hit, allowing their delinquent debtors to believe that they could end up like Gambini if they didn't take their debts to the Irishman very seriously.

It was confirmed that Nunzio had issued the threat to Mrs. Gambini, but he had not returned to White Plains after that, nor had he ever rented an apartment there. Kidder even had the names of witnesses who would testify to that in court, if necessary. In exchange for this confirmation, Nunzio was to be warned to get himself underground for a while, at least until Kidder arrested the guilty parties.

Everything was falling into place for Kidder's theory to be substantiated. Since it was not a professional hit, it had to be personal. If it wasn't Nunzio at the apartment complex, it had to be someone made up to look like him, right down to his earring. Although it had been inadvertent, Nunzio had apparently given the murderer a surefire way to make it look like a mob hit. Drew Marshall was tall, with dark features; with the right props, he could have disguised himself to look like the thug they'd all seen. For an emotionally based homicide, Kidder thought the plan was quite ingenious.

He was already certain Mrs. Gambini and Marshall were lovers. During a polite conversation with Marshall's cousin at Century Publishing, Kidder learned that the Marshall family had visited New York on two other occasions in the last ten years. Therefore, even though Marshall had just recently moved to New York, there had been an opportunity for him to have met Mrs. Gambini through his cousin prior to that. It was possible that no one had ever been aware of their long-distance affair.

But maybe the husband had found out. Maybe he'd refused to grant his wife a nice, clean divorce. Maybe the gambling fever had him wanting to hold on to her and her growing bank account whether she was faithful or not. That could be why no divorce papers had been filed, even though Mrs. Gambini insisted they were getting divorced. Marshall's divorce had been finalized only three months before. All they needed to live happily ever after was to get Rico Gambini out of the way.

Bingo! Kidder had the motive he'd been looking for. What he needed now was a third party who could verify the long-standing relationship and divorce problems—a confidante of one of them who wasn't bright enough to know she was betraying a friend—the giant, redheaded dingbat model, for instance.

The background check on Marshall supported his theory as well. The cowboy was a convicted felon. Kidder guessed the pressure of a cross-country affair, a growing family, and a high-stress job pushed him into using drugs. But every good cop knows it's a short walk from getting hooked to dealing to being capable of murder. Marshall *could* have done it. And without having a nine-to-five job to report to, he had plenty of opportunity.

There was only one hole that needed filling, and it was staring up at him from the autopsy report on his desk. He reread the findings for the third time. It made him think of completing a jigsaw puzzle only to find there's one more piece, but no place left to put it.

In spite of Captain Hart's repeated order to leave Teri Gambini alone, Kidder could think of no one else who might be able to shed some light on this problem. Besides, he had purposely stayed away for two days to let her think she could relax. That way,

141

his next attack on her nerves would be a total surprise.

Teri realized she was finally beginning to relax. With the unwinding, however, came the boredom, and by Friday morning, she was back at her easel.

Except for that one disturbing incident, Selena had been excellent company yesterday. Teri was especially grateful for that because Drew had been busy all day and hadn't called until late in the evening. Neither of them said anything vitally important; they hadn't needed to.

She had not expected to feel his absence so much, or so soon, but just hearing his voice before she went to sleep had been like a balm to her lonely soul. He had mentioned his needing to use the darkroom today. She told herself that had nothing to do with her own need to be in the studio, but she recognized the white lie for what it was and looked forward to his arrival.

Detective Kidder showed up instead. When he told her he had more questions, she almost closed the studio door in his face.

"It will only take a few minutes."

Teri resisted the urge to ask if he was joking. None of their previous encounters had taken only a few minutes. "Do you mind if I continue to paint? I just blended the tint I want, and I'd hate to have it dry on me.

"Not at all," he said, walking up to her easel. "You were working on this the last time I was up here, weren't you?"

"Yes, I believe so." She edged him out of the way so that she could sit down on her high stool.

"I guess it takes a long time to finish one of these, eh?"

"Sometimes." Teri decided politeness was no

longer required with the annoying man. She wished she could have dealt solely with that nice Captain Hart. "Detective, I don't want to be rude, but I *am* working, and you said you had some more questions."

"Yes. Yes, I do. Would you happen to have any of that delicious coffee of yours brewed?"

Teri growled under her breath. "No. I didn't make any today."

"Too bad. It's really very good. Is it some special blend?"

"Detective!" She could see his hearing aid in place, so she knew that was not his problem. He seemed to be purposely trying to make her blow up at him. She took a deep breath. "I'm sorry. You must understand, I'm not myself yet. My painting relaxes me, and I'd like to get back to it."

"Of course," he said with a great deal of false compassion. "I received the autopsy report on your late husband this morning. It contained something very puzzling." He let her hang for a moment before continuing. "When I first spoke to you, you were quite positive that Mr. Gambini had not been having an affair with another woman."

"I believe I said I couldn't figure out when he *would* have, since I could account for all his time. I wouldn't have sworn that he wasn't."

"I stand corrected. Then, shall we say, he probably was not in the midst of an affair at the time of his death?"

"Yes, I suppose, but what does it matter now?"

"I hope you'll pardon my insensitivity, but there's no way around this. Your husband was not only naked, with no clothes left in the apartment, he had recently ejaculated. The M.E. found clear evidence of it and, because of Mr. Gambini's tight time schedule, it had to have happened in that apartment."

Teri gasped. "I can't believe for one minute that Rico and that . . . that animal were . . . Impossible. Not Rico."

"Forgive me, Mrs. Gambini. I see I've led you down the wrong path. Whoever your husband had sex with — and I'm sure you know better than me whether that was a man or woman — that person did not have black hair. There was one foreign pubic hair tangled with Mr. Gambini's and according to the report, it was blond."

Teri's jaw dropped before she could stop it. As the blood rushed from her head, she grasped the edge of the table next to the easel to keep from falling.

Kidder immediately held out his hand, but he didn't quite touch her. "Are you all right, Mrs. Gambini? Do you know a blonde who might have been with your husband in that apartment?"

Her mind whirled with thoughts of blond hair and seduction. But they were horrible, impossible thoughts and she sent them away with a shake of her head. "No. I . . . I was shocked. There just doesn't seem to be an end to all this."

"Well, if anyone comes to mind, you be sure to call me right away so that I can check it out."

Kidder had no doubt whatsoever that Teri Gambini already had someone in mind.

The weather Saturday morning was all wrong. Teri wanted it to rain — a lightning storm would have been even better — then maybe none of the curiosity seekers would have shown up.

She had no idea how it had happened, but the private graveside service had been turned into a three-ring circus. Rico's relatives behaved as she'd expected and feared. The semiprofessional cryers that attended every Sicilian funeral had shown up in

144

force to sob loudly or faint whenever things got too quiet. But the usual strain of coping with Rico's family was made worse because Teri had refused to hold a wake. Even knowing she was breaking their rigid code of behavior and would probably be cursed for life, Teri could not push herself to sit in a flower-filled funeral parlor with all these people for three solid days.

Having somehow gotten news of how Rico was murdered and what the motive probably was, several reporters and photographers anxiously recorded every wail and teardrop for posterity. One television network had even sent a crew.

If she had to be there, she wanted Drew beside her, but he had convinced her yesterday that his presence at her side would be highly improper. He was here for her, in the crowd somewhere, but she had lost sight of him, and that upset her more than all the rest.

And Selena had worn that stupid red wig again. For some reason it was beginning to irritate the hell out of her. Unless Selena had guessed about the cameras and didn't want to be recognized, Teri could not understand why she would disguise herself.

To top it all off, Detective Kidder hovered along the fringes of the crowd. Watching. Waiting. But for what?

She still didn't understand why he thought Rico's having sex with some blonde before he was killed was so important. As she had told him then—and her assumption hadn't changed any through the long night since—it sounded to her like the killer used some blond woman, probably a prostitute, to act as a decoy to get Rico into the apartment. Drew had agreed with her when she had told him about it later.

And then there was the awful coincidence. She

could not erase the picture of Selena and her laughing about getting rid of Rico, nor could she stop the breathily voiced words that kept playing over and over like a broken record in her head:

Seducing him should be a cinch.
Sex with me would probably kill him.
That's what best friends are for.

It was only a joke, she reminded herself for the zillionth time. Nothing to feel guilty about.

Like this funeral! Kidder wasn't the only one watching her—they all were. The audience was waiting for the star to act out her role, and she couldn't do it! The family was going to string her up by her thumbs any minute.

As if Selena sensed her panic, she leaned over and whispered in her ear, while pushing something into her hand. "Tobacco. Put a bit in your eye. *Now.*"

Teri saw Kidder making his way toward her and she quickly did as Selena instructed.

By the time the priest led the final prayer, Teri's eyes were on fire, her face was streaked with genuine tears, and Kidder was standing next to Rico's mother. The last thing any of them needed today was a rude detective asking a lot of upsetting questions. Turning to one of Rico's sisters, Teri quickly requested that she help her round up the relatives and send them back to the house to save them from the press. Much to Teri's relief, the woman took charge without an argument.

Selena was determined to run interference with the detective to give Teri a chance to herd her sheep into cars and get away. Out of the corner of her eye she saw the reporters descending on Teri, but there was no way she could help with that, too. The tobacco trick had worked. Any pictures they took of

146

Teri would show a grieving widow. It had to be enough.

"Detective Kidder. How nice of you to come.

His gaze darted from Selena to Teri and back again several times before he accepted the fact that he wasn't going to be able to get to the widow.

"Good morning, Selena. How's she holding up?"

Selena shrugged and stepped into her "dumb" character. "Oh, you know. Teri tries to be so strong for everybody else, but she cries all the time when we're alone."

"Really?" he asked, looking skeptical. "I thought they were getting divorced."

"Who told you that?"

"Mrs. Gambini. Why? Wasn't that the truth?"

"Of course it's true. Teri never lies. I just didn't think she had told that to anyone but me."

"You two are very close, then?"

She nodded. "Best friends."

"Then perhaps you can help me help her."

Selena angled her head. "Sure. What can I do?"

"Just keep an eye on her. She's under a lot of stress right now. Does she have any other friends she can rely on?" When Selena didn't answer immediately, he got more specific. "Lady friends? Any men she's particularly close to?"

"I don't think so."

"What about that Mr. Marshall?"

"Drew Marshall? The photographer?"

"Yes. They seemed to be old friends."

Selena's mouth pursed. "No, they just met a few weeks ago. Now that Rico's gone, I'm the only person she's really close to. I'm sure.

"Did you know Rico Gambini as well?"

"I only talked to him a few times. He was usually at work when I was at the studio with Teri."

"Would you say he was a ladies' man?"

Selena saw Teri's car finally driving away. And

147

not a moment too soon. She did not care to answer many questions about Rico Gambini. "He liked women, if that's what you mean."

"No, not exactly. I'd rather you didn't upset Mrs. Gambini by telling her I talked to you about this, but you might be able to guide me in the right direction here. Do you know if there are any blond women among their acquaintances who Gambini might have been seeing on the side?"

Selena controlled her reaction to his question. "A blonde?" She pretended to wrack her pitiful brain. "No one comes to mind. Why?"

Kidder shook his head. "Nothing important. Just something that turned up with the body."

"How's the investigation going? I've got to tell you, I'm absolutely fascinated by what you do. But I guess it's almost impossible to solve a murder when the mob's involved. Do you think you'll ever find that guy?" She noticed how he stood an inch taller after she flattered him. The man had an ego to play to. Now she would see if he also had an active libido.

"I doubt it. But I do expect to catch the murderer."

"Ooh, Detective, that sounds like something the good guy would say in a movie." She made herself touch his arm and lean forward in a confidential manner. "Does that mean you already know who did it?"

He grew another inch, but backed away from her. Adjusting the waist of his slacks, he stated, "No, not yet. But I will. And I'd appreciate any bit of information you might think of to help me out. We both want to solve this case quickly so that Mrs. Gambini's life can get back to normal, don't we?"

Selena gave him a big, innocent smile. "You can count on me, Detective. I'd do anything for Teri."

Not until much later that night, when she was in her own bedroom, did Selena let herself consider what Kidder had said at the funeral.

What had she overlooked that they had discovered so easily on a decaying body? She had been so careful about her hair. Yet they knew Rico had been with a blonde. That word had to be a key. The detective hadn't said long, white, or silver hair; he had definitely said blonde, which told her precisely what kind of hair it was and where it had been found.

The fact that Kidder would not be given the opportunity to check the hair color between her legs was not enough. Nor could she be certain he wouldn't unexpectedly barge into the studio one day and catch her with her hair down . . . literally. The bottom line was that he now had a piece of evidence that could tie her to Rico's death, even if Kidder's suspicions weren't centered on her at this time.

But he was definitely suspicious of someone. Why couldn't the old man just accept the obvious? The average cop would have blindly followed the trail she'd left without hesitation.

She had not liked his harassment of Teri, but a certain amount of suspicion had been a possibility, until they saw the condition of the body. Kidder should have backed off by now, and he shouldn't still be hanging around the funeral asking personal questions.

If his sneaky little mind ever turned to her, all he needed was a DNA test on her hair to get a perfect match to the one he had. She'd read all about that method of identification. It was practically foolproof.

Selena picked up the doll resting on the pillow beside her. "What do you think, Juliette? Do we need to make the snoopy old policeman go away?"

Not yet. It wouldn't be smart to take another risk so soon when he may still go away on his own. Let's wait and see.

It seemed to Selena that she had spent half her life waiting to see how people around her were going to behave.

"But Mommy, why do you have to get married again? After Daddy died, you promised it would just be the two of us."

"And it has been, baby, for four years. I know it's hard for you to understand, but you will when you get older. Troy's good to me . . . to us. He's not at all like your father. I love him, baby, and I want him to share our life. I'll still love you just as much as ever, but then you'll have his attention, too. Doesn't he buy you pretty presents and treat you nice?"

Selena didn't want to give in, even if her mother did speak the truth. And she understood more about the man-woman thing than her mother imagined — especially after she had peeked into her bedroom late one night when her mother and Troy thought she was sleeping. Troy apparently made her mother very happy, happier than Selena could ever remember, but she still wasn't sure she wanted him living in their house.

"He's okay, I guess. Except for all that kissing and hugging."

Her mother giggled. "Oh, I don't know. I kind of like that part."

"Yeah, well, I don't. If he's going to marry you, tell him to keep his kisses all for you."

Her mother gave her a quick hug and laughed again. "Now, don't be such a pouty-puss. Troy is a very affectionate man. It's just his way to give hugs and kisses to people he cares about, and I know he already cares about you. I'll bet in no time he'll love you as much as I do. Don't worry, you'll get used to having a loving father for a change."

"Will I have to call him Daddy?"

"Not unless you want to. But don't you think it might seem strange if you continued calling him Uncle Troy?"

Selena shrugged. She would decide what name fit him after he'd been around awhile. If he kept her mother smiling, maybe she could agree to call him Daddy. If not . . . well, if not, what she called him wouldn't matter anymore.

Eleven

For three days after the funeral, Teri didn't feel like doing anything but vegetating. She slept, ate, and slept some more. A dozen movies made the trip in and out of her VCR, but she couldn't recall what any of them had been about. It was as if her body and mind had decided she needed a vacation after the fiasco at the graveside and afterward in her home.

One of the less obnoxious reporters had told her the media had received an anonymous tip about the murder, but that it was their unofficial opinion that someone within the mob had spread the news. It was typical of them to take advantage of such a situation to promote their deadly reputation. As far as the media was concerned, news was news, and the bloodier the better.

Unfortunately, one newshound staked out her frontyard so that he could take pictures and badger the relatives as they left. The result was that no one wanted to leave. Rico's family supplied the food and the womanpower to serve it and clean up afterward, but Teri was on the verge of collapsing when they all finally went home.

Everyone who had called since, even Selena and Drew, was asked to give her a few days before coming over.

By Wednesday morning she felt a bit more human, and when Selena called for the umpteenth time, Teri told her to come by. If nothing else, maybe she would sketch a little.

Drew's call that day also helped pick up her spirits. He had been asked to fill in for another photographer on a commercial shoot for an ad agency. He was optimistically hoping that the other's case of flu would be his lucky break, and Teri did also. It meant he would be out of town until Friday, but Teri assured him that although she would miss him, she would be fine . . . as long as he promised to come to dinner Friday night.

Kidder's time was almost up. In six days he had to report to Hell, and he knew he didn't deserve that sentence. The investigation that was supposed to save him had come to a screeching halt.

He now had the whole picture but couldn't prove it. Even his old pal Hart wouldn't listen to him unless he could produce some solid evidence, or at least one witness to support his theory, no matter how much sense it made. Normally, he would have kept plodding along, searching for clues, tracking down the mysterious blonde. Normally, he wouldn't have to worry about a deadline. He knew Hart thought he was crazy. If he didn't come up with something substantial before they confined him to the Property Room, the captain would never assign another detective to follow Kidder's leads. Mrs. Gambini and her lover would get off scot-free!

He had no alternative except to jangle the weak link until it fell apart. It was time to shove Teri Gambini's back against the wall with a direct assault.

"I'm sorry, Selena," Teri said disgustedly as she

153

set down her sketchpad. "I may as well forget it. My fingers don't want to listen to my brain today."

Selena clucked her tongue. "You're probably trying too hard. Let's just have some tea and talk awhile. I went to see that new musical comedy everybody's raving about."

For the next hour Selena kept Teri entertained with a blow-by-blow account of the play and what every person in the audience was wearing. They were both relaxed and smiling when someone knocked on the studio door.

Teri remembered to look out the window first. With an exasperated sigh, she told Selena it was Detective Kidder, and made herself count to ten before unlocking the door.

"Good morning, Detective Kidder. I hadn't expected to see you again so soon."

He nodded curtly. "I have an important matter to discuss with you. May I come in?"

She hesitated a moment, wishing she had the courage to refuse, then stepped aside. "We were just—" She looked around the studio. For a second she thought Selena had vanished into thin air, until she saw the closed bathroom door. Turning back to Kidder, she saw him eyeing the two cups on the table. "Selena and I were just taking a break. I'm trying to get back to work today. Would you like a cup of tea?"

"No, thank you." With hands clasped behind his back and a concerned frown on his face, he rocked back and forth on his heels a few times before speaking. "Have you given any more thought to our last conversation?"

Teri sat down and took a sip of her cooled tea. "To be quite honest, Detective, I don't *want* to think about any of it. In fact, I don't even remember what our last conversation was about."

He stopped rocking. "The blonde."

Teri couldn't stop the involuntary muscle twitch

of her eyelid, but she tried to ignore it as she calmly replied, "As I told you the other day, I think she was a paid lure."

Kidder took a few steps toward her, making her look up from where she was seated to continue meeting his eyes. "Come now, Mrs. Gambini, you can do better. You don't believe that at all. When I first told you about the hair, you almost fainted from shock. You barely managed to answer me now. Face facts, lady. You haven't got what it takes to pull this off."

Teri felt herself recoiling, even though her body hadn't moved an inch. "What . . ." She choked on the question, but it had to be asked. "What are you saying?"

He moved even closer and bent toward her, so that now she had to lean back in her chair to keep from feeling his breath on her face. "We'll start with the blonde. You know who it is, or you have a very good idea. I believe you were genuinely shocked, so I don't think you knew she was involved at first."

"That's ridiculous!" Teri pushed him away from her and stood up. How could she tell him why she had reacted that way without explaining everything? It would be like pointing an accusing finger at Selena, then turning it back on herself as an accomplice. He would never believe her shock was all because of a very bad joke. "Why *shouldn't* I be upset? My husband was not only butchered, but just before that he had no qualms about meeting some strange woman for sex in an apartment a few blocks from our home. Do you think I should simply accept all that like it was a daily occurrence?"

"You *were* getting a divorce . . . or did I misunderstand you before?"

Her hands balled into fists at her side. "Yes. We were."

"And yet there were no papers filed. I checked. I think *you're* the one who wanted a divorce . . . and

155

that your husband wasn't willing to go along with your plans. I think a man with a gambling problem as bad as his wouldn't let go of a wife right when she was about to start raking in the big bucks."

She was certain the truth of his statement was written all over her face, yet she had to deny it or fall into the trap she sensed being set. "No, that's not true. He was going to quit gambling. He swore to me it was the last time."

"But you knew he'd never make it that easy on you. He'd fight you every step of the way, and you were in too much of a hurry for that. Because we both know his gambling wasn't your real reason for wanting a divorce."

She felt the trap but couldn't see where it was coming from. "We may have had some other problems, but nothing as bad as his gambling."

"That's a *lie!*" he shouted, marching toward her, making her back away from his sudden anger. "His gambling was your excuse to cover up for your own sins. A wife who fornicates with a man other than her husband shall be damned in Hell. And in your case, I'm going to be the one to send you there."

Teri stopped backing away. "You're insane. I never cheated on my husband in the entire twelve years we were married."

Kidder regained his composure to deliver his killing blow. "Is that so? Well, I'll admit that the two of you have covered your tracks very well. But not good enough to hide it from me."

Teri was so bewildered by his words that she stood frozen in place, gaping at him as he continued.

"The two of you obviously got tired of your long-distance affair. He got his divorce, but you were having trouble with yours. So you plotted your husband's demise. I know the how and why. I just haven't figured out where the blonde fits in."

"What *are* you raving about? *What* long-distance

affair?" His smug expression told her he really believed what he was saying. That *she* had plotted with some man to kill her husband.

"Still playing the innocent, eh? Fine. I'll spell it out for you. Drew Marshall killed your husband, and you helped him do it."

She staggered to the bed and slumped down on the edge. "Drew? And me? Detective, I hate to blow up your theory, but I never even *met* Drew Marshall until a few weeks ago. Besides that, he's a very gentle man. He'd never be able to kill another person."

"Another lie, Mrs. Gambini? Save it for the jury. Your lover is an ex-con drug addict who very nearly killed several hundred people. I know *exactly* what kind of man he is. And I know what kind of woman you are."

Teri's mind reeled. What could she say to make him see how wrong he was? Massaging her temples, she realized the conclusions he had drawn were not all that hard to believe if you didn't know the truth. She had to appeal to whatever logic he had. "Please listen to me very closely, Detective. I met Drew the week before Rico disappeared. We have since become friends because of our work, but we *are* not, *have* not been lovers. And I did *not* need to have Rico killed. He had agreed to give me a divorce in exchange for bailing him out. The only reason the papers weren't filed yet was because I had a deadline to meet that didn't leave time for appointments with attorneys. And lastly, if I hated my husband enough to kill him, I would *never* have given him a gift of another woman as a going-away present!" Her conscience allowed her the two half-truths for salvation's sake.

Kidder glared at her for a long moment, but she straightened her shoulders and stared back.

"Have it your way for now, Mrs. Gambini. But let me tell you how it's going to be. When I'm through putting this case together, you and loverboy will be going away for a long time. Unfortunately, they don't have co-ed dorms in prison, so you won't get to be together in spite of all the trouble you went to. On the other hand, if you agree to testify against Marshall, tell me who the blonde is, and generally cooperate, I can almost assure you of a minimum sentence—maybe even probation, if you can convince the district attorney that you didn't really know what Marshall was planning until after it was over."

Teri's mind sorted out one important fact: he wasn't here to arrest her. Apparently it was all supposition—a hunting trip, as Drew called it—but would their innocence protect them from this hunter's trap? "Get out, Detective Kidder, and take all your false accusations with you. I've done nothing wrong, and neither has Drew."

"I'll go, Mrs. Gambini. But as the television detectives always say at this point, I'll be back."

Once he was gone, Teri's body gave in to the fear he had instilled. Her heart ran a race with her lungs, and she couldn't control the trembling in her arms and legs. But she didn't cry. There didn't seem to be any tears left in her.

When Selena sat down and put her arm around her, Teri was startled out of a full-fledged anxiety attack. She had forgotten all about Selena.

"Are you going to be okay?" Selena asked quietly.

Teri blinked at her. As dumb as it sounded, she had to ask, "Selena, were you in the bathroom all this time?"

"Yes, sorry I couldn't help you with him, but I seem to have picked up an intestinal virus. I felt a little queasy this morning when I got up. I probably shouldn't have come over at all. What are you going to do about Kidder?"

"He's nuts. Absolutely, certifiably insane. And I'm scared to death he's going to send me to the loony bin in his place. Maybe I should file a complaint against him for harassment. But then, that might only make things worse." She took a deep breath. "Look, hon, why don't you go on home and take care of yourself? There's no way I'm going to be able to work with these anyway." She held up her quivering hands as proof of her statement.

Selena gave her a look of sympathetic understanding. "Don't worry about me. I'll be fine. You will, too. Soon. I'll make sure of it."

Selena felt bad about leaving Teri alone, but she had something more important to do than sit there holding her hand until she calmed down. Although she had initially hidden in the bathroom to keep Kidder from seeing her without the red wig, the thin door had given her the bonus of being able to hear every word without either of them knowing she had eavesdropped.

She could not believe the false conclusions Kidder had drawn. There was nothing to substantiate them, yet he made it all sound entirely credible. Selena knew from all the cases she'd read about that circumstantial evidence, presented well, could get an innocent person convicted. Now she understood why he'd asked that question about Drew being Teri's old friend. He was trying to get her to provide him with proof that they were longtime lovers. How ridiculous!

Calling the media had been a risky thing to do, but she'd been certain that the more people there were who thought the mob was involved, the more the police would concentrate on that angle and leave Teri alone. Apparently Kidder wasn't influenced by the opinion of the press.

Juliette would have to be told they had waited too long. There was no time for a complex plan. They had to act quickly or Teri could be taken away from them, and that would be like losing Mommy all over again.

She hoped Juliette already had something in mind.

4 BESTSELLING HISTORICAL ROMANCES BY YOUR FAVORITE AUTHORS CAN BE YOURS, FREE!

Kensington Choice, our newest book club now brings you historical romances by your favorite bestselling authors including Janelle Taylor, Shannon Drake, Rosanne Bittner, Jo Beverley, and Georgina Gentry, just to name a few! Each book is filled with passion, adventure and the excitement of bygone times!

To introduce you to this great new club which is part of Zebra Home Subscription Service, we'd like to send you your first 4 bestselling historical romances, absolutely free! And once you get these 4 free books to savor at home, we'll rush you the next 4 brand-new books at the lowest prices available, as soon as they are published.

The way the club works is that after your initial FREE shipment, you will get our 4 newest bestselling historical romances delivered to your doorstep each month at the preferred subscriber's rate of only $4.20 per book, a savings of up to $7.16 per month (since these titles sell in bookstores for $4.99-$5.99)! All books are sent on a 10-day free examination basis and there is no minimum number of books to buy. (And no charge for shipping.) Plus as a regular subscriber, you'll receive our FREE monthly newsletter, *Zebra/Pinnacle Romance News*, which features author profiles, contests, subscriber benefits, book previews and more!

So start today by returning the FREE BOOK CERTIFICATE provided. We'll send you 4 FREE BOOKS with no further obligation: A FREE gift offering you hours of reading pleasure with no obligation...how can you lose?

We have 4 FREE BOOKS for you as your introduction to KENSINGTON CHOICE! To get your FREE BOOKS, worth up to $23.96, mail the card below.

FREE BOOK CERTIFICATE

Yes! Please send me 4 Kensington Choice (the best of Zebra and Pinnacle Books) Historical Romances without cost or obligation (worth up to $23.96). As a Kensington Choice subscriber, I will then receive 4 brand-new romances to preview each month for 10 days FREE. I can return any books I decide not to keep and owe nothing. The publisher's prices for Kensington Choice romances range from $4.99-$5.99, but as a preferred subscriber I will get these books for only $4.20 per book or $16.80 for all four titles. There is no minimum number of books to buy and I may cancel my subscription at any time, plus there is no additional charge for postage and handling. No matter what I decide to do, my first 4 books are mine to keep, absolutely FREE!

KF0697

Name _____

Address _____ Apt. _____

City _____ State _____ Zip _____

Telephone ( ) _____

Signature _____

(If under 18, parent or guardian must sign)

Subscription subject to acceptance. Terms and prices subject to change.

AFFIX
STAMP
HERE

KENSINGTON CHOICE
Zebra Home Subscription Service, Inc.
120 Brighton Road
P.O.Box 5214
Clifton, NJ 07015-5214

Twelve

Teri had stepped from one nightmare into another. Not knowing what had happened to Rico for a week had left her nerves ragged. Then the funeral had sapped what little strength she still possessed. But Detective Kidder was surely going to push her over the edge.

The morning after he'd made his outlandish charges, she decided to take a walk around the block. Rage flooded through her when she saw the detective sitting in a car parked across the street, watching her. She forced herself to take the walk, mainly to show him that he wasn't intimidating her, but she cut it short when he got out of the car to follow her.

Her rage turned to fear when she realized it wasn't the first time she'd noticed that car parked there. Since she hadn't seen him in it, she'd assumed one of the neighbors had bought a new car. Had he forgotten to duck down when she'd walked out of the house just then? Or did he want her to know he was there, watching her every move? How long had he been doing this?

Long enough to know Drew had spent a night in her house? Her stomach spasmed violently as comprehension dawned. He must have known about that! He might also have seen them the night Drew

161

had kissed her in the doorway. *That* was why he had come to the conclusion they were lovers. And that meant her denial of an intimate relationship had sounded like a bald-faced lie to the detective. Could she now turn around and explain the truth in more detail, or would that only compound her guilt in his eyes? She realized no one who'd witnessed their passionate embrace would believe she and Drew hadn't slept together the night he'd stayed over. And here all she'd been worried about at the time was what the neighbors would think if they saw them.

She felt as though she were caught in a spider's web constructed of her own half-truths. Would anyone believe her now if she told them the whole of it?

Would anyone understand how a bad joke had become reality and how she suffered from the guilt of knowing she had wished her husband out of her life?

Or that she and Rico not only knew a blonde woman, but one who had willingly offered to seduce Rico to set him up for an easy divorce, and that she had lied only to protect an innocent young woman from unnecessary harassment?

Or that she and Drew were only *thinking* of becoming lovers while her husband lay mutilated in the morgue, and she didn't feel the least bit guilty about that because she believed she deserved a little happiness?

She wasn't certain she believed it herself.

Staying inside her house kept her from having to see Kidder, but she knew he was out there. Her only consolation was knowing that if Vincent Nunzio decided to come after her for pointing him out to the police, she had a personal watchdog right outside. She wondered if Detective Kidder would finally believe her if something drastic did happen. She also found herself questioning whether he would actually do anything to stop the thug from hurting her. Telling herself he was still an officer of the law, regardless of his personal feelings for her, she was able to get a little sleep that night.

She woke on Friday, preoccupied with thoughts of Drew. She couldn't wait to see him. She thought she should stop him from coming, yet he had to be told about Kidder's accusations. She started to leave a message on his machine, then changed her mind. If Detective Kidder was staking out her house, he might have tapped her telephone. She couldn't take the chance of saying anything over the phone that might be misconstrued. She would have to talk to Drew in person.

As originally planned, she went shopping for a special dinner for Drew's homecoming. What she hadn't expected was an uninvited police escort everywhere she went, but she decided another confrontation with Kidder would serve no purpose.

When Drew called to let her know he was back, and started to say something more personal, she cut him off. Trying to keep the worry out of her voice, she told him she had a new project to discuss with him, and suggested he come over for dinner around six. Drew was clearly confused, but didn't question her peculiar behavior until he arrived at her house.

"What's wrong?" he demanded the moment she opened the door.

"Come in and I'll explain." She directed him to the edge of the front window in the living room and, holding the curtain aside an inch, told him to look across the street. He tossed his hat on the couch and went to look. "See the gray compact? Anybody in the driver's seat you recognize?"

"I can't really tell from here. Is this a new version of I Spy, or what?"

"It's Detective Kidder. He thinks . . . oh, God,

163

this is so nuts it's hard to say it out loud. He thinks you and I have been having an affair for some time, and that we killed Rico because he wouldn't give me a divorce."

Drew laughed sharply once before realizing she wasn't sharing the joke. "You're serious?" he asked, incredulously.

"It sounds impossible when I say it like that, but the way he delivered it to me, step by step, he made it sound completely rational."

"How can it sound rational when there's no truth in it?"

She related how the detective had spelled out his theory to her.

"Okay," Drew conceded. "There's some sense in it if you don't know the truth. But he can't prove we were long-distance lovers when we only just met. For that matter, we aren't lovers now." Her skeptical look caused him to add, "In the biblical sense."

She shook her head. "I don't think the truth matters. I think he's been watching the house for some time. Maybe he even took pictures."

Drew's eyes revealed when he recalled the incriminating incidents. "Oh. But we still didn't know each other long enough to plot a murder together. And if we had to, we could surely prove it."

Teri felt somewhat relieved to hear him say that, but there were still the other half-truths. "He was on target about Rico and the divorce."

"But no one else knows that, do they?"

"Selena does, and now you do, too."

"As one of the accused, I don't think I count. Are you afraid Selena might say somethin'?"

She frowned. "Not on purpose, but he's very tricky with his questions. And then there's that business about the blonde." She told him about the hair found on Rico's body. "When he asked if I knew any blondes Rico might have been seeing, I said something like, I don't know any blondes. I don't remember exactly what I said; I was so stunned. But I didn't want him bothering Selena with a lot of questions just because of her hair color."

"But she's not a blonde."

"What?"

Her hair might be called white, silver, or even gray, but not blond. Anyway, he could see Selena with his own eyes."

His logic was so clear that Teri wondered how she could have been so blind to it, until she tried to remember when Kidder had seen Selena. "It sounds strange, but I'm not sure he *has*. I mean, he has, but now that I think about it, I'm not sure he's seen her *real* hair. She's had a thing for this red wig lately. I'm just not positive about it."

"Either way, she *wasn't* havin' an affair with Rico, was she?"

"No, of course not. She's my friend." *A friend who would have seduced my husband if asked.* Teri kept that embarrassing episode to herself. As nice as Drew was, she didn't want him to know what truly wicked thoughts she'd once had.

"Then he has nothin' but a lot of suppositions. I think you should go see that Captain Hart and tell him what Kidder's doin' to you. I got the distinct impression he believed the guy we pointed out was guilty, and he couldn't wait to pin the whole thing on the mob. I can't help but wonder if Kidder's actin' on his own."

"You're right. I kept thinking Kidder was acting crazy, like it was something personal he had against me. Maybe he really *is* off-balance. That settles it," she stated firmly. "I'll go see the captain tomorrow and put an end to this nonsense."

"Good. So, what's cookin'?"

"Do you really think you should stay to eat? I mean, he's out there, probably counting the minutes we spend together."

"If he's tappin' your phone, which I doubt, since that's not such an easy thing to do legally, he knows you invited me to dinner to discuss work."

"Right. But I don't think you should stay long, do you? I mean, I want you to stay, but until we're off his prime suspect list, I think we should—"

"Cool it?" he finished for her. She nodded, with a blush for emphasis. He couldn't resist giving her a hug, but he set her away immediately after. "Until we're in the clear, we'll keep our relationship strictly professional—confined to the studio after tonight. Have you been working?"

"A little. It's been hard."

"I can't imagine why!" His sarcasm earned him a smile. "At any rate, he can't make anything of our both bein' in the studio from time to time."

"No, I don't think so."

"That's settled too, then. How about feedin' a poor, lonely cowboy who's been eatin' nothin' but trail dust for days?"

She found she could laugh after all, and led him to the kitchen. As they ate, Drew told her about his trip and his hopes for a lot more of those kinds of assignments from the same agency. It occurred to Teri that, even considering what a good week he'd had, Drew was not reacting as she'd thought he would when he learned of the detective's charges. Finally, she asked what was on her mind: "Are you pretending not to be worried for my sake?"

"Worried 'bout what?" he asked with a lopsided smile.

"You know damn well what I'm talking about."

He took her hand in his. "Listen to me, darlin'. Worryin' don't make a bad situation better, only worse. Ever since I hit bottom, I learned to live one

166

day at a time. The other slogan I have imprinted on my brain from my experience is 'Let go and let God.' I do the best I can and leave my future in His hands. I figure since He brought me to you, He had a good reason."

She pulled his hand to her lips and kissed his knuckles. "Oh, Drew, that's so like you to say the perfect thing. I don't want to send you home after that, but I'll console myself with knowing I'll see you tomorrow in the studio."

He hated leaving her alone, but it would add fuel to the detective's imaginary fire if he stayed any longer. As Teri said, they had the studio . . . *the studio?* Instantly making a decision, he said, "We still have work to do."

Her eyes opened wide. "We do?"

"Sure 'nuff. And we haven't got a minute to waste. Right now I want you to mosey on up to the studio. I'll only be a couple minutes behind you."

She didn't know precisely what he had in mind, but if it meant she could postpone saying good-night, she was all for it.

"Turn on the outside light and bang the kitchen door good and loud on your way out. Hopefully, he has his hearing aid in. We want to make sure he knows right where we are for the rest of the evenin'."

His deviousness made her laugh again, and she did as he suggested. A moment after she entered the studio, she heard a thud like a car door slamming and ran to the window. For a heartbeat she had feared Drew was leaving, but he was only getting his camera and bag out of the trunk. She also noticed he had a brown grocery bag with him. Her curiosity was peaking by the time he joined her, but she waited for him to explain.

He set down his equipment and handed her the grocery bag. "Go put this on."

167

She looked at the brown bag and asked innocently, "How should I wear it? Over my head?" He smirked at her, and she opened it to find her pink terrycloth robe. As she pulled it out, she asked, "What's this for?"

"You'll see. Just put it on."

She started to push one arm into a sleeve, but he stopped her.

"Not like that. Go in there," he ordered, pointing to the bathroom, "and put it on—the way you were last week when I put you to bed. *Exactly* the way you were. It looks like we've been accused of somethin' that's dang near impossible to deny. I figure that already makes us guilty of improper behavior without havin' enjoyed it. Unless you have an objection, I'd rather be guilty of somethin' I found considerable pleasure in."

Her stomach did a double flip as his words sank in. The waiting was over. They were going to become lovers for real, right under the detective's watchful eye. The move to the studio and the camera equipment were just a cover for Kidder's sake; they knew he couldn't possibly see anything inside because of the blackout shades over the windows.

She took the robe into the bathroom and immediately heard Drew moving things around in the studio as she undressed. What on earth was he doing now?

As she came out of the bathroom, her nervousness required her to make another joke. "I assume you didn't want me to put my head under the faucet to get the look *exactly*—" her words hung in the air as she took in the changes he'd made. One of her big lamps had been covered by a pink filter and was glowing on the bed, over which was draped a large piece of royal blue satin. The charming devil who had set the stage was fiddling with his camera as if he hadn't noticed her arrival.

"Just have a seat on the bed," he told her in a stiff, professional voice.

"Drew," she said in a warning tone, "what are you doing?"

He glanced up at her with a perfectly innocent expression. "I'm workin', ma'am. And so are you. Ever done any modelin' before, ma'am?"

"Drew!" This time she stomped her foot for good measure, but it did her no good. He was waiting for her answer. Why not play along, she asked herself. Because she didn't know the rules to this kind of game. But as she remembered how much she liked Drew's kisses, her body began warming up. She decided to leave the rules to him. "No, I haven't," she finally answered, sitting where he wanted her. "I'm too plain."

He shook his head at her. "Wrong attitude. We can't get this shoot right unless you know how good you look. You're beautiful, Teri Carmichael, inside and out, and I want your eyes to tell the camera you know it."

"All right. I'm beautiful. What I'm *not* is photogenic. That's why I usually stand on the *other* side of the camera." She made a funny face at him as he held his camera up to his eye and prepared to snap.

Click-whirr. "Wrong again, ma'am. This camera loves the way you look—the way your hair hangs loose around your face, restin' just so on your shoulders. Did you know it has just a hint of auburn when the light hits it? Muss it up a little, now." She started to make a joke of that, too, but somehow it seemed more fun to do what he wanted her to. She certainly had given instructions to enough models to know what he meant. As she threaded her fingers through her hair and tossed her head from side to side, he moved from one spot to another, clicking his camera repeatedly.

"Smile for the camera, pretty lady. It loves your

sexy mouth. Let it have a peek inside. That's it. Such a talented little mouth. The kind that makes a man willin' to suffer the fires of Hell to have that mouth on his." *Click-whirr.*

"And your eyes. Warm, sensuous eyes that tell a man everythin' he wants to know, nothin' held back. Don't hold it back now, darlin'. Let your eyes tell the camera what you're thinkin' 'bout."

She felt her heartbeat pick up as she remembered the night they'd almost made love. His sharp intake of breath told her he'd seen her explicit thoughts through his camera lens. Suddenly she understood this was a game for two, and that she could create her own rules.

His camera kept clicking as she ran her gaze over his body, imagining all the things she intended to do with it. When she ran her tongue over her lips, she watched his body change inside the snug jeans, preparing itself for her, and her breathing altered to accommodate her erratic pulse.

"Good. Very nice. Let's do a pose or two. Try lyin' on your back with your head almost off the side of the bed, and bring your hair out so that it hangs down over the edge. Yes, that's it. Now bend your far knee up through the robe's openin'. C'mon, darlin', show the camera what great legs you've got. Better yet, I'll help you."

He set down the camera and went to her. With great care and attention, he separated and arranged the robe so that nothing but her leg was visible. It was difficult to lie still as his hands smoothed her robe into place, but when he ran his fingertips up and down her inner thigh, she almost pulled him on the bed with her that minute. But he wasn't done with her yet. First he positioned her arms and hands. Then, touching her only through her robe, he loosened the belt and parted the top between her breasts.

170

"Time to close your eyes," he murmured, moving away. She did, and the camera began clicking again. "You're not sleepin', you're rememberin'. Your mind and body are filled with nothin' but memories of your dream lover. The feel of his calloused palm against your naked breasts. How his tongue teased your nipples until you nearly screamed."

Her hands automatically moved to ease the tingling his words created.

"You're rememberin' how he felt stretched out on top of you and how your thighs parted to make room for him."

Of their own accord, her legs opened and her body squirmed in search of its other half.

Click-whirr. "Now, darlin', nice and easy-like, sit up with your back to the camera.

She no longer thought to refuse him, as she could see and hear by the roughness in his voice that the game was clearly a tie at this point. Again he set the camera down and came up behind her to position her the way he wanted her.

"The camera liked that little bit of skin, darlin', but it wants to see some more." His fingers grazed the swells of her breasts as they closed around the robe's edges. "Let's show it some of this gorgeous back," he said, easing the covering off her shoulders. His knuckles caressed her skin as he slowly dragged the material all the way down her arms to her wrists. "Straighten your spine, darlin'," he whispered, and his finger stroked the length of that column.

The gooseflesh he raised had nothing to do with the temperature in the room.

"Such a beautiful back," he complimented as the rest of his fingers entered the play and made a shivery path over her shoulders. "Almost as beautiful as the front." His hands cupped her breasts, and she leaned back against him.

171

"Drew, *please*." She moaned when his fingers toyed with her nipples. "No more."

"No more?" His voice was husky with a need for quite the opposite. "Or more?"

In answer, she turned and unbuckled his belt.

Before she gave him what they both wanted so desperately, she begged a favor. "Please destroy that film."

His sexy grin was full of mischief. "What film?"

Thirteen

Juliette was not very happy about having to come up with a plan that had to be carried out so fast. She preferred plans that took time to prepare—the kind that showed how very smart she was. But Selena had explained why they must hurry, and Juliette did the best she could within the set rules.

Some rules couldn't be changed, however. First, no one must see or hear anything that happens to the bad person. Second, when the bad person is hurt, the police must believe it was an accident or that another bad person is to blame. And third, above all, the good person must be protected from both bad people and the police.

After Selena heard the terrible, hurtful things Detective Kidder had said to Teri, she went straight home to Juliette. It wasn't until the next morning, though, that they finally agreed on a safe enough plan.

The bad policeman was very eager to get some kind of proof that Teri and Drew were guilty of Rico's murder, and Selena had promised to contact Kidder if she thought of any little bit of information. All she had to do was offer a string that he couldn't resist pulling. By the time he realized what was on the other end of the string, it would be too late.

Throughout the day on Friday, Selena placed calls to the police station, asking for Detective Kidder in a variety of voices. Since she was aware that all incoming calls were recorded, she never left any messages, nor did she intend to talk to him if he was in, but she knew of no other way to track him down. The station would not give out his home number or address, and he wasn't listed in the phonebook. That meant the first part of the plan was going to depend on a little logic and a little luck.

Selena figured that if he wasn't at the station, he was either at home or out doing whatever detectives did. And in this one's case, that seemed to involve a lot of time bothering Teri. If Selena guessed right, she would have to act on the spot, which meant she had to be prepared.

Before leaving her apartment and heading for White Plains, she transferred one of the special packages from her freezer to a slightly larger bag with ice, then chose a purse big enough to conceal that and all the other items she might need, depending on how things moved along.

Juliette was definitely not happy with all the "ifs" in this plan, but they didn't seem to have much choice.

The sun was low in the sky as Selena drove out of Manhattan, but it was still light enough for her to wear her large dark sunglasses. She had pinned her hair up and covered it with a floppy hat—the red wig would no longer be necessary. Because of the unusually mild weather that June evening, her long, tan trenchcoat would not seem too out of place if anyone happened to see her. But all anyone would actually *see* was a tall, genderless person carrying an oversized denim shoulder bag.

The little luck she needed was waiting for her when she reached Teri's street and slowly passed the house. Everything was perfect.

The detective was sitting in a car across from the house and hadn't noticed her drive by. Selena wondered if Teri knew he was there, hoping to catch Teri in some naughty behavior, or simply hoping to push her into a confession by his constant annoying presence. It didn't matter. Soon none of his foolish suspicions would matter.

The second piece of luck was in Teri's driveway. Selena remembered Rico's car had been put in the garage until Teri had time to sell it, and her car now sat outside in the drive. That car, and the lights in the house, which were on, assured Selena that Teri was at home and, more than likely, some neighbor would recall that if asked. Selena hoped a neighbor might also recall seeing the other car parked in the driveway.

She knew Drew Marshall had gone out of town on a big assignment. Apparently he was back and didn't want to wait to develop his film. There was just a splinter of light visible at the edge of the window, but it was enough to let her know he was hard at work. If her luck held, he would be at it for hours, and he and Teri would be able to provide alibis for each other's whereabouts that night, with the neighbors as witnesses. It was absolutely perfect.

She found a parking place around the corner and quickly walked back to Kidder's car. As he was watching the house, he didn't see her approach on the passenger side of his car. Hunched down, she rapped on the closed window.

Kidder jerked around, his hand flying to the holster inside his jacket.

Selena briefly lowered her glasses to help him identify her. "It's me," she said in as loud a voice as she dared, and when he lowered the window an inch, she added, "Selena. Let me in. *Quickly!*"

He pressed the button to unlock the doors, but instead of getting in front as he expected, she dived into the backseat and lay down. The shocked expression on his face was worth the banging her knee had received for her graceless action.

"Hurry!' " she ordered breathlessly. "Get away before they see me!"

Kidder shifted his bulk in the seat behind the steering wheel, but he couldn't quite get around to see more than a tangle of long legs. Her head was too low behind his seat for him to see her, but he had no trouble recognizing her voice, even with the edge of panic in it. As he angled the rearview mirror, trying to get a look at her, he questioned, "Hurry *where*, before *who* sees you?"

"*Them!* They'll kill me if they know I'm talking to you."

His nose told him this could be a trap. The dingbat could be helping her friends lure him away from the house for some reason. "I'm not going anywhere, Selena . . . *you* are. I'll give you to the count of five to tell me what you're up to, or you can get out of my car."

"Oh, no-o-o!" she whined. "Not you, too. After the way you talked at the funeral, I thought you'd help me."

Her sob was pitiful; Kidder relented. "Okay, kid. I'll listen, but no promises."

She sniffed several times before choking out her plea. "Not here, *please*. Can't we go somewhere else to talk?"

"We could go down to the station—"

"*No!* Not there. I'm scared to death of police stations, and someone might see me, and then they'd find out, and then I'd be the next one dead." Her sobbing began in earnest.

"Okay, okay. Tell me two things and maybe I'll take you somewhere. Who are 'they,' and why should I care what they do to you?"

Between sniffs and hiccoughs, she told him, "Teri Gambini and . . . and Drew . . . Marshall. They . . . killed Rico and . . . and I'm pretty sure they know that I know."

Years on the force, as well as years of marriage, had made him too skeptical to accept a woman's tears as proof of sincerity. "Hmmm. The other day,

176

you didn't know anything that could help me in my investigation. You even convinced me that you didn't know about any close relationship between the two of them. Since you've gone this far out on the limb, why not tell me why I should listen to you now?"

"I was too scared. I thought I'd be safer if I kept quiet about what I knew." She sat up so that he could see her face in the rearview mirror. Slowly she removed the sunglasses and revealed her tear-streaked face. Then she took off the big hat. "I'm the blonde you've been looking for. I was there. I saw them."

"Bingo!" he shouted with a bang of his fist on the steering wheel. When he looked in the mirror again, she was gone from view. "Selena?"

"I'm down here," she answered from behind his seat. "Now can we *please* get away from this house?"

He started the engine and drove several blocks before he saw a suitable place to park — the empty parking lot of the elementary school. "Okay. There's no one around here at this time of night. Come up front and talk to me."

Kidder watched her sit up and look around before deciding it was safe to do as he suggested. He felt a little sorry for the dingbat. She really did look scared to death. "Come on, I don't bite." That seemed to reassure her enough to get her to move. Even after she settled herself in the front seat he had to urge her to speak again. "I was right, wasn't I? They were having an affair, and the husband didn't want the divorce, so they knocked him off and set it up to look like a mob hit. Right so far?" She hesitated, but nodded her confirmation. "Were you having an affair with Rico Gambini?" This time she lowered her head before nodding again. "Did they know?"

"I think so, but Teri didn't really care, you know? I think maybe she thought if he had somebody else, he'd go for the divorce, but he wanted the money more than me." Her lip quivered, but she held back the new flood of tears that threatened.

"If you were there, how is it they let you live?"

"I was there, but they didn't see me. Until you told Teri about the blond hair, they didn't know I'd been with him only minutes before they went into the apartment. Oh, Lord," she moaned, and hid her face in her hands. "If Rico hadn't sent me out of the apartment just then, I would have been there, probably still together, like . . . oh, dear Lord, what am I going to do? I'm too scared to figure it all out!"

"Let me help with a few questions so that I can get this straight in my own head." He wanted this to be the truth so badly, he hated to have to ask anything that might refute what she was saying, but if he didn't ask, Captain Hart would do the honors when he brought her in. "How is it you were in the apartment in the first place?"

She lowered her hands and steadily met his gaze. "I thought it was so romantic, him being a mailman and all. When I got the key and the typed note signed 'R' in the mail, I never thought it could have been from anyone else."

"What did the note say?"

"It was so-o-o cute. And sort of mysterious. But he liked to play pretend when we were together, so I thought it would be fun. It said I should go to such-and-such apartment on that day, take all my clothes off, and wait for a special piece of mail to be delivered to the door. So I did. When there was a knock on the door and I heard Rico say it was the mailman, and that I had to sign for a letter, I cracked up. I guess I don't have to tell you what happened when I opened the door. I thought he acted awfully surprised, but I figured that was part of the game."

"So you were sent there to receive a letter—naked—and he had a letter to deliver. And neither one of you questioned the other?"

She looked at him as if he was out of his mind. "Questions and Answers was *not* one of the games we played. Really, Detective, if I invited you into an

178

apartment while posing in nothing but my birthday suit, would you be asking questions? Well, he didn't, and I didn't, until I saw Teri and Drew sneaking into that same apartment with another key."

"When was that?"

"Well, we had just finished, you know, and Rico was really thirsty for something cold, but the refrigerator was empty—I mean *really* empty—so I got dressed, grabbed my purse, and went downstairs to the soda machine. I was on my way back up when I saw them going in. I didn't know what to do. I waited a while, then I left."

"Do you still have the note and key?" he asked hopefully.

She shook her head. "I threw them away. I got scared when Teri told me he was missing and started asking funny questions about getting things in the mail. I mean, it wasn't too hard to figure out they had wanted me to be with Rico when they did him in so they could get me, too. Maybe they had planned to make it look like a lover's quarrel. I don't know. Anyway, I just acted dumb, but I think she was suspicious. I know she figured it out when you told her about the hair, but she's been waiting for Drew to get back from his trip before doing anything about it. Now he's back, and I don't know what to do. I'm scared to death to go back to my apartment. Where can I hide that they won't find me?" She finished with a desperate cry.

Kidder couldn't believe his luck. The dingbat had just handed him his case wrapped in silver paper. She was his passport to freedom from exile. All he had to do was treat her like a princess until he could convince her to tell her story to Captain Hart. Considering how *scared* she was of everyone and everything, including police stations, and taking into account how great the possibility was that she could change her mind if left to her own devices, he knew what he had to do.

"Tell you what, kid—I'll take you to my place tonight. You'll be safe enough there. Then tomorrow, after you've had a good night's sleep and a chance to calm down, we'll work something out."

Nibbling her lower lip, Selena gave that some thought before asking, "Won't your wife mind?"

His teeth clenched automatically. "I live alone."

Selena's worried expression altered into a shy smile. "All right. I think I'd feel much better tonight sleeping under the same roof as you."

Selena tiptoed to the closed bedroom door and pressed her ear against it. She could hear nothing to guarantee Kidder was asleep, but neither was there any indication that he was awake. She would simply have to take a chance and hope the one beer he had before retiring had helped him enter dreamland.

She couldn't wait to tell Juliette that their first plan had worked and none of the others had been necessary. But then, as Juliette had told her in the past, being the Protector gave her a certain amount of luck that always turned up when she most needed it. The just-in-case plans were hardly ever necessary, but Juliette always insisted they have them ready anyway.

In the hours since she had jumped into Kidder's car, she had devoted a great deal of concentration to her movements. She left her hair in pins to prevent any strands from falling out. She had used a hanky when opening his car door and made sure his was the only hand that touched doorknobs after that. Once in his house, she sat down on his sofa with her hands clasped on her lap, and stayed there, declining his offer of the guest bedroom, food, drink, or even the bathroom. The less she moved, the less she had to remember to cover up. Before she got up from the couch, she had put on the pair of surgical gloves she had in her bag.

Quietly, she turned the knob on Kidder's bedroom

door, prepared to cry loneliness or offer herself to him if he was still awake. But neither excuse was necessary—he was sleeping soundly on his stomach, with his head turned toward her.

His revolver was on the nightstand next to him.

She had never fired a gun before, but she had read enough books and seen enough movies to know that the cylinder had to be loaded with bullets; the trigger had to be pulled very hard, if it wasn't cocked first; and without a silencer, it made a lot of noise. The windows of the house were closed, but she wasn't certain that would be enough if someone nearby was still awake at that hour. She spotted a small, thick throw pillow on a chair and decided, better safe than sorry.

With the pillow in her left hand, she picked up the gun with her right and tested its weight. She could easily manage it with one hand. Pressing the barrel of the revolver into the center of the pillow, she lowered them both to Kidder's temple.

And fired.

The resulting mess was much worse than she had imagined, but it was the noise that paralyzed her with fear. For several seconds she held her breath, expecting to hear the sounds of an abruptly awakened neighborhood, but nothing happened. She could go ahead with the plan.

She took the special package from her big purse and carried it to the kitchen sink. The ice had not entirely melted, and when she removed the inner plastic bag, she found her prop was still frozen. For a moment she thought she would have to forget about leaving the clue, then her gaze fell on the solution. After opening the storage bag, she placed it inside the microwave to thaw it out.

Thirty seconds later, Rico's right hand was almost as warm as it was the moment she'd taken it from him.

Fourteen

Raking his hands through his graying hair, Drew smiled at the lined face in his bathroom mirror. *You're not as far over the ridge as you thought you were, cowboy.*

He hadn't stopped smiling since last night. It wouldn't be gentlemanly to brag, even to his own reflection. However, he couldn't help but note that in four hours with Teri he had more than made up for his long abstinence. The face looking back at him might be forty, but this morning his body felt more like that of a twenty-year-old. Just remembering what Teri did to get back at him for teasing her with the camera had him as ready as a stormcloud about to burst. He couldn't wait to rain all over that sweet little body of hers again and again.

She had him thinking about all the things he'd once wanted but come to believe he'd never have. And more than hungry, mind-bending sex, she made him think of holding hands in a movie, talking politics over breakfast, planning a vegetable garden, and balancing a household budget. All the ordinary doings he'd thought a marriage was supposed to consist of when he'd married Brenda were now within his reach.

He laughed at himself for being such a romantic fool. The shrink would probably have him recommitted if he heard his patient had fallen in love with the first woman who'd cried in his arms after his sentence was up. On the surface, it was exactly the kind of relationship he'd been warned to avoid. But Drew knew what lay beneath the surface, and it ran hot and deep.

Last night he had broken his own promise to wait until they were both less vulnerable. He had no regrets this morning, though, only a sense of extreme gratitude to the nosy detective who had indirectly pushed him into breaking it.

It was almost prophetic that Detective Kidder had left his post by the time Drew and Teri said goodnight, as if he had given up his crazy notions and was going to let the couple get on with their lives in peace.

There was no way Drew could give consideration to Kidder's accusations. To consider them at all would be opening the door to where those accusations could lead. *Back to imprisonment.* Simply thinking of such a possibility could throw Drew into a cowering panic—a state of mind he was intimately familiar with and had only recently learned to block by sheer force of will. As he had told Teri, he had to live one day at a time and hope for the best. What he hadn't told her was that his recovery was taking place on the very edge of that attitude, and he knew the slightest nudge could push him over once again.

It was much more pleasant to contemplate his next rendezvous with Teri.

Unfortunately for Drew and his rejuvenated body, he had two models meeting him in the studio first thing this morning. It would have to be business before pleasure.

When he arrived at Teri's and noted the absence of the detective's car, he breathed a sigh of relief, in spite of how many times he had told himself that he wasn't worried about the man. The models were already in the studio, and he told them what costumes to put on while he went to speak to Teri. As he hurried down the stairs, the sound of her voice led him to the backyard, where she was filling bird-feeders and visiting with the cat he had seen before.

"Mornin'," he said politely from a distance. Teri spun around and the happy expression on her face was all the reassurance he needed. "Quick. Come in the house. I have somethin' to show you." He strode to the kitchen door and held it open for her.

The second after he pulled the door shut behind her, they were in each other's arms—tasting, touching, seeking the heavenly release they had discovered the night before. The feel of the wall against her back and the air beneath her feet as Drew raised her to accommodate them both was a reminder to Teri of her personal vow, but not enough to keep Drew from kissing her neck as she spoke.

"I swore I wouldn't do this again."

Responding to the breathless longing in her voice rather than her words, he moved against her until she moaned, then asked, "Do what?"

"Mindless hormones. I swore . . ." she kissed him in a way that made a lie of her vow, ". . . I wouldn't let them rule my life ever again." His mouth moved to her ear as his body and hands made her forget why she'd ever made such a dumb vow.

"And I swore I'd never fall in love again," he whispered, and went back to nibbling her earlobe.

"Are you? Falling?"

"Hat over bootheels."

"What are we going to do?" she asked, wrapping her legs tightly around his hips.

He stopped his attentions long enough to raise his head and look at her with a twinkle in his blue eyes. "We could always give up swearing." Although the ad lib made them both laugh, neither made an effort to separate. Breathing heavily, he leaned his forehead against hers. "I have work to do."

"Hmmm. Does that mean I have to get down?"

"Only if you really want to."

His deep chuckle vibrated through her. "I don't think I could if I wanted to," she answered, nuzzling his neck. "But I just happen to know a solution to our problem."

Matching her rocking motion, he stoked his fire with hers. "We call the fire department to hose us down?"

"Mmmm. Good idea. We can use the phone next to my bed."

Drew didn't need an explicit invitation to put off starting his workday. Given the frantic condition they were in by the time they reached the bedroom, the additional delay was hardly worth apologizing for when he returned to the studio.

Teri had no desire to bounce out of bed and get dressed after he left her, but decency demanded it. In the space of twenty-four hours, the world had gone from muddy brown to hot pink. Drew's brand of loving was a tonic for everything that ailed her.

And if tremendous physical satisfaction was not enough, her personal bloodhound seemed to have given up his vigil in front of her house. It was still hard to believe the man could make such horrid accusations based on circumstantial evidence. On the other hand, she had seen plenty of television shows where the detective made wild charges just hoping the guilty party would confess everything. Well, in this case, she hadn't broken down for him, because she wasn't the guilty party and there was nothing to confess. Maybe Kidder finally realized it. In fact, if he didn't bother her again, she would forgive him for being so obnoxious and wouldn't even file a complaint against him.

That's how good Drew's loving made her feel.

But the afterglow faded rapidly when the phone rang and she heard Selena's voice coming through the answering machine, pleading with Teri to talk to her. Just before Selena cut off, Teri picked up. "I'm here."

"Oh, good. Were you painting?"

"No, not yet. I, uh—" Teri stammered for an acceptable excuse.

"Well, don't worry about it. I've got some news that should put all your worries to bed and get those creative juices flowing again."

Selena's excitement was evident, and Teri tried to give her the attention she wanted, instead of thinking about what the word "bed" suggested to her. "Really? *All* my worries? It must be pretty terrific news."

"Detective Kidder will no longer be bothering you."

"That *would* be terrific," Teri said with a laugh. "But how can you be sure? Have you got a friend in the police department you neglected to tell me about?"

"He's dead. Murdered in his own bed."

Teri was certain she couldn't have heard right. *"What* did you say?"

Selena giggled. "I knew you'd be surprised. But it's true. He's out of your hair . . . permanently."

Permanently? Like Rico is out of my life permanently? Selena's usage of the word alarmed her in the same way Kidder's announcement about Rico's blonde lover had. The coincidence was unnerving. "Are you sure?"

"Oh, yes. I'm positive."

Selena's giggle was muffled this time, but Teri still heard it, just as she heard something in Selena's voice that made it sound like she knew a secret. "Selena? How did you find out?"

"Oh, I heard it on the news this morning, but I know how you hardly ever read the paper or watch TV, so I thought I'd be the bearer of the good news."

Teri was speechless. No matter how annoying the

186

detective had been, she could not refer to his murder as good news. It seemed that Selena had a blind spot when it came to sympathizing over someone's death, and it would serve no purpose for Teri to scold her about it again. "Did you hear how it happened, or whether they know who did it?"

"Um, no, I don't think so. But I'm sure it will turn out to be another mob hit. Probably even connected to Rico."

"But—" Teri started to argue the logic of that assumption and stopped herself. Although Kidder had been tailing *her,* believing *she* was guilty, he might also have been hounding someone in the mob. It was possible. "You're probably right."

"So, *now* are you ready to get back to work? I'm available to sit for you today."

Teri's mind was busy trying to absorb Selena's news and thinking how she needed to tell Drew right away. "Work? Yes, I should, but not today. I've got to go through Rico's things sooner or later. I might as well get it over with before I take on any new assignments."

"Tomorrow, then?"

Teri heard the whining tone and hesitated a moment too long.

"Teri? Are you still there? Maybe I should come and help you today."

"That's okay. I think I need to do this by myself, but tomorrow should be good. How about if I call you?"

"Promise?"

"I promise."

Knowing firsthand how much concentration Drew needed to do the shoot, she decided to wait until he took a break to tell him about Kidder. In the meantime, she drove to the store to get a newspaper. When she returned home, she turned on the radio to listen for the news as she scanned the paper for anything about a cop killing. Although there was nothing about Kidder's murder in the paper, she rationalized that it could have been a very late-breaking story.

She decided the chore she had mentioned to Selena would actually be a good one for that day and took the radio into the bedroom while she got started.

As the third hourly news update ended, Teri's stomach insisted she think about lunch. Her bedroom floor looked like an obstacle course of bags filled with Rico's clothes to go to charity and boxes packed with things that his family might want to go through later. The one possession of Rico's that Teri left right where she saw it was his handgun. Since he could no longer insist they keep a gun in the house, she wanted it gone. She wondered how to go about getting rid of one.

The second phone call that day almost wiped out Teri's memory of the first. The owner of the Forsythe Gallery happily informed her that they had just sold the most expensive of her paintings. By the time Teri hung up, she was raring to get back to work on the new series she'd been thinking about. And she couldn't wait to tell Drew.

She had heard the models leaving a short time ago. Drew hadn't come down from the studio yet, but he was probably hungry by now. Heading for the kitchen, she decided a picnic was in order. A number of summers had come and gone since she'd taken advantage of the redwood table and benches under the trees out back. In practically no time she had packed lunch for two in a basket, located a battery-operated radio, and gone outside to set it up.

Teri smiled when she saw Drew coming toward her before she had a chance to go get him.

"You must be readin' my mind again, darlin'," he said with a wink, then noticed the radio. "A little mood music?"

"Hardly." As he sat down, she took sandwiches, fruit, chips, and sodas out of the basket. "Selena called this morning. She heard on the news that Detective Kidder was murdered. I've been listening for more details."

"Murdered? Geez! He was parked in front of your house just last night. What happened?"

"I'm not sure. There was nothing in the paper, and I've been listening to the radio for the last three hours, trying different stations, but I haven't heard a word about it."

"That's odd. When a police officer gets killed, it's usually big news. Could Selena have been mistaken?"

Teri shook her head. "I asked her that myself. I couldn't believe it. But she said she was positive. That Detective Kidder was . . . now, what did she say? Oh, yes, that he was murdered in his own bed."

"Well, I can't say I'll miss havin' him around, but it's still a shame."

"I wonder if another detective will continue with his investigation."

Drew shrugged, then took her hand in his. "Don't be frettin' over somethin' that hasn't happened yet. Kidder's suppositions were so far off the mark, we've got to believe the next detective assigned to the case will toss those ideas out the window."

"God, I hope so. For a little while, though, I think we should still be, um . . ." She lowered her lashes shyly.

"Discreet?"

Their relationship was too new for her to feel completely at ease discussing the mechanics of it, and she steered back to the original subject. "You know, I had this really frightening thought. What if I *had* filed a complaint against Kidder, as we discussed? Then he was murdered. I could have ended up being a suspect again!"

189

"But you didn't."

Before either could say more, the news came on, and they both listened intently to each brief announcement.

"I don't get it," Teri said, five minutes later, when music began playing again with no information about Kidder's death having been related.

"Maybe the police are keepin' a lid on it for some reason."

"I suppose." For several minutes they ate, listening to soft rock and watching the birds battle each other for the choicest seeds, until Teri remembered to tell him about selling another painting.

"That's wonderful!" Drew said, leaning across the table to give her a congratulatory kiss that fell within the limits of "discreet."

"The gallery owner said there's been so much interest in my work lately, he wouldn't be surprised if the rest of my paintings sell before I finish this next series."

"Have you started it yet?"

"It's mostly in my head, but I've done a few sketches. I thought I'd call it 'Faces.' Each painting would be a collage of expressions of one person's face." Her hands drew abstract pictures in the air. "I was thinking of doing one of a little boy, another of an old woman, throw in an ethnic mix, and go from there."

"Sounds fascinatin'. Any chance you'll be needin' a photographer to help catch all those expressions? I happen to know one who's not very experienced, but accommodatin' as all git-out."

Teri fought to keep a straight face. "Oh, I already have someone in mind to ask, and he's also very accommodating. And he's proved he has a lot of experience in areas where it really counts. But those aren't the reasons I'd ask him to work with me."

"Oh?" Drew asked skeptically, trying just as hard to keep from grinning. "Then what out-standin' qualification does this someone have?"

She glanced from side to side, as if to make sure no one was listening, then secretively imparted her reason. "I wouldn't want this to get around, but I have a soft spot for lonely cowboys."

Drew laughed and gave her another quick kiss. "And I am mighty grateful for every one of your soft spots, ma'am. When do we start?"

"How about tomorrow? Maybe we could drive around looking for a good subject or two."

"Sounds fine to me. I'll just finish developin' the film I used today so I'll be free tomorrow. What are you up to for the rest of the afternoon?"

She couldn't help making a face. "I've been going through Rico's things. It's not that big a job, but it's depressing as hell." When he looked as though he was about to offer sympathy, she stopped him. "No, I'm okay, really. Sometimes, though, I forget what happened to him and I expect to see him walk in the door. It's a very strange feeling."

"And I'm makin' the adjustment that much harder," Drew said, looking away.

She reached across the table and touched his face. "I wish you'd stop doing that." He looked at her with one brow raised in question. "Whenever you feel guilty about something, you look away from me, as if you expect me to lay into you. I can only guess that it's a little something left over from your marriage, but I don't give a damn why you do it. Just stop. You're the best thing that's happened to me in years. I can't begin to imagine how much harder this all would have been without you."

With each word, she got a little more aggressive, and his face broke into a smile. "I'll bet it's like the Fourth of July around here when you really get fired up about somethin'!"

She raised her chin in a gesture of mock defiance. "Just don't try me."

His eyes instantly filled with mischief. "An' here

I was, countin' on *tryin'* you at least once more today."

Blushing prettily, she again moved the conversation to cooler ground. "Do you have any idea how to get rid of a gun?"

Drew choked on the soda he was drinking. Don't tell me—you did do the detective in, and now you've got to hide the weapon."

"I'm serious. Rico kept a loaded handgun in the nightstand next to our bed. It always made me nervous, and I want to get it out of the house. But he got it illegally—it was never registered with the police—so I'm not sure what they might do or think if I try to turn it in. I don't need to raise more questions right now. And I can't throw it away. Who knows what kind of person would end up with it? Do you want it?"

Drew waved a hand at her. "Not me. I've always figured if I had a gun, I'd probably be the one to get shot with it." He didn't mention that he didn't yet trust himself to possess such a sure means of self-destruction.

As they were cleaning up, the sound of a car in the driveway drew their attention, and they both went to investigate.

Teri's breath caught when she saw a police car, but the sight of Captain Hart getting out of that car released some of the fear that had automatically gripped her.

"Mrs. Gambini. Good afternoon," Hart called with a nod and a friendly smile as he approached. With an uncertain glance at Drew, he added, "I believe we met at the police station. I'm Captain Hart."

Drew stepped forward to shake his hand. "Yes, we did. Drew Marshall."

The captain's smiling expression turned grim. "Unfortunately, we haven't located the man you both identified. Actually, 'unfortunate' is not nearly a strong enough term. That's why I came by today. I wanted to speak to you personally, before you heard it elsewhere."

Teri felt the tension return as she noticed how uneasy he looked, and thought to put off whatever he had to say. "Would you like to come in for a cold drink, Captain?"

"No, thank you. I have to get back to the station before all hell, pardon me, before the news gets out. Do you remember Detective Kidder?"

Teri stiffened and felt Drew touch her back. "Yes, of course. He was here just—"

"He was murdered," Hart said over top of her words. "Shot with his own gun, right in his home. Someone broke in through a window while he was asleep. No one seems to have heard a thing. Obviously Bill hadn't either, since they . . ." The captain closed his eyes and took a ragged breath. "Sorry. Bill was a good cop and a friend of mine for over thirty years. I only came by to let you know what the lab boys already found out, before the press gets hold of it."

"But it was already on the news," Teri told him.

"Damn! We had this thing completely under wraps. There's no way it leaked out from our end. When did you hear it?"

"Well, actually, I didn't. A friend called about nine or so to tell me she heard on the news that the detective was murdered in his bed. She had met him when he was here and again at the . . . the morgue."

The captain slammed his fist onto the car's hood. "That cinches it! *We* only got the tip a little before nine—an anonymous phone call. But we didn't know what we would find at Bill's house until we sent two officers over to check it out, and that was well after nine. Those scumbags must have called the media even before they called us." Anger now replaced his sorrow. "They're as bad as movie stars, the way they grab publicity. It's sick!"

"I'm sorry, Captain. I don't understand—you know who did this?"

"Hmmph. There's no question about who's taking responsibility—the Irish mob. They've practically admitted it in public. You see, it's not unusual for them to want people to know what they're capable of. It keeps the fear level up." He briefly cited a few examples.

Teri remembered Rico's funeral and wondered if that was how the media had found out about that also. But it seemed extremely peculiar that she hadn't heard the news bulletin Selena referred to repeated at any time during the morning. Wouldn't one station pick it up from another? If the mob wanted it to be known, wouldn't they have chosen a popular station to leak it to? Wouldn't someone have called the police to verify the tip before reporting it? And why was Selena the only person who'd heard it? Teri stopped her thoughts. She didn't know that for a fact; someone else *must* have heard it. But for some reason, her stomach twisted with the feeling that this was another eerie coincidence.

Hart was continuing his explanation. "First they killed your husband for crossing them. They made sure to leave an obvious clue for the police—the missing hands—then they passed the news on to the press. But I mucked up their plan by insisting Detective Kidder track down the thug. I should have assigned it to someone else. He was getting on, slowing down, couldn't hear worth a damn."

Teri realized the captain blamed himself for Kidder's death, but she didn't know what consoling words would be appropriate, under the circumstances.

For a moment Hart seemed lost in his own thoughts. "He would have been off the street completely in another day or two. I should have left him alone."

"Was he retiring?" Drew asked, speaking up for the first time since greeting the captain.

"No. It was just a transfer. But Bill thought it was worse than a death sentence. He was so damned anxious to solve this case and prove he could still do his job." He went on talking distractedly about his co-worker for several minutes.

Comprehension of why Kidder had been pushing her so hard didn't make Teri any more appreciative of his investigative efforts against her and Drew. Apparently he must have found the time to push someone else as well. Someone much more dangerous than she was. But when? He had practically camped on her doorstep since she'd filed the missing person report.

The captain seemed to think that Kidder was concentrating solely on the mob. So, she and Drew must have been right about Kidder harassing her on his own. A complaint now, however, would serve no purpose, especially considering how badly Captain Hart was hurting for his friend.

"Forgive me," Hart said, pinching the bridge of his nose. "I got a little sidetracked there. The reason I came by was to warn you about the lab findings. The press is liable to be after you for a reaction. There were fingerprints picked up at the scene: outside the broken window and on the gun. They were identified as your husband's."

Fifteen

Teri splashed cold water on her face, then brushed her teeth. The nice picnic lunch had rebelled by the time she'd heard Captain Hart's full report. It was beyond her imagination how any human could be so perverted to do what had been done. But before he left, Hart had explained that it was a typical ploy of the mob.

"Teri?" Drew called through the bathroom door. "Are you all right?"

She dried her face and opened the door. His concerned frown let her know words were not necessary. He understood and took her into his arms. But the temporary comfort was interrupted by a telephone call from a local reporter. As the captain had predicted, the minute word about the fingerprints got around, the media wanted a statement from the widow.

Drew picked up the second and third calls, telling them Mrs. Gambini was in a state of shock and could not be disturbed. He finally took the phone off the hook and they went up to the studio for the rest of the afternoon. After one persistent reporter found them there, Drew finished his work and insisted they leave the house for a while. Teri quickly agreed and took advantage of the outing to drop off the bags of Rico's clothes at a Goodwill location. She was suddenly in a great hurry to get every reminder of Rico out of her sight.

Drew was reluctant to leave her alone that night, but they both knew it was best for appearance sake.

He was back, though, minutes after the sun reached a respectable level in the morning sky.

"You didn't sleep," he stated after examining the dark circles under Teri's eyes.

"I'll be okay. I had a little trouble dealing with the ghosts that kept popping up when I closed my eyes. They'll go away, just like they did after Rico was found. Anyway, you weren't my first visitor this morning. A reporter showed up at dawn since he couldn't get me on the phone. I never did put it back on the hook. I'm afraid he was very disappointed with what little I could tell him. But that's his problem, not mine."

Reassured that her mental condition was returning to normal, he kissed her to check on her physical state. Her warm response did much more than merely reassure him, and they soon made up for the previous day's lost mood.

Because of their later departure, they were just getting into Drew's car when Selena's white Cadillac Seville pulled into the driveway behind them. The glowering expression on her face as she slammed her car door shut served as a sharp reminder to Teri of their conversation the day before.

"Oh, dear," was all Teri said before Selena reached her.

"Why didn't you call me?" she demanded. "You *promised* you'd call. I hate it when people break their promises."

"I'm sorry, Selena. So much has happened since I talked to you, I guess I forgot."

"Forgot? I couldn't forget *you,*" she whined back. "I worry about you. You said we would spend the day together. I was counting on it."

Teri was fairly sure she had only promised a phone call, but Selena was acting more like a spoiled child than an adult friend, and Teri didn't

197

get the impression contradicting her would help. She had never dreamed Selena's dependence on her would go this far.

"Were you going somewhere with *him?*"

Teri was stunned to see Selena glaring at Drew as if he was an enemy she had never seen before. Teri's intuition told her to tread carefully. Although it didn't make sense, Selena was not only angry over being forgotten, she was showing serious signs of jealousy. "Drew and I were going in search of some subjects for my new series. You know, the one I started sketching you for. He's going to help with the photography." Before her eyes Teri watched Selena's body relax and her angry features soften. Almost too abruptly, the lovely adult replaced the spoiled, jealous child.

"You know how much your work fascinates me. Would you mind if I come along? I won't be in your way."

Teri minded. Without looking at Drew, she was certain he minded also. But guilt over forgetting to call Selena beat out irritation over the young woman's momentary childishness. "Sure. You might spot somebody we'd miss." As Selena got in the backseat, Teri threw Drew a glance that promised she'd make it up to him later.

Selena felt better after Teri invited her along. She understood how important Teri's painting was to her, and she supposed creative people tended to be forgetful. She had to remember to make allowances. Seeing Teri ready to work again with a happy smile on her face was enough reward for her efforts.

Teri's feelings toward Drew confused her, however. He was extremely polite and, unlike most men, never looked at her with sex on his mind. She considered the possibility that he was homosexual. If so, she might even get used to having him around. But he hadn't looked at the male models with any more interest than he'd looked at her. On the other hand, he'd watched Teri very closely. That could be for professional reasons, yet Detective Kidder had seemed certain there was something more going on between them. Drew would require more study before she could make up her mind about him. And this was the day to do it.

When they stopped at a park and got out of the car to walk around, Selena stayed a few steps behind. Whenever Teri turned around with that worried look on her face, Selena would give her a smile to let her know everything was fine. Selena knew she wasn't being much help in finding an interesting face, but at the moment it was more important to her to watch Drew.

He was a good photographer, she'd grant him that. When Teri convinced an elderly woman to let them photograph her, Drew put her at ease with his soft drawl and didn't take forever to focus his camera.

Before they left the park, Teri also found a maintenance man who agreed to have his picture taken, and Drew approved Teri's choice with a wink and a grin.

Selena's opinion of Drew remained unsettled until they were getting back into the car. It was such a small thing that alerted her—a small but familiar gesture. As Drew opened the door for Teri, he watched her get into the car with an intent look in his eyes. And when she was settled, he brushed her cheek with the back of his fingers.

Selena's mind flashed a memory of another man's eyes and the first time he had touched her like that.

"I *hate* you," thirteen-year-old Selena raged at her stepfather. "I'm telling Mom what you did."

"Now, baby, calm down," Troy said, blocking her way into the house.

"I don't want to calm down. I *saw* you. Through

the Eskers' kitchen window. You were kissing Mrs. Esker. And touching her where you shouldn't. How could you do that when you're married to my mother? I thought you loved her."

Troy gripped her arm and led her away from the house. "I do love your mother. I can explain. I swear you'll understand if you'd just listen to me."

Through teary eyes, Selena stared up at the man she had learned to love and trust in the last year—a kind, sweet man whom she called Daddy as a reward for making her mother so happy, and for helping her forget some of the nightmare she had known with her real father.

"Please, baby, come take a ride with me and we can talk. You always like our long talks."

Because she didn't really want the good times to end so quickly, she agreed to listen to what he had to say. But she knew from past experience that they wouldn't discuss anything while he was driving to their special place.

Right after Troy married her mother, he moved them to the country. When he had pointed to a spot on the map outside Kingston in Ulster County, New York, it hadn't looked all that far away from the big city. He had said it would be worth driving a little further to have a nicer house and own so much land. Selena's mother had liked the one-story ranch house right away and used a part of her first husband's insurance money to buy it. The rest of it, she always said, was for Selena's education. Her mother swore it didn't bother her that their nearest neighbor was over a mile away or that no one could even see the redwood house if they were out on the road. But Selena had the feeling her mother liked it because Troy liked it.

To get to the house, you could go up the winding one-thousand-foot dirt driveway to the top of the hill, or you could find your way through the pine forest that surrounded the house. Marking trails through the trees that only she could figure out became one of Selena's favorite pastimes. The second was canoeing on the Ashokan Reservoir with her stepfather.

That was what she'd had in mind today as she'd hiked through the forest to the Eskers' house in search of him. Her mom had told her he'd gone over there to help Mrs. Esker unclog her kitchen sink. Mrs. Esker always had something that needed fixing, and her husband was usually out of town on business. Now Selena couldn't help but wonder about all her stepfather's helpful trips to their neighbor's house.

When they reached the edge of the reservoir and parked among the trees, it took him another few seconds to begin talking. "I didn't want to tell you this, baby, but I don't know any other way to explain what you saw today."

He looked so sad, Selena almost forgave him before he explained anything.

"Your mom's got a weak heart. She didn't want you to know."

Her eyes opened wide. "What do you mean?"

"I mean, she shouldn't be overly excited, or it could . . ."

"You mean she could *die?*" Selena's eyes filled with tears at the thought.

Troy moved across the seat and pulled her into his arms. "Now, now. There's no need to cry. She'll be fine. As long as we take care of her and don't upset her too much."

Selena raised her head from his shoulder. "Then how could you cheat on her? That would tear her apart."

He squeezed his eyes shut and lowered his head. Selena thought he was going to cry, but since he wouldn't look at her, she couldn't tell for sure.

"It would probably kill her," he said quietly after a moment. "And I can't help myself. I love her so much, but I don't know what to do."

"I don't understand. You know it would kill her to find out and you say you love her. So why were you kissing Mrs. Esker?"

He took his arms from around her and turned away. "I'm a weak man, Selena, but I have strong physical needs. And, with your mom's health the way it is, I can't ask her to satisfy them as often as I need to. That's the only reason I was visiting Mrs. Esker. I don't really want to be with her, but she's willing to . . . to help me with my needs."

Selena thought about this for a moment. She knew men were different from women. Her own father had needs, but his hurt the body rather than the heart. There had been times before he died when Selena had drawn his brutal attention to herself, hoping to save her mother from punishment. She would have to protect her mother from pain again. "I won't tell. This time. But I'm afraid she'll find out anyway. I want you to promise you won't go see Mrs. Esker again." She heard him sigh, though he still had his back to her. "Daddy? Please?"

Slowly he faced her again and brushed the back of his fingers over her cheek. The affectionate touch was so typical of him, so tender, it made her young heart flutter with love.

"You're so beautiful, baby. When I first started dating your mom, you were just a kid. How could I have known how quickly you'd turn into a desirable woman?"

Part of Selena was pleased he had called her a woman, but she could see he was upset, and it had something to do with the compliment he had just paid her. I don't understand."

Again he caressed her cheek. "No. I don't suppose you do. It's not your fault that every time I see you, my . . . I ache with need. It wouldn't be so bad if I could go to your mother for relief more often. She'd understand how I love you both the same. But with her poor health, I can't expect her to make the ache go away all the time."

"And so you went to see Mrs. Esker." He nodded, his regret so obvious that Selena had to forgive him for his weakness. "And it's . . . because of the way I've . . ." She glanced down at her full breasts. ". . . Changed?" Hesitantly, he nodded again, and she made the only decision possible. "I meant it when I said I don't want you to go to Mrs. Esker again. Or any other woman. I don't want there to be any chance that my mother would ever find out you cheated on her. If you have to kiss someone besides my mother—and it really is partly my fault—I'd rather it be me."

He blinked at her in surprise. "And you won't tell her, or anyone else, about anything we do together?"

She bowed her head. "I promise. I won't tell." Then she raised her gaze to hold his. "And do you promise never *ever* to go to another woman and to keep making my mom happy?"

He kissed her softly on the mouth. "I promise."

"Should I call you Troy, now that I'm a woman?"

"I don't think so. Your mother would notice, and we don't want to upset her, do we?" She frowned and shook her head. "Just keep calling me daddy. I like it."

He stroked her arm in a way that made goosebumps rise. "Okay. Daddy?"

"Yes, baby?" His fingers brushed the sides of her breast.

She tried to ignore the way her body tensed with each touch. "I don't know very much about the kind of kissing you and Mrs. Esker were doing."

He smiled at her in a way Selena had never seen before, and didn't particularly like.

"You shouldn't lie to me, Selena. You know exactly what I need from you."

When she narrowed her brows in confusion, his smile tilted, making her suddenly nervous.

"I saw you watching your mom and me one night before I asked her to marry me. I knew you were curious, so I didn't send you away. I made your mom very, *very* happy that night."

"I know," she said, embarrassed, but unable to deny any of it. "I could tell. She sang to me while she made breakfast the next morning. I didn't remember her ever doing that before."

"Your mom's probably wondering where we are, so I think we'd better get back. But I'd like to make her very, *very* happy again tonight. Like the other time. I'll leave the door open."

Selena's heart was pounding. This was not what she had expected him to ask of her. She thought he wanted kisses or maybe to touch her breasts, as she had seen him do with Mrs. Esker, but now she understood how much more he needed from her to keep her mother happy. If she refused him, she could be risking her mother's life. With a reluctant nod, she agreed to peek into their bedroom one more time.

His smile broadened. "Now, give your daddy a kiss to seal our secret bargain."

That was the first time a man had pushed his tongue into her mouth. But it was only the first of many personal invasions to come in the years that followed.

As Selena watched Drew, she knew without a doubt what he wanted from Teri, and it was up to Selena to warn her friend before she found herself helpless at another man's mercy.

By midnight, Teri finally realized that neither Selena nor Drew were willing to be the first to call it a night. They had both stayed with the excuse of fielding reporters for her, but the media had apparently lost interest in her again. When they turned on the television to watch the nightly news, they saw Captain Hart assuring a reporter that the police would soon track down the people responsible for Detective Kidder's death. To the question "Was it a mob hit?" he was evasive, but no one watching would think he believed anything else. Not having had much sleep the night before, Teri decided it was no longer necessary to play the polite hostess.

"Listen, guys. I've had a great day and evening with you, but I'm dead on my feet. Drew, if you'll be developing that film tomorrow, I'll see you then. Selena, I'll give you a call as soon as I need you to sit, but it probably won't be for about a week. I've got a lot of other things to work on right now." Selena's frown made her add, "This time, I won't forget to call, I swear."

Drew looked as though he couldn't make up his mind about whether to go ahead and leave, or give Teri the kiss they'd both been thinking about all day. She made his decision for him by holding out her hand and saying, "See you tomorrow," but her eyes held a promise of reward for his patience today.

Teri stood at the open front door after he left, expecting Selena to walk out right behind him. One look at Selena's face let her know she was wrong.

"Close the door," Selena ordered abruptly. "We have to talk."

"Selena, I'm exhausted," Teri pleaded, but closed the door anyway. Weariness did not prevent her from noticing how distraught Selena suddenly was as she strode to the window and peered out through the drapes. There was something very unsettling about how quickly Selena's moods seemed to be changing. Had she always been like that? Teri didn't think so. She yawned in spite of the troubling thought.

"Good," Selena said, turning back from the window. "He's gone. You're going to have to insist he immediately make other arrangements for processing his film."

Teri was caught unawares by the demand. "Why would I do that?"

"I don't expect you to understand. You're just so innocent of the ways of men. But that's why you have to be extra careful now that Rico's gone."

Teri guessed what Selena was getting at, but didn't want to jump to any conclusions. "I'm not *that* innocent. I've lived with a man for quite a long time."

"And that man was recently murdered. The police may still suspect you of having something to do with it. You must make sure you're not compromised in any way."

"Compromised? Selena, I think I'm too tired to follow this tonight —"

"Yes, *compromised* — put in a position where it looks like you had a reason to kill your husband. You may not realize it yet, but Drew is intending to compromise you."

Teri might have laughed at the phrase, except that Selena's silver eyes had narrowed to glittering slits in her pale face. It put Teri on guard. "Drew is a gentleman. He —"

"Drew is a pig," Selena spat. "Just like every other man." She moved closer to Teri with each vindictive word, completely ignoring Teri's protests about Drew. "He wants to use you for his own needs, regardless of what danger it might put you in. Then, when he's tired of you, he'll betray you. I won't let that happen to you again."

For each advancing step of Selena's, Teri took a step backward, away from Selena's irrational anger. Teri could only imagine that the girl had been badly hurt by a man and now believed every man was rotten, but that didn't give her the right to insult Drew.

206

Although she didn't get the impression Selena would listen to her, she had to try. "You're wrong about Drew. Not all men are bad, any more than all women are good. And Drew knows about Kidder's charges. I told him. Even though Captain Hart seems convinced the mob was behind both Rico's and the detective's murders, Drew wouldn't do anything to bring suspicion back to me."

Selena's chest rose and fell sharply several times, making Teri think she was struggling to get herself under control. Teri hoped she would do it quickly. Selena's strange behavior was beginning to frighten her. As abruptly as Selena's fury had appeared it vanished, and the friend Teri thought she knew became solicitous once again.

"I'm sorry. I see I've upset you, and that's the last thing I wanted to do." Selena's eyes were back to normal and filled with concern. "I only wanted to warn you about him. He may not have done anything yet, but I saw the way he looked at you all day today, and it's only a matter of time before he starts tricking you into doing what he wants. The only way to prevent it is to send him away—now. Before it's too late for either of you."

Teri realized that although Selena had softened her voice and her words, she was still insisting she break off any relationship with Drew. What Teri couldn't understand was why the warning sounded like it carried a threat along with it. Surely Selena's jealousy wasn't *that* serious. Nevertheless, Teri knew the time had come to start severing their friendship.

Reaching out to touch Selena's hand, she tried to reassure her, without lying. "I'll think about what you said, and I'll be careful with Drew. Now, I really need to get to bed."

Selena allowed herself to be led to the door before saying what else was on her mind. "I've been giving some thought to moving out of Manhattan. I

207

spend a lot of time commuting between there and here. With you being alone now, I was wondering if you'd like a roommate."

It took Teri a moment to realize what Selena was suggesting, and then only incredible restraint kept her from revealing her instantaneous, horrified reaction.

Selena was encouraged by Teri's silence. "You know, I have money. I'd help with the expenses, and I could do things around the house, so you'd be free to paint. It would be good for both of us to have the company."

Teri knew this was not an issue she could let hang between them, even if it hurt Selena's sensitive feelings. A break in their relationship had to start here and now. "I don't think it would be a good idea, Selena. You know what they say about familiarity breeding contempt. I'm afraid our friendship would suffer if we spent every day under the same roof." When she saw the pout forming, she went a little further. "Please understand, it's not you. I don't want to share my life with anyone at the moment. I need some space, and time alone." Although Teri knew that wasn't entirely true, Selena seemed satisfied.

"I understand, but I'd still like us to spend more time together. Just so I know you're doing all right."

Teri was careful not to make another promise she couldn't keep, since that was apparently what had set Selena off that morning. "Let's see how my work goes on this new series. You know that once I get started on something I forget about everybody and everything except my painting."

Selena smiled and nodded, accepting the explanation. "You're right. I know how you are. And that's even more reason for you to get Drew out of your life. He'll soon become a distraction if you don't stop him. You may not want to get involved, but he's a charming man. And that's the worst kind of snake there is."

So, Teri thought after Selena finally departed, the girl once fell in love with a charming man, and he betrayed her. Not an uncommon occurrence, but Selena's hostile comments seemed too extreme—as if it happened only yesterday. Teri was fairly certain Selena would have confided in her if she'd been seeing a man, and never in the year they'd worked together had Selena even mentioned having a date. Teri hadn't given that much thought before, but combined with the way Selena had just blown up about Drew, she realized there was a reason for Selena's lack of social engagements that went far beyond her being shy.

If her own life was not on such shaky ground at the moment, she might have found the energy to help Selena through her problems. As it was, it took everything she possessed to work through her own.

Drew had used the word "smothered" when they had talked about how Selena occasionally made her feel. At that time Teri had thought the description was somewhat harsh. For whatever reason, in the short time since, Teri wasn't sure if the word was harsh enough. "Strangling" seemed to better define the way she'd felt in the last ten minutes—as if Selena's hands were choking her.

Teri's breath caught short as the image of Selena doing her hair came to mind, and again she felt the scarlet fingernails pressed against her throat. She exhaled, trying to banish the memory, but her heart was racing, and her mind was calling up other disturbing thoughts. *Coincidences.*

Selena offering to seduce Rico. A blond pubic hair on his dead body.

Selena wearing a red wig or disappearing into a bathroom whenever the detective was around. Her playing dumb in front of him.

Selena knowing so much about odd things, like being prepared with two hankies at the morgue, and knowing how to make tears flow when there weren't any.

Selena's hearing about Kidder's murder even before the police verified it.

Selena's peculiar, almost pleased, responses to both Rico's and Kidder's deaths.

Selena's automatic assumption that the murders were connected.

Selena's use of the word "permanently."

Coincidences. They had to be. If it hadn't been for Selena's hateful comments about Drew and the strange light in her eyes, Teri would never have stopped to tally them all. But tonight Selena's behavior bordered on unstable, and it made Teri think back to all the times in recent weeks that Selena had unnerved her in some way.

Teri shook herself. Her imagination was running amok. One thing she was certain of, however—she had to break Selena's dependence on her before the girl had her going completely crazy.

Sixteen

"And to think, all these years, I thought coffee was the best way to start a day," Drew said with a chuckle, then kissed the corners of Teri's smile.

"Let's not forget, you've also given me an excellent reason not to make my bed right after waking up." She shifted in his arms and smirked when his body responded to her movement. "I was sort of hoping you'd be the responsible one and insist we get to work sometime before noon."

"I'm makin' up for yesterday," he said with another laugh, but stopped short of kissing her when he saw the change in her expression. "What?"

"Oh, it's nothing—really. I'm just afraid Selena's problems are a lot worse than I thought." He stilled his hands, waiting to hear more. "She stayed a while after you left last night. I know this sounds crazy, but she wanted to warn me about you. Said you were going to *compromise* me, of all things. I think she's really jealous of you."

He eased away from her a bit. "Do you think you were mistaken—about her not wantin' you physically? I mean, she's as big, and probably as strong, as a man. Maybe the sexy exterior is a false front, no pun intended."

Teri shook her head. "I still don't think that's it. Her attention toward me is adoring, childlike. She only touches me occasionally—and then it's on the hand or arm—and has never attempted to give me even a friendly kiss, or hug the way other women *or* men do."

"Then maybe she's simply worried about you. As a carin' friend. Even you and I thought it was a bad idea for us to get involved." Her narrowed brows made him explain. "Past tense. And we were wrong. Seducin' you was the best idea I've had in years." For that, he received a kiss. "But I can see why she's concerned. You're very vulnerable right now."

"I don't think 'concerned' covers it. She was . . . I don't know, almost fanatical. It was kind of scary."

"Well, I wouldn't worry too much. She'll come around in time, I'm sure, when she realizes I'm not goin' to break your heart."

Teri smiled, feeling much better for his reassurances. She'd probably been so tired last night, she wasn't thinking clearly. She kissed him again, with purpose this time. "Thank you." To his unspoken question, she replied, "For promising not to break my heart."

Slanting his mouth over hers, he sealed the promise the best way he could, then whispered, "I love you, Teri. You've filled a place in my heart that's been empty for a long, long time."

"And I love you, more than I thought I could ever love anyone again."

Teri and Drew spent the rest of the day looking for more interesting faces. As they rode in the car they touched constantly. In public, however, they reminded each other that there was still a small possibility that another detective could have taken Kidder's place, following them unseen, waiting to accuse them of being lovers. Neither believed it, but it didn't hurt to be cautious, and they knew once they were back in the studio "working" that evening, all restraints would be removed.

Only after Teri watched Drew leave did she check her answering machine.

Her sister-in-law had called about something of Rico's that she wanted. Teri sighed. She was glad she had already sorted through everything. Tomorrow she would deliver the boxes of Rico's possessions to his sister and let the family squabble over them. They had never wanted any part of her while Rico was alive, and as soon as she performed this last ritual, she could put that part of her life completely behind her.

Since that meant a trip to New Jersey, she decided to make a day of it and visit her grandmother at the nursing home in Camden as well. Drew had two assignments that he expected to keep him busy most of the day, so the timing seemed perfect.

There were two more messages on the machine—both from Selena. In spite of Drew's certainty that Selena would eventually come around, Teri intended to stick with the decision to start backing away from her. Instead of returning the calls, she went to bed.

The ringing of the phone interrupted a pleasant dream. Teri strained her sleep-blurred eyes to focus on the illuminated numbers of her alarm clock: one A.M. Assuming it must be an emergency at that hour, Teri lifted the telephone receiver before the machine could pick up the call.

"H'lo?" Teri crackled, then cleared her hoarse throat.

"Teri? Is that you?" questioned a shrill female voice laced with panic, but still recognizable.

"Selena? What's wrong?"

"Nothing's wrong with me. What's wrong with you? I left messages twice and you didn't call back, and now you sound horrible. Are you sick?"

Teri took a deep breath before answering. "I

sound horrible because I was sound asleep. Selena, it's one o'clock in the morning. I heard your messages, but it was late and I thought it would be better to call you tomorrow."

"Are you alone?"

"What? Of course I'm alone."

"Good. As long as everything's all right, I'll talk to you tomorrow. I can't wait to hear all about how your project is coming along."

Teri was baffled. Selena's voice had gone from nearly hysterical to whining to cheerful in a matter of seconds. "Yes. Fine. *Whatever*. Good night, Selena."

It was some time before Teri was able to fall back to sleep, and then the dreams were disturbing, though she couldn't remember any of them when she woke in the morning.

As she got ready for her day, she thought she'd have to tell Drew how right he was the previous morning. Having him for breakfast was a lot better than coffee and toast. After making calls to her sister-in-law and the nursing home, she loaded up her car and headed off to do her duty.

The sun was shining, the traffic on the New Jersey Turnpike was light, and rock-and-roll music reverberated through her car. It was going to be another good day, in spite of the fact that she was on her way to Rico's sister's apartment in Newark.

A short time later, as she attempted to parallel park in a tight space near the apartment building, Teri was startled by a white Cadillac Seville speeding around her. She had no time to think about that, though, because half of Rico's family was waiting for her, or rather, they were waiting for the boxes she had in the car. Teri didn't expect a warm welcome or an invitation to stay for lunch, and they didn't surprise her with either one.

Teri might have forgotten about the car she had seen, except that at one point on her drive south to the nursing home, she looked into her rearview mirror before changing lanes and spotted a white Seville a few cars back. From then on, she kept checking to see if it was there. The windows of that car were tinted and there was nothing unusual about the car that would identify it positively, but she had the strangest feeling that it was Selena's.

When the Seville followed her off the turnpike, she began to worry. It continued to hang back a few cars, which made her worry that much more. Either someone was tailing her, or she was definitely becoming paranoid. She told herself it had to be the latter as she drove into the parking lot of the nursing home and the Seville continued on past.

The aides at the home had used Teri's warning phone call to good advantage. Her grandmother had been bathed and dressed and brought outside in a wheelchair. They had even applied a hint of lipstick and blush to get her ready for the visit. The preparation served to arouse Teri's grandmother to a state of awareness, so that by the time Teri kissed her on the cheek, she recognized her granddaughter, for a change.

"How pretty you look, Grams. Have you got a hot date for dinner?"

Grams smiled. They had forgotten to put her teeth in. "There's a couple of men around here that keep pestering me, but I told them they're too old. I'm waiting for a handsome, young Italian boy like you have. How is Ricky?"

Teri gave her grandmother points for getting his name almost right. "He's fine. He had to work today, but told me to give you a hug and kiss from him." Grams showed her gums again. On the few occasions he had visited the older woman, Rico had always flirted with her like she was a young girl, since he saw how much it tickled her. For that kindness, Teri had forgiven many of the wrongs he had done.

While driving there, she had decided not to tell her grandmother about Rico's death. At eighty-two, she found talk about anyone's death depressing, but when the deceased was much younger and someone cared for, the news was much more devastating. Considering the fact that her grandmother seldom remembered that her own daughter was dead, Teri was certain Grams would also forget anything she told her about Rico. Better to pretend he was still alive.

Teri stayed until after dinner. She kept up the conversation, even when Grams' mind clouded over, or she just held her hand whenever the elderly woman dozed for a few minutes. And, as she did after every visit, she promised Grams and herself that she would make the trip more often. Maybe without Rico's demands on every second of her free time, she'd be able to keep that promise now.

Minutes after she got back on the turnpike, she glanced in her rearview mirror. The last rays of the day's sun glaring in her left eye made her squint, but they didn't blind her to the sight of a white car a ways behind her. There were a lot of white cars in New Jersey, she told herself. She sped up, passing several cars by weaving from one lane to the next. It was worth a bit of risky driving to see the white car follow suit, as if it was attempting to keep the distance between them the same.

Teri slowed down to a snail's pace, letting the same cars she'd just passed go ahead of her. She ignored the drivers' honking and obscene gestures, and kept one eye on the white car, which had also slowed down. Her maneuver had brought it closer and for a split second there was enough of an opening for her to confirm it was a Cadillac.

She was almost certain it was the same car. Could another police detective be following her as Kidder had? If that was the case, she doubted the officer would be driving a Cadillac Seville. Not only was it

216

an extremely expensive car, it was easy to recognize.

Suddenly she thought of stories she had heard of women driving alone on a highway and being followed and forced off the road, then victimized or killed. Despite the air conditioner she began to perspire as she tried to think of what to do. If that was Selena following her all day, as she'd first thought, then the girl had truly gone off the deep end. If it was a stranger, she needed to seek safety, not let the person follow her home. *Dear God,* she prayed, *don't let him know where I live.* Thoughts of Rico and Detective Kidder and the Irish mob ricocheted around her brain. What if they were after her now?

She had to keep a level head. The only alternative she could think of was to drive straight to the nearest police station, but the only one she knew the exact location of was in White Plains. She gripped the steering wheel a little tighter and determined not to have an accident that would cause her to stop before she got to her safe destination.

All her worst fears abruptly proved groundless, however, when the Cadillac left the turnpike, taking the exit to the Holland Tunnel and Lower Manhattan. *Lower Manhattan?* Where Selena lived! Teri was trembling. She would find out if her shadow had been Selena, and if it was, there was no way she was going to excuse her this time.

The moment she got in her house she dialed Selena's number.

"Hello," Selena answered in her Marilyn Monroe voice.

Teri hesitated, realizing how terrible it would be to accuse her wrongfully, yet she was too angry to play guessing games. "Selena, were you following me today?" She heard the sound of sharply inhaled breath, then nothing for several seconds.

"It's not safe for a woman alone on the turnpike," Selena whined like a bad little girl who knew punishment was forthcoming and would say any-

217

thing to put it off.

"Selena! Answer me! Were you following me all day?"

"We-l-l-l . . ."

"Selena!"

"Yes, but I was only trying to protect you. It's not safe."

"Do you have any idea what you put me through? I was terrified! I thought it was someone with the mob, intending to kill me. I'm still shaking so bad I can hardly hold this phone. And how did you know I'd be driving on the turnpike or where I'd be going? *I* didn't even know until this morning!" Instead of calming down by venting her fury at Selena, Teri was getting angrier by the second.

"I didn't mean to scare you." Selena's voice was so high it squeaked, and there was a definite hint of tears about to fall. "Oh, please, don't be mad at me. I only drove to your house to see you for a minute this morning, and then I saw you driving away and I got nervous for you. I only wanted to protect you. I didn't mean to let you see me watching over you."

"Whether you meant to let me see you is not the point. You shouldn't have been following me at all. If I want someone to protect me, I'll hire a bodyguard!"

Selena sniffed. "I'm sorry."

Teri was no longer influenced by the timid little girl voice. "Just don't *ever* do anything like that again." She hung up without bothering to say goodbye.

Selena hung up the phone and went to bed. Rocking Juliette back and forth, she said, "Don't cry. Everything will be fine. She's just mad at us now because she doesn't understand. But she will. One day we'll tell her everything we know and why we had to make sure she wasn't with *him*. But I don't want to make her any madder right now, so I won't go see her for a few days. You'll see, the next time I see her she'll be happy again. Do you think she'd like a surprise?"

She likes Chinese food. You could bring it to her while she's working.

Selena bounced up and down. "What a good idea! She'll be so happy she'll forget she was ever mad at us. Let's see, now—today is Tuesday. She said she needed space and time alone. How long should I wait to surprise her?"

Three days. Surprise her on the Fourth of July.

Appropriately, Teri was awakened on the Fourth of July by the sound of firecrackers popping in front of her house. The neighborhood children had started their celebrating early this year. It was just as well—Drew would be here soon, and they planned to do some celebrating of their own.

With each day that had passed since Captain Hart's visit, they became more convinced that Detective Kidder was the only one who'd thought they were guilty of anything. Captain Hart had called Teri once, but he had made it clear that he just wanted to be sure she was all right and that she would call if anyone bothered her. No more questions had been asked. No one was watching them— no police, no messengers from the mob. Other than Selena, no one seemed the least bit interested in what Teri and Drew were doing. And even Selena had apparently straightened herself out after Teri had told her off. Selena hadn't called once since then.

As if Teri's thoughts had sent a message straight to Manhattan, the phone rang. Rather than pick it up, Teri waited for the machine to click on and the caller to identify herself.

"Good morning, Teri. It's Selena. Are you up? Pick up the phone if you hear me. Oh, I guess you're still in bed or in the shower. Please call me as soon as possible. I want to make sure you'll be home today. It *is* a holiday, so you shouldn't be working. You do need to take a day off once in a while, you know. Well, I guess you're not listening or you would have picked up by now. Okay. Call me."

Teri listened to the hum of the telephone until the machine cut off. From the chirping quality of Selena's voice, Teri could tell that she believed all was forgotten, or at least forgiven. Teri's stomach's reaction to the call told her this wasn't yet the case for her. There was no way she wanted to take the chance of Selena showing up uninvited again and ruining this day. In fact, she really didn't feel like dealing with Selena and her weird mood swings anytime in the near future.

Though she was still irritated at Selena, she knew she couldn't just tell her to stop calling and stay away. Teri hadn't even been able to say that to Rico after years of abuses. She would have to lie out of necessity—to avoid crushing Selena's feelings in one blow, and to insure that she and Drew would have their day of celebration. She dialed Selena's number.

"Good morning!" Selena said cheerfully.

"Good mording," Teri replied, unable to pronounce the "n" because she was holding her nose. "It's Teri."

"Dear heavens. You sound awful."

"I picked up a little cold."

"Are you taking anything?"

"Aspirin, tea, and lots of chicken doodle soup. I just deed to rest."

"I'd better come by and—"

"Don't do that! I'm dot that bad. And there's do sense in you catching it from me. Anyway, I'm the kind of person that would rather be left alone when I'm sick. I hear my kettle whistling. I'll talk to you in a couple days."

Selena smiled at Juliette. "This is even better than we planned. I'll get to show her how well I could take care of her if she'd let me move into her house."

But she said she wanted to be left alone. You don't want to make her mad again.

"Oh, that's just her way of being nice. You know how she's always thinking of other people first. She doesn't want to be a bother. But *everybody* likes to be taken care of when they're sick, even if they say they don't. I'll have to remember to get extra wonton soup when I pick up the food. Now, what else should I bring?"

How about the Story. It always makes me feel better when you read it to me.

Selena gave Juliette a happy hug. "That's the bestest idea you've had yet. Maybe after she hears the Story, she'll start to understand."

"Sit right there and close your eyes," Teri instructed Drew as she nudged him onto a stool in the studio.

Drew sat, but he was still staring at the white sheet draped over a board so large that Teri had used an easel on each end to prop it up.

"C'mon," Teri teased. "Close your eyes, or I don't take the sheet off. And until I take the sheet off and you *ooh* and *aah,* I don't take anything else off."

Drew laughed at her empty threat, but closed his eyes as she ordered.

Quickly she removed the sheet and tossed it on the bed. Standing to one side of the display board, she told him he could open his eyes. *"Ta-dah,"* she sang, waving her arm like a magician's assistant.

Drew came off the stool with an appreciative "Wow." Stepping up to the board, he studied each of the separate arrangements pinned there with a critical eye. Teri had selected five closeups each of six of the subjects he had photographed in the past week.

She stood quietly but impatiently, waiting for his opinion of her choices. When he made her wait a second longer than she thought necessary, she demanded, "Well? What do you think?"

He moved his gaze over each set again and rubbed his jaw thoughtfully. Finally, he pointed to one photograph of a little boy. "I think I could have gotten a better angle on this one, but other than that, they show the work of a pure genius."

She playfully slapped his arm. "You're supposed to build up *my* ego, not yours."

"O-o-h," he said, pulling her into his arms. "You were expectin' *oohs* and *aahs*. Well, I'm savin' those for the second unveilin', ma'am."

Her lower body had no trouble interpreting precisely what unveiling he was referring to. "Then I guess you'll have to come up with some other complimentary phrases regarding the first. Unless . . ." She made a grimace to express her doubt about the perfection of her arrangements.

Drew turned her around to face the board, but still held her close against his chest as he critiqued her choices. "When I was developin' all the film, I picked the same six subjects, but I didn't want to influence your selection." He dipped his head to kiss her ear and she squirmed against him. "I thought you wanted my opinion. I can't think if you're doin' that."

Teri laughed and moved again.

"Uh-uh. If you want to hear what I really think, you have to stand perfectly still."

She froze in place, knowing very well she wouldn't be able to stay like that with his breath fanning over her ear and his fingers stroking her bare arms, and he knew it, too. But she thought it might be fun to see how long she could hold out against the seduction he was obviously intending, and she played along.

She remained stiff as he discussed the first two arrangements, despite the chills running up and down her back from his kissing her neck.

She started losing ground on the next two, when his hands crept under her T-shirt and unhooked the front closure on her bra. But she knew he was slipping just as fast as she was from the way his body was straining to melt into hers.

By the sixth set, neither one of them had any idea what Drew's opinion was. And they didn't care.

Selena was a little surprised to see Drew's car next to Teri's in the driveway. She thought he'd be picnicking with his cousin's family today. But then, knowing he was struggling to get his career off the ground, perhaps he didn't want to take the time off. She hoped he hadn't bothered Teri, as bad as she was feeling.

When there was no answer at Teri's front door, she went around to the kitchen and knocked there. She chided herself for not realizing that Teri might be napping when she arrived. She should have brought the keys she'd taken from Rico. That way, she could have just gone on in and left the food on the counter. Making a mental note to put the keys in her purse when she got home, she headed up the stairs to the studio. Teri probably kept an extra house key up there.

Assuming Drew was in the darkroom, she tried the knob before knocking. The unlocked door opened easily and she stepped inside.

A moment later a bloodcurdling scream lodged in her throat and the box of food dropped out of her hands. She barely felt the splash of hot soup on her feet. She couldn't make out the words being hurled at her. All she knew was what she saw: a naked woman being held down on all fours by a naked, sweating, humping pig.

Selena ran from the reality and the memory it stirred. The part of her that knew who those two people were sped away in her car. The part of her that saw the other couple was screaming in silence all over again.

Sixteen-year-old Selena ran deeper and deeper into the pine forest in back of her house. She ran until she was certain no one would find her. She ran until her lungs burned and her leg muscles gave out and her body collapsed on the cold, damp ground.

He had lied. He had betrayed her mother and her.

Three years of following every one of his disgusting directions to *help him keep her mother happy and healthy.* Selena had taken the pills that made her sick to her stomach and bloated her body. She had suffered the agony and embarrassment of repeated visits to the doctor to treat the infections she'd contracted, infections the doctor had warned her were caused by allowing a boy to use her in unclean ways. She had learned to say the words he wanted to hear and perform the acts that made him groan with pleasure and grow weak with satisfaction.

And she had never told a soul.

She had never gone out on a date or even to a school dance because he didn't approve of anyone touching her but him.

She didn't have any girlfriends because she

couldn't share her secrets with them. To her classmates, she was a freak.

Because of two men. One had made her look different than everyone else by heredity, but they had each had a hand in making her view the world differently from other girls her age.

Until that day, she had thought she hated only the first man. For a while, she had even thought she loved the second.

But a bad head cold had brought her home early from school that day. And she had walked into her house to find that second man on the living room floor with Mrs. Esker, rutting like a pig. In that shocking moment, she also knew it was not the first time they had been like that.

He had lied. He had betrayed them. And now he would pay.

When she returned to the house much later, it was as if nothing out of the ordinary had occurred.

Her mother made dinner.

They ate and cleaned up.

Troy kissed and stroked her after she got into bed, as he had every night for the past three years.

After the house was quiet, Selena got up, went to her closet, and took a box down from the top shelf. When Troy had moved them to this house, Selena had insisted on carrying her special box herself and putting it away. She had always known it was there, even though she hadn't opened it since then.

She ran her fingers lovingly over the tape that held down the flaps of the box, then carefully peeled it off. The sight of her old friend lying among the roller skates, marbles, and other souvenirs made her smile right down to her toes.

Hello, Selena, said Juliette in the old familiar musical voice. *I've missed you.*

One week later, Selena and her mother were wearing black again and sadly accepting every sympathetic word offered.

"The poor woman," they murmured, "so young to have lost two husbands."

"That poor child," they whispered behind Selena's back, "having two fathers die by accidents. What a terrible thing for her!"

"I heard she was with him in the canoe when it capsized."

"They say he fell and hit his head. She almost drowned herself trying to save him."

"I heard she was with her real father when he died also."

"How awful!"

"Poor, poor Selena."

As the tears coursed down her fever-heated cheeks, Selena mentally thanked her drama teacher for the lesson on how actresses cry on cue.

Seventeen

"Dear God," Teri muttered as Selena tore out of the studio door.

"Excuse me, darlin'," Drew said, moving away from her and pulling on his briefs. A moment later he closed the gaping door and locked it with an audible *click*. "Sort of like closin' the barn door after the horses got out, but heaven knows who else is lurkin' out there."

"This is all my fault. I was so eager to show you the board, and then—"

"And then we *both* got distracted." He bent down and started putting all the little red and white boxes of Chinese food back into the carrying box. Only the wonton soup was lost.

Teri put on her pink robe, which had never made it back to her bathroom in the house, and got a towel to soak up the liquid.

"Anyway, Drew said, laughing a little, "what's the big deal, other than bein' embarrassed? So we were caught with our pants down, or off, I should say. Selena knows what men and women do together. Now she knows we're lovers as well as friends. She should have knocked, but it's too late to worry about blame. We'll all laugh about this years from now."

Teri shook her head. "I don't know. Did you see the way she looked? That wasn't embarrassment or surprise on her face. It was pure horror, like she had seen the devil himself."

"To be quite honest, I was too busy grabbing for a sheet to notice how she took it. And then she was gone. At least now I can hold your hand in front of her."

Teri didn't agree. "You wouldn't say that if you heard the awful things she said about men the other night. I think she really despises all of you. I've been thinking back on that conversation, and it hit me that jealousy isn't quite what she's feeling. She actually *warned* me about you. I think she's convinced I'll get hurt and she's trying to protect me from you. In fact, that was the word she used to explain why she followed me all day Tuesday." Teri had told Drew about that the next day, but it hadn't sounded quite so terrifying in the retelling.

"Maybe it would help if Selena and I had a chat."

"*No!*" Teri blurted out. "I . . . I don't know why, exactly, but I just have a feeling that would make things worse, especially considering her attitude toward men. I was going to try to back off from her slowly. You see, I lied to her this morning to keep her from coming by. I pretended I had a cold. Now she knows I've resorted to lying *and* consorting with the enemy. No, I'm the one who has to deal with this, not you.

"It seems so strange, though, that we were friends and worked together for a year, and nothing peculiar ever happened. Then, all of a sudden, she changed into this weird person."

"Split personality? Dr. Jekyll and Mr. Hyde?" Drew asked with a serious face as they cleaned up the last of the mess.

Teri cocked her head at him. "Maybe—what are you thinking?"

"Sounds like drugs to me."

Teri's eyes widened. She hadn't thought of it, but it certainly would explain a lot. "Her eyes are so unusual, I don't know that I could tell just from looking at them, as you would with someone else. But I have noticed how they sometimes seem to glow with their own light."

"There were people who helped me a lot when I needed it. Maybe it's time for me to help someone else. At least I can find out if she's on something."

Teri frowned. "I'm still not sure your talking to her will get through. The way her moods have been switching in mid-conversation, I wouldn't trust her not to haul off and punch you if you annoy her."

"Hmmm. I'll keep that in mind. She's one big woman." He laughed at the face Teri made at him. "We'll both talk to her, okay? Either she'll accept the fact that we're in love, or she'll have to find new friends."

Teri found herself wishing that Selena would just go straight to finding new friends. She stopped short when she realized she was about to wish Selena would just go away. That was what she had wished for Rico. And nothing had been simple since.

Drew gave her a hug. He had no intention of waiting until they were all together to talk to Selena. First of all, if it was drugs, he was more qualified than Teri to deal with that. Second, if Teri was right in her analysis, any hostility that existed was between Selena and him. So it was up to him, not Teri, to straighten it out, and the sooner the better.

The red haze over Selena's eyes finally began lifting when she was back in her own bedroom with Juliette.

"It's too late, Juliette," she moaned, rocking back and forth much too quickly to be calming. "He already sank his fangs into her throat, and now she's under his power. I know, because she lied to me. Teri would never lie to me unless he made her do it.

Remember how Troy used to make me lie to everybody, even Mommy? Drew is just like Troy, Juliette."

Will I get to meet him soon?

"No, I'm sorry, but I don't think there's time. We have to take care of this quickly. Do you have any ideas?"

Maybe he's a real vampire. Then you'd have to wear a crucifix and drive a wooden stake through his heart, Juliette giggled in her tinkly voice.

Selena frowned. "You must be serious. There's no such thing as vampires, and everybody knows it. I only described him like that because it's an a—an—" The grown-up word would not form on her tongue and she shrugged.

Analogy.

"Yes, that's it. What should we do?"

I'll give it some thought, but only if you stop rocking so hard. It's making me dizzy.

The next day Drew had a commercial shoot on Long Island that promised to take most of the day, so he and Teri made plans to get together the following day. When the shoot finished up early, he determined to take care of something that had been eating at him since Selena's surprise visit.

A quick search through his wallet unearthed Selena's card. There was nothing on it but her first name and a Manhattan phone number, and he recalled Teri telling him something about Selena legally dropping her last name. His time in therapy had him automatically wondering whether she merely wanted to seem more exotic, or whether she harbored some deep hatred of the name itself and the man attached to it. From what Teri had said, Selena talked like she despised all men, so her problems probably went back a few years. Regardless, he wanted to make it clear that he was no threat to

Teri or to the women's friendship. Better that he put his cards on the table now, before the situation got more uncomfortable for Teri.

"Selena? This is Drew Marshall," he announced when she picked up on the fourth ring. "I think we should talk." For a moment she was so quiet he thought she had hung up on him.

"What did you want to talk about?" she asked cautiously.

"We both want what's best for Teri. If we can't be friends, at least let's not be enemies. What do you say?"

"I'm not sure I follow you."

"Well, I'm not sure I follow you, either, so I propose a truce . . . over dinner, just the two of us. We'll have a chance to talk and hear what the other one has to say." Again Drew had to wait for her answer.

"All right. Dinner. But not here in town. Everything's always so crowded, you can't hear yourself think, let alone talk. How about something further out, maybe closer to where you live?"

"I don't know too many places yet, but there is one nice restaurant on the edge of Tarrytown." He told her its name and described the location, and they agreed to meet there in two hours.

Selena hung up the phone and turned to Juliette. "What do you think?"

I don't think you should have agreed to meet him. It gives him an advantage.

"But it might be the easiest way to get him alone without Teri. I have to meet him."

Selena, we mustn't do anything yet. We haven't got a plan. You know we must have a plan before we act.

"We didn't have a for-sure one with Detective Kidder, and that worked out perfectly."

No, but we had several different plans to pick from, depending on the circumstances. This time, we don't even have one good idea. Please wait.

"I can't let this chance pass. If you want a plan, think of one. But fast. I'm leaving in one hour."

Drew was waiting in the restaurant's foyer when Selena arrived. "Hi. Glad you could make it," he said, offering his hand. When she ignored it and limited her return greeting to a curt nod, he knew this wasn't going to be easy.

They had to wait a moment for the hostess to finish hanging the new menu on the wall. Using an unnecessarily large hammer, she gave each of the four tacks one last tap, then turned to Drew and Selena with a smile. They were soon seated. Except for giving her meal order to the waitress, Selena remained silent, her body rigid with hostility.

Drew noted how Selena wrinkled her nose at the offer of a pre-dinner cocktail and flatly declined any wine. Experience told him alcohol was not her problem. It had to be drugs. Since it looked as though she had no intention of opening the conversation, he began as soon as their salad and rolls arrived.

"I get the idea I should be apologizin' for somethin' here, but since I don't feel guilty about anythin', I figure an apology would be a lie."

Her expression of disbelief was followed by a sarcastic "hmmph."

"Look," he continued, "I called you so we could clear the air between us. That's goin' to be mighty hard if you don't tell me what's buggin' you."

Selena took several slow, deep breaths. She wanted to concentrate on coming up with a plan, but if she didn't talk to him, he'd soon be putting up his guard. Though she didn't know what she was going to do yet, she knew she had to put him at ease and make him trust her. But her change of attitude would have to be slow or he might become suspicious. With a greater effort than it usually took, she separated the angry Selena from the friendly one.

"Okay, Drew. I'll admit I'm bugged. Teri is my dearest friend. She's going through a tough time right now, and the last thing she needed was some smooth-talking cowboy screwing his way into her life." She felt the anger building again and fought it back. "She needs space, and time alone. She told me so herself. You should have let her be, instead of manipulating her while she was too bewildered to see what you were doing."

"Whoa, there—you make it sound all one-sided. It's not. Teri and I both tried to be reasonable and ignore the attraction we felt, but that just didn't work for very long."

"Then you should have gone away."

"I couldn't do that. I'm in love with her. And she loves me."

"Hmmph. 'Love' is an easy word for men to use. The problem is, you think it has to do with what's between your legs instead of what is between your ears."

"Selena, please try to understand. I know you're not upset just because of me. Teri thinks your . . . *distrust* of men goes back a ways."

Her chin lifted abruptly and her eyes narrowed to slits. "You made Teri tell you about our private conversations? How dare you!" She could barely hold back the red haze.

Drew delayed his response until after the waitress placed their meals in front of them. "I didn't *make* Teri tell me anythin'. She's worried about you. And you're worried about her. And I'm the one caught in the middle of all this worryin'. You don't have to like me, but you're goin' to have to accept my bein' around if you're goin' to stay friends with Teri. It took me a long time to find someone like her. I'm not lettin' go."

He continued talking, but all Selena heard repeating in her head was, "*if*" she was to stay friends with Teri. She knew it! He was planning to stop Teri from seeing her so he could keep her all to himself. She couldn't allow that to happen. There had to be a way to stop him before it was too late. Struggling to control the violent hatred, she ran through the useless inventory in her purse, then began looking around the restaurant for a weapon of some kind.

Drew stopped his threats long enough to eat. She picked up her steak knife, cut her meat, then lowered the knife to her lap, where she slowly wiped it on her napkin. A moment later the serrated knife was in her purse, but she was afraid it wasn't sharp enough to do much damage. She reminded herself that she needed to ease his mind about her.

Looking contrite, she forced her voice to sound sincere and a little weepy. "Drew, I owe you an apology. You're absolutely right. I was letting my personal experiences cloud my judgment. I've been under a lot of stress lately. I can see you really love Teri and you'd never do anything to hurt her." She stretched her hand across the table. "Friends?" Drew grinned, obviously pleased with himself for fooling her, and shook her hand.

"Friends. And now that we're friends, I'd like to talk to you about somethin' else. I told you Teri's worried about you. She's afraid you have a problem. Well, I had a problem myself for a time, so I understand how it can happen. Some of the things Teri told me about you are a little too familiar to me."

Selena raised an eyebrow at him. What could Teri have told him? Did he suspect her?

"You don't have to talk about it tonight. Just know that when you're ready, you can talk to me. I think I know what you're goin' through. Maybe I can help."

Selena held her breath. It sounded as if he knew

things he shouldn't. Suddenly she knew how Drew had forced Teri into obeying him. He had apparently threatened her with revealing secrets he had figured out about Rico and Kidder. She felt the panic bubbling inside her. She had to get out of here. He had to be silenced immediately. "Drew, I'm not feeling well. I need some air. Could you take care of the check, and I'll see you outside?"

"You do look flushed all of a sudden. I didn't mean to upset you. Go on out. I'll be there in a minute."

As she hurried through the maze of tables, her gaze darted back and forth. There had to be something better than the little knife in her purse. In the foyer the hostess was herding a large party into the dining area and Selena's mind flashed on the image she had seen when she'd entered. Quickly Selena searched around the reservation podium until she found what she was looking for, then rushed outside before anyone noticed her.

She dropped her purse off in her car and waited beside it in the parking lot for what seemed like hours. Juliette's voice was in her head, telling her to go home, warning her not to take any chances. But the red haze was stronger than Juliette's voice, and she prepared for her chosen role. Behind her back the fingers on her right hand clenched the handle of the hammer and her left hand clutched the knife.

When she saw Drew leave the restaurant, she called out, "Over here," and waited for him to come close. "A model friend of mine wants some new photos for her portfolio. I told her about you, but I didn't have your number. Do you have an extra card I could have for her?"

As she had figured, he was flattered and quickly pulled out his wallet to oblige. She glanced around the parking lot to make sure they were unobserved. The moment his attention was directed inside his wallet, she brought the hammer up and swung it toward his head.

The blow caught him by his ear. He staggered, the pain registering with the shock, but he didn't fall. Before he had the chance to protect himself or run, Selena swung again, this time aiming for the other temple. He swayed in place, his eyes rolled back in his head, and he collapsed.

But that didn't mean he was dead. Again she looked around to make sure they were still alone, then rolled the body over onto its back and dragged it by its feet so that it was lying between her car and the next one. She shoved his wallet into her purse, then checked for a pulse at his throat. It was weak, but she could still feel it. Setting down the bloodied hammer, she crouched beside the body. Knowing the knife wasn't sharp enough to slice the throat, she raised it above her head and brought it down into the area of the chest where she guessed the heart was.

But the knife barely tore the shirt. Behind her, voices carried from the front of the restaurant and she knew she had to get away. Frantic now, she ripped open his shirt and stared at the tiny prick the knife had made.

Juliette's words came back to her. *Drive a stake through his heart.* Holding the knife point against the chest, she picked up the hammer with her other hand and drove the knife through the chest wall. As the blood frothed from the wound, the voices got louder and she tried to extract the knife.

She pulled and pushed, but it was stuck. As fast as possible she tried to wipe any fingerprints off the handle with his shirt, but everything was covered with blood, and there was no more time. The voices were coming right toward her. She grabbed the hammer and her purse and jumped into her car. With her car's tires spraying gravel, she pulled out of the space and sped away in a cloud of dust.

She knew the people would see the body. She had to hope he was dead long before they could get help. She had to hope none of them caught her license number. She had to hope no one had seen her before she got inside her car. She had to hope no one inside the restaurant had paid enough attention to her and Drew during dinner to identify her later. It was too much to hope for.

You should have listened to me. You weren't even wearing a disguise!

Selena turned her head to the passenger's seat and was surprised to see Juliette there. She didn't remember bringing her, but just seeing Juliette helped Selena calm down a little.

"I couldn't help it. He knew things. I had to stop him before he told on me." She looked down at her bloodstained clothes and hands and realized she was spreading the mess all over the car's pretty white interior. "Now look what I've done. I can't go back to my apartment like this. I'd never get past the garage attendant or building manager without them seeing me. Juliette! Help me. I can't think."

You must protect Teri. Go to her. You'll have to explain now. She must understand in order for you to protect her.

Selena frowned. "That's what you said about Mommy, and she never understood."

Then you know what you must do.

When Selena reached Teri's house, everything was dark, but her car was in the driveway. It looked like Teri was already in bed. Knowing how tired she had been lately, Selena hated waking Teri up. She had no choice about that, but she would put it off a while.

Before getting out of the car, Selena moved Juliette to the backseat to make room for Teri, then she headed for the studio. Using Rico's keys, she let herself in. Quickly she stripped off the stained clothes and bagged them, for disposal later. Though the small bathroom had no shower, she was able to get herself clean, and the rack of costumes offered a variety of things to wear. She laughed at the thought of putting on one of the fancy Victorian ballgowns for their journey, but it wasn't practical. She ended up choosing a loose peasant blouse with an elastic neckline, and a long skirt.

After she was presentable, she soaked a towel in cold water and took it and her bag of ruined clothes to the car. She put the hammer with the clothes, then tucked the bag into the corner of the trunk. Turning her attention to the interior, she tried rubbing off the blood with the wet towel, but soon realized that the brownish stains would probably never come out of the white leather upholstery or beige carpet. They'd have to be replaced someday.

"I'm glad you decided to come along, Juliette. You'll finally get to meet Teri."

Don't be long. We have to get away.

The reminder renewed Selena's fear, and she hurried to the front door of the house. Again using Rico's keys, Selena let herself in.

When she saw how peacefully Teri was sleeping, she had to remind herself that they had no choice. There was no way of telling how soon the police might be looking for her car.

Lightly shaking Teri's shoulder, she singsonged, "Teri. Teri, time to get up."

Teri heard a familiar voice in her dream, but it didn't seem to fit there. And it didn't make sense because she felt like she'd just fallen asleep. A moment later she realized she wasn't dreaming. Someone *was* trying to wake her up. Her eyes blinked open, but all she could see in the dark was a huge shape hovering over her. She opened her mouth to scream, but was immediately silenced by a large hand.

"Hush. It's only me. Selena."

Teri blinked again, this time to clear her head. As soon as her mouth was freed, she asked, "Selena? What are you—"

"I'm going to turn a light on now, okay? I know how frightening the dark can be."

Teri sat up and was still trying to sort the dream from the reality when the lamp on her nightstand lit up the room. "Selena, what are you doing in my house?" Teri could not begin to imagine what her presence there might mean, but none of the possible reasons seemed good. Selena had her back to her as she walked around the room, touching this and that.

"Selena! Answer me! And why are you dressed in that costume?"

Selena turned to her slowly, and when Teri saw her eyes, she instinctively inched backward until she was pressed against the headboard. The odd silver glow in Selena's narrowed eyes seemed to pin her in place. Teri didn't need any other evidence to know something was very wrong. When Selena finally answered, her voice was neither a breathless whisper nor a childish whine. It was deep and flat, as if she had lost all emotion—as if it was another person speaking.

"I used my key." She flashed the keys that were still in her hand.

Teri knew she had never given her a key, but the keyring looked familiar. "May I see those keys, Selena?" Her quivering voice betrayed her suspicion.

Selena stepped forward, letting the keys dangle before her as she held onto the blue plastic penlight attached to the ring.

Teri's mind wanted to deny what her eyes told her. "They . . . they look like . . ." Her heart began to pound even before it was confirmed. She reached out to take the keys, but Selena snatched them away before she could touch them.

"Yes, Teri—they're Rico's."

Teri couldn't get enough air into her lungs. Her head began to spin, but she fought the momentary weakness, telling herself there had to be a simple explanation. "How did you get his keys?"

Selena smiled, a secret, know-it-all smile, and started wandering around the room again. "Juliette said I have to explain *everything* to you. You must understand in order for me to protect you."

Teri bunched the bedsheets in her clenched fists, as if that might keep her from flying apart. More questions. Who was Juliette? What did Selena have to protect her from now? Selena sounded calm, but Teri felt certain if she started getting hysterical, Selena would follow suit. Quietly, she dared to repeat herself. "The keys, Selena . . . *why do you have them?*"

"Do you remember the day you asked me to get Rico out of your life permanently?"

Teri's eyes opened wide. "Selena, that was a joke. And I didn't really ask you—"

Abruptly Selena giggled, and the little girl voice took over. "Oh, Teri. We don't have to lie to each other. Get ready. This is going to make you laugh like you did that day." She paused to make sure Teri was ready for her next words. "You were right. Sex with me *did* kill Rico."

Eighteen

Teri didn't laugh. She didn't breathe. She couldn't. All the air in the room had been sucked away by Selena's demented humor. But she had to know for sure. "You were the blonde Kidder told me about? You were *there?*" Selena nodded, but her smile began to fade as the seconds ticked by and Teri still wasn't laughing. "Selena . . ." Teri had to swallow hard before she could ask, "Who else was there?"

Selena's happy expression became confused. "No one else was there. I promised to get rid of him for you, and I did. Everything would have been fine if it hadn't been for that snoopy old detective."

Teri's knees same up to her chest in a protective move, and her whole body froze with horror. She ordered herself not to scream as she wanted to so badly. She had seen the clues. They *weren't* coincidences, after all. But what Selena was saying was completely unbelievable. And she knew in the next instant that it was completely true.

Selena had murdered both men and actually believed she had done it for her. *To protect her.* Selena wasn't simply a vulnerable child in a woman's body. She wasn't merely a jealous friend.

She was insane.

Teri lowered her face to her knees as the trembling set in. Was she next? Is that why Selena was here? Cautiously she raised her head and saw Selena frowning at her. Teri's fear spurred her to beg, "Please don't hurt me, Selena. We were friends."

Selena's confusion came back, and she sat down on the edge of the bed. "Oh, Teri, you still don't understand, do you? I would never, ever hurt you. I have to protect you and keep you safe. That's why I'm here." She patted Teri's leg, but withdrew her hand when Teri flinched away. "I don't know how much time we have, but I'm sure we can take a few more minutes for you to pack some things. And, of course, we'll take your canvases and paints so you'll have plenty to do." She got up off the bed and tugged the sheet away from Teri. "Come on, sleepyhead. We'd better get moving."

Teri stared at Selena, trying to curb her panic enough to think. Apparently, she wasn't in immediate danger of being killed, but Selena wanted to take her somewhere, and that didn't sound much better at the moment. Somehow she had to summon the police, but how could she distract Selena long enough to use the phone?

Slowly she rose from the bed, trying to make her brain work faster than her body. Selena outweighed her by at least fifty pounds. She could never hope to overpower her, and yet, she couldn't just go off who-knew-where with this madwoman without a fight. Perhaps once they got outside she could run for help. Her gaze strayed to the nightstand drawer across the room, and she remembered what was in there. Did she dare try for Rico's gun? She wasn't sure she had that much courage. Struggling to keep the anxiety out of her voice, she managed to say, "If we're going somewhere, I'd better get dressed." Selena's smile told her that she believed Teri would cooperate. "Where are we going?"

"I have a house in Ulster County. Upstate New York is very pretty in the summertime, and not nearly as hot as the city. Hurry up, now. We may not have much time."

Teri opened a dresser drawer and took out underwear. If she thought about survival instead of what Selena had done to Rico and Detective Kidder, she found she could function almost normally. "Why are we in such a hurry?" Selena stopped her pacing, and Teri watched her withdraw into herself. Selena's head dipped, her shoulders slumped, and she hugged her body protectively.

"I didn't mean to be bad," she said in the little-girl voice, which became more whiny with each word. "Everything went wrong, and now Juliette's mad at me. I didn't have a good plan, didn't change the way I look. People saw me. But I couldn't help it. I had to protect you from him!"

Teri clutched the clothes she'd been gathering. She had the most wretched feeling that Selena was not referring to Rico or Kidder. "What are you talking about?"

Selena seemed to age a little as she defended herself. "I had to do it. Don't you see? He was going to hurt you and stop us from being friends. I had to make him go away before he could do that."

Teri dropped the clothes on the floor and whispered, "Drew?" A little louder she demanded, "Have you done something to Drew, Selena?"

The girl stood there looking sheepish. "I think he's dead. But I couldn't be sure. The people came and I had to run—"

"No-o-o!" Teri wailed as she flew across the room, yanked open the nightstand drawer, and grabbed the gun. Her hands were shaking so badly she wasn't certain she could pull the trigger if she had to. But she aimed it in Selena's direction and hoped that would be enough. "Stay back, Selena. I'm going to call the police now, and we're going to wait for them to get here."

"You don't want to do that," Selena said in her

flat voice as she straightened her body to its full height. "I'd have to tell them everything. How we planned Rico's disappearance together. How you held tobacco to your eyes to make yourself cry at his funeral. How Kidder was right about you and Drew being lovers, and that's why the detective had to die."

"But none of that is—" She was about to say "true," but she immediately understood how Selena was twisting the truth to make it believable. Who would the police believe if it was her word against Selena's? Was she at fault for not seeing Selena as a vicious killer? Was she partly to blame for the murders? Maybe if she had told Kidder of the coincidences, at least he and Drew might still be alive.

Oh, God, Drew, I'm so sorry. She swiped at the moisture filling her eyes just as Selena stepped toward her. *"No!* Stay back. I don't care *what* you tell the police. I'm calling them." She moved to the side of the nightstand, balanced the heavy gun in her right hand, and groped for the telephone next to the bed.

"You'd better not do that," Selena warned again. "The evidence points to you being the guilty party." Abruptly she giggled. "Oh, I made a joke!"

Teri's left hand returned to help hold up the gun. "What evidence, Selena?"

She giggled again. "Rico's hands. Get it? They're *pointing* at you! I hid them somewhere very close to you. The police would know you were involved when I told them where to find the missing hands."

Teri tasted bile and swallowed several times. The image of Rico's mutilated body lying in the morgue flashed in her mind. She hadn't seen any part of him below his shoulders, but her nightmares had supplied her with gruesome visions of what the truncated arms had looked like.

Captain Hart had told her Rico's fingerprints had been used in Kidder's murder, so she knew the hands had not been disposed of. And now Selena was telling her the grisly evidence was hidden "somewhere close." The idea that she could have accidentally found shriveled body parts in her bedroom made the nausea harder to control. If she hoped to have a chance of convincing the police of the truth, she had to find the hands before she called for help.

"Where are they, Selena? Where did you hide them?" Teri's gaze darted frantically around the room.

Selena clapped her hands and gave a tinkly laugh. "I know! We could play hide-and-seek. I never win when I play with Juliette, but I can beat you. You'll *never* find them."

Teri ignored the childish challenge as she opened the nightstand drawer all the way. Keeping the gun and her gaze aimed at Selena, she pulled open one drawer, but thoughts of reaching in and touching dead flesh delayed her search a moment more. Swallowing her revulsion, she blindly pulled one item after another out of the drawer and tossed them on the floor in front of her. Selena's relaxed composure and self-assured smile grated on Teri's raw nerves, but she moved to the dresser, then the armoire, searching each drawer in the same manner, until the entire floor was littered with clothing.

The gun in Teri's hand grew heavier by the minute. Yet Selena, intent on the game she had set up, no longer seemed to notice the threat. She appeared perfectly content to watch Teri ransack her room in a state of raw panic.

"You'll never find them," Selena singsonged. "I hid them in a very, very hard place."

Teri abruptly stopped her search. Selena was right—she would probably never find the hands, and the attempt was only wasting time. The gun felt as if it had tripled its weight in her outstretched hand. She had to either use it or take her chances with the police. She realized if they could just see and hear Selena as she was now, they would realize she was unbalanced. If they held Teri partially accountable because she hadn't told Kidder everything she knew before he was killed, so be it.

Moving back to the nightstand, she spoke in a maternal tone. "I'm not playing any more games with you, Selena. You need help and I'm going to get it for you." When Selena bowed her head and put her hands behind her back, Teri thought she looked like a child preparing herself for her punishment.

Selena continued to stand still as Teri lifted the telephone receiver, but the moment Teri looked down at the buttons, Selena lunged across the room and clamped her hand over Teri's right wrist.

With all the strength she could muster, Teri was able to angle the weapon toward Selena's stomach. She tried to squeeze her finger against the trigger, but her hand was paralyzed by Selena's ferocious grip. Selena grabbed Teri's other shoulder and forcibly shook her, but Teri refused to release the gun. She pulled and twisted, trying to break free from the bigger woman. As hard as she could, she kicked Selena's shin, but Selena didn't even cry out.

A second later, Selena wrenched the gun from Teri's hand, then threw her across the room as if she were weightless. Pain exploded in a hundred places in Teri's body as she collided with the dresser and landed on the floor. But it didn't prevent her from seeing that the gun was now pointed at her.

"I don't want to hurt you, Teri. But I will do whatever I have to do to protect you . . . even from yourself. I'd ask you to promise to behave, but I already know you can't keep your promises any better than any other adult. Now get up and get your clothes on. We've wasted too much time already."

Teri struggled slowly to her feet, noting that nothing seemed to be broken, only bruised.

"Don't think of running from me, either. I can't let you turn us both in. I'd never be able to take care of you in jail. They might not let us room together there. If you run, I'll have to stop you, even if it means shooting you in the leg. I know how to use a gun, you know. I learned in one lesson." She giggled lightly. "You couldn't have shot me, though. I know you too well. You haven't got the ability to hurt any living thing. I saw that right away in your paintings. You create beauty and life, not ugliness and death. And inside you're pure and white, like new snow. That's why I love you so much."

Teri gasped. "How can you say you love me and threaten to shoot me?"

Selena narrowed her eyes. "Juliette thought you would understand, but you don't, do you? My mother never understood, either. Perhaps when I have more time . . . but we don't *have* more time now. You have five minutes to get your clothes and some personal things together, then we leave."

Teri's mind skipped back to thoughts of running. For that she had to get Selena to relax again. "All right, Selena. I'm sorry I didn't understand. I'll pack now." She took a large suitcase out of the closet, then picked some clothes up off the floor and placed them in the suitcase. It didn't matter what she chose, since she didn't intend to go anywhere, but Selena was watching her every move.

Thinking that if she made the suitcase heavy enough, Selena would have to carry it, Teri stuffed the suitcase so full she had to kneel on it to close it. If it slowed Selena down even a second or two, that might be enough for Teri to get away from her, then the darkness might keep Selena from finding her long enough to get help. "All set."

Selena raised an eyebrow. "Without a toothbrush or hairbrush? We won't be able to go shopping for a while, so you'd better get everything you need now."

Teri got out the matching overnight bag and took it into the bathroom. When Selena followed her to the doorway, she made a small show of choosing which toiletries and first aid items to take. As Teri caught sight of her reflection in the mirror, she was amazed to see herself looking perfectly normal, rather than terrified out of her skin—her complexion wasn't a ghostly white, her eyes showed none of the fear raging through her. Yet terrified was exactly what she was. She wondered what she would do if she couldn't get away from Selena and realized that no one would have any idea where to look for her. Her clients weren't expecting to hear from her for a while. Only Drew would have noticed her absence, and he was—no, she couldn't think about him now.

The mirror. She thought of scribbling an S.O.S. in lipstick on it, but she didn't know if anyone would ever see it . . . except Selena. She was afraid that even if she asked Selena to give her some privacy, the message would be visible when she opened the door again.

In an attempt to appear as though she was really trying to plan for an extended stay somewhere, while thinking of a way to leave a note behind, Teri checked every drawer and cabinet, then pulled the shower curtain aside to check the things on the ledge of the bathtub. The curtain accidentally caught on a bottle and knocked it into the tub. The loud crash in the small room made Teri's heart leap in her chest, but she couldn't afford to fall apart quite yet.

Selena came up behind her to see what had happened, and Teri fought a silent battle not to recoil from her.

"Oh, too bad," Selena said with sincere sympathy. "And that was your favorite, too."

Teri stared at the broken glass container and the sea of pink bath crystals, and an idea popped into her head. "I've got everything I need now, so I guess I'll get dressed." Selena stepped aside, but remained by the bathroom door as Teri got an outfit together. With her clothes and shoes in hand, she walked back to the bathroom. "If you'll give me a moment to wash up . . ." Selena frowned and Teri reworded her request. "I have to use the toilet. Look, there are no windows in here for me to climb out of, and I'll just be a sec." After a moment's hesitation, Selena allowed Teri her privacy, but her distrustful expression remained unchanged.

Teri didn't dare lock the door for fear of alarming Selena, but the second the door clicked shut, she turned on the water in the sink and tore off her nightgown. Hastily, she dressed, then flushed the toilet. She needed every second she could to leave her message. Using the handle of a toothbrush, she carved letters into the spilled bath crystals on the floor of the tub.

HELP SELENA KILLED

"Hurry up, Teri," Selena called from the other side of the door.

Quickly Teri began scraping out the destination Selena had named.

ULSTER C

Selena opened the bathroom door before Teri could complete the last word.

"What are you doing?" Selena asked, clearly suspicious.

Praying Selena would not come further into the room to investigate, Teri rose, drew the curtain closed, and turned around. "I . . . I was trying to clean up the mess I'd made, but I suppose it can wait until I come back." Selena's smirk convinced Teri that Selena never intended to let her come back to this house. Teri took a deep breath to conceal the shudder that rippled through her, shut off the water in the sink, and stepped out of the bathroom. She only exhaled after Selena followed her.

All thoughts of running when they got outside were wiped out when Selena grasped Teri's arm and ordered her to pick up her luggage. Selena retained a tight hold on her throughout the time it took to load the suitcases in the Cadillac's trunk and go up to the studio. There, in spite of the gun she held, Selena reverted to her usual friendliness, as she told Teri to pick out whatever materials she'd like to take with her. Again Teri tried to get Selena to carry a few things to the car for her, hoping to get the girl's hands too full to manage the weapon also. But Selena refused to help or let Teri walk without her *assistance*.

Teri furtively scanned her neighborhood as she loaded her supplies into the trunk. Anyone about or even looking out a window had sufficient light from the streetlamps to see Teri being led around at gunpoint. But there was no one to witness her abduction, and she could not be sure that a scream would be heard. In spite of Selena's insistence that she didn't want to hurt her, the throbbing in her shoulder from where she hit her dresser was proof that Selena had no qualms about causing her pain. Teri feared that the only thing screaming might gain her was another injury—or death.

She realized Selena was capable of shooting her without the least hesitation. It wouldn't do her any good to scream or fight if it only got her killed. No, Teri determined, she didn't want to die. Better to go along with Selena's plans until a fairly safe escape presented itself. Perhaps she could jump out of the car along the way . . .

"You drive," Selena ordered, breaking into Teri's thoughts and pushing her toward the passenger door. "Get in and scoot over." She opened the door and pushed Teri forward.

Teri winced at the increased pressure of Selena's fingers around her arm when she was too slow to respond. "But I'm so tired. Remember, you woke me up. I might fall asleep if I'm driving."

Selena paused for only a second before giving Teri another shove that got them both into the car. "I'll keep you awake. I would have let you sleep on the way, but you showed me that I can't trust you right now. If I drive, you might try to jump out of the car, and you could hurt yourself. I can't let you do that. Until I have time to help you understand, I'll have to keep a very close eye on you." She reached into her purse on the floor and handed Teri the car keys.

Just before Selena pulled the door shut and the overhead interior light went off, Teri saw the fresh stains. She told herself they could be from a paint spill—anything but what she instantly knew had caused them. Her hands hovered over the leather-covered steering wheel, but she gagged at the thought of placing them over the same spots where Selena's hands had been . . . spots still damp from Drew's blood. *Dear God, help me!*

Selena shook Teri's shoulder. "Drive."

Teri tried to put the keys in the ignition, but her hands were shaking too badly. "I . . . I can't . . ."

With a cluck of her tongue, Selena grabbed the keys away, inserted the proper one, and turned on the engine. "Stop wasting time. Let's go."

Taking a ragged breath, Teri forced her fingers to close over the steering wheel and gearshift, and she obeyed. She felt her mind shutting down from the reality of what was happening to her and knew she couldn't afford that luxury any more than she could afford to get hysterical. Selena had prevented every escape attempt Teri had thought of, and because of her bungled attempts, Selena had no intention of letting down her guard for a while. The only thing Teri could do was hope to convince her that she *understood* Selena's good intentions as soon as possible. Then perhaps Selena would let her go without a struggle. Unfortunately, though Selena was obviously insane, she was also extremely intelligent, and Teri knew it would take more than a promise of good behavior to wipe out the fact that she had pulled a gun on her.

Earlier, Selena had told her they were headed to Ulster County, but now she would reveal exact directions only as Teri needed to know them. In spite of what she told Selena, not only was Teri wide awake, but she was noting everything about the route they were taking so that she could relay it to the police later. Thus Teri made no attempt to converse with Selena, and as they were driving north on the Taconic State Parkway, Selena limited her comments to directions.

"Get off on Interstate 84 and take the Newburgh-Beacon Bridge across the Hudson River. From there you go north on the New York Thruway."

Teri nodded her comprehension, but out of the corner of her eye she saw Selena turn around and shake her head.

"I don't think so," Selena said looking behind them.

"What? Did I miss a turn?" Teri asked, lifting her foot off the gas.

"No. Keep going the way I said. I was talking to Juliette."

Juliette? Teri remembered Selena referring to Juliette after she had awakened her. But there was no one else in the car.

"She wants to meet you, but I think introductions should wait until we get home."

Teri immediately assumed Juliette was some imaginary friend of Selena's, such as a child would have. It occurred to her that if she pretended to see Juliette, she might convince Selena she *understood* that much faster. "I'd like to meet Juliette now, Selena."

"All right, but don't miss the exit." Selena leaned over the seat and brought Juliette up to sit on her lap.

Teri glanced at the old doll and back to the road. It may have been a pretty plaything at one time, but that had to be long ago. The blond nylon curls still had a shine to them, but the painted porcelain face was faded and smudged. There was a crack down one cheek, and the movable eyelid on that side hung at half mast. Teri imagined the lacy evening gown was once quite lovely, but now it was stained, mended, and yellowed with age.

"You don't hear her, do you?" Selena asked in a sad tone. "I had hoped you would."

Teri thought of lying, but there was no way she could pretend to have a conversation with Juliette if Selena truly thought she could hear the doll speak. "I'm sorry. I suppose you'll have to tell me what she says. She's quite . . . beautiful."

Selena's smile lit up her previously sour face. Yes, she is. Juliette's the most beautiful doll in the whole world. My mother told me that when she gave her to me on my fifth birthday. Mommy said Juliette would help me not to be so afraid."

Teri noted the changes in Selena's voice and posture as soon as she mentioned her mother. She even thought she saw Selena put her thumb in her mouth, but a second later Selena straightened up and put Juliette on the seat between them. Using the gun as a pointer, she made the formal introductions. "Juliette, this is Teri. Teri, Juliette. Juliette said to tell you you're beautiful, too."

Teri tried to remember what Selena had said about Juliette before, but she had been too horrified by everything else Selena had said to pay much attention.

"She's not mad at me anymore," Selena said, triggering Teri's memory. "She said everyone breaks the rules sometimes, and it all worked out okay anyway."

Teri clenched her jaws and squeezed the steering

wheel to keep from doing or saying anything to alert Selena to her true reaction to her words. Two, possibly three men were dead by her hand, and she believed "it all worked out okay?"

"Juliette knows I've always listened to her before. I do everything exactly like she says and nothing ever goes wrong."

Teri's stomach started clenching again as she analyzed Selena's words. Juliette—the doll—told Selena what to do and how to do it. She didn't need to be a psychiatrist to understand that Juliette was some evil part of Selena's personality. But she thought that kind of situation occurred only in horror movies or sensational newspapers. She wondered if it meant that eliminating Juliette would prevent Selena from hurting anyone else, herself included, or if it would cause Selena to lose completely whatever slight grip on reality she still had.

For the remainder of the trip, Teri had to pay close attention to Selena's instructions. Once they had left the thruway at Kingston and driven beyond that city, there were no more streetlights and the winding two-lane roads seemed narrower than they were because of all the trees along the sides. Teri noted each turn she made that took her further away from civilization, but it soon became obvious that Selena was guiding her by landmarks rather than street signs. As dark as it was, Teri realized Selena could be directing her in circles. She soon began to doubt whether she would be able to find her way back to Kingston.

Checking her watch, Teri noticed it had taken about an hour and a half to get to Kingston from White Plains, and they'd been driving about a half hour since. They were near water now. She caught glimpses between the trees of what looked like a lake, but which lake, she had no idea, as she had never been to Ulster County before. Occasionally she saw a house or a light through the trees that indicated a building off the road somewhere, but they were few and far between.

"Stop!" Selena ordered. "Back up slowly."

Teri did as she was told, but had no idea why. There had been nothing on either side of the road but pine trees and weeping willows for at least the last five minutes.

"There!" Selena said, pointing to Teri's left. "Turn up that drive."

Teri squinted at the overgrown dirt path that didn't resemble any of the driveways they had passed along the way, and there was no sign of any house beyond the woods, but she turned and eased the Cadillac up the hill, over the ruts and through the drooping tree branches. Another minute passed before the headlights illuminated a small, single-story redwood house.

"Pull around back to the garage," Selena told Teri. "I'll empty the trunk and put your things inside later."

Selena took the keys from Teri as soon as she turned off the engine, but Teri watched her drop them in her purse and decided it would not be that hard to get hold of them again. She just had to stay awake longer than Selena, which shouldn't be too hard, since Teri had already had a little nap and was far too overwrought to fall asleep under the same roof as a murderess.

Though Selena kept the gun pointed at Teri as they headed toward the house, she no longer bothered to hold onto her. They both knew Teri wouldn't get far if she tried to run.

"It's probably a little dusty," Selena said as she unlocked the door and held it open for Teri. "But I'll have it good as new in a few days—you'll see."

Teri walked inside and was surprised a second later when a light clicked on.

Selena switched on several more lamps around the room. "I never turned off the electricity. Tomorrow I'll go get groceries someplace where they won't know me. But for tonight I can at least offer you some tea."

Teri looked around the living room. The sofa and chairs had been covered by sheets, but the tables, lamps, and knickknacks were covered with dust and spiderwebs. She followed Selena to the kitchen and stood by as Selena tucked the gun into the waistband of her skirt, then removed the sheet that was covering the table and chairs.

"Have a seat. It'll only take a minute to wash out a teapot and two cups."

The suggestion of tea made Teri aware of what she hadn't taken care of before they'd left her house hours ago. "I need to use your bathroom. All right?"

"Sure. It's just past the living room in the hall. There's only one."

Since Selena suddenly seemed to trust her again, Teri gave a moment's thought to running right then, but Selena had her purse with the car keys in the kitchen. If she had to leave on foot, she'd have a better chance after Selena was asleep. Besides, she really needed to use the bathroom.

There were also two bedrooms off the hallway, and Teri took a peek inside each. One clearly belonged to an adult; the other, a little girl. When she saw the photograph on the wall of two adults and a white-haired child, Teri knew they were in Selena's mother's house. She didn't dare dwell on the fact that Selena's room was still decorated for a very young girl, even though she had left this place only a year ago. Nor did she want to think about why Selena would have left the utilities on, as if she intended to return all along. From the appearance of things, however, it did not look as if she ever had.

By the time Teri wiped up the bathroom enough to use it and returned to the kitchen, Selena had teabags steeping in two cups of steaming water.

"Feel better?" Selena asked cheerfully.

Teri did her best to answer likewise. "Yes, but I am awfully tired. I'll help you change the linens—"

"No need. You just have your tea and I'll get our beds ready. I already added sugar to your cup, but I won't have milk until tomorrow."

"This is fine," Teri said, straining her teabag, then taking a sip to prove her words. She looked at the label, satisfied to see that this was ordinary black tea, full of caffeine, and not a nice, relaxing herbal. But as the minutes stretched by, she finished her tea and found it relaxing her anyway. When Selena came back to the kitchen, Teri didn't need to fake the yawn that she had planned to convince Selena it was time to go to sleep. She could barely keep her eyes open.

"Well, look at you!" Selena said with a laugh. "If I'd taken two more minutes, you'd have been asleep on the table. Go on. You can have my mother's bed. I'll bring in your suitcase now."

Teri got up from the chair, but swayed back and forth before taking a step toward the bedroom. As Selena gripped her elbow, Teri told herself she had better take another short nap while waiting for her kidnapper to fall asleep.

Selena helped Teri to bed, then smiled as she watched her dear friend drift into a deep sleep. A half hour later Selena had brought everything in from the car and put it all away. Everything would be ready when Teri woke in the morning. Selena couldn't guess how long she would sleep. The pill she'd crushed in Teri's teacup was one the doctor had prescribed for her mother, but that woman had been much bigger than Teri.

Taking Juliette into her mother's bedroom, Selena whispered, "See how happy she is now? Nothing bad will ever happen to her again."

And no one will ever again come between us.

"Doesn't she remind you of Mommy lying there?"

Before Troy, Juliette amended. *We were all happy before he twisted her mind. Remember how we used to cuddle together?*

Selena smiled, letting the pleasant memory warm her. "I don't think Teri would mind, just for this one night." Carefully, Selena crawled onto the bed, curled up behind Teri, and hugged her close.

It was just like having Mommy back again.

Nineteen

Captain Benjamin Hart rarely read the reams of reports that flowed through the police station, unless some dignitary got himself arrested and required special handling. And, under normal circumstances, he would never see a routine report from another city's police department. The papers handed to him the moment he arrived that morning were definitely an exception to the norm. The incident had occurred in Tarrytown, not White Plains, and the victim was no one special in the usual sense of the word, but his name demanded Hart's personal attention nonetheless.

Unlike his friend Bill Kidder, Hart preferred administrative duties over detective work because of the predictability of it. Rather than dealing strictly in hard facts, a good detective also relied on his curiosity, intuition, and blind luck. The only reason Hart had received this particular report was because his day-shift desk sergeant, Ross Parkins, was curious, intuitive, and married to a Tarrytown police officer. Rumor had it Parkins was bucking for detective.

Hart knew Parkins had been studying Kidder's case files on his own time and discussing them with his wife. She'd been working the desk at her precinct last night when the fingerprint identification had come through on a mugging victim. His name had rung a bell, and she'd called her husband. Though Hart had never had an interest in becoming a detective himself, he knew that questioning coincidences was often the key to detection. Because of Hart's friendship with Detective Kidder, Parkins thought the captain would want to know about the coincidences he was certain were tied together.

Rico Gambini had been with a blonde just before his murder.

Drew Marshall accompanied Mrs. Gambini to the police station to report her missing husband and helped her look through the mug shots. Hart added his own note that Marshall was also with Mrs. Gambini the day he went by her house.

Detective Kidder was investigating the Gambini murder when he was killed.

Detective Kidder's tape-recorded notes, found in his house, indicated that Drew Marshall and Teri Gambini were lovers and had plotted her husband's murder. Because Kidder's theory was completely unsupported, except in his biased mind, and because the evidence pointed so strongly to the mob, the notes had been dismissed.

Drew Marshall was assaulted and robbed after having dinner with a tall platinum blonde, but the blonde was nowhere to be found.

Benjamin Hart decided young Parkins's instincts were valid. There was a connection here, and it wasn't just the absentee blonde. Teri Gambini was sitting right in the middle of the coincidence pie. Either she was guilty as hell, or she was the next one due to become a victim.

Although it went against policy to interfere in a case that was out of their jurisdiction, because of the coincidences and Parkins's good work, he ordered the man to follow up on Marshall's assault. Normally, Hart wouldn't be involved at all, but Bill Kidder had been a good friend for many years and Hart still held himself partly to blame for his death.

As he was going over Parkins's analysis of the three

cases, the sergeant himself appeared in the office doorway.

"Excuse me, sir?"

Hart waved the slightly built redhead toward a chair on the other side of his desk. "What have you got?"

"Drew Marshall's out of surgery, but he's listed as critical. The knife punctured a lung. The only reason he's alive is that the knife wasn't pulled out . . . plus, the paramedics got him to the hospital in record time. The nurse I spoke to said it's the head injuries that are the real problem now. She couldn't give me any guess about when he might regain consciousness."

Hart grimaced. Drew Marshall knew the explanations behind the coincidences and might not live to reveal them. "Anything more on the blonde or the car that sped away from the scene?"

"Nothing yet, but I'll hear if Tarrytown's detectives uncover anything more. The woman was apparently very striking, because several people gave similar descriptions of her, which as you know rarely happens. Unfortunately, the only information the witnesses agreed on about the car was that it was white and bigger than a compact. No one read the tag or saw who was inside."

"Okay. How about Teri Gambini?"

"I had a patrol car go by her house. There's a car in the driveway registered in her name, but no one answered the door, and all I got was her machine when I called. I thought I'd go by later today, and if there's still no sign of her, I'll talk to the neighbors."

"Good. Just keep me advised." As Parkins got up to leave, Hart told him, "You're going to make a good detective, son. Probably as good as Bill Kidder ever was, and that's high praise, coming from me."

Parkins's freckled face pinkened a bit, and Hart thought the young man grew an inch taller as he exited the room.

* * *

Awareness crept into Teri's consciousness one heartbeat at a time. Her mouth was so dry her tongue stuck to her teeth. As soon as she tried to move, she became aware of throbbing pain in her shoulder and back. For a second she thought she had fallen asleep on the uncomfortable bed in her studio again. Then she remembered.

Selena!

Even recalling the ghastly revelations Selena had made and what she'd put Teri through during the night didn't make the chore of raising her eyelids any easier. Depression filled her as she realized she'd fallen asleep and could have missed a chance to get away. But as she opened her eyes, she thought it might not be too late after all. It was still dark. She looked toward her wrist, but without light she couldn't see the time on her watch. For once she wished she wore a digital instead of a traditional timepiece.

She blinked several times, expecting her eyes to adjust, and when they didn't, she touched them to make sure they were truly open. It wasn't simply dark, there wasn't even a hint of light. She remembered seeing a window in the bedroom. Surely some bit of moonlight would find its way through the curtains, in spite of the dense woods around the house.

Trying not to let the absence of light frighten her more than it already had, she sat up and moved her hand to the left, where she had seen a lamp on a table next to the bed.

Her fingers met cool, rough stone.

Like a mime, she pressed both palms against what felt like a concrete block wall beside her and probed her way toward the foot of the bed. This wasn't right. And it wasn't a dream. There had been no wall on that side when she'd lay down last night.

At the end of the bed she rose, keeping her hands on the wall. There had to be a light switch or table lamp somewhere. But suddenly she could go no further. Her fingers touched cold metal and quickly examined what she had encountered. Narrow vertical rods, spaced about three inches apart, were lined up at a right angle to the wall. By running her hands up and down, she felt three horizontal metal bars crossing the vertical ones.

Bars?

That's what they felt like, but she couldn't recall seeing any security bars on the windows of Selena's house. Gingerly she continued to follow the row of bars until, about eight feet further, they made another right angle turn.

Her heart picked up speed as she felt her way along. *What is this?* Her hip nudged something hard and she traced its form. With panic slowing her thought processes, it took her a moment to identify a chest of drawers with her two suitcases on top and next to that, the art supplies she had taken from her studio. After a few more groping movements, she found a third corner where the bars again abutted a concrete wall. Inching along that wall brought her to a low wooden table next to a narrow bed.

Once more she felt her way around the limited space, not willing to believe there was no door or window. Desperately she tried to create a mental picture of what her hands had touched. Was it possible that she was in a jail cell somewhere? Had she reached the police and been arrested, as Selena had said they would? If that was the case, why didn't she remember it?

Better question — why wasn't there any light? A jail would be well lit, and there would be other people around. Could she have gone blind and deaf, *and* have amnesia?

"Hello?" she heard herself call in a shaky voice, confirming that at least she wasn't deaf or struck dumb. "Is anybody here?" Trembling from head to toe, she gripped two of the bars and tried futilely to shake them. This wasn't possible! She was in some sort of barred cage.

In total darkness.

Alone.

"Selena!" Teri screamed as loudly as she could. "What have you done to me?"

But no answer came. There was only silence and no way out.

All she could think of to explain how she'd gotten here was that Selena had carried or dragged her to this place from the bed she'd fallen asleep in. When she recalled how quickly she'd gone from wide awake to unconscious, she guessed that Selena had to have drugged her tea.

Everything Selena'd said had made Teri believe she had no intention of killing her outright. Otherwise, she'd be dead already. So, what *did* she intend? Starvation? Slow torture? Driving Teri as insane as Selena already was? No matter how terrifying those thoughts were, Teri knew she could do nothing but wait until Selena decided to let her in on her plans.

She made her way back to the bed and lay down. Somehow, she would remain sane. Somehow, she would fight her way out of this nightmare Selena had drawn her into. If only she knew Drew would be waiting for her, she would have no trouble handling whatever Selena had in store for her.

But he wasn't waiting. Teri knew she had to accept that. It would be pure foolishness to cling to the belief that he was still alive. Though Selena had said she wasn't sure if he was dead, Teri had every reason to assume that if Selena had cold-bloodedly murdered Rico and Detective Kidder, she would have been no less efficient with Drew.

Hot tears seeped from her eyes as she thought of how little time they'd had together. She could see Drew winking at her and grinning, the way he did when he teased her. She heard his soft drawling "ma'am," and his last "I love you, darlin'," and she cried until her throat ached and the tears would no longer come.

She cried until she heard a noise above her. With the edge of the bedsheet she wiped her face and listened intently. There was a creaking, as if someone was walking on a wooden floor above her head. Quickly she stood on the bed and reached up, thinking she could knock on the ceiling and make herself heard by whomever was there, but again she discovered bars blocking her way.

"Hello!" she yelled upward. "Is somebody there?" She got off the bed and moved to what she assumed was the front of the cage. Her excitement built as she heard the footsteps moving more quickly, followed by the sound of a lock being turned nearby. A second later a burst of light surrounded her and she squeezed her eyes shut against the strain it caused.

"I am so sorry, Teri," Selena whined, her voice coming closer with each word. "I didn't realize it would take me so long to do the shopping, and I'm afraid I forgot about leaving a light on."

Teri slowly raised her eyelids and focused on Selena.

"Oh dear. You've been crying. I used to be afraid of the dark, too, but my daddy wouldn't let me keep a light on at night, so I had to get used to it. Sometimes I forget about that."

Teri couldn't be certain, but Selena's speech seemed more childish than ever before. There was no question in Teri's mind that the girl was demented; she just didn't have any experience that would help her in dealing with such a twisted mind. The only thing that occurred to her was to talk to Selena as if she truly was a little girl. Perhaps she would even obey Teri as an adult authority figure. She stepped closer to the bars and gripped them to help steady herself.

"Selena, let me out of here, she said as firmly as her rattled nerves permitted.

"Oh, no, I can't do that. I have to protect you."

Teri stopped the explosion that threatened to come out of her mouth. Shrieking at a child rarely gained any ground for the adult. As she struggled to compose herself, she surveyed her surroundings. A flight of steep, narrow stairs rose from the center of a fairly large room walled in whitewashed concrete blocks. The concrete floor had also been painted white, although a white woven area rug covered the floor where she was standing. The cage itself took up one corner and reminded Teri of the kind that house large animals in a zoo. On the opposite side of the room, she could see a washer, dryer, stationary tub, hot water tank, and furnace. The only other thing in the area was a straight-back chair like one she had seen in Selena's kitchen last night. It sat just outside the cage. All of that, plus the fact that there were no windows, told Teri she was in an underground basement.

"Are we still in your house?" Teri asked in a cautious tone.

Selena giggled. "Well, of course we are, silly. This is the safest place I could think for us to go."

All right, Teri thought, at least she knew where she was . . . more or less. Now that there was light, she could also see the position of the hands on her wristwatch—quarter to three. She had been asleep for about twelve hours. Through the bars she watched Selena go to the stationary tub and fill up two gallon-sized buckets with water. The running water made Teri urgently aware of what was missing in her private cell. "I need to use the bathroom."

"The potty is under your bed," Selena answered as she carried the buckets back and placed them on the floor outside the cage.

Teri hoped she was kidding, but Selena's expression told her otherwise. Kneeling down, Teri pulled out an adult version of a child's potty chair. "You can't be serious." Selena looked baffled by her criticism. "This is humiliating. Now let me out of here so that I can go upstairs."

"You're really going to have to get over this shyness around me. I'll tell you what. I'll go make you a nice lunch while you get cleaned up. The water's hot, so be careful. There's a bar of soap, a washcloth, and a towel in the top drawer of the chest. All your things are still in your suitcases. You can arrange them however you'd like." She took a key out of the pocket of her slacks, bent down, and inserted it in a lock at the bottom of the cage.

Teri hadn't discovered it in her blind search, but now she could see the pass-through. Selena slid a small section of bars up, pushed the buckets through, and relocked the door. All Teri could think of was whether she could squeeze herself through the same space.

"When you're finished, you'll leave the buckets and potty bowl right there for me to take away. Same goes for your meal trays and dirty laundry. You won't have a thing to worry about anymore. I'm going to take *wonderful* care of you." Selena started to walk away, but at the foot of the stairs, she turned and smiled happily. "It will be just like it was before Mommy went away."

Teri had thought she was as terrified as a human could be, but as she gaped at Selena's retreating figure and digested the girl's last few comments, she felt as if she had been pushed off the edge of a cliff.

Selena had matter-of-factly informed her of the procedures to be followed as if Teri was a hotel guest and she was the bellhop. She had spoken as if it was a previously established routine.

As if Selena was accustomed to keeping someone in this cage.

Teri's knees buckled and she folded to the floor. *It will be just like before Mommy went away.* Selena's final words registered with chilling alarm. Teri stared at her prison bars, realizing what she had been too frightened to think of before. This cage wasn't thrown together in the hours while she was asleep. And Teri was also certain Selena's decision to bring her here last night had been a last-minute one. She knew with

267

appalling certainty that she was not the first guest in Selena's private hotel.

"Don't dawdle, Teri," Selena called down from the top of the stairs. "I'll only be about twenty minutes. Then we'll have a long talk."

Teri closed her eyes in an attempt to stop the sensation that the room was spinning out of control. In spite of the impossibility of her situation, she had tumbled into a nightmare . . . one that could only have been conjured up by a sick, deranged mind . . . one from which she did not know how to awaken.

Sounds of Selena moving about told Teri the door at the top of the stairs had been left open, and she was jolted out of her shocked state by the idea of having to attend to her personal needs in front of Selena if she didn't get to them immediately.

As she forced herself to perform normal functions, she began to think rationally once again. There *had* to be a way out. The bars were solidly cemented into the floor and walls, so shaking them loose was out of the question. The pass-through door didn't look large enough for her to slither through, even if Selena were to leave it unlocked. Teri could now see hinges where a section of bars made up a larger door, but it also had a lock at the top that required a key. She wondered if the same key opened both locks, or if Selena could ever be convinced to open that door.

Thoughts of picking the lock sent Teri rummaging through her suitcases for some sort of tool. The only thing she found was a safety pin, which she put back in her bag for the time being. She had no idea how to pick a lock even with the proper tool, but she figured it was worth a try later, when there was less chance of Selena catching her.

Abruptly, her mind latched onto Selena's comment that they would talk. Teri told herself that although she had never studied psychology, she was a fairly logical person. Surely if she could get Selena to tell her about why she was doing this, she might discover a way to talk her out of it. This helped her to gather some fragments of courage. She prepared herself to encourage Selena to reveal her reasoning and determined not to show any reactions but sympathy and understanding, no matter how atrocious the discovery. Somehow she had to convince Selena that it would be safe to let her out of the cage.

As Selena had promised, she returned to the basement with a tray of food shortly after Teri had washed and dressed. Using the pass-through again, she exchanged the tray for the items Teri left for her to take away.

Reminding herself not to let Selena know how upset she was, Teri picked up her tray and set it on the table beside the bed. "Thank you, Selena. This looks great." Teri considered the drugged tea and realized this food could also have something in it. Not wanting Selena to know she was wary of her, though, she sat down and took a bite of the ham and cheese sandwich and washed it down with some iced tea. "Mmmm. Good. Aren't you having anything?"

Selena smiled and sat down on the chair outside the cage. "I already ate."

Teri noticed a children's storybook in Selena's hand and tried to interpret the look on her face as Selena watched her eat. Contented satisfaction seemed to cover it. The child and the lunatic both had retreated, leaving the young adult Teri was more familiar with. She hoped that was a good sign. After swallowing another bite of sandwich, and using as friendly a voice as she could manage, Teri urged Selena to talk. "Did you grow up in this house?"

Selena shook her head. "Troy, my *dear* stepfather, moved us here when I was twelve. He bought a discount store in Kingston right after my mother married him. She still had most of the money from my father's life insurance policy, and Troy convinced her it was a good investment. Of course, he also convinced her to manage it for him so that he had time to pursue *other* interests."

The smirk on Selena's face told Teri more than her words had, but Teri needed more information if she was going to talk her way out of this. "You didn't like him?"

Selena raised one brow, then gave a dry laugh. "Like? For a while I thought I loved him, but he turned out to be a pig, like my natural father. They just had different . . . ways of entertaining themselves."

Watching Selena's eyes narrow thoughtfully as she stared at a spot on the wall, Teri urged her on. "You told me you'd explain things to me. I'd really like to understand."

Returning her attention to Teri, Selena sighed. "Good. I want you to understand, then we can both live happily ever after. While you're eating, I'm going to read you a story. It's Juliette's and my favorite." With great care she opened the thin cardboard cover and smoothed the first page in place. "Once upon a time there was a sad princess."

Guessing this story might have more significance than as a mere amusement for her while she ate, Teri listened attentively and smiled when Selena did. The tale began with the princess and her mother, the queen, living in a castle after the good king had died. A wicked magician wanted to steal the queen's jewels and take over the kingdom. He thought because she was only a woman that she would be helpless against his magical powers, and for a time, he was right. But a fairy appeared before the princess and told her how to trick the evil man into leaving the kingdom forever. After the princess got rid of the magician, the people named her Protector of the Kingdom and gave her a golden sword of her own.

Teri watched Selena turn the last page without reading it and go directly to "and they lived happily ever after." It occurred to Teri that in this type of fairy-tale, a handsome prince would have come along at the end to marry the princess or the queen, and that Selena might have skipped over that part for personal reasons. Rather than mention it, however, Teri only said, "That's a very nice story."

Selena rose from the chair and began to pace in front of the cage, but her gaze stayed on Teri most of the time while she spoke. "My father was what people call a good provider. My mother and I never wanted for anything . . . except protection from him. He was a respectable businessman during the day and a mean drunk at night. His favorite punching bag was my mother, but occasionally I got in his way, too. Troy was just the opposite. He *loved* women . . . and young girls. When he put his hands on us, it was meant to give pleasure, but in the end it hurt no less than what my father did to us."

Teri didn't need explicit details. She could read the story of an abused child between Selena's sentences. "I'm sorry, Selena. It must have been awful."

Selena stopped in front of Teri. "I survived. And so did my mother . . . for a while, at least . . . because of Juliette."

Teri tensed inside, but kept her outward expression one of curiosity. "How did . . . Juliette help?"

Selena's eyes seemed to glitter with an inner light as she stepped closer to the bars. In a hushed whisper, she said, "She's very smart. She always knows tricks to make things right. When I was too little to stop my father from beating my mother, Juliette kept me from being afraid, but later she told me how to make him go away. You see, it was my duty as The Protector to take care of my mother, but Juliette had to tell me what to do."

One part of Teri's mind noted that Selena was managing to relay her story without slipping completely back into her childish voice. But the other part struggled to hold back the horrifying awareness that Selena might have killed her own father. "How old were you when your father . . . went away?"

"Eight. You look surprised. Don't be. I told you, Juliette is *very* smart. It looked like an accident, of course, his being drunk and falling down the stairs and all. No one suspected a thing." Her voice abruptly changed pitch. "Mommy and I were safe and happy for four years; five, if you count the first year after she married Troy." She frowned and looked away. "It changed after that. And then I had to make him go away, too."

Teri took a slow breath as her stomach threatened to get rid of the food she had just eaten. She was no longer sure she could pretend to understand. The body count was rising, and Teri didn't want to know if she had heard it all, but Selena no longer needed encouragement to speak.

"My mother had a weak heart, but she also had a weakness for bad men. I thought when I got rid of my father I had protected her from being hurt again. But Troy twisted her around his finger until she believed anything he said, even when she suspected he was cheating on her. I had to protect her from him, too."

She sighed and returned to her chair. "I had hoped that would be the end of it, but not long after Troy's funeral, another man started coming around, playing up to my mother. I realized then that it would never end. She didn't have the willpower to protect herself from them. It was up to me to take care of her, but I couldn't get rid of every man who had an eye on her or her money. Sooner or later someone would have gotten suspicious. So Juliette came up with a way for me to protect my mother from herself." Her broad smile showed how pleased she was with the solution.

Teri had guessed it before, but having it confirmed was like being dunked naked into icewater. Apparently, Selena took her wide-eyed silence for a question and answered it.

"Mommy never had reason to deny me anything I

wanted, including my request to have a chimpanzee for a pet. She even let me give all the directions for how I wanted this cage built. I hated lying to her, but I had learned from Troy that there were some things she was better off not knowing. She had a bad heart, you know."

Teri was beyond acknowledging anything. She could only sit there, gripping the bedding at her sides and staring at the white-haired demon through the bars. She ordered herself to think unemotionally and not to react, but it was impossible. Icy fingers of fear coiled their way into her limbs until she felt frozen in place. Despite the voices in her head warning that she didn't want to hear the truth, she could not remain silent. "You put your own mother in this cage? You *imprisoned* her?"

Selena's chin rose defensively. "I *protected* her. And now I'm protecting you. Neither of you understood how terrible men are. But I do, so it's up to me to keep you safe from them."

Teri stood up on shaky legs and moved to the front of the cage. Clinging to the bars, she dared to ask the one question left hanging. "How did your mother die?"

Twenty

Selena seemed to curl into herself without moving from the chair, and when she spoke, it was the child who answered Teri. "She sometimes told me her chest hurt. The doctor she went to before Troy died gave me medicine for her without insisting I bring her into his office because of the long trip. But I guess the pain must have been too much for her. One morning I came downstairs and—" She paused and palmed her eyes for a moment. When she removed her hands, her eyes were glassy with moisture. "Mommy used the cord from a lamp to hang herself from the top of the cage. I couldn't protect her from the pain, and she couldn't stand it anymore."

Teri could not stop herself from glancing at the bars Selena referred to and recalling the day Selena had put her hands around her throat. She had no doubt the woman's captivity by her insane daughter drove her to suicide more than any chest pain.

"Juliette made me take Mommy down and put her in her old room upstairs before I called the doctor. I still remember those ugly marks on her throat. I changed her clothes to make her look pretty and put a scarf around her neck. The doctor felt sorry for me, being left all alone like that, and he told everyone Mommy died of a heart attack so people wouldn't gossip about me and I could get the insurance money. Things are different here in the country, you know. He was actually kind of nice, for a man."

"How long, Selena?" Teri asked quietly, afraid of the answer. "How long did you keep her locked up before she died?"

Selena cocked her head as if that was a very strange question. "Only about three years. But at least I was able to take care of her for a while. When she died, I thought she might need me to go with her. But Juliette told me it wasn't time yet. Someone might still need me. Her contented smile returned. "And she was right, wasn't she? I met you right after I moved to Manhattan and I knew immediately it was you I had to protect next."

Teri felt they had arrived at a point in the conversation where she should attempt to convince Selena she understood and would never speak to another man again, if she would just let her out of the cage. She knew the timing was right, but she also knew she couldn't keep the hysteria out of her voice if she tried to talk.

"I think you'll settle in faster than my mother did," Selena said, her voice returning to its adult version. "She was used to going out to work every day at the store, and she never had any hobbies. I brought her books to read and crafts to try, but she never really liked working with her hands. She wanted to watch television, but reception down here was impossible. For a while, I would go back and forth to the store to bring her the paperwork to do. But one day she tried to send someone a message—she really never understood, you see—and the people there kept asking to see her, so I had to sell the store for her.

"It will be different for you. I realized that right away. You're accustomed to being alone and keeping your hands busy. I was getting very concerned when I saw how disruptive Rico was to your painting. And Detective Kidder upset you so much, you practically stopped working entirely. Now you'll be able to work without any interruptions, and I'll be able to pose for you all day long. I'll bet you'll have another fabulous series done in no time."

"But I like to share my work with others," Teri carefully protested. "It isn't nearly as rewarding to paint if no one will ever appreciate it."

Selena frowned and worked her mouth back and forth. "I'll have to think about that for a while. Maybe after I'm sure no one is looking for us, I can act as your agent and sell your paintings. We'll see. Now, if you're through with your meal, I'll take the tray and you can finish unpacking. Then you can make a list of whatever you need. I don't want to leave the house again for some time, but I may have what you want upstairs."

As soon as Selena was out of sight, Teri slumped onto the bed in a state of shock. She had been wrong to assume she could talk her way out of this cage. It wasn't just Drew, and Rico, and Detective Kidder. Selena had just calmly admitted to murdering two more men—her father and stepfather. And whether Selena accepted it or not didn't change the fact that she was also responsible for her mother's tragic end. That brought the death toll to six that Teri knew of, but how many more had Selena not told her about?

Selena's reasons for killing went back too far to be rationalized away in one conversation. And her childhood was so far out of Teri's realm of experience that she wouldn't know where to begin to help Selena work through her problems. *Problems?* Teri thought she must be getting hysterical even to use such a mild word. A "problem" was fear of the dark, not committing multiple cold-blooded murders. It looked as though she would be better off concentrating on a means of escape before she became another one of Selena's dearly departed.

She had no idea how long it would be before someone might question her disappearance and check out her house in White Plains, so she couldn't count on her message being discovered in the bathtub. Even if someone saw it, she doubted if they would be able to interpret it, since she didn't get to complete it. And if someone found the message, might that person also find what she had not — *Rico's hands?* Wouldn't it automatically be assumed that *she* was guilty of his murder, if she was not there to defend herself?

There was the possibility that Selena would take one of her paintings to a gallery at some point. Perhaps she could figure a way to send a cryptic message on the canvas, but she would be taking the chance that Selena would see it first, as she had with her mother's attempt to contact the outside world.

The only way escape seemed possible was if Selena let her out of the cage on purpose. That was the goal Teri would have to work toward. Surely Selena would understand her need for natural light in order to paint, and fresh air to keep her creative juices flowing. Since Selena seemed to care about her painting, playing on that angle sounded the most sensible.

But first she had to get Selena to trust her and, considering the fact that it was not quite twenty-four hours since she had aimed a gun at the girl, it would probably take some time to earn her trust again.

The first thing Teri had to do was block out all thoughts of the violent acts Selena had committed in her life and go back to thinking of her as a vulnerable innocent. At the moment, that seemed an impossible feat.

"It's been a week and there's still no sign of her,"

Sergeant Parkins told his captain. "I believe a search warrant for the house is justified."

Captain Hart didn't agree, yet he was as eager as Parkins to break the present status quo. "Marshall's cousin—the one from Century Publishing—said Teri Gambini told her she was taking some time off. She may have simply gone away on an extended vacation."

"On the same day her friend was attacked? One neighbor is certain she saw Mrs. Gambini earlier that day. It could be another coincidence, but something else hit me in the middle of the night: Teri Gambini was an animal lover. The backyard has a dozen bird feeders, dishes for food, and water bowls on the ground. She took care of feeding a flock of birds and who knows how many cats. I don't buy the idea that she would go away without making arrangements for someone else to see to the creatures that depended on her. Neither you nor I believe she's guilty of any crime, so that leaves foul play."

It was exactly the kind of logic Hart had been waiting for to make a decision. "I think you're right about that. Start the paperwork for a search warrant, but check on Marshall's condition one more time before you go breaking into the Gambini house. This whole situation would probably be cleared up in ten minutes if he regained consciousness."

Parkins nodded grimly. "I know. The nurses at the hospital have promised to notify me if there's any change. At least he's off the critical list."

"Hmmph. A lot of help that is if he's going to be a vegetable for the rest of his life."

"They don't know that for sure. The injuries to his head were extreme, but the doctor believed the surgery was successful. We'll just have to cross our fingers that he comes out of the coma sometime in the near future."

* * *

Teri glanced from the just completed portrait to Selena and back. It was hardly one of her better efforts. Given the circumstances, however, it was a masterpiece. The dampness in the basement kept the paint from drying in the manner she was accustomed to, and the lighting was atrocious.

Because Selena had allowed her to keep her watch, Teri was able to keep track of days and nights, and she made up a calendar so she would remain aware of how much time was passing. The watch and that calendar became her anchor to the real world.

Selena had proved to be a considerate keeper as long as Teri behaved like a grateful pet. Once she got over the initial shock of the circumstances she had been trapped in, and recovered from the monstrous revelations about Selena's past, Teri found that she possessed a fair amount of acting ability herself. She pretended to adjust a little more each day, even thanking Selena for her thoughtfulness from time to time. She forced herself to stand still and paint because that was when Selena was most rational.

Without overdoing it, Teri made subtle complaints about her environment, always in relation to her painting rather than her captivity. In spite of her desperation to be free, she cautiously spaced hints that she needed to get outdoors once in a while to do her best work.

But as the eighth day dragged on, Teri was losing her patience. Selena had ignored every complaint and hint. She was happy, therefore Teri was happy. Suddenly Teri realized what her mistake had been. She was *too* complacent. Selena had no reason to alter their routine. Perhaps it was time to change tactics.

As she studied the canvas, Teri became aware of

something she had unconsciously accomplished. She had finally managed to duplicate the haunted expression she had glimpsed in Selena's eyes. The smile that Teri had always thought of as innocent or serene appeared slightly different in this portrait also. Teri stepped back to judge the whole painting, as opposed to a part, and she saw what had been hidden from her in the past: *madness*. The smile of a lunatic; the eyes of the damned. Selena was on the wrong side of the cage bars, Teri thought, and came up with phase one of her rebellion.

Quickly, she mixed a shade of silver gray to match the color of the bars, then painted three vertical stripes down the canvas over Selena's face. The result was a true depiction of what Teri saw when she looked at Selena sitting on her chair outside of the cage, but it looked as though Selena was in a jail cell.

"Can I see it yet?" Selena asked.

"Just another minute. I'm adding one final detail." In very small numbers, she painted the date below her signature, blending it in with the background as much as possible. Holding the painting by its wooden stretcher frame, Teri turned it around for Selena to see.

"You ruined it!" Selena shouted, bolting off the chair. "Give it to me right now!" She tried to reach through the bars, but the space was too narrow for her arm.

"I painted what I saw!" Teri shouted back. She propped the portrait on the bed and stepped aside so that Selena would have to come all the way inside the cage if she wanted to get her hands on it. "How can you expect me to be creative in this pit? It's damp and dark and all I'm looking at all day is bars and endless, barren white. I can't stand this lack of color around me! I need color! Light! *Air!*"

Selena's fury tinted her cheeks hot pink. "Give me that painting. *Now!*"

"No! If you want it, you'll have to open this door and get it yourself." Teri watched Selena fighting to control her anger. Her chest heaved and her wide-eyed glare darted around the room as if seeking a weapon. For a moment Teri feared that she had pushed too far too fast, but then Selena whirled around and charged up the stairs, her backless sandals clacking away like machine-gun fire. A few seconds later Teri was pitched into darkness.

"It doesn't look good, sir."

Benjamin Hart had been anticipating the interruption by his desk sergeant. The young man didn't know the meaning of the word "later." In the last eight hours, with his superior's authorization, of course, he had walked the paperwork through for the search warrant for the Gambini house, had enlisted a detective friend of his, John Morris, to enter the premises with him, and had the place dusted for fingerprints. His enthusiasm had Hart on the edge of his executive chair, waiting for each report. "All right. Let's have it."

Ross Parkins came forward like an Olympic runner hearing the starting gun. "I know something happened at that house, I just don't know what yet. No sign of forced entry. The house was neat as a pin, except for the master bedroom. Someone had been searching for something there. Drawers were left open or dumped on the floor; clothes were strewn all over the place. But it did *not* appear that a struggle had taken place.

"Now this is purely guesswork on my part, but I noticed one medium-sized suitcase in the closet — the kind that's usually part of a matched set — but it was the only one there. Then I looked through the clothes and noticed there was no underwear. Maybe she never wore any, or maybe she packed it all up along with some other clothes in the suitcases that weren't there. Maybe Teri Gambini went somewhere in a big hurry."

Hart frowned. "Suppositions don't hold up in court."

"No, but fingerprints do. And there were four sets picked up in that bedroom. Teri and Rico Gambini, Drew Marshall, and someone else whose prints weren't on record anywhere but in our forensics lab." He waited for the captain to digest that, then said, "They're a match to the ones picked up off the knife they took out of Marshall's chest. On top of that, we found two very long white or platinum blond hairs on the carpet by the bed."

Captain Hart opened his mouth, but not even a surprised obscenity came out before Parkins continued.

"I already checked out the cab companies and bus drivers for that area. No one picked up any woman with luggage anytime recently, Teri Gambini's car was in the driveway and her husband's was in the garage. If she went somewhere, it looks like someone else drove her."

"The blonde?"

"As you said, Captain, that would be a supposition. But we're at least past the coincidence stage, and it's looking more and more like Detective Kidder was right about this having nothing to do with the Irish mob."

Hart recalled similar conversations he and Bill Kidder used to have. "Tell me something, Parkins. What does your nose tell you? Is Teri Gambini mixed up in all this as a victim or a perpetrator?"

Parkins shook his head. "I don't know yet, sir, but I can't wait to find out."

Teri dreamed she was running in wet, sucking sand. She had to hurry, but the faster she tried to go, the harder it was to free her feet from the sand.

Her legs grew heavier with each step until she was barely moving at all.

Her struggle took on a reality that pulled her into wakefulness. The sheet was tangled around her legs, constricting her movements, but it took her several seconds to figure that out in the dark. She was drenched in perspiration and her heart pounded erratically against her ribs. All the fear she had tried to hold back had surfaced in her dream.

Before she fell asleep, she had waited for what seemed like hours for Selena to return or at least turn the light back on, but neither had happened.

After the first night, Selena had brought down a small lamp with a dim bulb and plugged it in outside the cage. Teri assumed that she wasn't being allowed access to an electrical cord because of how Selena's mother had killed herself. She supposed that made sense, but it prevented her from having any control over the light, which was apparently the second reason it was placed out of reach.

This was the second time Teri had been left in total darkness, but it was no less frightening than the first. From the way her stomach and head felt, she knew lunch and dinner had passed without food. The meals in Selena's hotel were unexceptional, but they were always served punctually, at the same times every day.

What if Selena never came back?

Teri had asked herself that question a thousand times since the light had gone out, yet she still had no answer. Nor did she have any idea how long it had been. She might have been asleep for ten minutes or ten hours. Without light, her anchor had been ripped away.

Gradually her body returned to its normal state and she was able to think past her panic again. Instead of convincing Selena to let her out of the cage, she had probably lost what trust she had gained in the last week. She couldn't help but wonder, if Selena did return, how much longer would it take to recover that trust once more.

With that in mind, she figured it was time to try picking the lock again. She had made an attempt the second night she was there, after Selena had gone to bed.

Since she could barely reach the lock at the top of the cage, she had used the small table to stand on, then had had to scrunch down because it raised her too high. She had had no trouble slipping her thin hand between the bars beyond her wrist, but no matter how she had stretched or twisted, she could not get the pin into the keyhole. Perhaps she had not been desperate enough.

Not hearing any footsteps overhead, she hoped Selena was either asleep or out of the house. Feeling her way, she found the safety pin she had hidden in her clothes and again moved the table to the cage door. With light, balancing on top of the narrow table had been awkward. In the dark, she felt like she was performing a dangerous circus act. This time she used her left hand to find the keyhole and, with the straightened pin in her right hand, she blindly searched until she pricked her finger. It took all of her strength to hold herself in her contorted position while she worked the pin into the hole.

She poked, prodded, and wiggled her makeshift pick, but nothing seemed to be happening. It looked so easy in the movies.

Suddenly she was bathed in light, her body jerked in surprise, and the pin fell out of her hand. Sheer terror gripped her as she pictured Selena finding her in the midst of an attempted breakout.

"Wait!" Teri cried out. "Please don't come down yet. I . . . I'm not decent." As she spoke she got off the table and put it back in place, but everything was not back to normal. The silver safety pin, bent out of its normal shape, was lying on the white floor, outside the cage. Selena would know immediately what Teri had been up to. "I'll just be a minute."

"All right," Selena answered testily. "But hurry up. I have your breakfast."

Teri didn't take the time to ponder what significance that pronouncement had. She was totally absorbed in trying to get the pin back. Lying on the floor, she squeezed her arm as far as it would go through the bars, but the pin was still a few inches further away. Desperately, she looked around her, until her gaze landed on a paintbrush.

"Teri! Your eggs are getting cold."

Teri grabbed the brush and laid back down on the floor. "Give me another minute." Trying to hurry without making the situation worse, she extended the brush through the bars until the bristles covered the pin. It took three strokes to bring her precious tool within reach, and by the time she had the pin securely hidden again, she was vibrating with panic. "Okay," she called out, aware that her breathless voice probably betrayed her. The look on Selena's face when she came downstairs confirmed what Teri feared. The girl suspected something.

"What were you doing?" Selena asked as her gaze scanned the basement and Teri's clothes and settled on her flushed face.

Teri instantly realized Selena knew she hadn't changed clothes and without water, she couldn't have been washing. "I was . . . I had to go."

Selena glanced beneath the bed where the potty chair was stowed.

"I mean, I felt like I did," Teri quickly amended. "I couldn't, though. It's probably my nerves. I don't like being left in the dark." With each sentence she could see Selena accepting her excuses, and she quit while she was ahead.

Selena placed the tray by the pass-through and, as she unlocked the door, she told Teri in a flat tone, "When you misbehave, you will be punished.

Remember that." After she had pushed the tray through and relocked the door, she stood up and smiled, her whole demeanor abruptly turning cheerful.

"Juliette and I made a decision last night. I hadn't thought about how your being creative would make you somewhat . . . eccentric. I want you to be happy, and I know you have to be able to paint to feel your best. I'm afraid I hadn't thought about the lighting down here. I'll have to do something about that eventually. But in the meantime, if you promise not to cause trouble, I will take you outside one morning a week, starting today."

Teri felt her heart jump with anticipation. She was going outdoors. Out of the cage. Freedom could be only moments away . . . if she was fast enough . . . and sly enough. "Thank you, Selena," she said, bowing her head contritely. "I know after what I did yesterday, I don't deserve your thoughtfulness." Her act brought the desired response from Selena. The lunatic was pleased.

Between her excitement and not having eaten for some time, Teri finished her breakfast within minutes of Selena leaving her alone, then hurried through her morning routine. She didn't want to question why Selena had such a drastic change of mind. It was enough that she did.

Teri imagined all sorts of escape scenarios ahead as well as how Selena could prevent them. The worst thing she could think of was that since Selena treated her like a pet, she might put her on a leash. The best she came up with—and it couldn't quite be called a plan—was that once they were outside, Selena would be distracted by something long enough for Teri to get a running head start. Since she had never been very athletic, she realized if she went straight for the road, Selena would probably catch up to her with no problem. But if she took off for the trees, she might have a chance of getting away or at least hiding until dark. Spending time cowering in the woods sounded like paradise after the cage.

In preparation for her outing, she collapsed her easel and placed it with a new stretched canvas, and a selection of supplies by the door. She kept reminding herself not to appear too anxious, to bide her time, and get Selena to lower her guard.

After about twenty minutes, when Selena hadn't returned, Teri began to worry that the offer to go outdoors had been only a tease — a different form of punishment for her bad behavior. Then, Teri was slowly able to see why Selena had been stalling upstairs. She also knew how Selena intended to control her after she let her out of the cage. A leash would not be necessary.

She had been drugged. She felt the strong tranquilizing effects from her brain to her toes. If she tried to run, she wouldn't get far in slow motion. As the minutes ticked by, she wasn't even sure she could walk.

When Selena finally came to get her, the fog had completely enveloped her. She tried to talk, but she kept forgetting what she was trying to say before she got to the end of a sentence. Selena took all the art supplies away first, then came back for Teri, but by that time Teri had to fight just to stay awake.

She knew they were outside, behind the house. She saw the woods and fought to dredge up enough anxiety to counter the drug, but she lost the battle. Selena had given her what she demanded with one hand and prevented her from taking advantage of it with the other.

Teri couldn't run, but she could still think. If she behaved properly today, there would be another chance. If she pretended not to understand why she felt so strange, Selena would most likely use the same control method next week. Then it would only be a matter of not eating or drinking anything Selena offered her before they went out, yet acting sluggish, as if she had.

With that resolved, Teri pulled herself together sufficiently to apply paint to canvas, but the result didn't bear any resemblance to the trees she had intended to duplicate. All the while, she mentally recorded how she was feeling and acting so she could fake it next week for her farewell performance.

When Selena announced that it was time to go in, Teri checked her watch. She had been given two hours of fresh air and sunshine and had not appreciated one minute of it. Next week would be different.

Knowing what was coming helped Teri get through the days that followed. She worked on another portrait of Selena, read a true-crime novel she'd been given, and empathized with everything Selena said. She even started criticizing the men she had known in her life, much to Selena's pleasure.

It occurred to Teri that there still could come a time when Selena would let her out, but she didn't have the patience to keep her act going much longer. Smothering her real feelings of revulsion, while pretending to accept and understand why Selena had committed a string of murders, had Teri's nerves strung to their limit. Watching the minute hand of her watch creep past the twelve and crossing each hour off in her mind became the high points of her days. But thoughts of escape pulled her through one more hour, then another, until Monday, or as she named it, Independence Day, finally arrived.

Selena had told her it had rained continuously the day before, and Teri could barely control her frustration as she waited for Selena to give her a weather report that morning. With freedom so near, she didn't think she could stand having it postponed because of rain.

The minute Selena unlocked the basement door,

Teri was on her feet, braced for bad news, yet praying for good. As she had done dozens of times in the past week, she counted off the fourteen steps as Selena's sandals flapped against each one on her descent.

"Good morning, Teri. I made blueberry waffles this morning. I hope you're hungry."

Teri felt as if she were waiting for sentencing. And Selena made her wait longer while she passed her the breakfast tray and fetched hot water. But Teri held her tongue, knowing a show of complacency was more important today than it had been for the last two weeks.

Just before Selena went back up the stairs, she made her announcement. "It's still very overcast today, but it's not raining. I think we could go outside if you'd like."

If she'd like? Teri took a deep, calming breath before answering. "Yes, that would be very nice."

As soon as Selena went back upstairs, Teri scraped the meal and poured the juice and coffee into the potty chair bowl, then pushed it back under the bed. She didn't want to take any chances as to which portion might be drugged. If Selena stuck with last week's routine, Teri knew there was no reason to rush, but her anticipation had her hustling nonetheless. When Selena returned, Teri was washed, dressed, and slumped listlessly on the bed, as she had been a week ago. This time, however, it was only an act.

Ten minutes after Selena had her set up outside, Teri was certain her performance had been outstanding. Selena was watching her, but not with suspicion, and occasionally her gaze drifted away. With exaggerated precision, she daubed her paintbrush onto the canvas, squinted at it, and yawned repeatedly without covering her mouth.

By the end of the first hour, Selena was clearly bored with the lack of progress Teri was making on the barn she was attempting to create. Out of the corner of her eye, Teri watched Selena move away from her and bend over to pull a clover out of the ground. Her entire body tensed, readying itself for action. Selena looked at the clover then tossed it away. A moment later, she plucked another. Teri felt like shouting with joy when she realized that the girl was hunting for four-leaf clovers. Afraid that, like any child, Selena could lose interest in the game any second, and worrying that this might be the best distraction she was going to get, Teri waited for Selena to bend over again, with her eyes on the cloverleaves.

The moment came a heartbeat later, and Teri bolted. She got to the edge of the trees before Selena shouted at her. "Teri! Stop! You'll get lost."

But the warning only served to spur her faster. She didn't care if she got lost, as long as Selena couldn't find her. Teri knew which direction she had originally driven from and approximately how far away the nearest house was. The woods had a maze of overgrown paths between the trees and she chose the one that seemed to head toward that house. For several minutes she stayed on that path, running as hard as she could, leaping over fallen branches, stumbling on rocks, slipping on the damp pine needles, but she could still hear Selena yelling at her. In fact, it sounded as if she was getting closer with each passing second.

Teri saw a fork in the path ahead and picked the one that led away from the road, hoping Selena would be fooled. She needed to find a hiding place soon. Her body was in no condition for a cross-country run, no matter how much adrenaline was pouring into it from the fear of being caught. The further she ran, the denser the ground cover became, until she could no longer make out a path at all.

The only sound Teri could hear was her own

strained breathing as she maneuvered her way between branches. Her face and arms stung from the sharp pine needles jabbing her skin, but she had to keep going. If Selena was still following her, she was being very quiet.

Suddenly the toe of Teri's shoe caught on a root and she tumbled to the ground. The voice in her head ordered her to get up and keep running, but her heart, lungs, and leg muscles had been pushed beyond their capacity, and now that she had been stopped, there didn't seem to be any reserves to draw on. For a moment Teri lay there, giving in to the exhaustion. Though there had been a good reason for not eating her breakfast, she now regretted that she hadn't had just a little. Her escape had burned what little energy she had stored, and now even the adrenaline high seemed to have worn off.

Rolling herself onto her back, she determined to catch her breath and get moving again. But in what direction? She had made so many turns onto different paths, she had no idea where the road might be, or, for that matter, which way Selena's house was. The sky above her was completely blocked out by the thick tree branches, so she couldn't go by the position of the sun. There, deep in the forest's shade, it seemed more like evening than mid-morning. As the pulse pounding in her ears slowed, she listened for any sign that Selena was nearby, but all she heard was the eerie whispering of the wind through the pines.

When she had thought getting lost would be fine, she hadn't actually considered the possibility. It seemed incredible that she could be so near civilization and not find her way out before she starved to death. The only thing to do was to keep moving and be prepared to duck behind a tree or boulder if she heard Selena coming.

Teri glanced at her watch, stunned to discover that a half hour had passed since she took off.

Surely by now she should have encountered another house, glimpsed the road, or at least found a suitable place to hide out until nightfall. One thing was certain: she couldn't let Selena get hold of her. Knowing what atrocities she was capable of and imagining what sort of punishment would be in store for her helped push another surge of adrenaline into Teri's overworked system. Forcing herself to stand, she ignored the dizziness that washed over her and the throbbing in the knee that she had fallen on.

Looking around, she noticed what looked like a path, and limped toward it. Her progress, if it could be called that, was much slower now, but going somewhere seemed to make more sense than lying on the ground.

Every time a creature scurried through the underbrush or a bird squawked overhead, her heart leaped into her throat. All of a sudden she saw sunlight a short distance away. Certain she would soon have her bearings or maybe even find a neighbor's house, she pushed herself into a faster hobble.

Her heart stopped completely when she exited the forest only to see Selena standing about twenty feet away, grinning like a victorious Amazon.

Teri had been going in circles! She spun around and headed back along the path. In spite of the piercing pain in her knee, frantic images of what torture might await her at Selena's mercy drove her beyond the pain. She didn't look back, but she heard Selena running after her and she sent up a desperate prayer for God to save her from this madwoman.

A second later Selena grasped a hank of Teri's hair and jerked her to a stop. Teri screamed out, both from terror and angry frustration. Ignoring the burning in her scalp, she twisted around and swung her fists at her captor. "Let me go! You can't do this to me!" But neither her furious demands nor her puny attack affected Selena, and Teri was too exhausted to continue. Tears flooded from her eyes as Selena yanked on her hair and proceeded to drag her back the way she had come.

"That was very naughty of you, Teri," Selena said in a tone dripping with lethal promise.

"Please, Selena," she cried, gasping for breath. "I'm begging you to let me go. I promise I won't tell a soul where you are." She tripped on a fallen branch, and Selena jerked her upright by her hair.

"Your promises are worthless. Just like my mother's were. You *promised* not to cause trouble, and look what you've done. I warned you, Teri. I love you, but now you will have to be punished."

Black despair filled Teri's soul as she stumbled along, unable to stop sobbing. "What . . . what are you . . . going to do to me?"

"I don't know yet. I'll have to discuss it with Juliette. She always knows just what to do."

Twenty-one

"Welcome back, Mr. Marshall," Ross Parkins said with a smile as he approached the hospital bed. "I'm Sergeant Parkins, with the White Plains Police Department. Since your doctor has restricted visitors for a few days, I'm here on behalf of the Tarrytown police as well."

"Where's Teri? Is she all right?" Drew's voice was raspy from lack of use. He tried to lift his head off the pillow, but the pain that movement caused in his head and chest was more than his weakened body was ready to handle. "The nurse told me . . . who had come. Teri wasn't one of them."

"We were hoping *you* could explain that. If you don't mind, Mr. Marshall, the doctor only gave me ten minutes with you, and I have a lot of questions."

Drew wanted to demand that the sergeant answer his question first, but his previous speech seemed to have zapped his ability to demand anything . . . either that, or whatever was dripping into his vein was very potent stuff. He managed a nod for the officer.

"Do you know who attacked you?"

"Selena. Doctor said . . . I was stabbed, but all I remember was her hitting me in the head with a hammer."

"Is Selena the blonde you had dinner with?"

294

Drew nodded. "Teri told me not to go. I didn't listen."

"Why did she hit you?"

Drew narrowed his brows. His body wanted to go back to sleep and his mind was rapidly losing the struggle to stay alert. "Jealous . . . crazy jealous. Hates men. Got to warn Teri." His eyes closed in spite of his need to say more. Whatever he was on felt very, very good.

"Just one more thing." Parkins touched Marshall's hand and the patient squinted at him. "I think this Selena might have taken Teri somewhere. What can you tell me about Selena?"

The thought of Teri being with Selena roused Drew sufficiently to answer. "She's a model. Lives in Manhattan."

"Do you know her full name?"

Drew shook his head. "That's it. Teri said . . . changed it."

"You mean legally?"

"Yeah," Drew whispered before sleep overtook him again.

Parkins didn't have all the answers he'd hoped to get, but he had a hell of a lot more than he'd had an hour before Drew Marshall had come out of his coma.

His next stop was the studio over the Gambini garage. Since Selena was a model, he figured there would be personal information on her in the artist's files for tax purposes. That deduction earned him Selena's address, phone number, and social security number. Within minutes of returning to the station, the computer identified her automobile. But it took several hours and some administrative arm-pulling by Captain Hart to discover Selena's former name.

Selena Lipschitz. She had changed it about a year ago, and Parkins understood the obvious reason for a model to drop that last name. Something told him there was more to it, though. He ran that name through the computer, but there was nothing at all—no police record, no fingerprints on file, not even a traffic violation. Nor did the local tax rolls show any property owned by her in either name.

With Captain Hart's approval, Parkins went after another search warrant—this time for Selena's Manhattan apartment. It was late Monday evening when he and Detective Morris gained access with the building manager's assistance. The man was certain he hadn't seen Selena in over two weeks and later, the parking garage attendant confirmed the number of days she'd been gone. The timing fit perfectly.

A quick tour of the one-bedroom apartment confirmed that Selena had an obsessive personality. Every inch of every room was snow white . . . except for one wall of the bedroom. There, with brilliantly colored paintings and black and white newsprint, they discovered Selena's tribute to Teri Carmichael Gambini.

And when they read the vow—*I am the Protector*—it appeared that they had the motive for two homicides and one attempt. Parkins realized he had misunderstood Drew Marshall's comment about Selena being jealous. It wasn't a man-woman problem in the usual sense; she was jealous of anyone who got close to her idol, Teri Carmichael.

All Parkins had to do now was find Selena and prove she was guilty of murder. Although he had no doubt that fingerprints picked up in this apartment would match up with those found on the steak knife and in the Gambini bedroom, that wasn't enough to connect her to the brutal deaths of Rico Gambini and William Kidder. Under his friend's direction, Parkins carefully searched the apartment for more solid evidence, but nothing turned up.

Until Morris told him how many criminals hide money, jewels, and drugs inside the refrigerator and freezer, and suggested he check it out just to be extra thorough. There, Parkins found the link he'd been searching for—a pair of hands in plastic bags.

Teri recognized her predicament even before she was fully awake. Her one chance at escape had failed, and it looked like nothing short of a miracle would save her now. Her empty stomach grumbled with a more immediate problem. The last time she had eaten was dinner Sunday night, and the only nourishment Selena had offered after throwing Teri back into the cage was a cup of drugged tea. She hadn't dared refuse to drink it—Selena's glowing eyes promised violence if she disobeyed. It must have been an extra strong dose, because this time she tasted it over the bitter black tea. As punishments go, however, being knocked out wasn't all that bad.

Teri stretched and let out a groan. Her futile run through the woods had gained her a body filled with aching muscles and a knee that throbbed like a migraine headache. Her eyes opened slowly. Much to her surprise, she had not been left in the dark. She had expected at least that much. So darkness was not her punishment and, more than likely, the drugged tea wasn't, either.

She began to understand when she glanced at her wrist to see the time and realized that not only was her watch gone, but she was nude. It became even more clear when she looked around her cell and found the area had been stripped bare as well. Only the bed remained—no furnishings, not even linens, were left behind for her to use to cover herself.

Fighting the dizzying hangover from the drug, Teri sat up and gasped in shock. Selena was sitting in the chair outside the cage, hugging her doll, and staring trancelike at Teri. Teri instinctively curled her legs up and tried to cover herself with her arms, but Selena didn't seem to notice. Afraid of the answer, but needing to know what her fate was to be, she asked, "Selena, may I please have my clothes back?"

Selena blinked as if returning from some distant place in her mind, then narrowed her gaze at Teri. The little girl answered, "No. You have to be punished for being bad. We could hurt you, you know, very easily, but we don't want to do that. People shouldn't hurt someone they love."

"You say you love me," Teri cut in. "But you're hurting me by keeping me here."

For a moment Selena looked confused, but instantly shrugged off Teri's accusation. "I told you how smart Juliette is. She thought about how shy you are and how much you like your privacy, and she decided on a punishment that wouldn't really hurt you."

The basement was warm, but Teri shivered nonetheless. She had not guessed that her captivity could get worse without adding physical brutality, but Selena had tapped into a different kind of weakness. First she had stripped her of her freedom; now she was stealing her dignity.

"If you need to use the potty, you will ask permission, and I'll pass it to you. In a day or two, if you have been very good, I will let you wash and brush your teeth and hair. We'll see how it goes after that."

Teri was stunned by the degradation Selena's twisted mind had invented, but reminding herself that her tormentor was a homicidal maniac made her aware of how much worse her punishment could have been. Her stomach growled again, and hunger won out over humiliation. "Will you starve me also?"

Selena stood and, looking down her nose, spoke in a reprimanding adult voice. "Getting snotty will only make things worse for you." She turned on her heels and marched noisily up the stairs.

Teri barely had a chance to regret her lack of caution when Selena returned carrying the potty chair in one hand and a small tray in the other.

"I cleaned this up after the mess you made yesterday," Selena said, placing the potty on the floor by the pass-through. "Since you apparently didn't care for the food I prepared, perhaps you'll like this meal better."

Teri smothered her dismay as she saw what was on the little tray being passed to her—one slice of plain white bread and a glass of water—just enough to keep her surviving for another day. Without moving from her huddled position on the bed, she tried to make amends. "Selena, I apologize for . . . getting snotty. I'm just very hungry."

"You should have thought of that yesterday."

Teri stopped Selena from closing the pass-through. "Wait. I need to go. She saw Selena smirk at her and realized what was required. "Please may I use the potty?" Selena nodded and pushed it through. "Will you at least turn around?"

"No."

Teri stayed where she was for another few seconds while Selena took her seat again. Her basic needs forced her to swallow her pride in spite of the silver eyes staring daggers at her. She told herself it was ridiculous to be so embarrassed, but the truth was, only two other people—Rico and Drew—had ever seen her completely nude, and both of them had allowed her privacy in the bathroom.

Throughout the day, if it was in fact daytime, Selena left her chair for only very brief spells. Otherwise she never took her eyes off Teri. Because of the lack of food and the remnants of the drug in her system, Teri had no energy to do more than lie on the bed. But even though she kept her back to Selena most of the time, she still knew the lunatic was there, watching her every move.

Teri fell asleep, woke up, and slept again. Selena brought two more "meals" of bread and water, but

Teri had already lost all sense of time and couldn't guess whether she was having breakfast or dinner. She was beyond hunger by then, just as she was beyond modesty. The only thing left to her was survival, and she was beginning to wonder how long that would be important to her.

Drew wondered what was taking the police officer so long. Sergeant Parkins had promised to come by the hospital to see him in a few minutes. It had been twenty so far. He remembered the officer being there right after he had come to, and he was fairly certain he had answered all his questions. What Drew didn't know was what had happened in the forty-eight hours since then. Had they found Selena? Had something happened to Teri? With every hour that passed, he had grown more impatient, until he had finally called the police station that morning and demanded that someone tell him what was going on.

He pressed the button to call the nurse. He knew his pain medication wasn't due for another hour, but his chest was killing him and the headache seemed to be coming back again. He needed to dull the pain so he could talk to Parkins without wincing with every breath. He also needed it so he could eat his lunch. If he didn't eat, they'd stick that nose hose down him again, and he couldn't stand that. A little voice asked him if those were the real reasons he wanted the medication, and he assured himself that they were. Needing a drug for pain was different than needing it to escape from reality, wasn't it?

This morning the doctor had told him he was doing very well for a man who'd been through what he had. He had already managed to walk down the hall twice without collapsing. And, at his insistence, even the tube in his arm was going to be removed tomorrow. He'd be given antibiotics and painkillers in pill form thereafter. But they wanted to keep him for another week of observation anyway. At the moment, he had nowhere else to go and nothing to wear if he did.

His cousin, Ann, and her husband had been by and brought him a decent pair of pajamas, and a robe and slippers, but that was the extent of his wardrobe. He had given Ann his apartment key, since she'd offered to pick up some of his personal items, and he hoped she hadn't taken him literally when he'd told her there was no rush.

He was on the verge of calling the police station again when Parkins walked in. "You certainly look a lot better today," he said by way of a greeting.

"I'd be doin' even better if I knew Teri was okay. Did you find her? Or Selena?"

"I'm afraid not. Your doctor suggested I spare you any seriously bad news for another few days, but I think you might be able to help if I fill you in, so . . ."

"Spit it out, Sergeant. If you don't tell me what's goin' on, I'm liable to have a stroke from worryin'. Whatever you have to say can't be worse than not knowin'."

Parkins nodded his agreement. "I was in Selena's apartment in Manhattan. She hadn't been back there since the night she attacked you, and Teri seems to have disappeared at the same time. The fingerprints in the apartment are the same ones that were on the knife they took out of your chest and picked up in the Gambini bedroom."

"The bedroom? Well, that's possible. They *were* friends."

"Teri's bedroom was torn apart and it looked like she might have packed for a trip. Maybe in a hurry."

Drew didn't believe that, and he guessed Parkins didn't, either. "Go on."

Parkins paced around the bed as he continued.

301

He described the all-white apartment and the tribute wall. "I don't think there's any question that Selena was more than just a devoted fan."

Drew had had trouble breathing before. Now it was almost impossible. "You think she believed she was *protectin'* Teri from me? That's why she tried to kill me?"

"It's a little more than a deduction, I'm sorry to say. We found something else in that apartment—a pair of severed hands. They've been positively identified as Rico Gambini's, and the right one was used at the scene of Detective Kidder's murder."

"Dear Lord!" Drew muttered in shock. "She killed them both . . . to protect Teri? I wasn't the only one?" He pulled himself upright and swung his legs over the edge of the bed, preparing to get up and leave any second. "So? Have you arrested her? Do you know where Teri is?"

Parkins shook his head with a frown. "I was hoping you might have an idea. The way I've pieced it together, Selena attacked you and went to the Gambini house. She either forced Teri to go with her or told her a story that got her moving willingly. Since her motive has been protection up to this point, we can hope she'll continue to keep Teri safe, but we have to assume we're dealing with insanity here, and—"

"And the motivation could change any minute. Okay, what can I do?"

"We've issued a BOLO, that's 'be on the lookout,' for Selena, Teri, and the Cadillac, but nothing's come in yet. I'd have to guess they're hiding out somewhere very secure and out of the way. There's no telling how far away they went, though. When she applied for her name change, she listed Philadelphia as her birthplace. I confirmed that and got her parents' names off the birth certificate. The father died thirteen years ago, and the mother sold their house four years after that, about the time she

302

married a man named Troy Nevins. Unfortunately, the data trail went cold from there, until Selena filed for a name change in Manhattan."

"What? No forwardin' address?" Drew asked, a bit sarcastically.

Parkins shrugged. "Computers can only put out what's put in. At any rate, my nose tells me they're not just holed up in a public motel room somewhere. It would be too hard for Selena to keep Teri under control in a place like that. Would you know of any place Selena might go to lie low? Family? Friends?"

"I'm positive Teri said she had no family. I think the mother and stepfather died, too. And she was pretty sure she was Selena's only friend."

"Do you have any idea where she lived last? Sometimes a psycho will return to a rock they crawled out from."

Drew rubbed his temples, trying to remember any other detail Teri had mentioned. "I don't know. Teri only said she moved to Manhattan about a year ago, but I don't remember if she said where she had moved from."

"And she changed her name at the same time." Parkins made himself a bet that when they figured out where Selena Lipschitz had been a year ago, they'd find another dead body or two. "Well, thanks anyway. If you think of anything, you know how to reach me."

"That's it? You're just givin' up?" Drew couldn't believe there wasn't something more he could do to help find Teri.

"No, Mr. Marshall. I'm not giving up. But sometimes waiting is the only thing we can do."

As the sergeant walked out of the room, the nurse came in with the painkiller Drew had been so anxious for just a short while ago. He knew all the frustration and fear he was feeling would be washed away with the pain a few minutes after the drug was

303

injected into his IV. All he had to do was lie back down and let it go to work. But the thought of giving in to it clashed with thoughts of Teri, out there somewhere, with a maniac killer, probably scared out of her mind.

"No, wait," he said abruptly, stopping the nurse as she was about to press the plunger on the hypodermic. "I don't want it anymore. Just get me some aspirin, okay?"

The nurse clucked at him, but withdrew the needle. "There's no order on your chart for aspirin. The doctor prescribed specific medication and that is all I'm authorized to give you."

Drew forced himself not to give in to the seductive pull of the drug in the nurse's hand or the rage building up inside him. "Look, I'm a recoverin' addict. This here's too easy, you see? Please call the doctor and ask him 'bout the aspirin." Fifteen minutes later, he had his Tylenol and knew what he had to do next.

He called Ann and told her his need for clothes had suddenly become urgent, since he was checking out tomorrow morning. Then he called the White Plains Police Department and caught Sergeant Parkins just as he walked in.

"I have an idea," Drew told him. "But you'll have to help me get out of here. I'm still weak as a kitten today, but they're takin' the tube out of my arm tomorrow mornin' and I think I'll be able to do a little more walkin' by then. I want you to take me to Teri's house. I know you said you already went through there, but maybe I'll see somethin' you missed, since I've been there before."

Parkins laughed. "I'd thought of that myself, but the doctor had threatened to perform delicate surgery on my private parts if I tried to get you out of there before another week."

"You just be here. I'll get myself out."

It was easier than he had expected. At ten thirty

the next morning, he and the sergeant took a walk down the hall and just kept on going. By the time they reached his car, however, Drew had accepted Parkins's smaller frame as a crutch.

Drew was able to catch his breath on the ride to Teri's house, but he now understood why the doctor had wanted to keep him in the hospital for another week. He promised himself to return, if he didn't find anything of importance at the house. Once he regained enough strength to talk, Drew told Parkins, "After you left, it occurred to me that Teri would not have gone willingly with Selena no matter *what* story she had concocted. Teri didn't trust her anymore. She couldn't put her finger on it, but she knew somethin' wasn't right. That was why she told me not to meet with Selena. The way I figure it, Selena had to force Teri out of that house, and, in that case, maybe Teri tried to leave me a message. That's assumin' Selena didn't tell her I was dead, of course."

"I'll buy that, although we didn't see anything."

And neither did Drew . . . during the first hour that he was in the house, going from room to room, and searching through the upheaval in the bedroom. He was so exhausted and disappointed at not finding any clues, he almost passed on checking out the master bathroom.

A memory of his walking through this house another time, looking for an intruder with Teri on his heels, had him smiling in spite of how awful he felt. He remembered her laughing about his braving the shower monster for her, and the night he had interrupted her strawberry bubble bath.

That was what he smelled—strawberries. Following the faint scent, he pushed himself into the bathroom and looked around. The shower curtain was drawn halfway along the tub, but a quick glance inside assured him no scary surprise awaited him there. He pulled the curtain the rest of the way

305

back and frowned over the broken crystal decanter. Had Teri broken it while Selena was dragging her away? There was no blood to indicate a struggle, only shards of glass and spilled pink crystals.

Then he looked again. "Sergeant! Come here quick."

Parkins was at his side a second later. "What is it?"

"Look. I almost missed it. There are letters scraped out in the bath crystals. Dust settled over them, but if you look hard, you can make it out. See? HELP SELENA KILLED . . . what do you think this name is? It's not as neat as the other three words. Teri must have been rushed away."

"Son-of-a-bitch! Pardon me, but two of us looked in here and didn't see that. The only excuse I can give is when I glanced behind the curtain, I was at an angle and half-expecting to see a body. When there wasn't even a drop of blood, I just kept going." Parkins knelt down and read off the letters: "V-L-S-T-E-R-C. Does that mean anything to you?"

"No, but there's definitely a space between the 'R' and the 'C'. Maybe it's the first initial of a last name."

Parkins moved his finger in the air over all the letters, tracing Teri's words several times. "Maybe that first letter is a 'U' not a 'V'."

"Ulster?" Drew asked, testing the sound of the name. "There's an Ulster in Ireland."

"And one in New York," Parkins exclaimed, slapping his forehead. "The 'C' could stand for 'County'—Ulster County, New York! Your lady left a message, all right." He rose and dusted off the knees of his dark uniform pants.

Drew felt a surge of success revitalize him. "Do you think that's where they were headed?"

"It's worth a shot. Are you up to going to the station with me, or should I take you back to the hospital? You're white as a ghost."

Drew just looked at him like he was crazy and Parkins laughed. He understood what it was like to want to be part of the hunt. He wouldn't deny Drew Marshall even if he did look like he was ready to fall on his face.

Twenty-two

"Bingo!" Ross Parkins shouted when he hung up the phone. "Selena Lipschitz gained title to a piece of property in Ulster County a little over a year ago."

"Let's go," Drew said, but the time it took him to get up from the chair betrayed his lack of energy.

"You'll have to stay here," Parkins told him.

"I'm going if I have to hire a cab and follow you there."

After several more arguing statements and Drew's promise to stay out of the way, Parkins gave in and went to clear his trip with Captain Hart.

Since the law enforcement agency with jurisdiction in Ulster was New York's State Troopers, Hart arranged for Parkins, Morris, and Marshall to go to the station nearest Selena's property and be accompanied to the house by troopers. There was no guarantee Selena was there, but they would be prepared to apprehend a crazed killer nonetheless.

Drew slept through most of the two-hour trip, but the morning's exertion took its toll in pain when he awoke. Every breath was like another knife in his chest. But it would all be worth it if they found Teri safe.

Through half-closed eyes Teri watched Selena take

the little tray away. This marked the ninth meal of bread and water rations . . . and she had actually been grateful when Selena brought it to her. Teri had thought Selena had already deprived her of all she could when she woke up naked in the barren cage. But at that time, she had still had two weapons left—her strength and her mind. The first was disintegrating from purposeful neglect. Selena was keeping her too hungry to stage another rebellion, and the slightest activity left her weak and dizzy.

At first she believed Selena couldn't break her will to live, no matter what torture she devised. But then, at first, Teri also believed that she could somehow talk her way out of her imprisonment.

In the time since her escape attempt, which she estimated as four days, Teri had apologized, pleaded, screamed in anger, and cried in desperation, all to no avail.

Her newest fear stemmed from the awareness that Selena no longer had any lucid moments. She talked only to Juliette and served Teri's needs like a robot. Teri was fairly sure her warden wasn't getting any sleep, either, since she rarely moved from the chair. She was sitting there, staring at Teri when Teri fell asleep, and she was always there when Teri awoke. When she did go upstairs, she would leave Juliette in the chair to keep her one good eye watching their prisoner. Sometimes the shabby old doll frightened Teri more than her owner did.

Selena also seemed to have forgotten her offer to let Teri earn back her privileges, or perhaps, she, too, was losing track of time. Teri and her cage were still stripped bare, and the only water she had received was for drinking. She knew better than to waste that on washing herself. Though she might be filthy and losing weight, as long as she had bread and water, she could survive.

And that fact made Selena the only lifeline Teri had. Without her, Teri would die of starvation. Depending on someone so insane for the merest existence left her totally helpless; and that helplessness was slowly chipping away at her will. Every so often she found herself wanting to curl into a ball and go to sleep, never to awaken again. So far, however, her mind had remained clear enough to push such thoughts away. Although her situation offered no sign of hope, she wasn't yet ready to follow Selena's mother's escape route.

Overhead, she could hear Selena moving about. Strangely, it sounded like she was running from one end of the house to the other. What could she be up to now? Having something to be curious about stirred Teri from her lethargy.

Suddenly she heard Selena bolt the basement door and saw her racing down the stairs with Teri's robe over her arm. With her long, white hair flying madly around her and her glazed eyes widened in panic, she looked as if she was being chased by demons . . . or was one herself.

Teri backed into the corner of the cage as Selena hurriedly unlocked the door, darted inside, and locked herself in with Teri.

Pocketing the key, she tossed Teri the robe and ordered, "Cover yourself. Quickly. And be very quiet."

What Teri saw in Selena's hand quieted her more effectively than the warning. Selena had Rico's gun, and, as far as she knew, it was still loaded. At least it wasn't pointing at her this time. She pulled on the robe and made herself wait for an explanation.

"Don't worry, Teri. I won't let them get you. I'll protect you."

"Them?" Teri prayed Selena wasn't just being paranoid. She listened intently for any noise that might indicate a rescue was imminent, but for several minutes the only sound in the empty basement was Selena's breath hissing through her teeth.

310

"That's the white Caddy we're looking for," Parkins told the men around him as soon as they opened the garage door. "I think we'd better assume our killer's in the house." The six troopers who had provided escort surrounded the house while Parkins and Morris went to the front door. Drew was ordered to stay by the police car until they had the situation under control.

When knocking, pounding, and shouting didn't produce any results, Parkins smashed a window and climbed in. Quickly he unlocked the front and back doors and let in Morris and the troopers. A brief search of the house proved that someone was living there, and a damp towel in the kitchen suggested the inhabitant hadn't been gone long. The only place they couldn't check was behind a door in the kitchen that had been locked from the other side. While two of the troopers worked at removing the hinges on the outside of the door, Parkins called Drew inside to take a look at the strange portrait in the corner of one bedroom.

"That's Teri's work, all right," Drew confirmed as soon as he saw the painting of Selena behind bars. He bent down to examine the signature. "Look here—it's dated July 13. Teri must have painted it after Selena took her away."

Just then one of the troopers came back to the bedroom. "We got the hinges off that door. You ready?"

Parkins turned to Drew. "You'd better go back outside. We don't know what we'll find behind that door."

Ignoring the suggestion, Drew followed Parkins to the kitchen, but was held back by Morris while the door was pried open and Parkins led three of the officers down into the basement.

* * *

Teri wanted to scream out a warning, but Selena had her pinned against her with one hand over Teri's mouth and the gun barrel pressed to her temple.

"Hush now," Selena whispered, tightening her grip on Teri's face. "I don't want to hurt you, but I won't let those men get their hands on you."

Teri understood instantly. Selena would kill her before allowing her pet to be rescued.

The moment the first police officer appeared, Selena pointed the gun at him and fired. That man jumped off the stairs and rolled on the floor while three others behind him did the same thing, only to discover there was nowhere to hide. Selena pulled the trigger three more times at the moving targets, but in spite of the bullets ricocheting around the basement, only one man was hit.

They all had their weapons out, but Selena kept Teri securely in front of her as a shield. As soon as it became obvious that they weren't going to shoot, she turned her gun back on Teri.

"You all want her alive, don't you?" Selena ranted at them. "You want to take her from me so you can play your man-games with her. But I'm not going to let you have her. I swore to protect her, and I will if it means ending both our lives right now. I have two bullets left, one for her, then one for me. But it would be better if you would all just go away and leave us alone."

The redheaded officer set his gun on the floor and got up slowly with his hands raised. "Selena, you can't kill Teri. That would break your vow as The Protector, and you've already made one mistake too many."

Teri felt Selena loosen her hold on her a bit.

"How do you know who I am?" Selena asked warily.

The officer took one step toward the cage and spoke in a gentle voice. "I found out from someone with greater powers than you. You failed once, Selena. If you fail again, you can no longer be called The Protector. Your title will be granted to someone more worthy."

Teri prepared herself as she sensed Selena's attention turning completely to the officer. Although the gun was still directed at her, it was no longer pressed against her temple. But Teri realized that even if she could break away, there was nowhere for her to run within the cage. If only she could slip her fingers into Selena's pocket while she was distracted and get the key to this bright officer, he might be able to get the door open and end the stalemate.

Selena was obviously confused by what the officer was telling her. In her little-girl voice, she asked, "What do you mean, I failed?"

The redheaded man looked up the stairs behind him and called, "Mr. Marshall, why don't you tell her how she failed?"

"Marshall!" whined Selena in disbelief and pointed the gun at the stairs.

"No-o-o!" Teri screamed as she slammed her elbow into Selena's stomach, then bashed the girl's forearm with her doubled fists as hard as she could. The pistol fell from Selena's hand, clanged against the bars, and slid under the bed. In a blur of movement, Selena dived to the floor to retrieve the gun, and Teri threw herself on top of her. While Selena groped beneath the bed for the gun, Teri dug her hand into Selena's pocket, pulled out the key to the cage, and tossed it through the bars.

The redheaded officer grabbed the key and inserted it in the lock, but he wasn't quite fast enough. In the same seconds that it took him to open the cage door, Selena found the gun, bucked Teri off her back, and hauled her up in front of her again. The other two officers had moved up beside the redhead and were prepared to shoot, but Selena had her gun pressed against Teri's temple again. Se-

313

lena cocked the weapon and Teri's breath caught in her throat. She knew her slightest movement could mean her death.

"Put down your guns and back away from the door," Selena ordered angrily. "You, too," she shouted at the downed officer beneath the steps. As soon as they were out of the way, Selena brought Teri out of the cage and moved toward the stairway. "Okay, all of you, get into the cage." She waited impatiently for them to drag the injured man inside with them, then demanded, "Now call everyone else down here to join you."

Parkins knew he had to make a quick judgment call. If Selena saw Marshall, she would probably try to shoot him on sight. Her aim was lousy, but coming down the stairs in his weak condition, with her at the bottom, he'd be a sitting duck. Also, if he left Morris and another officer up there, they might be able to overpower her when she got to the top. But Selena knew someone was up there, so he called, "Kirby. Smith. Come down here." He hoped they'd all get the intended message, since they'd surely been listening to every word.

"With your hands up," Selena added. When they reached the basement she made them remove their gun belts and get in the cage also. "Okay, where's Marshall?"

"He's not really here," Parkins told her. "I lied about that. He is alive, but he's still in the hospital." For a moment he thought Selena was going to turn the gun on him, but all she did was sneer. He kept watching her trigger finger on the cocked weapon and hoped Teri was smart enough not to jar her now.

Towing Teri along with her, Selena shifted the gun from one hand to the other, closed and locked the cage door, and returned the key to her pocket. Still considering the officers a threat, she kept Teri in front of her and started up the stairs backward.

Teri gagged when Selena's forearm cut off her air passage as she pulled her up onto the first step. After several steps, Teri learned to anticipate the moment she needed to step up by listening for the clack of Selena's sandals right before she would yank Teri up by the throat. Teri wondered how Selena was navigating the stairs backward with those floppy shoes, then scolded herself for thinking of something so silly when her life was about to end, but her brain didn't seem to be functioning any better than her starved body.

Three-quarters of the way up the stairs, a stray memory came to her about how, if you are ever being forcibly held, going completely limp could help you get free. Anything was worth a try at this point. Drew was alive and she was determined to see him again.

Teri waited until the next step up. One sandal landed, and as Selena lifted her other foot, Teri went slack.

She had only meant to slip out of Selena's grasp, but as Teri drooped, Selena lost her shoe, then her balance. With a hard jerk, Teri twisted aside, causing Selena's heavy body to catapult forward. Clinging to the railing, Teri gaped in shock as Selena toppled down the stairs, shrieking and flapping her arms and legs like a huge ragdoll as she tried to stop her fall. With a sickening crunch of bones, Selena landed on the white concrete floor.

No one moved or spoke for several heartbeats. Suddenly Selena's eyes popped open and she raised the gun toward Teri.

Teri wanted to move, but her body refused to cooperate. She could only stand there, quivering with terror. But Selena couldn't seem to pull the trigger. Her head turned slowly toward the chair where Juliette was perched, as if she was listening to something the doll was telling her. A moment later, Selena's hand began to spasm.

With a keening cry, she pointed the gun at Juliette and squeezed the trigger. As her mentor exploded into pieces, Selena brought the gun to her own temple.

And fired again.

With the ear-splitting sound of the gunshots still echoing throughout the basement, two more officers sped down the stairs past Teri as she collapsed onto a step. She was not sure she had the strength to get up on her own, until someone sat down beside her and stroked her cheek.

"Drew!" she cried, throwing her arms around him. For a long time they merely held each other, oblivious to the gruesome scene below them. There was so much to say, but not yet. When one of the officers needed to get by, they rose to go upstairs also, but Drew hesitated when he saw Teri turn to look back at the creature on the basement floor.

"May she rot in Hell," he said, without an ounce of sympathy.

As for Teri, her time in Hell had ended . . . permanently.

Twenty-three

"Congratulations, Ms. Carmichael," the owner of the Forsythe Gallery said, beaming from ear to ear. "I think this is the best showing we've had since your exhibit last year. Your idea to share the spotlight with your husband was sheer genius! I'm not suggesting your 'Faces' series isn't magnificent, but displaying the paintings alongside his original photography showed brilliance, pure brilliance!"

Teri blushed with pride. "Thank you. We couldn't be more pleased. Pardon me, but Drew seems to need rescuing from one of your more enamored blue-haired patrons." She made her way through the champagne-sipping crowd to Drew's side. Smiling at his fawning admirer, she linked her arm through his and politely excused the both of them.

"Thanks, darlin'," he murmured with a wink as Teri led him to a quieter corner of the gallery.

"My pleasure." She raised up on tiptoes and softly kissed his mouth.

He couldn't resist wrapping his arms around her in spite of the lack of privacy. "They love you."

"They love *us*," she corrected, then let her gaze scan the collection on display. "It *is* good."

Drew watched her closely and knew the precise moment when she looked at the final collage of the series: Selena . . . in all her faces and moods . . . including insanity. Simultaneously fascinating and repelling, it had drawn the most attention at the exhibit. "You okay?"

Teri nodded and smiled for him. It had taken a year before she could work on that last painting, but she had felt driven to do so. With its completion, she was able to put an end to her nightmares.

And now, snuggled safely in her love's embrace, Teri could almost forget about the girl who had deceived her with innocence, lied to her about hiding gruesome, incriminating evidence in her home, and then dragged her through the terrifying corridors of dark obsession.

Almost.

HORROR FROM HAUTALA

SHADES OF NIGHT   (0-8217-5097-6, $4.99)
Stalked by a madman, Lara DeSalvo is unaware that she is most in danger in the one place she thinks she is safe—home.

TWILIGHT TIME   (0-8217-4713-4, $4.99)
Jeff Wagner comes home for his sister's funeral and uncovers long-buried memories of childhood sexual abuse and murder.

DARK SILENCE   (0-8217-3923-9, $5.99)
Dianne Fraser fights for her family—and her sanity—against the evil forces that haunt an abandoned mill.

COLD WHISPER   (0-8217-3464-4, $5.95)
Tully can make Sarah's wishes come true, but Sarah lives in terror because Tully doesn't understand that some wishes aren't meant to come true.

LITTLE BROTHERS   (0-8217-4020-2, $4.50)
Kip saw the "little brothers" kill his mother five years ago. Now they have returned, and this time there will be no escape.

MOONBOG   (0-8217-3356-7, $4.95)
Someone—or some*thing*—is killing the children in the little town of Holland, Maine.

THE MYSTERIES OF MARY ROBERTS RINEHART

THE AFTER HOUSE   (0-8217-4246-6, $3.99/$4.99)

THE CIRCULAR STAIRCASE   (0-8217-3528-4, $3.95/$4.95)

THE DOOR   (0-8217-3526-8, $3.95/$4.95)

THE FRIGHTENED WIFE   (0-8217-3494-6, $3.95/$4.95)

A LIGHT IN THE WINDOW   (0-8217-4021-0, $3.99/$4.99)

THE STATE VS.   (0-8217-2412-6, $3.50/$4.50)
ELINOR NORTON

THE SWIMMING POOL   (0-8217-3679-5, $3.95/$4.95)

THE WALL   (0-8217-4017-2, $3.99/$4.99)

THE WINDOW AT THE WHITE CAT
                              (0-8217-4246-9, $3.99/$4.99)

THREE COMPLETE NOVELS: THE BAT, THE HAUNTED
LADY, THE YELLOW ROOM
                              (0-8217-114-4, $13.00/$16.00)

Available wherever paperbacks are sold, or order direct from the Publisher. Send cover price plus 50¢ per copy for mailing and handling to Penguin USA, P.O. Box 999, c/o Dept. 17109, Bergenfield, NJ 07621. Residents of New York and Tennessee must include sales tax. DO NOT SEND CASH.